Contract with the King

To: Deborah
I hope you enjoy this
adventure!
Paul Pullen
8-13-08

by
Paul Pullen

Bloomington, IN   Milton Keynes, UK

AuthorHouse™
1663 Liberty Drive, Suite 200
Bloomington, IN 47403
www.authorhouse.com
Phone: 1-800-839-8640

First published by AuthorHouse 2/13/2008

ISBN: 978-1-4343-0741-5 (sc)

Library of Congress Control Number: 2007904726

Printed in the United States of America
Bloomington, Indiana

This book is printed on acid-free paper.

I would like to thank the following individuals
for their editorial assistance:

Kristin McDermott
Betsy Cotton
Martha Baker

ELDORADO

Gaily bedight,
A gallant knight,
In sunshine and in shadow,
Had journeyed long,
Singing a song,
In search of Eldorado.

But he grew old—
This knight so bold—
And o'er his heart a shadow
Fell as he found
No spot of ground
That looked like Eldorado.

And, as his strength
Failed him at length,
He met a pilgrim shadow—
"Shadow," said he,
"Where can it be—
This land of Eldorado?"

"Over the Mountains
Of the Moon
Down the Valley of the Shadow,
Ride, boldly ride,"
The shade replied—
"If you seek for Eldorado!"

E.A.P.

What is the grst?

Chapter One

Paul walked into Dave's dark bedroom and paused, waiting for his tired eyes to adjust—tired from staring at the road and rearview all the way from Memphis. He stretched the stiff muscles in his back and neck then sat in an old armchair beside his roommate's bed. A burnt-orange University of Texas curtain reached out from an open window. The faint smell of stale marijuana smoke ascended from a mound of dirty clothes between Dave's bed and desk. A page in an open medical book fluttered. "Dave, wake up."

Paul rubbed the goose bumps from his tanned arms then combed his fingers through his curly brown hair. The early morning breeze was unusually cool for Austin in March, but he knew it would not last. KLBJ had predicted a high of 86°. The alarm clock on Dave's nightstand read 3 a.m. As Paul watched Dave sleep, he wished he, too, was snuggled in bed, drifting off to dreamland, but before he could even think of sleep, he had one more important task to complete. He shook Dave's shoulder. "Dave, wake up."

Paul, Dave, Brooks, and Rob, the Four Musketeers, had met in third grade but had not become close friends until junior high and high school, a time when forever friendships are formed. While growing up, they had reveled in numerous exploits, from painting zebra stripes on the Buckholzs' prize-winning bull, to setting the town dump on fire, but they were now 24-year-old college students, embarking on what might prove to be the greatest adventure of their lives. The others had already joined the game, and now it was time to invite Dave, the cautious one, the one Paul had wisely saved until last. "Dave, I did it. I got him."

Dave stared at Paul's blurred image through half-open eyes. He reached for his wire-rimmed glasses then peered at his alarm clock. He pushed himself up on one elbow, brushed back his sandy-brown hair, and stared at his friend. "Paul, you've got to stop smoking that pot. We've both got to stop, or we'll never get through this semester alive. I bet you smoked all the way from DeSoto."

"Dave, you know I don't smoke anymore, and I didn't go to DeSoto. I went to Memphis. I pulled it off, Dave. I nabbed the King. We've got him hidden in Detox. Tara and Brooks are keeping the first watch. He's not lookin' too good, Dave. We're going to need your help."

Dave was used to his friends waking him up at all hours of the night, for the strangest reasons, and past experience had taught him to humor them if he ever wanted to get back to sleep. He fell back onto his pillow and stared up at the ceiling. "Okay. Okay. I'll play along with your little game, but this had better not take long. I have to be at work at ten, I've got classes all afternoon, and it'd be nice to get a full night's sleep for a change."

"Yes, it would," Paul replied, watching Dave pluck a Longhorn T-shirt and pair of jeans from the top of the dirty laundry. While Dave dressed, Paul closed his eyes. Please, God, protect Dave during this one. Please protect *all* my friends.

Dave climbed into Paul's old Malibu, noticing an expensive guitar in the back seat. "Where'd you get the guitar?"

"Graceland," Paul answered.

Dave laughed. "Well, young man, I guess we can add theft to kidnapping."

Dave often emulated his father by beginning sentences with "Well" or "Well, sir."

"What else did you take?" Dave asked.

"That's about it—except for an envelope full of pills—and of course, Elvis."

Dave shook his head, leaned back in his seat, and closed his eyes. Paul glanced at the car's speedometer, easing his foot off the accelerator. He did not relish the thought of Dave telling some cop they were just in a hurry to check on *Elvis*.

"How'd you get the King out of his castle?" Dave asked.

"It was easy, just like in the dream I told you about last summer. The side door was unlocked. Two guards, passed out in the living room. I ran upstairs and found him in pretty much the same condition as his guards. I shook him half-awake. I told him he had to eat, that I knew a place that served the best cheeseburgers in the world, but that we'd have to hurry or they'd be closed. I half-walked, half-carried him right out of his castle."

"Well, that was smart," Dave mused. "I would have never thought of that. You offered *Elvis Presley* a cheeseburger, and he just followed you right out of the gates of Graceland."

"That's pretty much the way it happened. Wait till you see him, Dave. It's really sad."

Dave studied Paul curiously then chuckled, as if reassuring himself it was all a joke, just a big joke.

Detox, short for the Detoxification and Drug Rehabilitation Unit, was located at the Austin State Hospital, one of the state's oldest mental institutions. The hospital consisted of eight two-story, wood and brick units. Detox was one of the older structures, built during a time when *Asylum for the Insane* hung on the front gate. The unit housed Austin's hard-core drug addicts. Seventy percent of its patients were court-committed, so the entire hospital was surrounded by a tall, chain-link fence.

Paul, Dave, and Brooks worked at Detox as part-time nurse's aides. Their duties there consisted of distributing food, pillows, and blankets, observing patients' behavior, and logging appropriate comments in the Progress Notes section of each patient's file. Aides also took part in between-shift briefings and were sometimes called upon to restrain and lock up those individuals choosing a more physical means of expressing their displeasure with the unit.

The guard at the entrance recognized Paul's car and waved them through.

"I bet security was happy to see the King?" Dave joked.

"I had him covered up in the back seat," Paul replied.

Paul parked the car near the back entrance, unlocked the unit's heavy steel door, and pulled. He slowly closed and locked the door behind them, hoping not to wake their patients. The smell of disinfectant filled their nostrils as they walked down a long hallway lined with sixteen tall lockup doors. Each door contained a small window, protected with a metal grid for safe observation. Each lockup contained one mattress and one pillow, sealed in plastic for easy cleanup. The lockups were cold, poorly ventilated, and usually vacant, except on those busy Friday and Saturday nights when Austin's finest ran out of jail space for the city's more violent drunks and addicts.

At the end of the hallway, a nurse's station separated two twenty-bed dorms, one male and one female. Paul was glad to see the station empty and their patients apparently sound asleep. Besides Tara and Brooks, two other employees were normally scheduled to work the graveyard shift, but Tara had given both the night off so that she and Brooks would have the place to themselves. Paul led Dave down the steep basement stairs, unlocked the door, and relocked it behind them.

The basement was used primarily for storage but contained four additional lockups that could be used for emergencies. Brooks sat beside the only closed lockup door, feet crossed over a desk, arms crossed nonchalantly behind his head. He wore his usual short-sleeved, plaid shirt, jeans, and tennis shoes. His short, straight, black hair was parted to one side. A legal pad rested on his lap. Brooks' full name was David Michael Brooks, but his friends called him Brooks, Brooksie, or Mr. Brooks. Brooks was the group's journalism major, and Paul had pulled him into the venture by suggesting he keep a journal or write a book about the kidnapping.

"Good morning, Dave," Brooks greeted.

"Is it?" Dave asked, giving his friend a cross look.

The lockup door opened and Tara Benoist, Detox's head nurse, stepped out carrying a stethoscope, thermometer, keys, and several files. Paul studied the curves of her tall, slender body before focusing on her green eyes and bright-red lips. Tara wore a dark tan beneath her white nurse's uniform, and at one time or another, every male in the unit had wondered exactly how far the tan went. At the sight of Dave and Paul, she pushed the door shut with her foot and dropped everything onto the desk. "Good morning, Dave," she greeted, giving him a big hug. "Sorry we had to pull you out of bed so early, but it was for a good cause." She surprised Paul with a big hug, too. "Paul, you're amazing. You pulled it off. You single-handedly nabbed the King of Rock 'n' Roll. You're truly amazing."

"Thanks," Paul, replied, elated by the feel and scent of Tara's soft skin. During the long drive from Memphis, he had talked himself through long periods of fear, paranoia, and loneliness. On more than one occasion, he had questioned his own sanity. Tara's warm hug and kind praise had instantly removed all traces of doubt and fear.

Unfortunately for Paul and Tara, their jubilation was cut short. Dave's face had suddenly turned ash white. He rushed to the lockup and pressed his nose against the grid-protected window. Elvis was sound asleep, and long strands of black hair hid most of his bloated face, but there was no mistaking the sideburns, no mistaking that familiar curl of his upper lip.

"Dave Turner—Elvis Presley," Brooks joked. "Elvis Presley—Dave Turner."

Dave's face turned red as he whirled to face the others. "Are you *crazy*!"

Tara touched an index finger to her lips. "Shhh," she said, pointing upstairs to where their other patients slept.

"Have you lost your *minds*!" Dave yelled, spinning to take another look. "This better be a joke! I hope to God this is a joke, because if that's really Elvis Presley, y'all are in *deep* shit."

Brooks whistled a few bars of "Suspicious Minds," an Elvis tune about a man caught in a trap.

Dave spun to face Brooks. "Why are you doing this!"

"Because I've been awarded exclusive rights to the story and screenplay," Brooks answered.

"*Story and screenplay*!" Dave echoed. "Does the fact that you'll be writing them from a cold, dark jail cell bother you at all!"

"I won't be going to jail. Paul kidnapped him."

"You're holding him against his will!"

"Seventy percent of our patients here are being held against their will."

"They're court-committed! Like you're going to be!"

"I don't think so, Dave. I don't think the King's been a happy camper lately. Just look at him. Do you think it's his will to be in this condition?"

Dave took another look through the window then faced Tara. "I won't be a part of this."

"You're already a part of this," Tara replied.

Dave could not believe his ears. And Tara was right. He *was* a part of this. He had suddenly stumbled right into the middle of a big trap and could easily feel the rope tightening around his legs. He closed his eyes and felt himself dangling upside down, blood rushing to his head, wind blowing through his hair, watching helplessly as his bright future passed away beneath him. There went his hopes for a medical degree. There went his successful career plans. There went his dreams of one day having a beautiful wife and family. His whole future was passing beneath him like so many rustling leaves—quite suddenly, *way* out of reach. He shook the image away and began pacing in front of the door, occasionally stopping to glare inside. Elvis looked like he had been hanging upside down, too. In a meat locker. Dave faced his friends. "What if he *dies* in there? Anyone think of that? What if he *dies*? *Who* do you think they'll blame?"

Tara emptied the envelope full of pills that Paul had lifted from Graceland. Like agitated insects, the brightly-colored tablets and capsules scampered across the desk toward the King's cell. "I'd say he has a far greater chance of dying in Memphis than in Austin."

Dave glared at Tara, shook his head, then continued pacing. "This is just a bad dream," he mumbled, more to himself than to the others. He stopped and faced his friends. "This is just a bad dream. And I can tell you this—it *won't* have a happy ending."

Tara leaned back against the desk, casually swinging her long, light-brown hair behind her while staring at the ceiling. "Dave, how many individuals do you think we help here? How many of our patients experience a complete recovery?"

"I don't know. Forty percent? Thirty percent? Is *this* our punishment for not doing better? How many will we be able to help in prison?"

"Twenty percent," Tara continued undaunted. "All these physicians, psychologists, and psychiatrists—all these nurses, aides, and volunteers—all this time and energy spent, and 80 percent go right back to the street, to some other institution, or worse. We're spinning our wheels here, Dave, and I can no longer be a part of it."

Dave scanned the bleak basement before taking a deep breath. "Tara, I know this place is in desperate need of change. I know you've been working hard to make that change. And now you're telling me you can no longer be a part of it. But what in God's name does all *that* have to do with *kidnapping* Elvis Presley!"

"We prefer *intervention*," Brooks corrected. "The experimental procedure is showing positive results in New York and California. The process gets everyone involved: courts, counselors, family members, employers . . ."

"I'm *familiar* with interventions!" Dave interrupted. "This is *not* an intervention! This is *kidnapping!*"

Tara nodded reflectively. "Yes, regardless of our honorable intention, the courts will certainly see it as such. All the more reason for us to make sure *this* kidnapping has a happy ending." She opened Elvis' file to make a few notes.

Dave watched her a moment, shook his head, and looked inside the lockup. "You kidnapped the King of Rock 'n' Roll, drove him across state lines, and locked up in a state mental hospital. A *state mental hospital!* That, alone, should get you an extra twenty years." He scanned their faces, waiting for some response, but none was given. He continued pacing. "*Elvis Presley.* Out of all the drugged-out rock stars, you picked *Elvis Presley.*"

"His celebrity status will, of course, present a few problems we're not used to dealing with," Brooks admitted.

"A few problems! You mean like the FBI? The CIA? The Texas Rangers? Those sorts of problems? I bet every cop from Memphis to Austin's looking for him right now. And what *about* Memphis? What about his family, friends, girlfriends, bodyguards, managers, lawyers, doctors, psychiatrists, gurus? What about *them*?"

"What about them?" Paul asked. "Judging from his present condition, they haven't been doin' a very good job."

"And you'll do better?" Dave scoffed. "A nurse and two nurse's aides will miraculously *save* Elvis?"

"That's three nurse's aides, counting you," Brooks corrected. "And Rob's on the way, too."

"Good, he can take my place," Dave replied, looking toward the King's cell. "I can't believe you got him this far without gettin' shot—or worse."

"What's worse than gettin' shot?" Brooks asked.

"Gettin' all of us shot," Dave replied, glaring at Brooks. He faced Paul. "This isn't about Tara and some noble search for a better form of treatment, is it? This is about you and your stupid dream. You saved Elvis in dreamland and saw it as some sort vision, some sort of green light." He looked at Brooks and Tara. "And you two idiots followed blindly. You followed this—*dreamer*—into God knows where." His eyes fell to the desk and a magazine displaying a picture of the Texas State Capitol. "What if he'd dreamed of the Governor? What if he'd dreamed of Congress?"

"Don't be silly, Dave," Brooks replied, "we don't have enough lockups for Congress."

Dave shook his head then scanned the windowless basement, searching for the quickest route of escape. His eyes fell on the locked basement door. "Take him back, Paul. I'll help you. If we leave right now, we might can get him back before the whole world finds out."

Paul closed his eyes and pictured himself loading Elvis into his car, driving him back to Memphis, pushing him out onto Beale Street, and pretending none of this ever happened. His eyes quickly opened. "Sorry, Dave, I can't do that." He looked toward the desk, focusing on a copy of *Rolling Stone* magazine. "Dave, Hendrix is dead. Janis, dead. Morrison, dead. You don't have to look much further than that to see what's going to happen to Elvis. What a waste. He's forty-two years old. Only forty-two years old."

"I was hoping to see forty-two, myself," Dave replied, "and I'll tell you exactly what's going to happen. This whole thing is going to blow up right in your face?"

"We've discussed the risks, Dave," Paul replied, "and we all have our fears. I fear we might be too late, that Elvis might be too far gone for us to help. I fear if we fail, our lives could be forever ruined. But more than that, I fear waking up one day discovering we missed a valuable opportunity to save the King."

Dave stared at Paul a moment before bowing his head.

"We saw no other way, Dave," Tara said. "We felt we had at best, one chance, and all you have to do is look at him to see that this is very possibly *his* last chance."

A loud cough echoed from behind the closed door, followed by the sound of phlegm splattering against the hard linoleum floor. Tara stepped to the widow and watched as Elvis rolled over and fell back to sleep. "Dave, you once told me you envisioned yourself becoming the type of doctor who might have to take chickens and eggs instead of cash, the type of doctor who'd never refuse an uninsured patient. Well, I'm telling you this man's insurance has run out, and you're turning your back on him? Why? Because his name's Elvis Presley? Because it's too risky? Because we might fail? Sorry, Dave, that's not good enough. This man is extremely ill, he's in urgent need of help, and we're in a unique position to offer him that help."

Dave opened his mouth to rebut but seemed at a loss for words.

"We're going through with this, Dave," Paul assured his friend. "We need your help. We want you with us. But whether you're with us or not, we're going through with this."

Dave scanned the pills, files, keys, and magazines covering the desk, eyes pausing on a boating magazine. The ship had already set sail, with his best friends in all the world on board, and there he stood with his feet planted firmly on the dock, hands grasping the boat's railing—body stretching, stretching, seconds from falling into the abyss.

Dave reluctantly reached out and picked up the file labeled EAP. "Rob's really in this, too?"

"He said he wouldn't miss it for the world," Paul answered.

"Everyone's in but you, Dave," Brooks said, "and I have to admit, jail won't be much fun without you."

The trace of a smile appeared on Dave's face. As his mind raced back and forth between staying and leaving, his smile vanished. Both choices left him cold, but deep down he knew there was only one way out of this mess, for himself *and* his friends. He had to climb aboard this ship of fools and help them *save* Elvis. "Unbelievable," he said, shaking his head. He opened the file, scanned the first page, then looked up at his friends. "Anyone got the name of a good lawyer?"

"Yes!" Paul and Tara replied.

"All for one and one for all," Brooks said excitedly.

"You won't regret it," Tara said, giving Dave another big hug.

"I already regret it," Dave replied.

Paul's heart leaped as he stepped inside the lockup to check on Elvis. The last piece of the puzzle had just fallen into place, and it was a very big piece. Paul could not imagine taking on a venture of this magnitude without Dave's help. He watched Elvis' chest rise and fall a moment before rejoining his friends.

"Now might be a good time to start our first briefing," Paul said. "Dave, I bet you have a ton of questions."

"Where are the cops?" Dave asked.

"I think I nabbed him without sounding any alarms," Paul answered. "His guards might not even know he's gone yet, and when they make that unpleasant discovery, they'll be slow to call the cops."

"Why do you say that?"

"Because his drug use, mood swings, gun play, and between-concert disappearances haven't exactly been good publicity," Paul answered. "And judging from the contents of his coffee table, his guards were mixin' cocaine and Jack Daniel's before crashing for the night."

"His *Memphis Mafia* has had quite a bit of experience covering for him," Tara said. "We think they'll try to cover up their own negligence, clean out all the illegal drugs, look for notes and clues, and perhaps use a private security firm to help them search for the King as quietly as possible—before calling the police. All this will take time, however, and during that time, I'll be working hard to convince Elvis to stay."

"We're hoping he'll be dried out enough in a few days to make an intelligent decision," Paul said. "If he elects to stay, we'll ask him to call his family and friends to tell them he's okay and that for health reasons, he's decided to take an extended leave of absence."

Dave studied his friends a moment. "Sounds like you've got your work cut out for you."

Tara smiled. "*We've* got our work cut out for *us*."

Dave looked up at the basement ceiling. "How long can *we* expect to keep him hidden down here?"

"We're hoping for three or four days," Paul answered, "depending on his behavior."

"Then what?" Dave asked.

Paul looked at Brooks.

"I found this old, five-bedroom ranch house about an hour from here," Brooks replied, "just past Lake Travis. Tara named it *The Vineyard* because of the dried-up grapevines out back. It's very secluded. The closest neighbors are a mile away." He glanced toward Elvis' cell. "Perfect for anyone wanting a little anonymity. Rent will cost us $300.00 a month. I've already paid the security deposit, and our landlord's letting us rent it month to month. So, if Elvis decides not to accept our little invitation, we can get our deposit back and forget the whole thing."

"What's in his system right now?" Dave asked.

"We won't know for sure until we have his blood and urine tested," Tara answered. "Based on our research, he goes down with a strong mixture of sedatives, tranquilizers, and sleeping pills—his bedtime snack." She used the envelope to scoop the scattered pills into a large pile. "*This* is his breakfast in bed—basically, a strong mixture of amphetamines, antidepressants, and appetite suppressants." She held up a bright yellow capsule. "This one is a synthetic form of heroin. Highly addictive." She returned the pills to their envelope. "You can bet, at some point during the next few days, he'll contemplate killing to get this envelope."

"Vital signs?" Dave asked.

Tara opened the file and read. "Blood pressure—160 over 90. Temperature—98.7. Weight—260. He's pretty congested, either from a cold, sinus infection, or allergies. I have a friend, a retired physician named Dr. Smith, who has 20 years' experience helping drug-abuse patients. He owes me a favor, and I've called it in. He'll examine Elvis today, complete with blood and urine analysis. He's also agreed to be on call the next few months, if needed."

"Must have been a *big* favor," Dave commented.

"It was," Tara replied.

"Next?" Paul asked.

"How long do you plan on keeping him at the ranch house?" Dave asked.

"Five months," Paul answered. "Through mid-August. We think he deserves at least that much time to get his life back together."

"Five months is an awfully long time," Dave said. "What about his friends and family members? What about his music, his concert schedule? What about his daughter?"

"He's used to spending months at a time away from his family," Paul replied. "As for his concerts." He looked at Tara.

"During the past five years, Elvis has been operating under an extremely grueling concert schedule," Tara replied. "One year alone, he gave 165 live performances, a daunting task for even a young, healthy Elvis. For five years, he's been sacrificing his physical and mental health so the show could go on. For the next five months, the show will *not* be going on." Tara thought about Lisa Marie. "I *am* a little concerned about the length of time he'll be spending away from his daughter. After he's through withdrawal and well into recovery, we can discuss flying her out for a visit."

Paul noticed Dave's concerned expression. "The first few months will be hectic, all right, because of our classes and work schedules. But Rob should be able to take over a lot of the watches during April and May, since he won't be working or taking classes this spring. None of us planned to take summer classes, so if we can just make it until June, things should get a lot easier."

Dave closed his eyes, recalling Elvis' lifeless body sprawled across the plastic-covered mattress. "He'll be under a lot of stress."

Brooks looked up from his legal pad. "Dave, you're beginning to rain on our parade."

"No, he's not," Tara defended. "He's asking important questions, and I seem to recall you having similar concerns."

"Yes, well, that was before . . ."

"Before you saw a golden opportunity to write a best seller?" Tara joked.

"Well, well," Dave scoffed, "*that* should come as as no surprise to anyone. Brooksie's just in this for the money, the root of all evil."

"Let's just say I became more enthusiastic once my own role was clarified," Brooks replied.

"Getting back to your concerns," Tara said to Dave. "Yes, withdrawal and recovery will be difficult for Elvis—the process is difficult for all our patients. Are you afraid he won't be up to the challenge?"

"I just want a glimpse of the big picture—the worst-case, best-case scenarios."

Tara looked at Paul.

"Worst-case," Paul replied, "something happens to him during the next few days, before he's made his decision to stay, before he's contacted Memphis. We all go to jail. Do not pass Go. Do not collect $200.00."

The basement walls began slowly closing in on Elvis' kidnappers.

"And the best-case scenario?" Dave asked.

Paul looked at Tara.

"Elvis gets his life back," Tara replied, standing. The walls stopped. "He experiences health, happiness, and a future that he in large part, controls himself." The walls moved back as Tara walked to the lockup to look inside. "In a nutshell, he gets everything he's not getting now."

"We're hoping for the best-case scenario," Paul said. "To this end, our short-term goal will be to keep him safe, secluded, and far away from drugs. Because Tara has a lot more experience helping addicts than the rest of us, she'll be calling the shots. Any other questions?"

Dave thought for a second. "I'm sure I'll have more later, but I can't think of any now."

"I had better check on our other patients," Tara said. "If they're sleeping soundly, I'll be right back."

"I'll go with you and check on our male patients," Brooks said, accompanying Tara.

Paul watched the basement door shut then listened for the sound of footsteps ascending the staircase before speaking. "Dave, I might have one more, small reason for kidnapping Elvis, which I might have neglected to tell the others."

"Finally, we get to the bottom of this insanity," Dave replied.

Paul took a deep breath. "Remember Miss Jamison, our high school counselor?"

"Sure, how could I forget her? Every boy at DeSoto High had the hots for that woman, myself included. She moved to New York after our sophomore year. I heard she's become a successful psychologist."

"Yes, she has, I got a card from her last Christmas. Anyway, after one of my high school fisticuffs, she informed me that sixteen was a little old to be fighting over ones childhood idol. She said most young men do good to handle one emotion and that when it came to Elvis, I seemed to be juggling quite a few. She described it as a big weight on my shoulders, a weight that could grow heavier if it wasn't addressed and resolved. She suggested counseling. I suggested she mind her own business. Like any teenager with half a brain, I completely blew her off. I wasn't crazy. I didn't need counseling."

Dave chuckled. "Miss Jamison thought everyone needed counseling. I wish she'd called me in for a few sessions. If she'd worn her dresses any shorter she would've had to counsel me for trying to jump her bones."

Paul grinned. "Yes, but with me, I think she might have been on to something. I've matured a little since high school. I'm majoring in psychology, myself. And during the long drive back from Memphis, I kept wondering if what I was really doing was some sort of attempt to resolve this matter the only way I knew how."

Dave leaned back, struck a reflective pose, then burst out laughing. He stood and peered through the window at Elvis. "Well, sir, I'll say this for you. If that's what this is really all about, you certainly have taken the bull by the horns." The two friends were still laughing when Tara and Brooks returned to the basement.

Tara stepped inside Elvis' lockup and soon returned, leaving the door wide-open. "What did you say he had to eat last night?" she asked Paul.

"Cheeseburgers, fries and a soda," Paul answered, grinning at Dave.

"If you men wouldn't mind, there's half-digested cheeseburgers, fries, and soda all over the floor in there."

Paul's grin quickly vanished, causing Dave to laugh.

While the others cleaned up the mess, Tara asked Elvis a series of health-related questions, but his responses were unintelligible, and he quickly fell back to sleep.

"I can't keep *my* eyes open either," Paul said. "I think I'll take a nap in one of the lockups."

"Paul, you should really go home and get some sleep," Tara replied. "We can handle things here."

"What about you, Dave?" Paul asked. "I robbed you of a good night's sleep."

"I got more than you, and how can I possibly sleep now? I'll keep watch until my shift starts upstairs."

"Thanks, Dave," Paul replied.

"Does this phone work?" Dave asked.

"Yes," Tara answered.

"I'll call the nurse's station when he wakes up. He'll probably want to use the toilet, and I have a feeling that'll be a real chore."

"I can be back at ten," Paul said, glancing at his watch. "That'll give me six hours sleep. I'll keep the phone by my bed in case something happens."

"Nothing will happen," Brooks said. "Get some sleep. We'll brief you at ten."

Paul stood to leave then paused. "What if someone tries to come down here?"

Tara smiled at her exhausted friend. "We've discussed the possibility countless times, but for Dave's benefit, we should probably discuss it once more. The basement's off limits to all our patients. Staff only comes down here for supplies, and I've just supplied the nurse's station, both dorms, and all three restrooms. We've also installed a new lock on the basement door, and we're the only ones with keys." Tara removed two keys from her chain and handed them to Dave. "One's to the basement door, and the other's to the lockup."

"Thanks," Dave replied.

"I'll be in the nurse's station if anyone needs me," Brooks said, picking up his pen and pad. "Dave, I'll smuggle you down some breakfast after our upstairs briefing."

"Thanks," Dave said.

"I'll walk you to your car," Tara said to Paul. "I could use some fresh air."

Tara held Paul's arm as they climbed the basement stairs, knowing he had mixed emotions about leaving. She also knew he needed sleep—a big day lay ahead. As they stepped outside into a cool breeze, goose bumps formed on her bare arms. She pulled Paul closer. "When this is over, I'd like to visit the coast for a few days. Perhaps Corpus."

Paul closed his eyes to picture Tara walking along a white, sandy beach, half-nude, her bare feet stepping just where the waves were bestowing their treasures. He visualized an aqua-green ocean complimenting her jade-green eyes as one of her breasts slid out from beneath the strands of her long hair. He shook the image away as Tara waited patiently for some reply. Paul's tired mind, however, was somewhat confused by the remark. Was she asking him to go with her to Corpus, or does she want him to check her mail and water her houseplants like last time?

"Corpus sounds like a good idea," Paul replied. "Perhaps we'll get some time off for good behavior."

Tara laughed, studying her partner in crime. "You did a good job with Dave."

"Thanks, so did you."

"And you and Mr. Brooks were right to save him until last."

"We know the conscience of the Musketeers pretty well. Right now, his main motivation for helping is a strong desire to keep us all out of jail."

Tara smiled, but as her thoughts turned to Elvis, her face saddened. "It was a shock seeing him like this. I pretty much knew what to expect, but it was still a shock."

"Be careful, Tara," Paul said, as they reached his car. "Looks can be deceiving. When those drugs wear off . . ."

"Thanks, but I can handle myself."

"I know you can—but if something were to happen to you—I—I."

Tara blushed then impulsively kissed her friend on the lips. "Don't worry, honey. I'll be fine. Now you go home and get some sleep."

As Tara spun to walk away, Paul could feel the sudden burst of heat rushing to his face. Although he had imagined it often, they had *never* kissed, and she had *never* called him *honey*. He watched until she was safely inside the building, his face beaming. Wow. And all he had to do was kidnap the King.

Chapter Two

While driving home from Detox, Paul's thoughts kept returning to his and Tara's first kiss. He tried to focus on more serious issues. Would Elvis' condition worsen? Had his Mafia boys already called the police? Would the King ever in a million years agree to stay with them? But after each of these questions, Paul's heart won out over his tired mind, and his thoughts returned to Tara. Although he had often yearned for more than friendship, she had drawn a clear line, which he had been unable to cross. During the planning stage of the mission, their friendship had evolved into a businesslike partnership, which made the kiss stranger still. Had their relationship suddenly evolved into something else, or was he reading way too much into one kiss—one heart-throbbing, earthshaking kiss?

Paul soon arrived at his and Dave's rental house, showered, turned on his window air conditioner, and placed the phone by his bed. Images of Tara strolling by the seashore eased him off to dreamland. Six hours later he lay half-awake feeling the warmth of the late morning sun while listening to the faint sound of a police siren. The distant siren melted easily into his peaceful dream of dancing dolphins and flying fish, but when his telephone rang loudly, he bolted straight up out of bed and grabbed the receiver. "Hello!"

"Good morning," Tara said cheerfully.

Paul's alarm clock blared loudly, causing him to jump. He spun and struck the snooze button. "Is everything okay?"

"Everything's fine. How'd you sleep?"

"Like a rock. How's he doing?"

"Compared to our other patients, he's been a saint. At this moment, he's sound asleep."

"Does anyone suspect anything?"

"Not a thing—our staff's been a little preoccupied. Hear that?"

"Yeah," Paul said, listening to a loud argument in the background.

"One of our long-terms is trying to clarify the pecking order for one of our new arrivals. I should probably separate them. Mind if I fill you in on the rest later?"

"Not at all, I'll see you in half an hour."

Brooks snuck down to the basement carrying a plate of bacon, eggs, and toast for Dave. "How's he doing?" Brooks asked, pressing his nose against the window.

"Still out cold," Dave answered, digging into his breakfast. "He's probably making up for all those sleepless nights in Vegas."

"Yes, I've read about those wild nights," Brooks said, scribbling on his pad.

Between bites, Dave studied Brooks curiously. "Are you really writing a book about this?"

"I certainly am."

"And that's how Paul suckered you into this mess?"

"Suckered? Mess? Is that any way for a future doctor to talk about saving a man's life?"

"My mistake," Dave replied. "What exactly motivated you to join this noble venture?"

Brooks stared at his pad a moment, gathering his thoughts. "Nine months ago I decided to branch out from essays and short stories, to writing a book. I quickly discovered the hardest part of writing three hundred pages is writing the first page. I'd been staring at my blank pad for quite some time, trash can overspilling with wadded up ideas, when Paul and Tara divulged their plan to kidnap Elvis. From that moment on, my pen's been racing across this pad like the frenzied brooms in *Fantasia*."

"So you threw caution to the wind because it seemed like a good idea for a *book*?"

Brooks smiled. "Hmm, I guess that's one way of putting it, but I think I'll describe it in more passionate terms." Brooks looked his friend in the eye. "Listen, Dave, you want to become a doctor, right? You love everything about it: the research, problem solving, looking for better treatments, and on and on. You're also looking forward to the numerous perks like the good pay, prestige, country club membership, and expensive house and sports cars."

Dave smiled, picturing himself in a new Mercedes, hands tucked snugly around its leather-wrapped steering wheel.

"And Tara's a nurturer," Brooks continued. "She's most alive when she's helping others—patients, coworkers, friends, garden plants, whatever. And she, too, thrives on making positive changes in the health industry.

"Paul loves the outdoors—jogging, hiking, and pushing himself physically. He also likes playing guitar, reading poetry, and let's not forget romance. He's been in love with *someone* or *something* since the third grade. He's most alive when he's in love.

"As for Rob, he's always asking, Where's the party? He's not happy unless he's immersed in one of his latest exploits: football, paintings, sexual conquests, and whatever.

"And, I'm a writer. I *love* to write. I'm most alive when I'm writing. So, how could I possibly say no to this great opportunity? I feel more *blessed* than suckered."

Dave took another bite of eggs, staring at Brooks' filled legal pad. "Well, sir, you should feel doubly blessed, because unlike the rest of us, you'll be able to pursue *your* talent in jail."

Brooks chuckled, pulled out a clean pad, and continued writing.

At 10 a.m. Paul returned to Detox, passing Phyllis, a dayshift nurse, at the door.

"What are *you* doing here, Paul?" Phyllis asked.

"I need to check out the work schedule."

"Good luck. Tara's been playing havoc with it all morning, scheduling some of us around the clock, and others three and four days off."

"Exams," Paul said. "I could surely use some extra time off to study."

"I hope you get it," Phyllis replied, leaving the unit.

Paul greeted Tara and an aide named Shelly at the nurse's station.

"Are you working day shift?" Shelly asked Paul.

"No, I just stopped by to check out the work schedule."

"Shelly, would you mind updating the progress notes on the women while I check on the men?" Tara asked, picking up several files.

"Not at all," Shelly answered.

"Then I need to run to admissions for a while," Tara added.

"We'll be fine," Shelly replied.

"Paul, if you'd like to come along, we can discuss the work schedule," Tara suggested.

"Where was Phyllis going?" Paul whispered, as they neared the men's dorm.

"I sent her out for breakfast tacos. We've been too busy to eat—a blessing in disguise. Dr. Smith examined our patient."

"Already? That's great. What'd he find?"

"Nothing serious," Tara answered, glancing back at the nurse's station. "Brooks and Dave are waiting for us downstairs. We'll fill you in there."

In the basement, Brooks sat in his usual position behind the desk while Dave stood at the lockup door wearing a white smock and stethoscope.

"Good morning, Paul," Brooks said to Paul. "Sleep well?"

"Yes, thank you," Paul answered. He looked at Dave's smock and grinned. "Doctor Livingston, I presume?"

Dave faced Tara. "Nurse Benoist, would you be kind enough to begin the day's first briefing?"

Tara picked up Elvis' file. "Doctor Smith found our patient fit under the circumstances. He prescribed an antibiotic for Elvis' sinus infection and Valium for withdrawal. He advised us to hold off on both medications until we've received the results of the blood and urine tests, hopefully by this afternoon.

"Elvis thinks he's been committed to a Tennessee state rehab clinic. We saw no reason to tell him otherwise. Along with his sinus congestion, he's experiencing headaches and nausea, especially when standing for long periods. He was very open about his health problems and the various drugs he's been using to fight them. He was polite and well-mannered during the exam and even said *sir* and *ma'am* when answering our questions. During our later visits, he began calling me *girl* and *hon'*, and Brooks, *son* and *boy*."

"You can take the boy out of the country," Dave joked.

"Or he's making a statement about our age difference," Brooks guessed. "He *is* eighteen years our senior."

"I think it's cute, whatever the reason," Tara said, "and I hope it means he's growing comfortable in his new surroundings."

"He calls me *Doc*," Dave said, flicking an offensive piece of lint from his smock. Brooks rolled his eyes.

"He hasn't eaten this morning," Tara continued. "Dave and Brooks have been listening to the news every hour. No word out of Memphis, yet. We've also been debating the length of his stay in Detox."

"We like the added security of a lockup," Dave said, "but the longer we keep him here, the riskier it becomes."

"Did you install that deadbolt on the pantry door at the house?" Paul asked Brooks.

"Yes, but that door's pretty flimsy. If he gets mad enough, he should be able to bust it right off its hinges.

Unfortunately, the pantry's the only room in the house without windows."

"It might serve as a good threat, if nothing else," Paul said. "Tara, what do you think about moving up his departure?"

"Four days here would have been ideal, but I agree, that might be pushing it. I'm also a little uncomfortable about letting that much time elapse before calling Memphis. At the very least, his father and daughter need to know he's okay. And that news would be better received if it came from Elvis, himself."

"Why don't we keep him here tonight and tomorrow night," Paul suggested, "then move him out day after tomorrow."

"That would still give me two full days to work on him," Tara replied. "It might be enough."

"How much progress have you made so far?" Paul asked.

"He seems to like me. I think I'm gaining his trust. But we're a long way from that big talk. I want him as relaxed as possible when I inform him that things aren't exactly what they seem. I've also been making some improvements in our speeches."

"Speeches?" Dave asked.

"We've prepared strong arguments to convince him to stay."

"Please tell me you didn't prepare those little speeches you used to bamboozle *me* into this venture."

Tara grinned.

"I feel hoodwinked," Dave said.

"You'd have felt more than that if you'd said no," Brooks joked. "That lockup next to Elvis' had your name on it."

"We needed you with us," Tara said to Dave. "Our arguments had to be persuasive, with nothing left out, so they were prepared in advance, and rehearsed, too, I might add."

"I'm touched," Dave replied. "When not working hard to reduce my own culpability in all this, I'll be working hard to keep you folks out of jail."

"I wish you luck," Brooks said. "If you succeed, I'll give you an autographed copy of my first book."

"Thanks, but I already have a doorstop. I'll take a Mercedes 450 SL."

"What's next on our agenda?" Paul asked.

"Dave and I don't feel comfortable calling him *Elvis*," Tara answered.

"What's wrong with *Elvis*?" Brooks asked. The room fell silent. "Let me guess. You're afraid one of us will be standing in line at the grocery store, behind a Texas Ranger working on the case, and they're going to slip up and blurt something out like, '*Damn*, I forgot those jelly-filled doughnuts for *Elvis*.'"

Everyone smiled.

"Perhaps we'd just feel more comfortable calling him something else," Dave said, "especially while we're in Detox."

"Fine with me," Brooks replied. "What should we call him?"

As the others discussed new names, Paul felt a tinge of guilt. They had already robbed the King of his freedom, privacy, and dignity. Now, they were casually discussing the theft of his name. On the other hand, he could not deny the name *Elvis* was long overdue for a change. For twenty years, it had been used to sell newspapers, magazines, and tabloids. During the past ten years, it had been used in literature, movies, and thousands of television sitcoms. Now, the name was being used to get laughs—by every comedian, disc jockey, and talk show host in the country. Paul's jaw tightened. No, he thought. *This* theft was justified. The name *Elvis* needed a change, almost as much as the King, himself.

"How about *Aaron?*" Dave suggested. "It's his middle name, and we won't get arrested using it at the grocery store."

Paul immediately thought about his younger cousin, also named Aaron, and the fun they used to have playing their childhood summers away.

"Aaron," Paul said, listening as the name filled the basement. "Smart, Dave. I like it. And you can't get much more unassuming."

"I like it, too," Tara agreed, watching Brooks write the name on his pad. "That's with one A, Mr. Brooks. It was misspelled on his birth certificate, and until recently, he continued spelling it that way."

"Got it," Brooks said. "Four letters like Paul, Tara, and Dave. Begins with an A, the first letter of the alphabet. It says we're giving him a new start. I like it."

"Perhaps we should ask *him* first," Paul suggested, motioning toward the King's cell.

"Good idea," Tara said, looking inside the lockup. "I'll ask him as soon as he wakes up." She glanced at her notes. "Next, I'd like to discuss his mood swings."

Inside the lockup, Elvis slowly opened his eyes, squinting at the bright, grid-protected light bulb hanging in the center of the ceiling. The light reminded him of the projects—small, beige rooms lit with lone bulbs—their missing fixtures either stolen or busted. How strange to have leaped from that single bulb, to the countless bright lights of movie sets, concert stages, and Las Vegas. He glared at the lonely bulb above his head, feeling as if he had come full circle. Hey, where in the heck was he? He closed his eyes and slowly inhaled the sick mixture of body odor, vomit, and disinfectant. Oh, yeah, he was in a hospital. Some kind of—state hospital. He opened his eyes and stared at the plastic-covered pillow and mattress glued to his face and arms. Couldn't they have at least given him a sheet? What were they afraid of, that he would try and hang himself? He pictured himself feeding one corner of a clean white sheet through the small grid covering the ceiling light.

The King lifted his face from the sticky pillow, rolled over onto his stomach, and pushed himself up to his knees. He waited for his nausea to pass before crawling across the floor—dry hands dragging across the hard linoleum like fingernails scratching across a cracked chalkboard. He sat against the wall, quickly lifting his hands off the floor. He pulled his knees up beneath his chin and wrapped his arms around his legs, a common pose for lockup visitors. The room was so quiet, he could hear his dry eyelids scraping across his pupils. He closed his eyes and pictured himself straddling his Harley. He imagined the powerful rumble between his legs—his moist hands tightening around the hog's warm handlebars—that exhilarating lurch forward.

He could almost feel the wind blowing through his hair as the Harley's deafening crescendo filled his ears.

A sliding deadbolt startled Elvis from his daydream. From his crouched position on the floor, he glared at the four intruders.

"Mr. Presley, I'd like you to meet Paul Roberts," Tara introduced, guessing Elvis would have little recollection of the previous day's events. "He's one of our best nurse's aides."

Elvis closed his eyes, trying to bring back the Harley.

"Good morning," Paul said, extending his hand.

The King recognized something in Paul's voice and quickly opened his eyes.

"We're glad you're here, Mr. Presley," Paul said, still holding out his hand.

Elvis reached up and lazily shook hands.

"We're confident we can help you recover from your addiction," Paul added.

Elvis' eyes narrowed.

"How do you feel?" Tara asked.

"Like I wanna die, and this place ain't helpin'."

"You'll be leaving in a few days," Tara replied. "Where exactly do you hurt?"

Elvis clenched his teeth, trying to hold down the small amount of undigested food still tormenting his stomach. He began massaging his throbbing temples. "I have a stomachache and my head's killin' me."

Tara reached into her her skirt pocket for a packet of aspirin. "Here, take these. Would you like some water?"

Elvis gulped the aspirin then began running off a long list of needed medications. Between each request, he glared at Tara, wondering why she wasn't writing them all down.

Paul stared at Elvis' soft, puffy hands, recalling the King's weak handshake. It was hard for Paul to believe that those same karate-trained hands had once shattered thick boards. He studied Elvis' face. Swollen eyelids sagged over bloodshot eyes. Clownish sideburns hung from pale, bloated cheeks. Dirty strands of long, black-dyed hair framed a three-day beard—curtains closing over a hobo face. Rounded shoulders slumped forward like an old man's. A large white belly bulged between a tightly-stretched T-shirt and the straining waist band of a dirty pair of black sweat pants.

Paul recalled the first pictures he had seen of his child-hood idol, Elvis Aron Presley—the young man's tanned, muscular body and strong, squared shoulders. He recalled Elvis' blue eyes, pompadour hairstyle, and neatly trimmed sideburns. He remembered Elvis' chin held high, and most of all, the King's brilliant smile. He stared at the sad individual slumped before him now. No way. No way, could *this* be the same man.

As Paul's eyes moistened, he quickly looked away, scolding himself for almost crying. As the team's leader, he could ill afford to let his emotions get in the way. He forced himself to focus on the business at hand.

"Mr. Presley, would you mind if we called you *Aron?*" Tara asked.

Elvis' eyes rose from Tara's tanned, panty-hosed legs, to the seductive curves of her hips and waist. He noticed the subtle movement of her breasts, pushing against her thin blouse with each breath. He felt that all too familiar stirring in his groin.

"Mr. Presley?" Tara asked again.

"What?"

"Would you mind if we called you Aron? We think it might give you some degree of anonymity during your stay here."

Elvis *Aron* suddenly recalled Jesse *Garon*, his stillborn twin brother. In the Old South, parents often rhymed the middle names of their twins. Throughout Elvis' life, he had often thought of Jesse Garon. He thought of Jesse the day he walked into Sun Studios, the day he married Priscilla, and the day Lisa Marie was born. He thought about his twin the day he performed live via satellite for over a billion fans. He thought about Jesse Garon the day their mom died and the day Priscilla asked him for a divorce. He was thinking about Jesse now.

Over the years, Elvis had often wondered why God had allowed Jesse Garon to die and Elvis Aron to live. At that moment, he would have gladly traded places with Jesse, wherever he was. And where *was* that, exactly? For nine months, they'd shared the same womb, only to be sent in completely opposite directions. Had God allowed his twin to grow up in heaven? Or because he'd died so young, without enjoying a single breath of air, had God allowed him a quick reincarnation? Could he be walking the earth this instant? Elvis Aron, may I present, Jesse Garon? Jesse Garon, may I present, Elvis Aron. And what would Elvis say to his twin after all these years? Hey, Jesse! How's it goin'? What's it like on the other side? Boy, my boy, you'll never in a million years guess what happened to *me*.

The thought made Elvis smile. For the first time since leaving Memphis, the King smiled. Suddenly, he was very thankful for the small connection he still shared with his twin. He looked up at Tara, "No, hon', I wouldn't mind being called *Aron*." His eyes fell to a splotch of dried vomit on his leg, face saddening. "I'm kind of tired of being *Elvis*."

"Very good, then, *Aron*," Tara replied, "do you need anything else?"

"Yeah, out of here."

Aron glared at the backs of his intruders as they left the lockup. The hard thud of the dead bolt faded, again leaving him in silent, solitary confinement, mind drifting back to the projects. Back then, he had often used music to escape the bleakness of his embarrassing poverty, failing grades, and awkward youth, the bleakness of those small, bare rooms. He searched his mind for the just right tune and was soon humming a childhood favorite, an old gospel about faith, hope, and redemption.

Outside Aron's lockup, Paul glanced at his watch. "Dave, they'll be expecting you upstairs. And again, I'm sorry for robbing you of a good night's sleep."

"I'll catch a nap in Dr. Raymond's physics class this afternoon," Dave said.

"Tara, why don't you and Brooks go home and get some sleep," Paul suggested. "Elvis and I—I mean *Aron* and I—will be just fine."

"I need to talk to him as much as possible while he's awake," Tara replied. "If he takes a nap this afternoon, I'll do the same."

"What about you, Mr. Brooks?" Paul asked.

"I'd like to start moving some things to the house, but I'll need Rob's truck for the bulky items—and Rob, too, unless you want him here."

"We'll be okay today," Tara said, "but I'd like everyone back here just past seven, after the day shift's left the building."

"No problem," Brooks replied.

"I'll be upstairs if anyone needs me," Dave said, standing. "I'll order extra meals at lunch and sneak them down after we've fed our other patients. Good luck."

"Thanks," Tara replied, watching Dave leave the basement. As Brooks stood to leave, the phone rang loudly, causing all three to jump.

"That's probably Rob," Brooks said, reaching for the phone.

"This is the police," Rob joked. "We have the place surrounded. Drop your weapons and come out with your hands up."

"Rob, where are you?" Brooks asked.

"Thirty minutes outside of Austin. Did Paul get him?"

"Right out from under their noses, and without a fight, and drove him all the way here without a hitch."

"*Yahoo*! I knew it! I knew he'd pull it off! How's . . . ?"

"*Aron* is just fine, all things considered."

"*Aron*, eh? Smart. Did Dave freak?"

"Did he ever. You should've seen him. Screaming, yelling, pacing back and forth, looking inside the lockup every ten seconds. And during the whole time, I kept wondering how he could say no. Can you imagine him nonchalantly working his shift upstairs, as if nothing at all unusual was happening below?"

"With us calling to ask him if he'd mind sending down a couple of fried peanut butter and banana sandwiches," Rob laughed. "So he's in?"

"He's in, thanks to some powerful persuading by Paul and Tara. I've got it all documented."

"I bet you have. So where do you want me?"

"Can you help me move some furniture to our safe house?"

"Sure, but we'll have to empty my stuff first. I've come to stay."

"I'll meet you at my apartment in thirty minutes. We can move furniture until six—Tara wants us back here at seven. Here, I'll let you talk to her."

"Rob, I'm glad you made it safely," Tara said.

"Safe and sound," Rob replied.

"I bet you're tired. Before I forget, I hope you and Brooks get some sleep today—we might be in for a long night."

"Spoken like a true nurse. He hasn't gotten physical has he?"

"No, but for most of our males, it's just a matter of time, which reminds me, are you having second thoughts about leaving football for the art world?"

"None at all. I can't get my canvases stretched fast enough. Wait till you see my latest."

"I was hoping you brought *all* your paintings. I'm eager to see how you've progressed."

"All thirty-two, and I'm growing by leaps and bounds."

"What are you doing to stay in shape?"

"I switched to light beer. Hey, I read Aron used to love playin' football. Maybe after things settle down, he'll be up for a little two-below."

"I'll ask him."

"Tell him he can play quarterback."

"I will. In fact, I should be talking to him now. Thanks again, Rob, for joining our team."

"It's going to be a real blast, Tara. I'll see you tonight."

Tara passed the phone to Paul before returning to the lockup. "Did the aspirin help?" she asked Aron.

"Listen, hon', I don't know how I landed here, but I'll give ya $50,000 to get me out right now. I can have it wired to your account. Just give me the numbers."

Aron's eyes searched the lockup as if looking for pen and paper.

"That's very generous of you, Aron, but that's not how it works here. Get well, and you'll be released."

Aron's jaw tightened.

"Please try to use this time to rest," Tara suggested.

"I'm not tired."

"You mentioned to Dr. Smith that you suffer from chronic fatigue, that you sometimes check yourself into Baptist Memorial just to rest."

"Yeah, I do, hon'." Baptist is a great place to rest, and they've got plenty of drugs, I mean medications, to help. Can ya get me a PDR (Physicians' Desk Reference)?"

"Yes, but you're not in Graceland. You won't be allowed to order from it."

"What medicines can I get in here?"

"Aspirin, now. In a day or two, Valium and Demerol for withdrawal."

"*Withdrawal!* What in the heck you talkin' about? And I'm gonna need something a lot stronger than Valium and Demerol."

"Did you once say you'd rather be unconscious than miserable?" Tara asked, recalling a recent magazine article.

"Yeah, I did, hon'. I wish I was out right now."

"There *are* other choices, you know."

"Not for me."

"Nonsense. There's a whole world of options out there, Aron. The same world that existed in 1954, the day you walked into Sun Studios—only bigger, only better."

"What are *you* on?"

Tara scanned the bleak lockup. "I'll admit, our options are sometimes difficult to see, but they're out there, nonetheless." She scanned her notes. "You mentioned during our last visit that you were tired of being Elvis. What would you say if I offered you a break from being the King—not just an overnight stay at Baptist Memorial—but a five month stay where most of the pressures of being *Elvis* will be far removed, a place you might one day describe as pure heaven?"

"Ha! Now I *know* you're on somethin'. Who do you think you are, God?"

"No, but I can sometimes help others see their choices."

Aron scanned Tara from head to toe. "How old are you, hon'?"

"Twenty-six."

"Twenty-six," Aron scoffed. "A 26-year-old nurse, workin' in a stupid state hospital, is gonna create heaven for *Elvis*. Look around you, hon'. *This* is what you've created."

Again, Tara scanned the room. "You raise a good point, but we're working on something better, and I suggest you give my offer some serious consideration, should the opportunity present itself."

Aron shook his head in disgust. "Boy, my boy," he replied, looking toward the door.

"I have to check on my other patients, then I'll be right back."

Just past 1 p.m. Dave snuck two lunches down for Tara and Paul. "How's he doing?" he asked, looking inside the lockup.

"Sleeping soundly," Tara answered, taking a bite of her peanut butter sandwich, "and I'm happy to report, we've had several productive conversations."

"Does anyone upstairs suspect anything?" Paul asked.

"No, it's been really hectic up there," Dave answered. "Mrs. Baker had an allergic reaction to penicillin—we had her rushed to Brackenridge. Mr. Samuelson, the new patient we were warned about, went ballistic on an aide and will be spending the rest of the afternoon in lockup. And Phyllis and Dr. Wilbur are no longer on speaking terms, thanks to a blowout over the good doctor's treatment of the nursing staff. Everyone up there's fighting, patients and staff alike. I don't think they'd notice Aron if he came up singing 'Blue Suede Shoes.' I'm glad to be off."

"Brooks and Rob called a minute ago," Paul mentioned. "They've already moved two truck loads of furniture to The Vineyard."

"Isn't that a little premature?" Dave asked.

"Rob's fallen in love with the place," Paul answered. "Says he's staying regardless of what Aron decides."

"It's good to have him back in Texas," Dave said, "although I *will* have to bust his chops for keeping me in the dark about all this."

"I'm exhausted, guys," Tara said, pushing back her tray. "I think I'll take a nap in the lockup next to Aron's."

"Pleasant dreams," Dave replied, reaching for the other half of her sandwich.

Tara looked at Paul. "You'll wake me when he awakes?"

"You can count on it. I don't think he cares too much for me."

Tara smiled. "Until he's through withdrawal, he won't be caring too much for anyone."

Tara retrieved a pillow and blanket before entering the empty lockup.

Dave stood to check on Aron, glanced at his watch, then returned to his chair. "Well, Paul, I have a half hour before class, and I'd just love to hear the specifics."

"The specifics?"

"Of the kidnapping. I'm very curious just how you pulled it off?"

"Where would you like me to begin?"

"How about from the moment you entered Memphis."

Paul closed his eyes, picturing the Memphis city limit sign passing by his car's window. "I entered from the west on I-55 in the middle of rush-hour traffic, most of it headed in the opposite direction. Graceland wasn't hard to find, just a mile off 55. I parked 50 feet from the entrance, raised my hood to fake car trouble, and strolled up to the front gate."

"Why'd you go alone?" Dave asked.

"Tara and Rob both wanted to go, but I thought it best we limit the risks. If I got caught, then I could just pretend to be some crazy fan trying to meet *Elvis*."

"Why in broad daylight?"

"It's a twelve hour drive from Memphis to Austin, so I couldn't both take him and deliver him under the cover of darkness. Detox can resemble Grand Central Station during the day, and I wasn't at all sure what condition he'd be in, so I thought it best to nab him in the afternoon and deliver him before sunrise."

"Just out of curiosity, in that dream you had last summer, did you kidnap him during the day?"

"Yes, as a matter of fact, I did."

Dave shook his head. "So you're telling me your dream had nothing to do with your decision?"

"It might have played a small part."

Dave rolled his eyes.

"Whatever my reasons, it worked out for the best. At two in the afternoon the place was wide-open. At night, it might have been locked up tighter than a drum."

"What do you mean, wide-open?"

"The front gate and side door were both unlocked."

"So you just marched right inside? Without having any idea what to expect?"

"During our research, we discovered Aron had become lax in every aspect of his life. His health, diet, finances, drug use, relationships. He'd even become uncharacteristically lethargic during his latest concert performances. We expected security at Graceland to be lax, and it was. We also read that even when security was tight, a fan or two managed to sneak in from time to time." Paul stood to look inside the lockup. Aron's lifeless body hung over all four sides of the small mattress. "Of course, in light of his present condition, his guards probably weren't all that worried about Elvis fans breaking in to get a glimpse. I guess that's another reason why security was so lax."

Paul returned to his seat. "I snuck straight into the living room. The smell of stale cigarette smoke and spilt booze filled the air. Long drapes covered the room's tall windows. A guard was asleep in a recliner and another asleep on the sofa, curled up around an empty Jack Daniel's bottle. The coffee table was covered with empty glasses, small pieces of aluminum foil, and several white lines. Guns lay everywhere—a rifle and shotgun against the wall, pistols on the end tables, and what looked like a machine gun near the television."

"Did you bring any weapons?"

"No."

"You broke into a house full of guns and coked-up bodyguards without so much as a pocketknife?"

"I had a gut feeling I wouldn't need any. Plus, I didn't want to give anyone an excuse to blow my head off. I brought a syringe full of Thorazine, along with some ropes and duct tape. But barging in with ropes and tape seemed almost as conspicuous as arriving with drawn guns, so I left everything in the car. And again, if things turned nasty, I wanted the option of pretending I was just another crazy fan trying to get a glimpse of *Elvis*."

"Where was Lisa Marie?"

"Early in the planning stage, I told Tara there was no way I could kidnap the King with his daughter in the house. I could just imagine her waking up screamin' and cryin' for her dad—and me trying to explain to a little 9-year-old girl that I was taking her father for his own good.

Tara called Graceland pretending to be a reporter for Teen Magazine and asked if she could interview Lisa Marie in mid-March. They informed her that Elvis' daughter would be staying with Priscilla in California during the month of March. Of course, schedules *do* change, so I was still a little worried she might be in the house, until I saw the contents of the living room. At least, I hoped they wouldn't leave guns, cocaine, and booze lying everywhere with a small child running around the house.

"I climbed the stairs to the second floor and began searching rooms until I found him lying face down on black silk sheets. We read he never drinks, but his breath reeked of alcohol. We also read two of his former body-guards were writing a tell-all book about the king and that he'd been taking it pretty hard. I guess he was lookin' for relief wherever he could find it.

"I searched for his billfold and car keys, so it'd look like he'd left on his own accord, but I struck out. That's when I found the envelopes on his nightstand. I crammed the full one in my pocket, put tennis shoes on his feet, and tried shaking him awake. I pulled him up to a sitting posi-tion and slapped his face until I got a response. Without even opening his eyes, he pushed me away and fell back down. I couldn't see dragging 260 pounds of dead weight down the staircase and past two sleeping guards. I needed him at least half-awake, so I pulled him back up and con-tinued slapping his face, trying anything that might entice an aging, drugged-out rock star to leave his comfortable bed. I offered him cocaine, Harley's, Lamborginis, a new guitar, young, naked women, and whatever else I could think of off the top of my head. Strangely enough, it was the cheeseburgers that got his attention. He opened his eyes and grinned. I sat beside him on the bed, wrapped his left arm around my neck, circled my right arm around his waist, and stood.

"At the top of the staircase, he rocked forward and backward, drunklike. As I adjusted my grip, I almost laughed at the thought of us tumblin' head over heels all the way to the bottom of the staircase and landin' at the feet of two angry, gun-totin' bodyguards. I listened intently for any sign that the guards had awakened. The house was eerily quiet. We negotiated the first couple of steps without a hitch, right up until he decided to sit down. I'd braced for him falling forward or backward but never expected him to just plop straight down on the steps. My first instinct was to hold on tight, which turned out to be a big mistake. His weight pulled me straight over. I somersaulted once then clung to the steps like a big spider.

"He found my fall quite amusing and was about to laugh when I raced up and quickly covered his mouth. He pushed my hand away, but kept quiet. Again, I wrapped his arm around my neck and stood. At the bottom step, right as I turned toward the door, a guard coughed and rolled over. I froze. With Aron's weight slumped over my shoulders, I couldn't easily turn to look toward the living room. Plus, if the guard was staring at us through half-open eyes, I didn't want him noticing any movement. So, I just stood there, frozen, holding my breath and prayin'. After a long, quiet minute, we made a beeline for the side door.

"Just outside, he collapsed, but this time, he was out cold. I stretched him out beside some shrubs and was about to shut the door when I noticed a really beautiful guitar leaning against the wall. Without much thought, I snatched it before closing and locking the door behind us. I folded his arms around the guitar as if it was a teddy bear, then ran. As I opened the gate, a big, black crow perched on top squawked so loud, I almost jumped out of my skin. It flew to a nearby branch as I ran to my car. I shut the hood, jumped behind the wheel, and turned the key, but nothin' happened. I sat in shock, staring at the dark instrument panel and listening to the most sickening silence.

"A few months back, I'd had some starting trouble and thought replacing the battery had solved the problem. Again, I tried, and again, nothin' happened. I quickly grabbed a pair of pliers from under my seat, opened the hood, and tightened the battery cables. I searched for any other loose wires, jumped behind the wheel, said a quick prayer, and turned the key. The engine started. I slammed the hood, threw the car into gear, and raced through the front gate. After a ten minute struggle, I got him sprawled across the back seat, pitched the guitar up front, and stopped just long enough to close the gate behind us, and to give the stupid crow another opportunity to scare the piss out of me, which it took full advantage of.

"We stopped three times for gas, and once for cheeseburgers, and here we are."

Dave stared at Paul a moment then shook his head. "And he slept all the way?"

"All the way, except when I coaxed him to eat a bite."

"And you did all that alone," Dave commented, shaking his head.

"Yes, and no. Now that I've had more time to think about it, I don't think I was as quite *alone* as I first thought. There were just too many coincidences. The front gate and side door unlocked. Both guards sound asleep. Aron just conscious enough to make it down the staircase, but not conscious enough to put up a fight. I think Someone was pulling strings, Dave. Someone with quite a sense of humor, who let me stumble at the top of the staircase but kept me from falling all the way to the bottom, who watched me open my car hood to fake car trouble and thought it'd be funny if I experienced some *real* car trouble. Someone who wanted me to escape with the King, undetected, but not without experiencing a few curves along the way."

Again, Paul stood to check on Aron. "Of course, I didn't see the humor until Memphis had completely vanished from my rear view mirror. Then, I had a good laugh, after which, I thanked God for His help *and* His sense of humor."

Dave studied Paul seriously. "You know, this might not be kidnapping after all. I mean, it's not like you held a gun to his head."

"I'm glad you see it that way," Paul replied. "I hope the judge sees it the same way."

"I'd play up the God angle. You know, look him right in the eye and tell him you heard voices directing you every step of the way. Maybe a good lawyer can cop you an insanity plea."

Inside the open lockup, Tara rolled over on her mattress, smiling at Dave's joke. Paul's twice-told description of the kidnapping seemed like a bedtime story, easing her off to dreamland. Tara was pretty sure God had more important things to do than help a group of college students bent on saving *Elvis*. But just in case He *had* been pulling strings, she thanked Him for His help before falling fast asleep.

As Dave left for campus, Paul continued keeping watch while studying for an upcoming Perceptual Psychology exam. At 4:30 p.m. Aron began to stir. Paul immediately awakened Tara, and she and Aron were soon discussing ineffective medications and the proposed length of his stay at the unit. Paul sat an earshot away, ready to rush inside the cell, if needed. He found it difficult to concentrate on Tara and Aron's conversation while reading his dull textbook, so he soon traded his text for a collection of poems.

Dave returned to the basement at 6:30 p.m. "No mention of Aron on the six o'clock news," he reported to Paul. "How long's Tara been in there?"

"Off and on for two hours," Paul answered.

"How's our patient?"

Paul picked up Aron's file to read Tara's latest entry. "Nervous, anxious, verbally hostile, demanding to be released."

"Hi, Dave," Tara said, locking the cell door behind her. "How'd your classes go?"

"I had a little trouble concentrating. Bunsen burners and petri dishes just can't compete with kidnapping the King of Rock 'n' Roll. I hear he's feeling the effects of withdrawal."

"Yes, he is, and he's being quite a handful. I'm glad the day shift will be leaving soon," she added, picking up the phone.

The men listened quietly until Tara had finished her phone conversation with Dr. Smith.

"Mind if I talk to our patient?" Dave asked.

"Not at all," Tara answered, "but I don't want anyone going in there alone. And let's be sure to keep the basement door locked, so if he escapes the lockup, he'll still be confined to the basement."

"I'll go with you," Paul said, picking up Aron's file. "Here," he added, pitching Dave the white smock. "I assume you want to continue your doctor masquerade."

"You assume right," Dave said. "He wouldn't dare hit a doctor."

"I'll go in, too," Tara said, "but only for a minute. I'd like to begin the upstairs briefing as soon as possible so the day shift can leave on time."

They entered the lockup to find Aron in his usual position against the wall, knees curled up beneath his chin.

"I informed Dr. Smith that the Valium wasn't helping and that you wanted something stronger," Tara reported. "He wants to increase your dosage of Valium, first, before prescribing anything stronger."

"Stupid doctors," Aron grumbled.

"He's a good doctor, Aron, if at times a bit cautious. Don't worry, I'm on your side. Let's try a higher dosage of Valium for forty-eight hours before asking . . ."

"Forty-eight hours!" Aron interrupted, placing his fists at his sides, knuckles digging into the hard floor. To Aron, every second in the cell felt like an hour. Forty-eight hours would feel like a life sentence. "You must be crazy!"

Aron looked at Tara for some response, but none was given. His eyes fell to the ugly linoleum floor and a big, black cockroach, down for the count—its brittle, spindly legs pointing toward the ceiling. That would be *him* if he stayed there another minute. The King of Rock 'n' Roll would be entombed with a stupid cockroach. His heart began to race as the wall at his back pushed him toward the dead bug. He dug his feet and hands into the floor, trying to brake his forward momentum. The wall pushed harder as his feet began to slide—a big, fat rat being pushed steadily toward the edge of a very steep cliff. Aron's eyes darted across the faces of his intruders stopping on Paul. "What are *you* lookin' at?"

"Nothin'," Paul replied, leaving the lockup and soon returning with two sheets and a pillowcase. He covered Aron's mattress and pillow then used a tissue from his pocket to remove the dead roach.

"I have to attend a short briefing, then I'll be right back with your Valium," Tara said to Aron.

After Tara left, Aron stood and began pacing the short distance between the cell's walls. "Either of you have a cigarette?"

"I didn't think you smoked," Paul replied.

"*Son*, you don't know a *thing* about me! Maybe I just started!"

"Smoking isn't permitted in lockup," Dave answered, "but you're welcome to smoke after you're released."

"Released?" Aron asked.

"Yes," Dave replied, "to a—halfway house."

"A halfway house! You're moving me to a *halfway house*!"

"We're experimenting with this big, comfortable ranch house in the country," Paul explained. He scanned the lockup. "We think some of our addicts may benefit from a shorter stay here, and a longer stay in a more healthful environment."

"You're forcing me to move to a stupid *ranch house*!"

"No, we're not forcing you," Paul replied. "We just want you to look the place over—and maybe—think about staying for a while."

"I don't need to think about staying for a while! My answer's no! Now let me out here!"

"Aron, you're going through withdrawal," Dave said. "I know this lockup's uncomfortable, but right now, it's the best place for you."

"Did John and Ed put y'all up to this?"

"Who?" Dave asked.

"You know who!" Aron shot back. "They threatened to have me locked up if I didn't get help, but I never thought they'd go through with it. Stupid fools. How could they *do* this to me? I'm *Elvis Presley* for Christ's sake. The tabloids will *crucify* me."

Aron continued pacing, mind racing, head throbbing. John and Ed could not have done this alone. Ricky and Joe must have helped. Wait till he got a hold of *them*. His dad and Ginger (Aron's girlfriend) probably helped, too. And Priscilla. His eyes darted to Paul and Dave. "They're *all* against me!" he shouted. "How could they do this to me! When I get out of here, they're history. All of 'em. Out of Graceland. Out of Memphis. Out of my life! Forever!"

"Aron, who are you talking about?" Dave asked.

"My family! My friends! My *ex*-friends!"

"Aron, your family and friends aren't the enemy," Dave replied. "Your addiction to drugs is the enemy."

"Addiction! What are you *talkin'* about! My drugs are prescribed by doctors! I need them to stay *healthy*!"

While Dave and Aron argued, Paul focused on the crisp, thin file resting in his hands. Newly admitted patients with files like Aron's had a very good chance of recovery, unlike the unit's long-terms. Files belonging to long-terms grew as thick as gas station phonebooks, complete with worn corners, torn pages, and coffee-stained margins. Long-terms' files followed their patients through countless hospitals, mental hospitals, and rehab clinics, collecting years of toxicology reports, blood and urine analyses, psychological profiles, progress notes, court orders, and quite often, criminal records. Picking up a long-term's file was like fishing an old tire from the bottom of a river—tugging on the line as the heavy tire gathered moss, seaweed, branches, a corpse or two. Paul stared at Aron's thin file, praying it would never look like those belonging to long-terms.

A flash of movement caught Paul's eye. He looked up, but in slow motion compared to the large fist 12 inches from his face and moving in fast. His head exploded with pain just before everything went black.

Dave had instinctively stepped back to block the doorway and suddenly found himself five feet away, watching helplessly as Aron jumped onto Paul's lifeless body, pressed his knee into his chest, and squeezed his hands around his neck.

"Stop!" Dave shouted, leaping forward to grab Aron's arms.

Paul regained consciousness with his neck on fire and his lungs straining to pull in air. He grabbed Aron's wrist and pushed as Dave pulled. Aron tightened his grip. Paul swung his fist with all his might. Aron shook off the blow and squeezed harder. Paul swung again. Dave jumped to his feet, clasped his hands together in a tight fist, and raised them high above Aron's neck. Tara's loud scream filled the lockup. A large, paint-splattered boot caught Aron in the gut, sending him sprawling across the floor. Paul rolled over onto his stomach and pushed himself up to his hands and knees. He tried to breathe, but his collapsed lungs refused to open. As the room darkened, he slowly lowered his head to the floor. Just before passing out, his lungs relaxed then filled. As his chest heaved, the room brightened. While his lungs frantically sucked in air, he stared intently at the bright puddle of red filling the beige square beneath his head.

"Paul, can you move?" Tara asked.

Paul was so busy breathing, the question failed to register.

"Let's get him out of here," Tara said. "Is anyone else hurt?" Heads turned toward Aron who was curled up in a ball, arms wrapped tightly around his stomach. The red skin around his left eye had begun to swell.

"He'll be okay," Rob answered, kneeling beside Paul. "I caught him below the rib cage. Paul, we're liftin' you up, okay?"

Paul nodded, wincing in pain.

"Stomach down, head first," Rob said, as the others nodded.

Paul closed his eyes as eight strong hands lifted him up, up, and away. He felt like Superman—after an ill-advised flight through a hailstorm of Kryptonite. He tried to sidetrack his mind by focusing on the cold basement floor against his warm chest—on the soft, scented hands cradling his head as they rolled him onto his back. But his focus quickly returned to the excruciating pain shooting from his head, face, and neck. He felt like leaving his body. Even the contents of his stomach wanted to flee. *Superman* wanted to die.

Tara eased Paul's head to the floor, slammed and locked Aron's door, then returned to Paul's side. "How many fingers do you see?" she asked.

Paul opened his eyes and raised two fingers.

"Was he unconscious?" Tara asked.

"For a few seconds," Dave answered.

Tara studied his pupils. "Paul, can you speak?" He could only manage a painful nod. "Can you feel this?" she asked, squeezing his arms. Again, he nodded. She applied pressure to his hands, legs, and feet, watching for his reaction each time. She next examined the deep cut on his face and darkening bruises on his neck. "Besides your face and neck, what hurts?" He raised a hand to the back of his head. Tara's fingers gently searched and soon located a large bump.

"His head must have hit the floor when he landed," Dave said.

A loud knock shook the basement door. "Tara, are you down there!" a voice called out. All heads turned.

"Shit!" Tara said, lowering Paul's head to the floor. "Yeah! Just a second!" She ran to the supply shelf, grabbed a box of sanitary napkins, pulled one out, and ripped off its wrapper. "Brooks, apply pressure to this," she said, carefully placing the napkin over the cut on Paul's face. She ran back to the shelf and filled her arms with facial tissue, toilet paper, and soap. "Don't anyone make a sound. I'll be right back." She rushed to the basement door, stuck her key into the lock, then turned off the lights before unlocking and opening the door. "I was getting supplies when a shelf broke," she said, dropping a roll of toilet paper. "Could you help me carry these up, please?"

The basement door shut, leaving the men very much in the dark. The dim light crawling across the floor from Aron's lockup cast a faint halo around their wounded Musketeer. As their eyes adjusted, Brooks and Rob began asking question after question about the attack. Dave answered their questions, occasionally peering down at his injured friend. "I thought you said God was watching after you," Dave said to Paul.

"That was in Graceland," Paul whispered hoarsely. "I don't think He spends much time in Detox."

"You sound *terrible*," Brooks said, still pressing the napkin against the cut.

"I can hold that," Paul whispered, tapping Brooks' hand. "I'm okay." He took several deep breaths then slowly sat up. He waited for the room to stop spinning before taking inventory of his injuries.

Rob glared at the door to Aron's cell. "Would it make you feel any better if I went in there and kicked his butt?"

Paul focused on Rob's broad shoulders and muscular arms. "No, but thanks for askin'."

Tara returned carrying a First-aid kit and ice pack. She locked the basement door behind her before flicking on the lights. "Why is he sitting up?"

The men squinted guiltily in the bright light.

"Please lie down," she said, again cradling Paul's head in her hands. "We need to get you to Brackenridge. This cut will need stitches, and they'll want to take X-rays of your head and neck." She delicately removed the blood-soaked napkin. "I'll take you."

"Tara, you're the only nurse on duty tonight," Dave reminded. "Don't you think you should stay here?"

"Let me take him," Rob suggested. "Nobody'll miss me. And y'all are obviously going to have your hands full here."

Tara carefully cleaned the cut, mind wrestling with her difficult decision. Although her head was telling her to stay, her heart was screaming at her to go with Paul to the hospital. She applied a clean bandage, occasionally glaring at the lockup door.

"They're right," Paul whispered, staring into Tara's green eyes. You should stay here. Rob and I'll spend a half-hour at Brackenridge then hurry back."

"No one spends a half-hour at Brackenridge," Tara argued.

"Yes, you're probably right," Paul agreed. "All the more reason for you to stay here. This could take hours, and there's really no good reason for you to risk being gone that long."

Tara's heart could think of *one* good reason, but her mind was coming up with a number of good reasons to stay. She inspected Paul's bruised neck before gathering her supplies and standing. Paul sat up to prove he was okay. He waited for his head to clear, then slowly stood, but not without a little help from his friends. Tara handed him the ice pack and watched as he wrestled with where to put it first. She shook her head then helped him raise the ice to his swollen face. "Ten minutes on your face then your throat then the back of your head then repeat the process."

"Got it," Paul replied.

Tara studied Paul's eyes before taking a deep breath. "Okay," she conceded. She looked at Rob. "Do you know the way to Brackenridge?"

"Oh, yes, I've sung that tune before."

"We'll be fine," Paul assured Tara.

Tara forced a smile then peered through the lockup window. "No one opens this door without my say-so," she said, turning to watch until every head nodded. She then walked Paul and Rob to the basement door, giving them further instructions on the way. "Wait here while I check upstairs. Two knocks means it's okay to come up." She turned off the lights before carefully opening the door and closing it behind her.

Paul and Rob listened to her footsteps ascending the tall staircase. In the dim light sneaking in around their feet, Paul focused on Rob's paint-splattered boots and overalls. As his eyes adjusted, he studied Rob's red, shoulder-length hair, bearded face, and big brown eyes. "Welcome to Detox," Paul whispered, with a painful grin.

"Thanks," Rob chuckled, "I think I'm gonna like it here."

Chapter Three

Rob Carpenter raced his pickup through the yellow light at Guadalupe and 38th. The former Colorado running back had one goal in mind, and the traffic lights, stop signs, and rushing pedestrians were merely defensive backs to be outmaneuvered along the way.

"Now, wouldn't be the best time to get pulled over for speeding," Paul said hoarsely.

A passing streetlight brightened Paul's bruised neck and face.

"One look at you and the cops will be givin' us an escort," Rob replied, slowing for a red light.

Paul moved the ice pack from his face to his throat. "Do you miss football?"

"Yep, but I don't miss sittin' on the bench watchin' Colorado's pass-oriented offense."

"No, I can't picture you sittin' on the sidelines for very long." He glanced at Rob's paint-splotched football jersey. "I like your fashion statement. It says you're evolving from a football player to an artist."

"To an abstract expressionist, to be precise. And *evolving* is a good word. It's a great feeling discovering your passion, discovering why you're here on this planet."

"And just how did you make that discovery?"

Rob stepped on the gas. "One day Beverly and I were on our way to a movie when she suggested we stop by the art department to see one of her professor's latest abstracts. Never in my life, had I seen such an array of bright colors, suggestive swirls, and erotic images. The painting excited Beverly, too—we ended up blowin' off the movie. The next morning I sat in on one of her art classes, and the rest is history."

"I'm happy for you, Rob. We were a little concerned about you—with all the drugs, changing majors every semester, and dropping out of football."

"I was a tumble weed all right, but my life's got direction now, and except for an occasional joint or two, *art* has become *my* drug of choice." He swerved to avoid a bicyclist, then hit the horn.

"You certainly seem in your element now," Paul chuckled. "You look like you're riding in the front seat of a roller coaster."

Rob glanced at his friend. "Nothing personal, but you look like you were just thrown off the back."

Paul moved the ice to his head as Austin's Brackenridge Hospital came into view. "Remember those boxing lessons you gave me in junior high?"

"Yep."

"We should have worked a little more on duckin'."

"It was a suckerpunch, Paul. Not much you can do about that."

Paul closed his eyes, recalling the attack. "After our patient's safely through withdrawal, and well into recovery, I'm going to kill that suckerpunchin' son of a gun."

Rob laughed as his truck screeched to a stop in front of the emergency entrance. Five minutes later Paul was filling out medical forms while a frustrated, overworked, Aunt Bea-looking receptionist fastened a plastic identification bracelet around his wrist. She looked at Rob, scowling at the big jock's long hair and paint-splattered clothing. There was something about him that she just did not like. She looked at Paul. "How'd you say this happened?"

"It was a bar fight, ma'am," Rob answered for his injured friend. "Over a woman. It's always a woman, ain't it, Aunt Bea?"

Aunt Bea glared at Rob, adding *rude* to the list of adjectives growing in her head.

"Rob, I can answer," Paul said, pain shooting from his throat. "It was a bar fight, ma'am."

Four questions and three forms later, Paul and Rob sat in the waiting room watching the hospital drama play itself out between two swinging doors. A hunter had shot himself in the foot, a golfer had broken his leg falling off a golf cart, and a small, freckle-faced girl had had a nasty run-in with a dog. Paul and Rob's barroom brawl had only added to Aunt Bea's workload, and she could not help showing her displeasure by glaring at the men.

"Lady, what's your problem?" Rob asked.

"Rob," Paul scolded.

After noticing water dripping from Paul's ice pack, Rob stood, barged through the swinging doors, and soon returned with a fresh pack.

"Thanks," Paul said, smiling at his friend. He chuckled. "Hey, remember when Brooks said you arrived on the scene a few seconds late, that you'd obviously lost a step since leaving football?"

"Yeah."

"Well, I think you arrived just in time, Rob, and I'm glad you're here—and not just to drive me to the hospital and get ice packs. I'm glad you're here on our team."

"Thanks. There was no way I was going to miss *this* one."

Paul removed the ice from his face and leaned forward. "Listen, Rob, if things don't go as planned, if things turn . . ."

"You can stop right there," Rob interrupted. "You're about to apologize for something that hasn't even happened. We're big kids, Paul, and I don't remember you twistin' anybody's arms. We knew what we were gettin' into, and I for one am in this for the long haul, whatever happens. Do you understand me?"

"Yes, I understand you, but I still feel . . ."

"Responsible?"

"Yeah, for *whatever* happens."

"Of course you do. This is your baby. But like you said, we're a team, and we all have our responsibilities. You've already accomplished the hardest part. You nabbed the King, drove him seven hundred miles, and smuggled him into the basement of Detox without a hitch. You did an unbelievable job, Paul. Now, I think you should trust us to do ours. I think you should close your eyes, save your voice, and concentrate on healin' those injuries."

Paul closed his eyes, leaned back against his chair, and pressed the ice against his face. Fifteen minutes later an attractive nurse walked through the swinging doors. "Paul

Roberts?" she called out. Both men stood. "Goodness, what's the other guy look like?" she asked.

"He's got a black eye and a stomachache," Rob answered.

"And you are?"

"Rob Carpenter," Rob answered, shaking the nurse's hand. "Friend of the victim."

"Karen," the nurse introduced, "nurse of the victim."

Their eyes locked for what Paul thought was an awfully long period of time.

"Ah, I'm the victim," Paul interrupted.

"Yes, I gathered as much," Karen replied.

"Mind if I come back, too?" Rob asked.

"The more the merrier," Karen answered. "Follow me, gentlemen."

Paul was quickly examined by a physician then taken to X-ray. Twenty minutes later he lay on his back staring up at a bright circle of light while a doctor prepared the cut for sutures.

"I gather he was a lot bigger than you," the doctor joked.

"Yes, sir," Paul answered, "the biggest guy in the bar. I've never seen anyone so fat, move so fast." He closed his eyes as the sharp needle pierced his skin.

The doctor glanced at Rob. "Where was your bodyguard?"

"I'm afraid I was about twenty steps too slow," Rob answered.

"Some bodyguard," Paul joked. "I guess I'll have to get someone with a little more foot speed."

"You and Elvis both," the doctor replied, again, sticking the needle into Paul's face.

Paul's eyes shot wide-open. "Elvis?" he asked.

"Yeah, it was on the seven o'clock news. The King's missing."

"Missing?" Paul echoed.

"Yeah, apparently his bodyguards dropped the ball."

"Was he—kidnapped?"

"No, they don't think so. No signs of foul play. No ransom notes. Besides, who'd be foolish enough to kidnap Elvis Presley?"

"Who, indeed?" Rob laughed.

"He's apparently flown the coop before," the doctor continued. "They'll find him, probably passed out at a Mr. Donuts. Right now, I'm more concerned about *your* condition," he added, noticing the color had vanished from Paul's face. "Are you sure you wouldn't like to stay the night? I can offer you a room with a view of the Capitol."

"Thanks, but no thanks," Paul replied. "I'll be fine."

The doctor tied off the last suture then inspected his work. "There, that should heal nicely, provided you stay out of the bars for a week or two."

"My bar-hoppin' days are over."

"Do you have any drug allergies?"

"No, sir."

"I'll have Karen give you two injections—a painkiller and an anti-inflammatory. The latter will help reduce the swelling in your neck. I'll write you a prescription for both. You can begin taking them tomorrow morning. If this cut shows any signs of infection, I want you to see your personal physician immediately."

"Thank you, sir, I will." Paul waited for the doctor to leave before speaking. "Great. I hoped we'd have another day or two before Aron made the national news."

"Well, he *is* Elvis Presley," Rob replied. "The good news is they won't be lookin' for him in Texas. They'll be turnin' up every donut shop, gun store, movie theater, and motorcycle showroom in Tennessee before broadening their search. Plus, I read he sleepwalks."

"You've been doin' your homework."

"Colorado *does* have a library or two."

Karen gave Paul two shots and the prescriptions before writing something on a piece of paper for Rob. Before leaving, Paul signed another form for Aunt Bea, who glared at the men once more as they rushed toward the parking lot.

"What's that?" Paul asked, motioning toward the piece of paper sticking out of Rob's pocket.

"That, my fellow Musketeer, is Karen's phone number."

"What! In the middle of all *this*, you got that chick's phone number!"

"I'm a handsome man. She'd be a fool not to jump at the opportunity."

"What about me?"

"What *about* you? You're not looking all that handsome right now—a big loser in a stupid bar fight. Even a nurse would have to think twice. Besides, from the way Tara was frettin' over you, you've already got yourself a nurse."

Paul smiled at the thought of Tara gently squeezing his hands, legs, and feet. As his thoughts returned to Aron, his face hardened. "I can't believe he got so violent his first night in Detox. Keeping him hidden down there might be harder than we thought."

"When were you planning on movin' him?"

"Day after tomorrow."

"We might should move that up. That secluded house in the country's lookin' better all the time."

The security guard at the State Hospital stopped Rob's truck at the entrance.

"I crashed my car and hitched a ride with a friend," Paul said to the guard."

The guard's phone began ringing. He picked up the receiver, waved them through, but stared suspiciously as they passed.

As Paul and Rob entered the basement, Tara stood to greet them. "How do you feel?"

"Not good," Paul answered. "But the painkiller should be kicking in shortly."

"*Holy cow*, have you seen your neck?" Brooks asked.

"No, but if it looks anything like it feels, I don't want to see it."

"You look like Clint Eastwood in *Hang 'em High*," Brooks said.

"Sound like him, too," Dave agreed.

"What about the X-rays?" Tara asked.

"Nothing broken," Paul answered.

"Did he give you a prescription?"

"Two, but I haven't gotten them filled yet."

"I'll fill them for you," Brooks offered, glancing at his watch. "There's a pharmacy on Guadalupe open late."

"Thanks, Brooksie," Paul replied.

Rob strolled up the lockup and glared inside. "What an idiot."

"It's not his fault," Paul said, "I should've been paying attention."

"Not his *fault*! He *suckerpunched* you, Paul! How's that not his fault?"

"Aron's going through withdrawal," Tara said to Rob. "He's not himself, and won't be for several weeks." She studied Paul curiously. "Nevertheless, our patients are still responsible for their actions."

"I feel partly responsible," Dave said. "I thought he was making a break for the door. By the time I realized he was going for Paul, it was too late to do anything but watch."

"I should have seen it coming," Tara said. "His violent outbursts have been well documented."

"Okay," Paul said, "now that we've evenly distributed the blame, I think we should move on to more important things, like *Elvis* making the seven o'clock news."

"What?" Brooks asked. The room fell silent.

"What'd they say?" Dave asked.

"We heard about it secondhand from the doctor who stitched Paul's cut," Rob answered.

"The King's been reported missing," Paul said. "No signs of foul play or ransom notes, and he's apparently flown the coop before."

"Paul and I were wondering if we should get him out of here earlier than planned," Rob said, looking at Tara.

"In a straight jacket?" Dave asked.

"I don't think that'll be necessary," Paul replied.

"If we can't control him in here, how will we control him out there?" Dave asked.

"We won't need to control him out there," Brooks argued. "He can blow up all he wants, and no one will be the wiser. We're lucky day shift had already left the build-ing. If they'd been anywhere near that basement door, they would've heard something."

"Some of our patients have been questioning our fre-quent trips to the basement," Paul mentioned. "We're having to do too much explaining." He pointed to his face. "And now we'll have to explain *this*."

"Tara, what do you think?" Dave asked.

"I think Detox has served its purpose. I can change the work schedule to get us off earlier than planned. The Vineyard may not have the security of a lockup, but we'll have a five-to-one advantage."

"I thought you wanted him more relaxed before your heart to heart," Dave said.

"Yes, another 24 hours would have been nice, but I just don't think it's worth the risk. We no longer have that luxury."

"What do *you* think, Rob?" Paul asked.

Rob motioned toward the basement door. "I like our chances better out there."

"Brooks?" Paul asked.

"The sooner the better. I say we remove him early to-morrow morning, before the day shift arrives. And don't forget, once we've left this institutionalized setting, we'll look like, well, a bunch of kidnappers, and that's not what we want. We want him on our side, as soon as possible, especially since they've already called the cops."

"I agree," Tara said. "I think we should have our say the minute we get him to The Vineyard then give him the choice to stay or leave."

"But what if he leaves?" Dave asked.

"Then, he leaves," Paul answered. "End of story." An eerie silence filled the basement.

"What!" Dave replied. "I just got invited into this little party, and now you're telling me it could all be over tomorrow morning?"

"Or not," Tara replied, pulling a syringe and vial from the desk drawer. "I have plenty of sedatives and the rest of the night to soften him up."

Everyone watched Tara fill the syringe.

Paul looked toward Aron's cell. "If we can just win him over long enough for him to call Memphis, it'd take a lot of the heat off."

"I can do it," Tara said confidently.

"What do you *think*, Dave?" Paul asked.

Dave scanned the basement. "Well, we probably *would* be pressing our luck by staying here another day, and I've heard so much about The Vineyard, it'd be nice to actually see it." He glanced at the lockup door. "I just hope Aron feels the same way."

"Okay, then," Paul said, "we move him out early tomorrow morning."

"I'll ask Phyllis to come in at six," Tara said. "She's always looking to pick up extra hours. If I can persuade an aide or two to come in early, we can all leave before the rest of the day shift arrives."

"I'll fill up the hospital van on the way to the pharmacy," Brooks said.

"How's our patient?" Paul asked, looking through the window.

"He has a pretty good shiner from the right hook you gave him," Dave answered. "This won't look good on your résumé."

Paul laughed, wincing in pain.

"Right now, I'd like to give him this shot of Valium," Tara said. "He'll probably jump through hoops to get a sedative, but just in case I'm wrong, let's be prepared to pin him to the floor."

Dave and Brooks reached for the white smock.

"I'll thank you to keep your paws off my smock," Dave said.

"That smock belongs to a *real* doctor," Brooks replied.

"I'm in medical school, and that's a lot closer to a *real* doctor than you."

"Fine, take it, but if I end up looking like Paul, it'll be on your shoulders."

"I can handle the weight," Dave replied.

Aron glared at his intruders, but the pain in his stomach and two hours of solitude had weakened his resolve to fight. At the sight of the syringe, his eyebrows lifted. After his shot, Rob, Dave, and Brooks accompanied him to the restroom while Paul and Tara cleaned the blood-stained lockup. During Aron's return trip from the restroom, he contemplated escape, but something about Rob's muscular build caused him to reconsider. The sedative was also having its desired effect. Aron knew that in a few minutes, most of his problems would be drifting far, far away. He plopped down on the mattress and stared at the ceiling, listening to the sounds of fading footsteps and the sliding deadbolt.

"I'll give the sedative twenty minutes before returning," Tara said. "I'd prefer talking to him alone, but it might be prudent if someone sat nearby."

"I'm your man," Rob said, moving a chair beside the lockup door.

During the next two hours, Tara had several constructive conversations with Aron before leaving him alone to sleep. At 5:45 a.m. Rob and Brooks awakened Aron and escorted him to the toilet while Paul gathered up all evidence of their presence in the basement. Upstairs in the nurse's station, Tara thanked Phyllis for coming in early before leading her to the female dorm. Dave greeted the dayshift aide arriving early then led him to the male dorm.

Paul watched from the top of the staircase until the nurse's station was empty then rushed back to the basement. "All clear," he announced to Rob and Brooks.

"The King's still sittin' on his throne," Rob replied, motioning toward the restroom.

"What did you tell him?" Paul asked.

"Just that we're moving him to a halfway house in the country," Brooks answered. "He's not completely awake, but I'm sure he's glad to be leaving *this* place."

Sunrise was still an hour away, and a thick, early-morning fog provided perfect cover as the four men strolled across the parking lot. The hospital van appeared to bob through the rolling fog like a boat floating in a harbor. The men climbed aboard and waited for Dave and Tara as a distant train whistle mimicked the sound of a foghorn. Just past 6 a.m. the van left the Austin State Hospital. Brooks sat behind the wheel and Tara rode shotgun. Aron sat in the center seat between Dave and Rob. Paul sat alone in the back. The fog turned to haze just past an Austin city limits sign and began to lift as they reached the Hill Country.

To Paul, the land surrounding Austin was so unlike the rest of Texas, at least, the flat part of Texas around DeSoto, where he and his fellow Musketeers had grown up. As the sky lightened, he stared at the soft, purple and blue hills, which seemed to roll into each other forever. Paul had spent countless hours hiking those hills, and it was during those hikes that he discovered they were anything but soft. Most were thickly covered with mesquite, junipers, and thorn bushes—providing a perfect canopy for the rattlesnakes, armadillos, and fire ants living below. Huge spider webs stretched between the trees, forcing hikers to look high and low as they trekked. It was rough country, much to the delight of the turkey vultures usually circling high above. There were no lions, tigers or bears, but it was always a good idea to carry a big stick along with your compass and snakebite kit.

Paul found hiking the hills fun and exciting. He recalled sitting alone one windy evening, chin held high and imagination running wild, as the dark trees danced and swirled against the pink sky. He remembered the mesquite resembling the animated characters in a Disney film and recalled having little trouble imagining them picking him up and tossing him from tree to tree all the way to the horizon.

The van hugged the two-lane blacktop as the road curled, rose, and flattened high above Lake Travis. They glided by a serene church overlooking the lake then swooped down past several marina entrances and lakeside bars before crossing over the Mansfield dam. Paul spotted two turkey vultures circling high in the early morning sky. He never saw the vultures as omens of doom, preferring to view them as guides for the joggers, bicyclists, and water sports enthusiast who frequented that blacktop—those worked-out, studied-out, and perhaps drugged-out city dwellers looking for a good place to air out their heads.

Aron rubbed the sleep from his eyes then peered out the window. "Where am I?"

"Rural Route 620," Brooks answered, "headed west, just outside of Austin, Texas."

Aron looked at Brooks to see whether or not he was joking. Again, he stared out the window as a fingernail curve of bright orange peeked above the horizon. Thin rays of yellow shot above a wide stretch of lime-green farmland. A farmer's irrigation system shot long sprays high above the field. The tops of the sprays glistened as they reached the early-morning rays.

"Austin, Texas!" Aron said, suddenly wide awake. "How did I get here!"

"I drove to Memphis and got you," Paul answered.

Aron turned to stare at Paul, pulse quickening. His eyes darted to Dave and his white smock. "Are you a doctor?"

"Well, not exactly," Dave replied, "at least, not yet."

Brooks slowed to make a right turn. Aron's eyes darted to the door handle just above Rob's leg.

"Don't even think about it," Rob said, propping his foot on top of the handle.

"Where are you taking me?" Aron asked.

"To an old ranch house in the country," Brooks answered.

Tara turned in her seat to face the King. "Aron, I know you have a lot of questions, but we'd rather wait to answer them at The Vineyard. After that, you'll be free to go, if that's what you want."

"I've—been—kidnapped?" Aron asked.

Tara turned to gaze out the front window. Ten minutes later, the van bumped over a cattle guard and onto a narrow dirt driveway. "We've got water," Brooks mentioned, as the house came into view, "but the electricity and gas won't be turned on until tomorrow, at the earliest. No phone. I'm not sure if we want one."

Tara caught a glimpse of the grape arbor out back and smiled. The others focused on the house's wide, wraparound porch, canopied by long eaves to shade it from the sun and shelter it from the rain. Paul gazed up at the cloudless sky, wondering when the house had last seen rain.

They let the dust settle before exiting the van and climbing the six steps to the front porch. Brooks turned left then led everyone to the south side of the house and view of a large pasture encircled on three sides by thick woods and the broken remnants of a barbed-wire fence. Purebred quarter horses once grazed the pasture, but now gophers, rabbits, and snakes called it home. To Rob, the pasture was the perfect place for football. A large evergreen that had been split in half by lightening stood like a goal post near one end zone. The thick woods circling the playing field resembled stadium bleachers filled with excited fans, eagerly awaiting the kickoff.

Brooks led them to the back porch and a panoramic view of the surrounding countryside. A small grape arbor and two dozen rows of dried grapevines filled the backyard. Behind the grapevines, the woods sloped slightly for a mile then lifted upward toward a stretch of high bluffs. A narrow deer trail zigzagged through the woods all the way to the bluffs. To the right side of the backyard, grooved farmland stretched toward a white farmhouse and red barn perched on the horizon.

The porch's walls and eaves amplified their every footstep, mimicking a small amphitheater. Paul wondered how the porch's acoustics might affect the sounds of tambourines, guitars, and harmonicas. He looked at Aron, wondering if the songs sung there would hit deeper. He glanced at his friends, curious if the laughter there would sound louder. He thought about the countless stories probably told there, wondering if the porch made the fish longer, the bears taller, and the ghosts scarier. It seemed to possess that sort of power.

The multitude of mesquite surrounding the house watched closely as the group made a complete circle, returning to the front porch. The screen door had fallen off its hinges and leaned on its side. Brooks unlocked and opened the front door then stepped back so the others could enter first. The house's big living room was sparsely furnished with an old sofa, coffee table, and several armchairs. Rob's thirty-two brightly colored paintings leaned against the walls.

"The bedrooms are pretty empty," Brooks mentioned. "We didn't want to move the rest of the furniture until . . ." He looked at Aron. ". . . until we knew the length of our stay."

"Have a seat, Aron," Tara said.

A four-day beard splotched the King's dirty face. The skin around his left eye was black and blue, compliments of his stay in Detox. He had worked up a sweat just walking around the porch, and his body reeked. He scanned the room, plopped down on the sofa, which seemed to

bow from his weight, then began massaging his wet temples.

To Aron's kidnappers, the room felt a little warm,
so they began opening windows. To Aron, it felt like an
oven—and the temperature was rising fast. While the
others sat in chairs or on the floor, Tara stepped into the
kitchen to retrieve two glasses of water. She set one in
front of Aron and handed the other to Paul, giving her
injured friend a reassuring smile. "Would you like to
begin?"

Paul took a painful swallow then stood. He began by
explaining how he and Tara had grown up idolizing *Elvis*
and that because of numerous tabloid articles describing his heavy drug use, mood swings, and deteriorating
health, they feared he would soon be dead. Paul described
the strange summer dream, in which he had successfully
pulled off a kidnapping, and divulged his and Tara's sudden realization that they were working in the perfect place
on the perfect shift with the perfect friends to pull off just
such a kidnapping. He explained how they had pulled
Brooks, Rob, and Dave into the plan and admitted that
although Tara had four years' experience working with
addicts, Rob had no experience and the rest of them
were just rookie nurse's aides. Paul admitted that the doctor who had examined Aron in Detox had been coerced
then ended his speech by telling Aron that because of his
violent behavior, they had decided to move him to the
ranch house earlier than planned and lay all their cards
on the table.

Paul returned to his seat on the floor and took another
painful sip of water. Aron stared at him wide-eyed, mind
racing. John and Ed had nothing to do with this? His fam-

ily had nothing to do with this? He'd been kidnapped! By a stupid nurse's aide! But where were his guards during all this? Where was *he*? How could he have been kidnapped and driven all the way to Texas without even realizing it? Stupid sleeping pills.

Tara set Aron's file on the coffee table then gathered her thoughts a moment before speaking. "Aron, we had no right to take such action. We've broken numerous laws and may end up in jail. But we saw no other way." She glanced at the file. "Since your arrival in Detox, we've witnessed nothing that would indicate our fears were unwarranted. The tests on your blood and urine revealed that you had enough chemicals in your system to kill a horse. Either you've built up quite a tolerance, or Someone up there likes you. Either way, you're lucky to be alive, and we thought *now* would be a good time to offer you a little relief—a long break from your overuse of drugs, brutal concert schedule, physically demanding lifestyle, and all the other pressures of being *Elvis*. We also thought you might enjoy being somewhat anonymous for the first time in your adult life.

"If you elect to stay, we'll help you in every way we can, but only as it pertains to our primary goal, which is to provide you with a healthy environment from which you can free yourself from your addiction to prescription drugs. We will *not* be your bodyguards, doctors, psychiatrists, gurus, maids, or cooks. One day you may regard us as your friends, but I have a feeling that day will be a long time coming.

"The first weeks will be difficult. I'm not sure what you know about detoxification and withdrawal—whether or not you've ever tried to come clean. I personally haven't experienced the process, but I've spent countless hours with those who have, and they describe it as pure hell. Most addicts attempting to quit never make it to first base. This nation's most successful rehab clinics have only a 50 percent success rate. Our record at Detox is considerably worse. With this venture, I've begun a search for a more successful form of treatment, less focused on chemical solutions, and more focused on environment."

Tara scanned her friends. "These are good people, Aron. They've risked much to give you this opportunity, and I suspect they, too, have their ulterior motives. But whatever their reasons, they are indeed giving you a wonderful opportunity. Now all *you* have to decide is whether or not to accept it." She walked up to a window and stared outside a moment before turning to scan her friends. "Does anyone have anything to add?" Heads shook. She turned and gazed out the window. "Well, then, I guess that's it."

Aron glared at Tara, fists tightening. Beads of sweat rolled down his forehead and into his burning eyes as his whole body began to tremble. "That's *it*!" he screamed. "That's *it*! You kidnapped me! Drove me a thousand miles from my home! Stuffed me up in a stupid cell! Hauled me out to this *oven* in the middle of nowhere! And that's *it*!"

Tara stared out the window without so much as a blink.

Aron's mind raced. No way could this really be happening. He was on some kind of trip. A bad trip. But he could not even remember the last time he had dropped anything, so how could he be tripping? Maybe he was dreaming. That could explain it. This was all just a bad dream. But it was all so *real*—the pain in his head, the

itchy couch against the small of his back, his intense urge
for a fix. He needed a fix so bad he could scream. He had
to get out of there—and fast. "I'm free to go?"

"You're free to go," Tara answered, without turning
from the window.

Aron put his fists on either side of his legs and pushed.
His knuckles sunk deep into the sofa, but his body hardly
budged. His head dropped as he glared at his big gut.
Over the years, he had waged a holy war against his belly—trying diets, stimulants, laxatives, girdles, and all sorts
of fat-concealing clothing. And now look at him. He
was—pregnant. America's once great sex symbol was six
months pregnant. Boy, my boy.

Aron looked up to glare at his kidnappers, none of
whom seemed even remotely interested in him *or* his
stomach. Unbelievable. A cocky bunch of college kids
had kidnapped the King of Rock 'n' Roll—and were *now*
preaching to him about being an *addict*.

Aron had never referred to himself as an addict,
not even when kneeling helplessly beneath 150 vials of
prescription drugs, shaking uncontrollably as the tears
flowed. But his kidnappers had surely used the word.
What had someone said in that cell? "Some of our *addicts* might benefit from a shorter stay here and a longer
stay in a healthier environment?" Aron scanned the hot,
half-furnished dump. So *this* was the healthier environment? He would rather be in that stupid cell—at least it
was air-conditioned. He would rather be dead than stay
another minute in that oven.

Perspiration trickled uncomfortably down Aron's back
and into the cleavage of his posterior. He pushed the small
of his back into the sofa as his saturated underwear tried

desperately to soak up one more drop. His breathing was quick and labored. His heart raced to keep up. His head was now throbbing with pain. He needed a fix—short of that, a painkiller—short of that, a shot of Valium or a stiff drink. He glared at Tara. "Can I have a drink?"

Tara glanced at the glass of water on the coffee table before returning to her view of the pasture, now bathed in bright sunlight. Aron's eyes darted to the glass then back to Tara. His jaw tightened. There was something about that nurse that he just did not like. He scanned the others. Dave was nonchalantly gazing out the window. Rob, balancing his chair on its back legs while staring up at the ceiling. Brooks, scribbling on his stupid legal pad. There was something about all of them that he just did not like—their thin bodies, cocky arrogance, matter-of-fact attitudes. They reminded him of himself at their age.

Suddenly, Aron recalled that young rebel that had exploded onto the American music scene in the late fifties, that soon-to-be idolized rock star destined to hold the world in the palm of his hands, that confident young man who had existed before depression, self-doubt, and drugs took center stage in his life. *That* young man had vanished without a fight, and Aron despised his kidnappers for reminding him of his existence. Stupid fools. Why would he want to stay with *them*? He was out of there.

Aron leaned forward, crammed his fists into the sofa, and pushed with all his might. The King stood, shins bumping against the coffee table. The glass of water tilted then fell. Water spread across the table before trickling onto the floor. He was free to go. Nobody was stopping him. Nobody was even looking at him.

Aron stepped around the table and turned toward the open door. The brilliant sunrise caught him by surprise, giving him pause. He squinted at the streaks of orange shimmering above a sea of tangled browns and greens. The house's winding dirt driveway had vanished. The two-lane blacktop was just a memory. He took another step. He was free to go. But where? Back to Memphis? Back to Graceland? Did he really want *that*? The doorway seemed to move further away. He rubbed his eyes and looked again. What had Tara offered him instead? A long break? A break from the pressures of being Elvis? How often had he dreamed of *that*? He forced another step, but the effort took every ounce of his strength. All of a sudden, his body felt so tired, so sluggish, like it was pushing against an invisible barrier between himself and the door. What was happening to him? Who was doing this?

Aron whirled to face his kidnappers, eyes focusing on Paul. As the sun inched higher, a ray of light shot through an open window, illuminating Paul's injured face and neck. What happened to *him*? Aron closed his eyes and immediately saw himself pacing inside a small cell. He remembered the walls closing in and his unbearable urge for a fix and his intense rage. He recalled his fist crashing into the aide's face, his right knee pressed into his chest, his hands squeezed around his neck.

Aron opened his eyes to the thumb-shaped bruises and swollen, discolored skin surrounding the sutured cut, a big lump forming in his throat. Oh, yeah. *That's* what happened to him. *I* happened to him. His eyes fell to his thumbs. He felt them digging into the boy's neck. He felt someone pulling frantically at his arms. He heard Tara's scream and the others rushing in to save their friend from the monster. And *he* was the monster. *He* was the monster that had done this—this *horrible* thing to—to somebody—who was just trying to help him. "Oh, God," he whispered. "Oh, God—please—no—what have I done? What have I—become?"

Aron wanted to run from the terrible memory of what he had done, from the nauseous feeling in the center of his stomach, and from the sudden pressure building in his eyes. He whirled to face the doorway and tried to take another step, but his feet felt glued to the floor. All of a sudden, he was falling. Intense pain exploded from his knees. A tear jarred loose and trickled down his cheek, just before the floodgates opened. The King bowed low, buried his face in his hands, and burst into tears, head resting just inches from the open doorway.

Out of respect for Aron, no one watched. Rob focused on one of his paintings. Dave stared at the wall. Paul watched a spider crawling toward the hallway. Brooks watched the last drop of water slowly roll over the edge of the coffee table and fall into the puddle on the hardwood floor.

Tara studied the early-morning sunlight shining through the top branches of a mesquite. She did not need to look at Aron to see the big picture—she had seen it often enough. Most addicts had to reach rock bottom before experiencing that sudden shift in consciousness. But because she had always held the King so close to her heart, *this* picture was difficult for her to stomach. She reached up to brush away a tear.

Paul, too, was having trouble holding back his tears. He forced himself to concentrate on the steady hum of spinning tires against a distant blacktop—the King's only accompaniment as he cried.

Paul's fellow Musketeers, however, were viewing the scene from a far less melancholy perspective.

Looks like The Vineyard is open for business, Rob mused to himself—open, and just received its first guest. The artist scanned the living room walls, looking for the best place to hang his first painting.

"Unbelievable," Dave whispered beneath his breath. "We may not be going to jail after all."

Brooks wrote furiously. Yes! Yes! We did it! We did it! This is great! This is fantastic! Why's everyone crying?

Quite some time passed before Aron slowly raised his head from the tear-stained floor. The hard cry had left him physically and emotionally drained, but it had left his mind clear and his senses heightened. A light breeze floated through the doorway to cool his wet skin. A salty tear rolled over the curve of his upper lip and into his mouth. A blue jay called from an open window. He stretched his arm through the open doorway. The invisible barrier had vanished, along with his headache, cravings, and other physical discomforts. Suddenly, an image of Lisa Marie filled his mind, causing a broad smile to quickly illuminate his face. He thought about his dad, Priscilla, Ginger, and the other individuals who might be affected by his decision. He thought about the countless responsibilities waiting for him in Memphis. Suddenly, he recalled the name of a good lawyer.

The King stood and faced his kidnappers. "I'll need to make a few phone calls—to Los Angeles, to Las Vegas, and to Memphis."

Chapter Four

While Paul and Tara drove Aron to the pay phone, Dave stood in the doorway staring at the sunrise that had so captivated the King. "He's calling Memphis," Dave said, in disbelief. "He's actually staying."

"Of course he's staying," Brooks said, picking up the tipped glass and mopping up the water. "How could anyone refuse such hospitality?"

Rob selected a large painting and with Brooks' help, hung it on the living room wall. "What do you think, Dave?"

Dave scrutinized the abstract without offering an opinion.

"How rude," Brooks scolded. "I think it's a masterpiece, Rob, and can only be described as comically erotic. Look right here, Dave. What's that remind you of? And over here. What do you think that is?"

Dave rolled his eyes.

"You don't like it, do you, Dave?" Rob asked.

"Well," Dave replied, "nothing personal, but abstract expressionism does seem a little out of place in an old ranch house."

"I guess you'd prefer Norman Rockwell," Brooks scoffed. "Some cute little fifties family sittin' around the kitchen table."

"In the *living room*?" Rob objected.

"You've got a point," Brooks agreed. "He'd hang the kitchen scene in the kitchen. In here he'd want something grandiose. I'm seeing a couple hundred thousand buffalo stretched out over a grassy plain, harnessed in some sort of thick, gaudy, western-looking frame. And I don't even want to look in his bedroom."

"Hmm," Rob said, rubbing his chin. "In his bedroom, I'm seein' a lone, Black Angus bull, with a blue ribbon pinned to his chest, lookin' at Dave with big, bedroom eyes."

"Or maybe winking at him," Brooks joked, "as if thanking him for last night. Hey, could you paint Dave an Aberdeen Angus abstract for his bedroom?"

"I'd consider it an honor. I'll use lots of black mixed with some suggestive pinks—hot pink for his balls. I'll make 'em low hangers, the size of watermelons, so big we'll have to put 'em on separate canvases and hang 'em beneath the main attraction."

"And we can hang it at the foot of his bed," Brooks suggested. "See how the art critic likes waking up to that every morning, no pun intended."

"None taken."

"Laugh it up, boys," Dave said, gazing toward the driveway. "Because I have a feeling, when Aron gets back, laughter will be a scarce commodity around this place."

*   *   *

Paul and Tara sat in silence until Aron finished his phone conversations and returned to the van.

"How'd it go?" Paul asked.

"I kept 'em short, like ya asked. I said I was stayin' at an out-of-state rehab clinic and wanted to try life without drugs for a while. I told 'em for this to work, I needed a few months away from Memphis. I told Yisa (Lisa Marie) that I loved her and that I'd call her every day. I told my dad he could tell the press whatever he wanted. I asked my lawyer to get me out of my contractual obligations for the next six months." Aron thought for a second. "I guess, that's it."

During the drive back to the house, big smiles graced Paul and Tara's faces. Aron studied them curiously. There was something he had missed earlier, something in addition to their youth, arrogance, and naive confidence. Ten minutes later the van hit the raised cattle guard, bounced high, and dropped. As Paul and Tara laughed, that something hit Aron square in the face. His chief kidnappers were happy. It was written all over their faces, and he had not recognized it until now. Was he so far removed from happiness that he could not even see it staring him in the face? His eyes began to moisten. He bit his lower lip, trying to regain his composure. He had not cried so much since his mother died. He needed an upper. He held out his hand and stared at his trembling fingers. "Got anything for this?"

Tara turned in her seat to focus on Aron's hand. "I've got just the thing at the house," she answered, facing forward. She thought for a second then turned and stared into the King's sad eyes. "Aron, earlier I mentioned that this nation's most successful drug clinics have only a 50 percent success rate. During our research, we read quite a bit about your persistence, patience, tolerance, sense of

humor, and endless generosity. It's because of these positive traits, I'm confident you'll be arriving on the happy
side of that 50 percent."

Aron, however, had his doubts. At that moment, he
felt no closer to the positive Aron, than he did to the
happy Aron. "Whatever you say, hon'," he replied, head
bowing.

At the house Tara gave Aron a sedative then suggested
he rest in the shade of the back porch. "Until we have
electricity, this will be the coolest place," she said, facing
a rocking chair west.

"Thanks," Aron replied, face etched in worry. Five—
long—months without drugs. What had he gotten himself into? He needed a Valium just to think about the
prospect. His thoughts turned to his phone conversation
with Lisa Marie. Yisa had always been so appreciative of
what little time he had had to give, and now she would be
receiving even less. Guilt climbed atop sloped shoulders
already weighted down with worry. He wished he was in
Graceland, where relief from such feelings was just a few
pills away.

In the living room Tara began The Vineyard's first
briefing. "Aron has just made a big decision, one that will
bring about some big changes in his life. From Memphis,
to Austin. From Elvis, to Aron. From a heavily-drugged
lifestyle, to a drug-free lifestyle. From a luxurious castle
where he was the King, to an old ranch house where he
may one day become an equal partner. No doubt, he's
already second guessing his decision to stay. Let's do all we
can to help him adjust to these changes. And let's remind
him often during the next few weeks that he's made the
right decision.

"For most addicts, withdrawal is a one to two week process. During this process, Aron will be nervous, agitated, confrontational, and violent, as we witnessed in lockup. Detox has become a testing ground for a wide array of medications designed to help addicts through withdrawal and recovery. The milder drugs do little more than offer temporary relief. The more powerful ones can have dangerous side effects and can become addictive themselves. These medications are *not* a cure and can actually impede a patient's progress through recovery. During the next three weeks, I'll give him mild sedatives and pain relievers, but only when he asks for them, and only to help him through withdrawal. In one month, I want him off all prescription drugs.

"What about mild antidepressants?" Dave asked, "or perhaps psychotherapy?"

Tara contemplated the question a moment before answering. "I think he deserves a chance to experience the natural highs and lows of a drug-free lifestyle, without interference from mood-altering drugs, at least during the first few months. I also think he deserves a chance to discover, on his own, a motive or two for staying clean. If he asks for additional help during some point in the future, or if Dr. Smith feels he needs professional help, there are ways we can do this. I know an excellent therapist who specializes in mood disorders, a Dr. Jane Bennett. She even makes house calls."

"Group rates?" Brooks asked, scanning his friends.

Tara grinned. "She's a therapist, not a miracle worker."

"But think of the books I could write sitting in on *those* sessions."

"Think of the look on that shrink's face when Tara introduces her to Elvis Presley and his five kidnappers," Rob laughed.

Dave rubbed his chin reflectively. "Before inviting her out, let's make sure she understands the Texas laws governing confidentiality and patient-client privilege."

"Really," Brooks agreed.

Tara scanned her notes. "Aron orders medicines from his PDR with the ease of someone ordering merchandise from a Sears Catalogue. He uses drugs to sleep, stay awake, lift his mood, get up for concerts, come down after concerts, curb his appetite, numb his pain, and address a number of other health issues. Like many prescription drug addicts, he also uses drugs to try to abate the negative side effects of many of the other drugs. I told Dr. Smith, I was a little concerned about abruptly removing so much chemical *help*. He gave me a list of adverse reactions to watch for, but reminded me that these reactions were rare and that Aron's body would soon be benefiting from not having to fight off the toxic effects of so many powerful drugs. I'm also hoping Aron will soon be benefiting from an improved diet, a reduction in stress, and regular periods of much-needed sleep. Any questions?"

Heads shook.

"Because drugs have played such a huge role in Aron's life, a huge void will be created by their absence. Part of our job will be to help him fill this void. To that end, Brooks and I have created a two-month Vineyard schedule." Tara passed everyone a copy of the schedule. "During the first two months, no fewer than two people will be assigned to watch him at any given time. We were careful to plan your Vineyard schedules around your class and work schedules. However, when not watching Aron, attending classes, or working, we ask that you stay close in case of emergencies.

"Brooks said the schedule reminded him of church camp—extremely structured. Keep in mind it's a necessary evil, temporary, and subject to change. We'll let Aron's health and behavior be our guide. Rob, because you're not presently working or attending classes, we scheduled you the most one-on-one time with Aron. Will that be a problem?"

"Not at all," Rob answered.

"Perhaps you could put a few of your sexual conquests on hold for a while," Brooks suggested.

"Or better yet, send them my way," Dave joked.

"Man does not live by sex alone," Rob said, chin held high. "I'm an artist, now. The King and I will be spending our spare time mixing paints and stretching canvases."

Tara smiled, turning a page in her notebook. "Aron's sleep habits are highly irregular, even for a rock star. If given a choice, he prefers staying up all night and turning in the following morning. I'll ask him to try to conform to a more normal sleep pattern during his stay here. If you're assigned to watch him during the day, please try to keep him awake and active. At night, let's encourage him to sleep."

Heads nodded.

"When not rehearsing, touring, or battling health issues, he enjoys racquetball, Harley rides into the country, renting entire amusement parks, playing with his arsenal of guns, and satisfying his sex drive. Needless to say, these activities won't be offered here."

"It was a sad day in this state's history when they boarded up the Chicken Ranch," Rob grumbled.

"A sad day, indeed," Brooks agreed. "I'd like to rent *that* place out for a night or two."

"Or three," Dave added.

"Paul, you mentioned trying to interest Aron in hiking," Tara continued.

"Yes, during my assigned time with him, from six until dusk. Brooks and I found a deer trail that stretches between here and the bluffs. It's rough country, and Aron's not in the best shape, but he's in desperate need of exercise. If he's physically exhausted by the end of each day, it might help him sleep. And because he's been cooped up in a lockup for two days, I'd like to start his first hike this evening."

"What about *your* condition?" Dave asked. "You can't even turn your head without turning your whole body."

"Really," Brooks agreed, "you look like the Tin Man in *The Wizard of Oz*. Oil. Oil."

"My legs are fine, and a hike might loosen my neck."

"Did you take your medicine this morning?" Tara asked.

"Not yet," Paul answered.

"Please don't forget, and please don't exert yourself between now and the hike."

"Tara, we still have a lot of furniture to move," Paul argued, "and a lot of work to do to make this place livable."

"Yes, we do, but it doesn't all have to be done today. We need you healthy, for the long term, and your injuries will heal much faster if you're getting plenty of rest. I've also adjusted the schedule so that you'll be able to get eight hours of sleep the next two nights. I see you have classes scheduled today."

"Classes that I'll be skippin', in light of my injuries. I wouldn't be able to concentrate, anyway. I'll stay close by for emergencies."

"That would be appreciated," Tara replied, closing her notebook. "Do we have anything else to discuss?"

Paul glanced out the window, noticing a tall weed resembling a Marijuana plant. He recalled how he and his fellow Musketeers had quickly enrolled in *Recreational Drugs 101* their first week in Austin. Brooks was the first Musketeer to leave the drug scene far behind. Paul, too, quickly lost interest, preferring more natural highs, like those experienced while jogging, listening to ones favorite songs, or laughing uncontrollably with close friends. Dave and Rob, however, had continued their lab work in the course.

"I have something I'd like to discuss," Paul replied. "I'm afraid a few of my fellow Musketeers are still suffering from the use of alcohol and other recreational drugs— mainly marijuana."

"You don't say," Tara replied.

"Where's the *suffering*?" Rob laughed.

"I think it goes without saying, this place should be drug-free," Brooks commented.

"Marijuana's not a drug," Dave replied, "it's an hallucinogen."

"Regardless of its classification, it's illegal," Tara said.

"Like kidnapping isn't?" Dave rebutted.

"Touché, Dave," Tara replied, "but for the time being, we've escaped the kidnapping charge. The last thing we

need right now is for one of us to get busted for possession."

Rob's shoulders drooped. "No sex, no pot, no alcohol." He looked at Dave. "What have we gotten ourselves
into?"

"I'm beginning to wonder."

"You still have your art," Brooks joked, patting Rob
on the back.

"Unlike our Detox patients, we have no problem controlling our occasional use of recreational drugs," Dave
defended.

"Good, then you'll have no problem controlling your
use down to zero," Paul replied.

Dave's expression soured.

"Dave, sooner or later all mature, intelligent individuals leave these drugs behind," Tara said.

"Ha! Half the students in medical school use stimulants to study and pot to unwind. I'll be at a distinct
disadvantage."

"We're only talking about five months," Paul reminded.

"I hope you're not talking about beer, too," Rob said,
"because if you are, you might as well lock me in the
pantry right now, and you're gonna need more than two
people watchin' me."

"I doubt an occasional beer will hurt," Tara said. "Alcohol's not Aron's problem. But please drink responsibly.
I'd like him searching for less-chemical ways to lift his
mood."

"Thank goodness," Rob said, "let's hurry up and vote
before someone adds masturbation to the list."

"Are we all in agreement?" Paul asked.

Everyone nodded, Rob and Dave reluctantly.

Brooks shook his head. "We may need that therapist sooner than we thought."

"Ask her to pick up a six-pack on the way out," Rob suggested. "All this talk about abstinence is makin' my throat dry."

"Any other business?" Tara asked.

The room fell silent.

"I need to get the van back to Detox," Brooks mentioned, "and we'll need to ferry cars back."

"Beds would me nice," Tara said.

"We'll need a washer and dryer," Dave added. "I can donate mine—they're not getting much use at *our* house."

Rob pitched Dave the keys to his truck.

"We'll need everyone's keys," Brooks added, "and a list of what you want moved."

"I won't need a car anytime soon," Tara mentioned, "but I'll need a few personal items from my apartment. Oh, and would you mind watering my plants, picking up my mail, and checking my answering machine?"

"Anything else?" Brooks asked, eyebrows raised.

"Thank you, that will do," Tara replied.

While the others spent their first day at The Vineyard moving furniture and cleaning house, Paul and Aron spent the day sitting in rocking chairs on opposite sides of the porch. Paul tried initiating conversations with Aron, but the King was in no mood for talk. Paul made numerous attempts to help with the housework, but each time, he was escorted back to his rocking chair.

Paul was only twenty-four, and Aron, only forty-two, but they sat on the porch like two old men watching the hot day slowly pass. Paul had no idea what was going through Aron's mind, but his own mind had been racing since his trip to Memphis. He soon grew content to just sit and observe his thoughts coming and going. It didn't seem possible, but at that instant, his childhood idol, Elvis Aron Presley, was sitting on the same porch 30 feet away. If not for the sharp pain that Paul experienced whenever he turned his head, he would have swore he was dreaming. He recalled Tara predicting that Aron might one day become an equal partner, but because Paul had spent most of his life idolizing *Elvis*, he had a little trouble picturing the King on his hands and knees scrubbing the toilet. He chuckled, deciding to assign Aron the kitchen and himself the bathroom.

Paul reflected on the stark differences in their lives. Paul was just a face in the crowd, literally just one of the forty-five thousand faces streaming across UT's campus every semester. Aron's face was quite possibly the most recognized in the world. Paul and his fellow Musketeers had grown up in all-white, middle-class DeSoto, Texas. Aron had shot from multiracial poverty to great riches, leapfrogging Paul's world altogether. Paul thought about their lives' similarities. Aron had a twin brother, although briefly. Paul had a twin sister. Aron's mother passed away at age forty-six. Paul's father passed away at forty-five. Paul thought about the number reversals in their birth dates and ages. Paul was born in fifty-three. Aron, in thirty-five. Paul was twenty-four. Aron, forty-two. Paul thought about the huge task that he had undertaken at age twenty-four and wondered how Aron might have been spending *his* spare time at that age. Paul did not have a clue. Aron turned twenty-four in 1959. Paul turned six that year, and he had a very good idea how he had spent his spare time at that young age. In March of '59, Aron's fourth movie, *King Creole*, hit their one-theater town, and Paul could easily picture himself sitting in the front row watching *Elvis*. In the weeks and months that followed, he saw the film seven times.

By late afternoon all five bedrooms were furnished with beds, dressers, and lamps. A table and six chairs were placed in the large country kitchen, a second sofa and two more easychairs placed in the living room, and a washer and dryer installed in the pantry. Four wooden chairs were added to the two rocking chairs on the porch. Six window fans stood beneath six windows, eagerly awaiting electricity. Rob's brightly-colored paintings decorated almost every wall, along with a few photographs, mirrors, and calendars. An hour before dusk, everyone congregated on the back porch to escape the house's heat and to discuss dinner.

"Aron, I'm going on a short hike before supper," Paul mentioned, "if you'd like to come along."

Aron was not a hiker, but he had become extremely bored sitting on the porch, and there was also that big apology he had been putting off. He was not sure how you apologize to someone for trying to kill them, but guessed it was better done in private, perhaps on a short hike.

"I don't have any boots," Aron replied.

"What size do you wear?" Rob asked.

"Eleven."

"Me, too. I've got three pairs you can choose from."

"You two aren't in the best of shape," Tara said to Aron and Paul.

"Thanks, hon'," Aron replied, standing, "but I think I can handle a little walk."

Paul noticed Tara's concerned look. "We'll be back before sunset," he promised.

"Hopefully, we'll have dinner figured out by then," Brooks said.

Paul and Aron left the shade of the porch, stepped into the 94° heat, and soon entered the shade of the thick woods. As endorphins pumped through Paul's veins, the pain in his upper body lessened and his pace quickened.

"Son, what's your hurry?" Aron grumbled, as the distance between them widened. Paul slowed his pace, reminding himself that he was hiking with a 42-year-old, out-of-shape, rock star who was struggling through withdrawal. He began forging the easiest possible route to the ridge. As his body melted into the steamy thicket, armadillos, rabbits, and snakes began appearing from nowhere, but only when in motion. When motionless, they disappeared like the creatures in one of Rob's abstracts.

Paul's 5'9" frame just missed the numerous branches, thorns, and cob webs. Aron's 6' frame missed nothing. A thorny branch struck him across the face. He cursed the tree as a bright streak of red suddenly underlined his black eye. A minute later he spotted his first rattlesnake and while giving it a wide berth, plunged face first into a big cobweb. A hairy spider scampered down the back of his neck as he jumped and screamed. Paul flicked the spider to the ground then continued hiking.

"Wait!" Aron yelled, frantically trying to rub the sticky web from his sweat-drenched neck and face. "What in the *heck* are we doin' out here!"

"Just gettin' a little exercise," Paul answered.

"Exercise! That's what racquetball courts are for! *Air-conditioned* racquetball courts! With *no* snakes! And *no* spiders!"

"Sorry, Aron, we're a little short on racquetball courts."

"I can't believe I'm hiking through a stupid *jungle*! I could be hibernating in my jungle room right now, falling asleep in front of a good movie, my head in Ginger's lap."

"You'll be back in Graceland soon enough," Paul said, turning to hike.

"Not soon enough for me," Aron said, following at Paul's heels. "Why'd you kidnap me, anyway?"

"I thought I explained my reasons this morning—to save my childhood idol."

Aron stared at Paul suspiciously. "I was the childhood idol of a million other kids, but I don't recall seein' too many of 'em standing in line in front of Graceland—waitin' for a chance to kidnap me."

"Good point, but if you're looking for ulterior motives, you're wasting your time. Let's just call it a humanitarian gesture."

"Ha! How old are you?"

"Twenty-four."

"Twenty-four. I've never met too many 24-year-old humanitarians. When I was twenty-four, my primary goal was gettin' laid."

Paul laughed. "Gettin' laid's important to me, too, but it's not the reason I kidnapped you, although, there was that kiss I got from Tara."

"Ya got a kiss from Tara for kidnapping me?"

"Yes, I did."

"I would have held out for more than that."

"We're just friends."

"Sure you are. Do you love her?"

Paul's face reddened. He glanced around the woods, making sure they were alone. "Yes, just between you and me, I fell in love with her the first moment I saw her."

"That's what I thought," Aron said, shaking his head. "Boy, my boy, one minute you're gettin' kissed by the beautiful princess, and the next, you're gettin' attacked by the evil monster."

"All adventures have their surprises—that's what makes them adventures."

"Right," Aron scoffed.

"Stick around, Aron. Whatever our motives, I think we'll all benefit from this venture."

Aron studied Paul's swollen neck and face. "I can't see that you've benefited a whole lot so far."

"I'm optimistic things will improve."

"I'm not," Aron grumbled, glancing toward the house. "I haven't been optimistic about anything since—since Mom died."

"I find that hard to believe," Paul replied. He motioned toward the ridge. "Maybe we can find a breeze up there."

Aron looked up at the tall ridge. A tight thicket of thorn bushes and cacti encircled the ridge like a moat, a strong warning for intruders. "You've *got* to be kidding."

"Brooks and I found an easier way up."

The men circled to the left side of the ridge and after a fifteen minute struggle, were rewarded with a panoramic view of the surrounding countryside. To their right, green and brown juniper, evergreen, and mesquite stretched from the bluffs to their safe house in the distance. To their left, freshly-grooved farmland curved toward their neighbor's house and barn perched on the horizon. A green tractor stood in the center of the field. A breeze rustled the trees below then climbed up the ridge to cool the hikers. Paul reached into his backpack and handed Aron an apple. Aron watched the fruit change into a chicken-fried steak right before his eyes. He was dying of thirst, however, and quickly gobbled it up. Paul slowly chewed *his* apple, studying the tractor below.

The quiet reminded Aron of the rehab cell, but there, the comparison ended. The view from the ridge was truly majestic—not a cloud in sight—except for the big one that had followed him up the ridge. He stared at Paul's injuries before taking a deep breath. "Listen, son, I'm sorry for what I did to you in that cell."

Paul's jaw tightened, causing a sharp pain to shoot from the stitched cut on his face. "It was nothin'. And I'm not your son."

"Nothin'! I tried to kill you! How can you say it was *nothin'*!"

Paul's eyes narrowed. "There's nothin' you can do to me that I can't recover from."

Aron's head dropped, eyes staring guiltily at his thumbs.

Paul, too, felt a sudden tinge of guilt. He had just been offered an apology and had responded like like a hurt, angry child. He took a deep breath. "Thanks, Aron. Apology accepted. I guess we just got off to a bad start."

"Boy, my boy," Aron laughed, "is that ever puttin' it mildly."

A farmer wearing blue jean overalls and a white T-shirt appeared from nowhere and climbed atop the tractor. A low rumble broke the silence below as the machine crawled toward The Vineyard. Fifty yards from the first mesquite, it made a U-turn and inched back toward the center of the field on its way toward the horizon. Paul focused on The Vineyard. "What do you think of our house?"

Aron recalled his first hour in the sweltering heat—his intense cravings and rage. He remembered wanting to run, and the strange force stopping him. He recalled breaking down in the doorway. He sighed. "I think it's gonna be bitter medicine, and I wasn't exactly lookin' for a cure."

Paul smiled, handing Aron a bottle of water.

Aron took a long drink, studying The Vineyard's rooftop in the distance. "What do *you* think of it?"

Paul closed his eyes and pictured the house's long eaves, wraparound porch, big rooms, and tall windows. He pictured Rob's colorful paintings and the plants Tara had used to decorate the kitchen and bathroom. "I love everything about it, I think it'll be good medicine, and I think on some level, we're all searchin' for a cure."

Aron studied Paul curiously. "Is that why you became a nurse's aide? Searchin' for a cure?"

"No, I became a nurse's aide because I was waiting tables and working as a clerk in a library, and thought I should move on to something related to my major, psychology."

Aron watched the tractor make a U-turn at the horizon and begin another slow crescendo across the field.

"My mom once worked as a nurse's aide in Tupelo. She hated every minute of it."

Paul laughed, wincing at the sharp pain shooting from his sore neck. "I can certainly sympathize with her."

Aron's thoughts floated from his mother, to Lisa Marie, to Priscilla. As the tractor neared, he focused on the old farmer and was reminded of his father. "My dad was pretty worried about me. I should probably give him another call."

"The pay phone's only fifteen minutes away," Paul mentioned.

"Where are *your* parents?"

"My mom lives in DeSoto, a small town south of Dallas."

"Does she have any idea what her boy's up to right now?"

"Are you kiddin'? She'd have me committed."

"Where's your dad?"

"He passed away when I was two."

"Sorry to hear that. You must really miss him."

"You can't miss somethin' you never had," Paul said, giving the same pat answer he had given often over the years.

"I miss Jesse, my twin brother. I never really knew him, but I used to talk to him all the time. When I got older, talkin' to Jesse seemed kind of crazy, so I guess I grew out of it. But for a long time, I missed talkin' to him. I once told my guru that I often felt alone, even when surrounded by people. He said I was just missing Jesse, the twin I never had."

Paul thought about his own twin. "I have a twin sister, and a younger sister, both living in Austin, and an older brother living in Dallas. I guess I should remind myself from time to time that I'm lucky to have them."

"Yes, you should, and yes, you are."

Paul noticed the sun lowering toward the horizon and glanced at his watch. "We'd better head back."

The tractor stopped in the center of the field, its low rumble fading. In the still quiet that followed, the farmer climbed off his tractor, turned, and waved at the two hikers.

"Wow," Paul said, returning the wave, "he must have the eyes of an eagle." He nudged Aron's arm.

Aron slowly lifted his arm and waved. To Paul's amusement, the King continued waving long after the farmer had turned to walk away.

"Wow," Aron said, with a grin, "maybe Tara was right. Maybe I *can* be anonymous out here."

They climbed down the side of the bluff and entered the forest. Its fading colors and cooling temperature warned the hikers nightfall was near. They quickened their pace but exited the woods well past dark.

To Paul, the house appeared quite romantic. Candlelight radiated from its open windows. Laughter drifted from the back porch to welcome them home. The sound of Tara's voice caused his heart to smile. The smell of food caused his stomach to growl.

To Aron, the hike was nothing more than a temporary diversion. Now that it was over, his intense cravings and physical discomforts quickly returned. To him, the house looked quite ominous. Its brooding eaves hung low like the long brim of an old witch's hat. Black fans perched like vultures in the windows. Trees reached out from the shadows—strong-armed pallbearers. A light breeze blew.

A fan blade turned. Aron could feel the fan yearning for that familiar rush of electricity through its veins, aching for that low-pitched, medium-pitched, and high-pitched buzz.

"Well, boys, I hope you enjoyed yourselves," Dave said, sounding more like his father, than his father.

"Sorry, we're late," Paul apologized. "It gets dark fast out there."

"How was it?" Rob asked.

"Rough, but fun," Paul replied.

"What did *you* think of it, Aron?" Tara asked.

Aron was busy watching the house's veins and arteries bulge and shrink faster and faster as its electric meter's tiny little hands spun wildly out of control.

"Aron?" Tara asked again.

"What?"

"What did you think of the hike?"

"Oh. Rough. It was rough. I've got the cuts to prove it."

"There's antiseptic in the bathroom, and clean towels and washcloths, if you'd like to take a shower before dinner."

"How 'bout an upper before dinner?"

"How about a Valium?" Tara asked, stepping inside and soon returning with medicine and water for both men. Aron gulped his before trudging to the bathroom to look for more. Tara focused on Paul in the dim candle light shining from a window. "How are *you* feeling?"

"Fine, except for my face, neck, head, and a slightly sprained ankle."

Tara shook her head.

"It was worth it, Tara. The view from the ridge is really spectacular."

"We picked up dinner," Brooks mentioned. "How does chicken, mashed potatoes, black-eyed peas, corn on the cob, and buttered rolls sound?"

"It sounds like heaven. Where'd you get it?"

"Found a little restaurant on Lake Travis," Brooks answered.

"How much do I owe you?"

"Just consider it a gift from The Vineyard's newly appointed chief financial officer," Brooks replied.

"You missed our first business meeting," Dave mentioned. "We elected Brooks treasurer because he's so cheap."

"Frugal," Brooks corrected. "I'm opening a joint account tomorrow morning. One hundred and fifty, per person, per month should be enough to cover rent, utilities, and a few groceries. Those in attendance refused to make it a paid position, so I guess I'll be skimmin' off the top."

"We're going to need an auditor," Paul replied.

"How much does that position pay?" Dave asked.

"We'll pay you twice what we're paying Brooks?" Tara joked.

"Did I miss any other important business?" Paul asked.

"As a matter of fact," Rob chuckled, "six people and five bedrooms presented a small problem that we rectified in your absence."

"May I make a motion that no further business be discussed without a quorum?" Paul grumbled.

"Sorry, the business meeting's already been adjourned," Dave answered.

"When's the next one?" Paul asked.

"None scheduled," Brooks replied.

"We decided to trade off bedrooms," Tara said. "During the first months, we'll be sleeping at different intervals anyway, so it shouldn't be a problem."

"Until we get electricity, I'll be sleeping on the porch," Paul replied.

"The house *is* a little hot," Tara agreed.

Aron trudged into the candlelit bathroom and scoured through the cabinets and drawers before angrily stripping off his sweaty clothes. As the cold water struck him in the chest, he jumped back, cursing loudly. He hurriedly soaped his body, cuts and scratches screaming, then held his breath before stepping back into the frigid spray. As his body grew used to the temperature, it began to relax. His exhaustion from the long hike, and Valium seeping into his bloodstream, was also having a calming effect. While drying off, he noticed that the house was still pulsating but not as wildly as before. The antiseptic he applied to his cuts was the same brand his mother had used on him when he was a small child, and the familiar scent filled his mind with fond memories.

Aron dressed in a clean, cotton T-shirt and shorts, which Tara had hung over the towel rack. He paused in the dark hallway, listening to the noises floating from the candlelit kitchen. The light banter, clink of dishes, and smell of fried chicken took him back to a distant time and place. He took a detour through the living room and grinned. Someone had placed a candle beneath each of Rob's color-splattered paintings—a British art museum during a blackout. A soft patchwork quilt now covered the room's itchy sofa, reminding Aron of his grandmother, Minnie Mae. There was something comforting about the living room's old furnishings, something Aron had missed during his first hours at the house.

Their first supper at The Vineyard was reheated with Sterno. Tara opted for stoneware, silverware, and glasses instead of the paper plates and plastic utensils included with the purchase.

"I'd like to plant a vegetable garden," Tara mentioned, while setting the table, "and perhaps later on, a flower garden."

"I'd like to clear the pasture for football," Rob said, filling glasses with water.

"I'd like to sell fifty-thousand copies," Brooks commented, scribbling beneath a lone candle.

"I'd like to get through this semester with a B average," Paul joked, as Aron entered the room.

"Sit wherever you like, Aron," Tara said, setting another candle on the table.

"Thanks," Aron replied, as he and the other men took their seats. "Are all of y'all in college?"

"Just three of us, right now," Paul answered, passing Aron the fried chicken. "I have a few semesters to go before getting my B.S."

Dave passed Aron the mashed potatoes. "I'm enrolled in UT's Graduate School of Medicine."

Brooks helped himself to the black-eyed peas. "I received my journalism degree last spring and am patiently waiting for one of Austin's local papers to come to their senses and give me a job. In the meantime, I'm taking two creative writing classes."

Tara took her seat. "I received my premed degree this past summer and I'm presently doing some independent research while looking into graduate school."

Aron looked at Rob.

"I dropped out of the University of Colorado to pursue my art," Rob said, motioning toward the brightly colored painting above the kitchen table. "No sells, yet, but one day soon I'll be hittin' the art world the way you hit the music world."

Aron smiled, thinking about that sunny day in July of '54 when he hit the music world with "That's All Riht (Mama)." In one week, the song sold 5,000 copies. Aron focused on the erotic forms in Rob's abstract and grinned. "Boy, I don't know much about art, but that one seems a little erotic for the kitchen." Laughter suddenly filled the kitchen. As it died, Aron again stared at the painting. "But I like it, Rob, and I hope ya do hit the art world."

"Thanks," Rob replied.

"Corn?" Tara asked, passing the bowl to Aron.

"Thanks, hon'."

"Anyone have any gardening experience?" Tara asked.

"I ordered a garden salad once," Brooks joked.

"Impressive," Tara replied.

As Tara discussed the various plants growing around the house, Paul could not help staring. When Tara mentioned mountain laurel, a breeze pulled the plant's grape fragrance into the kitchen. When she mentioned honeysuckle, the wind changed direction and the sweet scent of honeysuckle filled the room. Paul looked to see if anyone else had noticed the strange coincidence. Was Tara's voice attracting the scents, or was the breeze playing tricks on him? Was the house playing games, or was it just his imagination?

Paul recalled his first month at Detox, and Tara asking him to watch her apartment while she vacationed in Corpus. At the time, he was quite puzzled by the request—they had only known each other a few weeks, and he was sure she had closer friends and neighbors to call on for such favors. He was happy to oblige, however, and during his first visit to her apartment, he made a surprising discovery.

Tara's bedroom was filled with bright-green comforters and pillows. Green plants lined the room's windowsills, and her perfumed scent filled the air. Photographs of Tara with her mother covered the walls. But it was two rectangular-shaped movie posters that gave Paul pause. The first advertised *Flaming Star*, and Elvis was dressed in boots, jeans, and a long-sleeved shirt with the collar turned up—pistol resting at his hip. The second poster advertised *Blue Hawaii*, and Elvis wore a colorful shirt and lei while holding a beautiful woman in his arms. Diamond Head rose from the ocean just above his right shoulder.

The discovery was surprising because ten years had passed since the Beatles, Stones, Zeppelin, and Fleetwood Mac had thoroughly dethroned the King. During the mid-seventies, no one was decorating their walls with *Elvis*, that is, almost no one. To Paul, the discovery was important, but he would not realize how important until months later, after reading those first tabloid articles about the King's deteriorating health.

"More rolls, Paul?" Brooks asked, passing the basket.

Paul was lost in thoughts of Tara and failed to hear the question.

"Paul, more rolls?" Brooks tried again.

Tara's eyes directed Paul's focus to the basket of rolls.

"What? Oh. Thanks." He reached for a roll.

Brooks noticed the untouched roll on Paul's plate and made a few notes on his legal pad. Paul grinned, wondering how much the writer's eye had seen. He then inquired about the progress Brooks was making on his book.

As the others discussed Brooks' writing, Tara focused on the suggestive forms in the painting above Paul's head. She imagined herself slowly standing, removing her clothing, and climbing on top of the table, hands pressing into the baskets of rolls, knees in the mashed potatoes and black-eyed peas, a juicy ear of corn caressing the soft skin on the inside of her legs. She could easily feel her naked body melting like warm butter in Paul's strong arms.

"Tara, I can't sleep without sleeping pills," Aron said.

Tara was not listening.

"Tara," Aron repeated, stirring her from her daydream.

"Yes?" she asked.

"I can't sleep without sleeping pills."

"When was the last time you tried?"

"Boy, my boy," Aron laughed, shaking his head. "I can't remember that far back."

"Please try tonight."

Thirty minutes later Aron lay in bed listening to the house's strange noises. Cricket's called from an open window. Laughter scampered down the hall. The shower was turned on, followed by a loud curse, spurring laughter from the kitchen and living room. Noticeably absent were the sounds of televisions, radios, and phonographs.

Aron's thoughts returned to "That's All Right (Mama)" and the moments leading up to the first time he heard it played on the radio. At the time he was sitting in his old Lincoln Zephr, thinking about his dad's trouble keeping a job and his mom having to sweat over a hot ironing board just to put food on the table. He recalled staring at his car's AM radio, wondering if their ship would ever come in. It was at that moment, that their ship not only came in, but crashed into the car's bumper, up its hood, through its windshield, and right into the car's radio. He remembered listening in shock as the disc jockey played the song over and over, listening in awe as caller after caller begged for the song again and again. Aron smiled broadly before falling into a deep sleep.

Paul took a cold shower, checked on Aron, then un-rolled his sleeping bag on the front porch. He lay on his back, listening to the soft sounds emanating from the house—hushed conversations, the flipped pages of a textbook, a striking match. He slowly inhaled the faint aroma of oil paints, house plants, and a cinnamon-scented candle. He thought of Tara. He recalled Aron referring to her as the beautiful princess and smiled because that was exactly how he saw her. A strong breeze blew through the army of mesquite surrounding the house—taking roll call. One by one, the trees responded by shaking their leaves—all present and accounted for—all ready, willing, and able to protect the princess, the King, and their castle—to the death, if necessary. Paul soon fell fast to sleep.

Tara walked barefoot into the dark bathroom carry-ing a maroon-colored towel, washcloth, and candle. She lit the candle, slowly inhaling the bathroom's moist, cinnamon air. She closed the door before removing her shirt, bra, and blue jean shorts, stopping just short of her white cotton underwear. There was something exciting about standing half-nude—the only woman in a ranch house full of horny, hot-blooded, testosterone-filled men. It occurred to her that just minutes before *Elvis Aron Presley* had stood in that very spot—nude. How often had she dreamed of *that?*

When Tara was twelve, the mere *thought* of *Elvis* caused her body to tingle with excitement. Her introduction into puberty was fraught with images of him dancing into her bedroom, *his* lips on *her* lips, his hot hands exploring every inch of her trembling body. On more than one occasion, she had fallen asleep with her phonograph's stylus rubbing against the label of one of Elvis' 45's.

During Tara's mid-teens, she continued idolizing the King, but Steve, her first love, became the object of her more intimate feelings. At that moment, however, she was not thinking of Elvis *or* Steve. She was thinking of Paul—his slender, muscular body, warm smile, and searching eyes. Paul, too, had just stood in that very spot—nude. She closed her eyes and imagined him returning to the bathroom, his hands caressing her waist, his lips brushing across her earlobes, neck, and shoulders. Shivers ran up her spine.

Tara placed her thumbs inside the elastic band of her underwear and gently pushed until her last article of clothing had fallen to the floor. She turned on the shower and took a deep breath before offering her warm body to the cold spray. She picked up the wet bar of soap that Paul had just used and slid it up her arms, across her shoulders, and over her breasts. She imagined his soapy hands slowly sliding over her erect nipples and down to her tingling stomach before slipping between her legs.

As the day's dirts, oils, and scents fell from Tara's body and swirled down the drain, she chided herself for both pushing and pulling when it came to her relationship with Paul. She recalled her excitement the day he asked her out and how she had reluctantly declined the offer. She remembered desperately wanting to give him the keys to her heart and how she had settled for giving him the keys to her apartment. She recalled surprising even herself by impulsively kissing him in the Detox parking lot. As she rinsed her clean body, one thing became perfectly clear. She had brought quite a bit of excess baggage to The Vineyard, baggage that would need to be unloaded to make room for Paul.

Chapter Five

The following morning Paul awakened on the porch to the sound of Brooks and Tara discussing Aron making the 6 a.m. news. "What'd they say?" Paul asked, rubbing the sleep from his eyes.

"It seems *Elvis* is in a California hospital recuperating from exhaustion," Brooks replied. "The colonel has canceled all the King's concert appearances scheduled during the next six months."

"That's perfect," Paul said. "The legend will go on just fine without him."

"And now for the bad news," Brooks said. "He's been up since three."

"And *not* in a very good mood," Tara added.

"I'll talk to him before leavin' for campus," Paul replied.

Paul took a quick shower then found Aron on the back porch. "Good morning. Sorry about your trouble sleeping."

"I'll need downers to sleep."

"Getting used to your new sleep schedule will take some time. If you stay awake today, you'll probably have less trouble sleeping tonight."

"Okay, then I'll need uppers to stay awake today."

"Sorry, no stimulants."

"Boy, you said it. I've been staring at the walls since three this morning. This is the most boring place on earth. No television, no movies, no Harley's, no racquetball courts, no guns."

"Guns? What do you want with guns?"

"What do ya think I want with 'em? I want to have a *blast*. This is a great place for a little target practice. Picture this—life-size targets, just like the ones used by the FBI and DEA, hidden from here all the way to that ridge. We can blow away doctors, reporters, comedians, talk-show hosts, ex-bodyguards, Priscilla's boyfriends . . ."

"Nurse's aides," Paul suggested.

"Nurse's aides," Aron agreed. "Anybody that needs killin'. This is *Texas*, right? There's gotta be a gun shop and lumber yard close by. And Rob's got plenty of paint."

"Sorry, Aron, this should probably be a gun-free zone. And we're kind of tight on cash right now."

"I've got plenty of money."

"Yes, and we voted not to take one cent of it during your stay here."

Aron angrily stood and walked to the porch railing to glare at the woods. He closed his eyes, a sudden image of Graceland filling his mind. The Castle Graceland, had everything: sex, racquetball, billiards, poker, a 24-hour kitchen, 800 albums, 200 movies, 37 guns, 20 telephones, 16 televisions, 15 guitars, 7 cars, 3 motorcycles, a grand piano, and a partridge in a pear tree. Not to mention—drugs. And he had traded all that for this dump in the middle of nowhere.

"Rob has all sorts of fun activities planned for you to-day," Paul commented. "And don't forget to call home."

Aron's jaw tightened. There was something awfully irritating about this *kid* reminding him to call home.

"I saw some recent pictures of your daughter last month," Paul mentioned. "She's a beautiful little girl. You must love her very much."

"Yeah, I do, and I'm deserting her now."

"Aron, you're not deserting your daughter. You can talk to her whenever you want, and you're doing this for her, too."

"Is that right?" Aron replied, glaring at Paul.

"Yes, that's right, and you might want to spend the day thinking about those closest to you and how they'll benefit from you kicking your addiction."

Aron's face turned bright red as he whirled to face Paul. "Listen, *boy*, I don't need you tellin' me what I should spend the day thinkin' about!"

Paul's fists tightened. "It was just a suggestion, and I'm not your *boy*."

"You're not my *guru* or my *shrink* either, and you can *stop* actin' like it!"

Paul tried to calm his quickly-growing anger by slowly counting to ten. "Whatever you say, Aron," he replied, glancing at his watch. "I have to leave for class now." He paused at the door. "I hope the rest of your day goes better."

Aron spun to glare into the woods. His eyes narrowed as he pictured a big target resembling Paul, centered in the crosshairs of his rifle scope.

Paul spent the morning on campus then made a quick stop by the store where he ran into one of Brooks' friends,

Beth. While waiting in line, they discussed Paul's face
and neck injuries, the spring semester, and their classes
and professors. As the line crept forward, Paul noticed a
rather unflattering picture of Aron on the cover of one of
the checkout's tabloids. To his surprise, the headline read,
"KING ENTERS REHAB!"

"Is David (Brooks) out of town?" Beth asked. "He
hasn't been returning my calls."

"No, I think he just started some big writing project.
I might see him this afternoon."

"Would you tell him I split up with Chris and that I
have some extra time on my hands, if he needs help with
his project?"

"Sure. He'll be glad to hear it."

After leaving the store, Paul stopped by his and Dave's
house to pick up his mail, books, and clean clothes. He
remembered Aron saying The Vineyard was the most boring place on earth, and filled his trunk with footballs,
Frisbees, a chess board, poker chips, jogging shoes, and
an extra pair of hiking boots. He scanned the living room,
eyes falling on his most valuable possession, an old Gibson guitar. He had purchased the $300.00 acoustic for
$50.00, from a Dallas musician down on his luck. Al-
though Paul's guitar skills were limited, he loved to play,
and his Gibson had become a close friend, sticking by him
through three moves, four girlfriends, eight pairs of jogging shoes, and six years of college. He could not imagine
leaving it behind now. He carefully set the instrument in
the front seat, smiling broadly. From the age of six, he had
dreamed of one day jamming with the King of Rock 'n'
Roll. Suddenly, that dream appeared to be coming true.

He raced back to The Vineyard, arriving just in time for their noon briefing.

Tara opened Aron's file. "Rob, since you've spent the most time with our patient this morning, would you like to begin?"

Rob leaned back in his chair, looking out the window. "We began the morning nailing the porch's loose boards, repairing doors and windows, and stretching canvases—not exactly exciting stuff for someone used to more stimulating activities. I suggested fishing, swimming, and football, but he wasn't interested. I drove him to the pay phone, hopin' a call home might lift his spirits, but all it did was make him more homesick. The only thing he showed any real interest in was Tara's Physician's Desk Reference, and I have to tell you, the way he eulogized the uppers made my mouth water.

"If I haven't lost him by this afternoon, I'd like to coax him into runnin' wild on a 4 X 6. Maybe there's a great artist hiding behind the great performer."

"Perhaps there is," Tara agreed. "Thanks, Rob. At this point in the process, keeping him occupied is half the battle, and you're doing a good job."

During the remainder of the briefing, they discussed Aron's mood, behavior, and health before moving on to their finances and supplies needed from town.

"Anything else?" Tara asked, scanning her notes.

Paul recalled his grocery store conversation with Beth. "Yes, I think we need to discuss our friends in Austin, classmates, neighbors, relatives, and dating."

"Relatives and dating!" Brooks echoed. "We don't date our relatives, Paul. That's farther up north around Arkansas."

Paul smiled then continued. "For our plan to work, it's important we keep tightlipped in all of our other relationships. Think about what could happen if all of Austin found out Elvis Presley was living out here. We could certainly kiss his anonymity goodbye."

"Is anyone involved in a close relationship?" Tara asked.

"I left my close relationship in Colorado," Rob answered.

Brooks looked up from his legal pad. "Would you care to elaborate?"

"Let's just say I picked a good time to be leavin' Colorado, and thanks for pryin'."

"How about you, Mr. Brooks?" Tara asked. "Are you dating anyone?"

"No, I'm holding out for Beth, who's always on and off with her boyfriend."

"Right now, she's off," Paul said. "I ran into her at the store this morning. She said you haven't been returning her calls and that she's got some free time on her hands, if you need help with your writing."

"All right! What luck." His face suddenly saddened. "And rotten timing in light of our new responsibilities."

"You can see her in five months," Rob joked, patting Brooks on the back.

"After she's gone back to her boyfriend," Dave chuckled.

"I'm sure we'll be able to relax the schedule soon," Tara said. "Dave are you involved?"

"Well, before being shanghaied, I'd planned a second date with a cute little filly I met in Photography 302."

"Filly," Brooks echoed. "Perhaps you should be a Veterinarian."

"Perhaps you should be my first patient," Dave replied.

"Does this *filly* have a name?" Tara asked.

"Susanne," Dave answered, smiling broadly while staring at the ceiling.

"I think Dave's in *love*," Rob commented.

"Hmm, that possibility *does* exist," Dave replied. He looked at Paul. "And what about *your* love life?"

"I'm not dating anyone right now, but I *do* ask Tara out from time to time. Unfortunately, she keeps shootin' me down."

"I thought we were on a date last night," Tara replied. "Candlelit table, stimulating conversation, wonderful dinner. What more could a girl ask for?"

"Something a little more intimate?" Paul suggested.

"And what about you, Tara?" Brooks asked.

"I'm not dating anyone at this time." A worried look crossed her face. "But my mom's planning a visit next month."

"You're datin' your mom?" Brooks asked.

"That's disgusting," Dave agreed.

"Where are you from, anyway?" Brooks asked.

"She's from San Angelo," Dave answered.

"Remind me never to go there," Brooks said.

"Okay, gentlemen, to summarize, none of us is involved romantically at this time. Before you *do* become involved, please give serious thought as to how you'll explain your long absences. Also, while we're out here, no one's answering our phones in town. We don't want our friends and family members worrying, so please keep in touch. I'll call my mom today and ask her to postpone her trip until August." She glanced toward Aron's bedroom. "Perhaps we'll have something to celebrate by then, and everyone can invite their friends and families out for a visit."

Paul glanced out the window. "What about our neighbors? I know they're far away, but neighbors *do* drop by."

Brooks looked at Dave and grinned. "I've got an idea. How about we tell them we'd like to invite them in, but poor Dave's caught hoof and mouth disease."

Everyone chuckled.

Dave studied Brooks seriously then grinned. "How about we tell them Mr. Brooks just beat a murder rap with an insanity plea and he's been released under my care? That should keep the neighbors away."

Again, everyone laughed.

"How 'bout we tell 'em nothin'?" Rob asked. "How 'bout, we tell 'em to hit the road or we'll beat their brains out."

"Rob, we're talking about our neighbors," Tara said. "Surely, we can think of a more neighborly response than that."

"Why don't ya tell 'em the truth?" Aron asked, leaning against the doorway. "Tell 'em ya have a sick friend who's goin' through withdrawal."

"The truth," Tara echoed. "What a novel idea. Why didn't *we* think of that?"

"And this *is* a big place," Aron added, "I can make myself scarce when neighbors drop by."

"You could make yourself a lot more scarce if you cut your hair and lost those sideburns," Brooks suggested. "They're a dead giveaway."

Aron stepped up to a mirror and ran a hand through his long, black hair. "Yeah, you're probably right. And I could quit dyeing it, too. Boy, has that ever been a hassle." He wiped the sweat off from his forehead then lowered his hand, watching his fingers tremble. "Can I have a Valium?"

Tara glanced at her watch. "I'll be right back."

Aron gulped his sedative then sat alone on the porch.

That afternoon The Vineyard received its first guest, an electrician from Texas Power & Light. Santa Claus could not have been more welcomed, and six window fans soon applauded from six windows. The three on the west side of the house sucked cool air in while the three on the east side blew warm air out. It was not air conditioning, but the circulating breeze cooled the house considerably, and the fans brought other changes, as well. Dave noticed the living room's soft hum drowned out the house's numerous other noises, making it the perfect place to study. Rob liked the way the fans flickered sunlight across his paintings. Paul liked how the fans stirred the house's many aromas.

The electrician was followed by a representative from Lone Star Gas. The house's propane tank was filled, the lines checked for leaks, and the hot water heater and oven lit. Aron shaved off his thick sideburns and six-day beard before taking the first hot shower. Afterwards, he met Tara on the back porch for a haircut while the others sat in the living room discussing whether or not to add televisions, stereos, and telephones to the house.

"A stereo would be nice," Brooks said. "But a television would make this place seem a lot less remote."

"I went without television in Colorado," Rob mentioned. "Not having a TV surely frees up time for more *fun* things."

"I could do without the distraction," Dave said. "I've got a ton of reading between now and the end of the semester."

"I say we continue giving Aron a break from all the bad publicity," Paul suggested. "One of the national tabloids already has 'KING ENTERS REHAB!' plastered on its front cover, and they used the most unflattering picture they could find. Television and radio won't be treating him any better."

"We can entertain ourselves without them," Rob said. "We have tons of paint, lots of books, four footballs, and three guitars."

"Four guitars counting the one Paul stole from Graceland," Dave corrected. All eyes fell on Aron's expensive Martin.

"I wonder if we'll ever get to hear him play it," Rob said.

"I wonder if we'll ever get to hear him sing," Paul said.

"You folks are dreaming," Dave scoffed. "He's light-years away from playing guitars and singing."

"Just curious if it'll ever happen," Rob said.

"What about a telephone?" Brooks asked.

"I think we should hold off on that, too," Paul answered. "I can just see him calling 911 the next time he loses his temper."

"We'll just have to get used to driving to the pay phone," Brooks said.

As Tara and Aron entered the living room, jaws dropped.

"Wow, you could get into Texas A&M with *that* haircut," Rob joked."

"Put on a John Deere cap and a pair of sunglasses and you're just another good old boy from Texas," Brooks added.

"Just the look I was goin' for," Aron said, stepping up to the mirror. "Boy, it hasn't been this short since boot camp."

"You buzzed him good," Dave commented.

"Sorry, Aron," Tara apologized, "I got a little carried away."

"That's okay, hon', I wanted to lose weight."

"I'd say you lost about 10 pounds," Brooks said, glancing toward the porch, "which gives me a great idea how we can bring in a little extra money."

"Don't even think about it," Tara said.

"Ten bucks a lock could pay the electric bill," Brooks argued.

"Pump him full of Vitamin E and we can grow enough hair to pay the rent," Dave suggested.

Aron stared in the mirror, trying to come to grips with yet another drastic change.

"You'll get used to it, Aron," Rob encouraged. "And it has to be cooler."

"Next?" Tara asked, holding up her electric shears.

"No, thanks," the men replied.

Aron's buzzed head and puffy, clean-shaven face made him look more like Curly of The Three Stooges than Elvis Presley. But his body showed the hint of a tan from the previous day's hike, and he had, in fact, lost 10 pounds since Memphis. He was changing, at least on the surface, and the others liked the change. On the inside, however, the war continued to rage, making his second day's hike more torturous than the first. Paul made several attempts at conversation during their hike, but Aron preferred to fight the battle alone.

Years earlier millions of happy little cells were drafted to fight an escalating bombardment from an array of toxic chemicals. These cells recently heard rumors the war was over, but just as they began celebrating a joyful return to their homes, families, and loved ones, they were told their tours had been extended, that they must now serve as peacekeepers and reconstructionists, that before ever seeing their homes again, they must first accomplish the monumental task of returning a sick, obese, and depressed rock star back to health. Suddenly, every cell in Aron's body was reacting vehemently, and he could not blame them one bit. How easy it would be for him to relieve them of their duties, to end this insanity for himself and everyone involved, to chalk himself up as just another casualty of the Rock Generation. During the long hike home, Aron longed for God to lift him up, as He had lifted Jesse.

As the house came into view, Paul noticed Dave standing over a hot charcoal grill. Paul stopped to talk to his friend and savor the unexpected smell of burning coals and sizzling meat. Aron trudged up the porch steps, ignoring the grill, as well as Dave's friendly welcome. He walked to the bathroom, rifled through a backpack lying on the floor and found a near-empty bottle of aspirin. He turned up the bottle then chased the pills with a handful of water.

The others met Paul and Dave at the grill. "Tonight's menu," Rob announced, "barbecue ribs, pinto beans, brown rice, and cornbread. Oh, and one cold beer each, in honor of our first home-cooked meal at The Vineyard."

"I owe y'all, big time," Paul replied. "I'll cook tomorrow."

"The second batch of ribs will need another ten minutes," Dave commented.

"Good," Tara said, "that'll give me time to talk to Aron."

Aron left the bathroom to find Tara waiting in the hall with Valium in hand. "Listen, hon', I have a million health problems that I need medications for and . . ."

"What health problems?" Tara asked.

"My head's killing me, my whole body's sore from hikin', and I haven't had a bowel movement in three days."

"Here's your sedative. I'll be right back with a pain-killer and laxative."

"Wait! My skin's itchin' all over, and that *stupid* Valium's not workin'. I'm jittery and nervous, and I thought you said we were gonna try somethin' more powerful."

"After we've upped the dosage of Valium for a few days," Tara reminded.

"But . . ."

"Aron, it's been five hours since your last sedative. You'll naturally begin to feel edgy as the medication wears off. Take a warm shower, lie down for a few minutes before dinner, and give the sedative time to work. I have some cortisone cream if your skin's still itchy after your shower. I'll be right back with your other medications."

Aron's fists tightened as he watched Tara spin and walk away. At dinner he ignored all attempts at conversation and only picked at his food. The light banter and joking that usually accompanied their meals was noticeably absent, even after Aron left the table.

During dessert, Paul's head and neck began to ache, causing him to second guess his decision to hike so soon after his injuries. He helped with the dishes, took his medicine, and soon fell asleep while studying for an important psychology exam. He awakened the following morning, thankful to be experiencing only mild neck pain. He quickly showered, dressed, and gathered his books before joining Tara, Brooks, and Aron at the kitchen table.

"Good morning," Paul greeted.

"Good morning," his friends replied.

"What's good about it?" Aron growled, storming back to his bedroom. The sound of a kicked chair and slamming door boomed down the hall.

"How do *you* feel?" Tara asked Paul.

"Much better. You were right to insist I get eight hours' sleep."

"I *am* a nurse," Tara said, standing to pour Paul a cup of coffee. She returned to the table, leaned back in her chair, and closed her eyes.

Brooks pushed the morning paper in front of Paul. "The spring drought's in its seventh week."

"Any rain in the forecast?" Paul asked.

"Scattered showers this weekend, but they're not expecting much accumulation." Brooks crossed his arms on the table and rested his head on his arms.

"You two look exhausted," Paul said, feeling a little guilty. "How much sleep did y'all get last night?"

"A few hours," Tara answered.

"Three hours," Brooks answered.

"And I got eight," Paul said, shaking his head. "Now, I *really* feel guilty. Promise me you'll get some sleep this morning."

"I'll be sound asleep before you cross the cattle guard," Tara said.

Brooks glanced at his watch. "I'll wake Rob and Dave in a half hour, brief them, then hit the sack."

"I'd better get to class," Paul said, pouring his coffee into a paper cup. "I've got that big psychology test this morning."

"Good luck," his friends replied.

Halfway into town, Paul's head and neck began to stiffen, a painful reminder that he'd neglected to take his medicine before leaving the house. Two hours later he found himself massaging his temples while laboring over an extremely difficult exam—made more difficult by the fact that he had missed several classes while working on his mission to save the King. He searched his backpack for aspirin, but only found an empty bottle without a lid. *Aron*, he guessed, eyes narrowing. He threw the bottle back into his pack and returned to the test.

Paul's psychology professor, Dr. Singh, was famous for creating multiple-choice questions with more than one correct answer, forcing students to pick the *most* correct. Paul read the next question, narrowed the choices to two, and guessed before moving to the next question. Stupid professor, he thought, massaging his sore neck. Was he *intentionally* trying to make him flunk the test—fail the course—drop out of college? Halfway through the exam, Paul knew he had bombed it, big time. After guessing at the last question, he trudged to his professor's office, hoping for an extra assignment to raise his score. Dr. Singh informed Paul that extra work was not an option so late in the semester and that he would just have to study harder for the final.

"Thanks a lot," Paul replied sarcastically, whirling to leave the office. He cursed his professor under his breath while trudging down the long hallway.

The office door opened. "Paul," Dr. Singh called out.

"Yes," Paul answered, turning.

"Today's test covered the course's most arduous material. The final won't be inclusive, or as difficult. Study chapters nineteen and twenty and memorize the tables in twenty-one, and you'll do fine."

"Thanks," Paul replied, anger slowly dissipating. "Thanks," he repeated, "I appreciate that."

Paul trudged across campus, thinking about his sudden anger and rush to blame his professor. Dr. singh didn't want his students to fail. He just wanted them to know the material inside and out. Paul had only himself to blame for flunking the test, and the reason was obvious. He had taken on far more than he could handle—two difficult psychology classes—the graveyard shift at Detox—leading his friends on a Holy Grail quest to save the King—trying to win the hand of the beautiful princess—plus, whatever else he was trying to accomplish. He had taken on a huge load. And now, he would have to make an A on the final to pass the class and maintain a B average for the semester—the minimum goal he had set for himself after years of average, and sometimes below average, grades. To make an A on the final he would need even *more* study time. Something would have to give. Perhaps he should just drop the class, or better yet, drop out of college all together and focus on saving Aron, which was very possibly another pipe dream headed for disaster.

During the long drive back, Paul's worries over his test grade, fears that he'd taken on too much, and throbbing head caused his mood to plummet. He hit the cattle guard a little too hard, painfully jarring his head. "Medicine," he pleaded, as Tara met him on the front porch.

"That seems to be the request du jour," Tara replied.

"I felt so good this morning, I forget to take my pills."

An angry shout echoed from inside the house, followed by a crashing lamp.

"What's *his* problem?" Paul asked.

"No uppers, no downers, boredom, nothing to eat, and the temperature—along with his usual list of physical discomforts. How'd your test go?"

"Terrible. I had to guess at half the answers."

"I'm sorry to hear that. I wish I had better news to report on Aron, but I'm afraid he's been quite difficult. The others are in the kitchen waiting for us to start the briefing. I'll get your medicine."

"Thanks, Tara."

"How'd your test go?" Dave asked.

"Help," Paul answered.

"You *do* realize you're taking the hardest undergraduate course combined with the hardest professor."

"Yes, unfortunately, I sometimes have to discover things the hard way. I had to crawl into Dr. Singh's office and beg for an extra assignment to bring my grade up. He said no but he *did* throw me a bone by telling me exactly what would be covered on the final. I doubt it'll be enough, though. After today, I'll need an A on the final to pass the course. I'm thinking of dropping the whole semester."

"What!" Dave replied. "Because of *one* test? That's nonsense. I think I aced my final in that class. I'll help you study. With my tutoring, you're guaranteed to ace it."

"Thanks, Dave," Paul replied, massaging his temples, "that'd be great."

Tara returned with Paul's medicine then began the briefing.

Aron stormed into the room, glaring at Tara. "I need to talk to you! Now!"

"Of course," Tara said, following him to the porch.

Paul's whole body tensed. Aron outweighed Tara by 130 pounds and towered over her as he yelled. "Has he gotten physical?" Paul asked, staring out the kitchen window at Aron.

"Not yet," Rob answered.

Aron raised a hand to wipe the sweat off his forehead. Tara mistook the move and jumped back. Paul raced to the porch with Rob, Brooks, and Dave at his heels.

"Aron, *what's* your problem!" Paul shouted.

"There's no problem," Tara answered, "we're just clearing the air on a few things."

Paul's jaw tightened. "Why don't you take a cold shower! Then we can hike early today! Maybe it'll help you get rid of some of that excess energy."

Aron wanted to get rid of some excess energy, all right, by knocking someone's head off, but the five-to-one disadvantage made him reconsider, and he was, in fact, burning up from the heat. All of a sudden, a cold shower seemed like a good idea. He spun and stormed toward the bathroom.

"Paul, taking him hiking in the heat of the day might not be the best idea," Tara said.

"Tara, he needs to get outside and involved in something physical," Paul argued.

"Paul's right," Rob agreed. "The walls have been closing in on him all morning. A hike will do him good. As a matter of fact, I think I'll go, too."

"But . . ." Tara said.

"Tara, he's got a thousand problems right now," Paul interrupted. "Out there his only problem will be trying to get to the ridge and back without gettin' killed."

"Someone getting *killed* is exactly what I'm worried about," Tara replied. She faced Rob. "Rob, don't misunderstand me, I'm glad you were there in that lockup to kick Aron in the stomach, but we normally use less evasive means to subdue our patients."

"I won't lay a hand on him unless it's absolutely necessary," Rob assured Tara.

Tara faced Paul. "Paul, you're not harboring any ill feelings toward Aron, are you?"

"No," Paul answered, a little too quickly. He studied Tara's strained expression then took a deep breath. "Aron apologized for attacking me, and I accepted his apology. I'm harboring no ill feelings. Trust me, Tara, I won't touch him."

Tara searched Paul's eyes then slowly nodded. "Okay."

Aron exited the bathroom to find Rob and Paul waiting with a pair of clean shorts, thick socks, and hiking boots. He hesitated, grabbed the clothes, and stormed back into the bathroom.

During their hike, Aron's anger toward his kidnappers quickly turned toward himself. He realized that although it was *their* decision to kidnap him, it was *his* decision to stay—possibly, the worst decision of his life. As he struggled through the thick woods, he focused on other stupid decisions he had made during his life: cheating on Priscilla, trusting others to run his career, neglecting Lisa Marie, ignoring his health then looking for a quick fix. He tripped and landed hard, wondering if he would have to pay for all his life's mistakes in that one hike. Several branches felt the wrath of his anger, but by the time he reached the bluff, his anger was spent. He even surprised Rob by reaching down and helping him up the last few feet to the top of the ridge. The three men were soon guzzling water and chomping apples while enjoying the view. After their break, they explored the creek side of the bluff before returning home. Aron paused at the last row of grapevines then willed his tired body up the six giant steps to the back porch. After a warm shower, he took his sedative and painkiller, ate a few bites of dinner, and collapsed in bed.

"I think I'll try to sleep a few hours, too," Tara said.

"You should really get eight hours," Paul suggested.

"I agree," Brooks said, studying Tara. "Don't forget, you're working Detox tomorrow night. This might be your last chance to get a good night's sleep for a while."

"I'll take over your watch," Paul added. "I got plenty of sleep the last two nights, and tomorrow's Saturday. I don't have classes or work."

"Okay, gentlemen, you talked me into it," Tara replied.

Dave and Rob kept watch until 1 a.m. then awakened Paul and Brooks to take over. Brooks spent the rest of the night writing while Paul read two unusually dull psychology chapters in preparation for his final. At 6 a.m. Paul took a transistor radio to the front porch to listen to the news and weather. He closed his eyes to pray for rain and to picture water dripping off the porch's eaves.

The screen door opened and Tara stepped onto the porch. "Thanks, Paul, you were right to insist I get eight hours sleep."

"You're welcome," Paul replied, "and I *am* a nurse's aide."

"How long has he been sleeping?"

"All night, for the first time since Detox."

"That's a good sign."

The sound of a kicked chair echoed from Aron's bedroom.

"That's a bad sign," Paul joked.

Aron stormed onto the porch. "I need a painkiller."

"Where do you hurt? Tara asked.

"All over."

"I'll be right back."

"Hey, Aron, is all that commotion really necessary?" Dave asked, stepping onto the porch. "I was trying to get a little beauty rest."

Aron glared at Dave until Tara returned with his medicine. He quickly gulped the pills then glared at Tara. "I need to go back to Memphis for a few days—to check on my family."

"Aron, let's get you through withdrawal and a few weeks of recovery before discussing trips to Memphis."

"But . . ."

"Aron, please. You know what will happen if you go back to Memphis now. And you can use the pay phone to check on your family whenever you like."

Aron opened his mouth to argue then paused. Deep down, he knew she was right. He stomped back to his room and slammed the door.

"I'm glad it's Saturday," Paul said. "Something tells me we'll need a full staff today." He glanced toward the kitchen. "Who wants breakfast?"

"I'll help," Dave offered.

"Did somebody say *breakfast*?" Rob asked, stepping onto the porch.

Everyone helped cooked a big breakfast of bacon, eggs, hashbrowns, and biscuits while discussing their plans for the day.

"I need my car from town, so I can drive to work tonight," Tara mentioned.

"I need to pick up some art supplies and call my folks sometime today," Rob mentioned. "If anyone wants to tag along, we can grab Tara's car on the way back."

"I'll go with you," Brooks said. "I need to get some things from my apartment."

"Paul, I'm caught up on my reading," Dave mentioned, "if you'd like to start cramming for that final."

"Thanks," Paul replied, "I'll put on a fresh pot of coffee."

"How about some two-below later?" Rob asked. "I mean, it *is* Saturday."

"Good idea," Paul agreed. "Maybe we can talk Aron into playing."

"He *has* to play or the sides will be uneven," Brooks replied.

"Let me try to interest him in breakfast, first," Tara suggested, walking back to Aron's room with a plate of food.

Aron was in no mood for breakfast and spent the morning fighting bitterly with his kidnappers, especially Paul and Tara. Before leaving for town, Rob and Brooks discussed the issue with Dave.

"I think Paul and Tara have reached their limit with Aron," Rob mentioned.

"Perhaps we should blow off going into town," Brooks added.

"I should be able to keep the peace for a few hours," Dave replied. "I *have* had some experience at that in Detox."

After Rob and Brooks left, Dave persuaded Aron to write to Lisa Marie, suggesting it might be therapeutic for both the King *and* his princess. He then asked Tara to bake a batch of her famous oatmeal cookies. Tara was not at all interested in heating up the kitchen, but Dave moved another fan into the room and began assembling ingredients while making a big mess. Tara felt forced to take over, and the smell of fresh-baked cookies soon filled the house. Next, Dave called Paul out onto the front porch where he had placed two guitars and a stack of sheet music. "This place could use some music," he commented, handing Paul his Gibson.

Paul was in no mood for music but reluctantly took his *friend*, noticing a thick layer of dust between its frets.

During the past six months, other priorities had pushed guitar playing completely out of the picture. He guiltily dusted it off with his shirttail then smiled broadly as Dave began playing one of their favorite Bob Dylan songs, "Mozambique."

By the early seventies, Paul's infatuation with Aron's music had waned. The King's seventies' hits, "In The Ghetto," "Don't Cry, Daddy," and "I've Lost You" seemed so morose, especially compared to his earlier, fun-loving hits. Paul turned to Dylan and quickly compiled a large collection of the singer-songwriter's albums and sheet music.

Dave was singing "Mozambique's" reggae beat way too slow, however, forcing Paul to join in on rhythm to speed the tempo. Paul helped Dave sing the chorus then took over lead vocals. Dave bowed out of the next song, leaned back in his rocking chair, and closed his eyes. He chuckled, quite pleased with himself for so skillfully bringing peace to the house.

Paul's guitar, aside from collecting dust, had also become out of tune. Its sour chords combined with his less-than-professional singing voice was more than Aron could stand. He pitched aside his letter to his daughter and stormed onto the front porch. "Stop!" he shouted, towering over the two men. The music stopped. "That's the worst screeching I've ever heard!" Aron shouted at Paul. "And that guitar's a piece of crap, too! It's not even worth a new set of strings! Do yourself a favor and pitch it! And *please* stop singin'!"

Paul's face turned bright red. Suddenly, his long-held dream of one day singing with the King seemed like nothing more than the silly delusions of a naive child. Never, had he felt so embarrassed. Never, had he felt so small. He squeezed the neck of his guitar as if it were a sword and slowly stood to face Aron.

"Now, boys," Dave said, jumping between the two angry men.

Tara ran onto the porch holding a washcloth full of ice against a burn on her arm. "Aron, how would you like to spend the rest of the day in the pantry!" she shouted.

Aron's fists tightened. The sound of two cars bouncing over the cattle guard slowly drew their attention toward the driveway. Rob's truck and Tara's car soon rolled to a stop in front of the house. After the dust settled, Rob and Brooks climbed out and began unloading sacks and boxes.

Aron glared at Paul, jaw tightening. He would have loved the adrenaline rush of a good fight, but again, his timing was off. He was greatly outnumbered, and being locked in a hot pantry was not the sort of rush he was looking for. He whirled and stormed inside, cursing the hot house on his way to the back porch.

Everyone helped unload the vehicles then gathered in the kitchen for their afternoon briefing. "I'll be right back," Tara said, walking toward the back porch with a plate of cookies and a glass of milk. Aron ignored the kind gesture, forcing her to set the snack beside his chair before returning to the kitchen. She bumped her injured arm against the door frame as the sound of a shattered plate and glass followed her inside.

"Guess you should have used Tupperware," Brooks joked.

"That's not funny," Tara said, snatching the washcloth of ice to press against her arm.

"You're right, it wasn't," Brooks replied guiltily. "I'm sorry, Tara."

Tara stood at the head of the table and scanned the latest entries in Aron's file before beginning the briefing. "Aron is growing increasingly bitter, cynical, and antagonistic. He continues to complain of nervousness, headaches, muscle pain, and constipation. He's still demanding stronger medications." She glanced at Rob. "I wouldn't plan on him playing football today."

"I'll talk to him after the briefing," Paul said.

"I don't think that's a good idea," Dave replied. "Your last conversation with him almost ended in fisticuffs. I think you and Tara are both taking his behavior far too personally, and the reason is obvious. You're much closer to him, emotionally, than the rest of us."

"Thank you, Dr. Freud," Paul scoffed.

"I just think you two need a break," Dave replied.

Tara studied Dave seriously. "Dave, just because Aron's getting on our nerves, doesn't mean we can't do our jobs. He's getting on everyone's nerves."

"Yes, but the rest of us have been getting plenty of breaks. You and Paul haven't. In addition to your scheduled time with him, you've been spending every waking minute talking to him, waiting on him, making decisions about him, and worrying about him, and I don't think that's healthy, for you *or* him. I think both of you should take the rest of the day off. Go into town. See a movie. Get as far away from this place as possible."

Tara looked at Brooks and Rob. "Are you two gentlemen a part of this coup d'etat."

"*Coup d'etat*," Brooks laughed. "That's a little melo-dramatic, don't you think? Let's call it an *intervention*. It's for your own good."

"Nanci Griffith's playing at Z' Tejas tonight," Rob mentioned.

Tara looked to Paul for help.

Paul gazed out the window toward Austin. A big smile graced his face just before he burst out laughing. "Sorry, Tara, but all of a sudden, the image of us dining alone at some romantic restaurant seems far more appealing to me than fighting with Aron."

"Are you asking me out?"

"When was the last time you watched the sun set from Mt. Bonnell?"

Tara thought for a second and smiled. "I can't remember that far back, and I accept your invitation."

"Yes!" Paul replied. "Guys, if we don't make it back for a month or two, good luck with your adventure."

Brooks raised eyebrows caused Tara to laugh. "We'll drop you a postcard from Cancun, Brooksie," she joked, "if we can remember the address." A worried expression suddenly crossed Tara's face. "Wait. I have to work to-night."

"So," Paul replied, "if we leave now we can eat an early dinner, watch the sunset, and be back here in time for you to take a nap before work."

"What about his medications?" Dave asked.

Tara glanced at her watch. "He can have two Valiums at six, and if he asks, a nonprescription pain reliever. I'll leave you a key to the lock box."

"Got it," Dave replied.

"What about his evening hike?" Rob asked.

"He's assured me that his hiking days are over," Paul answered. "Let's give him a day off. I'll try to get him started again tomorrow."

"If you'll excuse me, gentlemen, I think I'll freshen up for my date," Tara commented.

After Paul and Tara left for town, Aron doubled his efforts to provoke those left behind. Dave responded with either kindness, or by retreating to the opposite side of the house. Rob narrowly escaped a jar of paint brushes hurled at his head then casually turned and walked away. After spending two years blowing off the provocations of 300 pound defensive linemen, he found Aron's childish behavior pretty easy to ignore. And Brooks was having so much fun documenting Aron's outbursts, it never occurred to him to get pulled into the fray.

By dusk, Aron found himself stewing alone on the back porch while the others sat on the front watching an unfamiliar sight, smoke-signal clouds peeking over the horizon.

*   *   *

Paul and Tara enjoyed an early dinner at a popular Sixth Street restaurant. The live music and festive, happy-hour crowd was a pleasant change from their challenges at The Vineyard. They discussed music, movies, politics, and Tara's growing desire to attend graduate school. After dinner they climbed to the top of Mt. Bonnell and watched the sun set, snuggled in each other's arms. Not until the long drive home, beneath a band of billowing cumulo-nimbus clouds, did their thoughts return to Aron.

"Dave was right," Tara commented. "We needed a break from Aron."

"How about another break tomorrow night?" Paul asked.

Tara leaned over and kissed Paul on the cheek, causing him to miss his turnoff. Tara laughed.

"It'd be a shame to run out of gas out here," Paul said, looking for someplace to turn around.

"Not *that* much of a shame, but I really *do* need to get some sleep before my shift tonight."

Paul and Tara arrived home to find the house quiet and Aron sound asleep. After inquiring about Aron's mood and behavior, Tara took a nap while Paul entertained his friends with a detailed description of his first date with Tara. Rob and Dave were the next to hit the sack, leaving Brooks and Paul keeping watch. Brooks took a blank legal pad into the living room while Paul sat on the front porch enjoying the unusual smell of rain. Just past 10 p.m. a strong wind shook the house, prompting Paul to awaken Tara.

"How's he doing?" Tara asked.

"Sound asleep," Paul replied.

"Good."

"The storm's closing in. I thought you might want to leave before it hits."

"I'll take a quick shower," Tara agreed.

Paul returned to the porch to watch the trees dance and swirl. Tara soon joined him, resting the palms of her hands on the railing while leaning into the wind. The long strands of her brown hair whipped behind her like summer wheat before a storm. She glanced at Paul's curled up sleeping bag resting near the railing. "The porch might not be the best place to sleep tonight. You're welcome to sleep in my bed?"

Paul had little trouble imagining himself snuggled between Tara's soft sheets, but the thought of her driving alone in a thunderstorm weighed heavy on his mind. "I'd prefer you call in sick and sleep there yourself."

"The thought *did* cross my mind. Unfortunately, I have two prospective nurse's aides scheduled for interviews."

"Can't Phyllis interview them?"

"Yes, but she's not authorized to hire. I've spent six months pleading for more aides, and now that I've been given the okay, I should really be there to interview and hire—as soon as possible. Otherwise, you men will have to take up the slack, and needless to say, I'd rather have you out here the next few weeks."

The wind stirred the dusty driveway as the porch light flickered. A large drop of rain crashed at their feet. Tara noticed Paul's worried expression. "I'll be fine, just promise me you'll call if anything happens."

"I promise," Paul replied, doubting any such call would be made. The nearest phone was fifteen minutes away, and Tara would soon be an hour away, too far to help out in any emergency. Also, Paul was quite worried about Tara driving alone, late at night, on treacherously slick roads, and not at all worried about anything that might happen at The Vineyard. "Tara, promise me if you get caught in a downpour, you'll pull over and wait till it passes."

"I promise."

"And if the weather's bad tomorrow morning, promise me you'll stay in town till it blows over."

"I promise," Tara said, doubting she could keep *that* one. She was far more concerned about Aron's behavior during her absence, than she was about driving in a little rain. With this in mind, she began making plans to leave work early. Her interviews were scheduled during the first half of her shift, so if she could hurry through them, complete a few changes to the Detox work schedule, and persuade one of the other nurses to come in a few hours early, she could cut her shift in half.

Paul walked Tara to her car and opened the door. They embraced and kissed before Tara drove away. The angry trees reluctantly opened then slammed shut as her car's taillights vanished. Paul closed his eyes and prayed for her safe return.

The storm shook and rattled the old house for several hours but left little moisture. Just past midnight, the winds stilled. Paul and Brooks turned in for the night, as Rob and Dave took over the next watch. An hour into their watch, the lights flickered before everything turned black. Twenty-four fan blades slowed to a stop as an eerie silence filled the house. "Houston, we've lost power," Rob joked, as he and Dave lit candles throughout the house. Suddenly, huge drops of rain began pelting the roof, spurring them to remove the fans and shut the windows against the ensuing downpour. Hurricanelike sheets blew from the southeast, leaving one dry spot on the northwest side of the porch, where Rob and Dave huddled beneath the eaves to watch the storm.

An hour later Aron awakened in his sweat-soaked sheets, craving a fix, and instinctively reaching for the envelope of pills on his nightstand, which was 700 miles away. His whole body tensed at the realization that he had again, awakened in hell instead of Graceland. He leaped out of bed, glaring at the candle melting over the side of the dresser like a Salvador Dali clock. His eyes darted to the closed windows and lifeless fan sitting on the floor. *What* were they trying to *do! Kill him!*

Paul awakened to the sound of a loud crash, and shot straight out of bed. He held his breath, listening intently as a second crash echoed throughout the house. He glanced at the candle on Tara's dresser, grabbed a flashlight, and ran in the direction of the noise. Brooks arrived in the living room just after Paul, flashlight in hand. The two men looked as if they had just jumped out of a Sears underwear ad.

Rob was crouched in front of Aron's door, both hands squeezed around the doorknob, Dave standing at his side. The room's furniture was in disarray, and smoke from a tipped candle hung in the air. Splintered pieces of wood covered the floor.

"What's going on?" Brooks asked.

"Just Aron blowing off a little steam," Rob replied.

"What was that crash?" Paul asked.

No one answered.

Paul's light beam scanned the floor, pausing on what looked like a big spider made of twisted wires and shredded pieces of wood. His light beam rose to the gaping holes in the living room wall.

"He busted his guitar?" Paul asked, in disbelief.

"Well, not exactly," Dave answered.

Paul knelt to inspect one of the splintered pieces of wood and immediately recognized something in its color. His eyes darted across the room, searching for his Gibson, the only guitar missing. His heart saddened as he focused on what was left of his *friend*, scattered across the floor. Again, his eyes fell to the small piece of wood resting in his hand. He recalled dusting off his guitar the day before and the guilt he had experienced for neglecting it the previous six months. The sudden realization that he would never play it again hit him hard. He recalled Aron calling it a piece of crap and saying it was not worth a new set of strings. Paul's sadness quickly turned to anger. He dropped the piece of wood, slowly stood, and faced Aron's door.

"Now, Paul, you can buy another one," Brooks said.

"No," Paul replied, "I can't buy another one, and he knew. It was my most valuable possession, and that son of a bitch knew, and this time, he's going to pay." He stepped forward, anger quickly turning to rage.

"Now wait, Paul," Rob said, turning his back on Aron's door, "you don't know that. Maybe it was just the closest guitar to him when he exploded."

"Get out of my way, Rob," Paul said, tossing his flashlight to the floor. The room dimmed as the light burst open and two batteries rolled across the floor.

"Paul, wait!" Dave shouted.

Paul's tall shadow followed as he leaped forward and swung at Rob's head. Rob raised an arm to deflect the blow. Suddenly, Aron's fist burst through the top panel of the door, grazing Rob's shoulder. Paul cocked back his arm to throw another punch as Dave and Brooks rushed to stop him.

The front door flew open. "Paul!" Tara screamed, running into the room. A bowling ball-like rumble echoed from Aron's bedroom, just before the door exploded off its hinges. Falling bodies and splintered pieces of the door crashed to the floor at Tara's feet. Paul jumped up, raised both fists, and waited eagerly for Aron to slowly stand. He swung with all his might.

"Aron!" Tara screamed.

Aron raised his arms, but the brunt of Paul's punch caught him square in the jaw, sending him falling against the wall. He shook off the blow and leaped forward. Rob threw a quick block, which sent the King sprawling across the floor. Brooks pitched his flashlight on the sofa and stepped in front of Paul, fists raised. Aron jumped to his feet. Rob and Dave grabbed his arms and pushed him back against the wall. Paul grabbed Brooks by the shoulders and tossed him to the sofa.

"Paul!" Tara yelled. "Stop!"

As Paul stepped forward, Tara jumped in front of him, raised an open hand, and swung hard. The unexpected blow stopped Paul dead in his tracks. Blood from a burst stitch filled the open cut then trickled down his cheek. Paul stared at Tara in disbelief. Tara stared at the drip, drip, drip onto his bare chest, her cupped hand slowly covering her mouth—a little girl having just said a bad word in class. Her eyes quickly filled with tears.

Water dripped off the porch's eaves. Distant thunder shook a loose window pane. Hearts raced and lungs heaved as Aron's kidnappers stood frozen in time. Their whole mission was suddenly unraveling, right before their eyes, and all they could do was watch.

Aron also stood motionless, but only for a moment. He was reeling from his adrenaline rush, and except for the blow to the door panel, he had not thrown a single punch. No way, could the fight be over now. He lunged forward as Rob and Dave tightened their grips and shoved him against the wall. "You lunatic!" he screamed at Paul. "You stupid lunatic!"

Paul slowly turned his focus from Tara, to Aron, fists tightening. "Let him go," he pleaded. "Let the stupid fool go."

"You're the fool!" Aron shouted. "You broke into Graceland! You kidnapped *me*! *Elvis Presley*! You locked me in a cell like I was some kind of *monster*! I'm not a *monster*! Do you hear me! I'm not a *monster*!" He lunged again as his ghoulish shadow climbed up the wall.

"You're not?" Paul replied. "Look in the mirror."

Rob and Dave held on tightly as Aron struggled to break free. "*You're* the monsters! All of you! And you're all goin' to *jail*!"

"Are you going to testify, Aron?" Paul asked. "Are you going to tell them you were so doped up you didn't even know you were being kidnapped?"

"I won't have to tell 'em a thing! *You're* the ones who'll be on trial! And my name's not Aron! It's *Elvis*! *Elvis Presley*!"

"Whatever you say, Aron," Paul replied.

"That's it! I'm out of here! I'm going back!"

"Back to where?" Paul asked. "To your rotting castle and what's left of your coked-up guards? To your silly toys and childish temper tantrums. To your . . ."

"That's *right*! And you can go back to your minimum wage job in a stupid nut house, to flunking out of college, to planning your next kidnapping before *jail*."

"And you can go back to your gemstone-studded jumpsuits and silly capes and scarves, back to your plastic scepters and even more plastic performances. You were the King, Aron. You were the most talented, idolized and sought after entertainer in America, and now look at you. You're a fat clown in a stupid, Las Vegas carnival act. Look what you've done to yourself! Look what you've done to *us*!"

"To *us*! *What* are you *talkin'* about!"

"You sold out, Aron. You sold your soul."

"So what if I did! It was *mine* to sell! This is *my* life! Do you hear me! *My* life! It's got nothin' to do with you! *Nothin'*!"

The ball was placed squarely in Paul's court, and all heads turned. Paul, however, was at a loss for words. Aron had made a very good point. On one level, the King's life, career, and lifestyle had nothing to do with Paul—nothing—they had only just met. But on another level, Aron's life had everything to do with Paul—everything—and he could not even begin to explain.

For Paul, the room's temperature had suddenly risen to its boiling point. He turned his back on the others, opened a window, and took a breath of cool, rain-cleansed air. He walked back to the center of the room, kneeled, and began picking up the larger pieces of his guitar. He slowly stood, pressing them against his blood-splotched chest—a little boy holding an injured puppy. "Leave, Aron, or Elvis, or whatever your name is. If *this* is your only *business* here, I think you should leave."

Paul turned, walked toward the screen door, and kicked with all his might. The door slammed against the front of the house and crashed at his heels as he stomped down the porch steps. The sound of footsteps against the puddled driveway faded, leaving the living room eerily quiet. The tension in Aron's arms vanished. Rob and Dave cautiously relaxed their grips.

"Did he say—*business?*" Aron asked.

"Yes," Brooks answered.

Aron slowly sat on the floor right where he had stood, mind racing back to the afternoon of his kidnapping, back to a strange dream, trip, or hallucination that he vaguely remembered experiencing just before leaving Memphis.

"Is there some significance in the word *business?*" Brooks asked, studying Aron curiously.

Aron stared intently through the dark doorway.

"Aron?" Brooks tried again, but for all practical purposes, the King had left the building.

Chapter Six

Tara lit a candle, picked up the flashlight, and walked to the backyard to inspect the storm damage to their grapevines and arbor. Rob, Brooks, and Dave straightened furniture and carried out pieces of the shattered door. Aron sat on the living room floor, staring into space. As his eyelids grew heavy, he slowly stood and returned to his bedroom, pausing in the doorless doorway to rub his sore shoulder and chuckle. He opened the room's windows to a cool, moist breeze then lay in bed, pondering the many questions tugging at his mind. Why had Paul's use of the word *business* jarred a faint memory of a distant dream? Why did he suddenly feel a need to learn more about the dream? Why had Paul shouted, Look what you've done to *us*? What was all *that* about? And why, all of a sudden, did finding the answers to these questions seem more important to Aron than returning to Memphis? He rubbed his sore jaw, shook his head, and laughed.

Brooks looked in on the King then returned to the living room.

"What's he doing?" Dave asked.

"He's laughing," Brooks answered.

"Laughing," Dave replied. "I must have missed some-thing."

Rob placed the smaller pieces of Paul's guitar on the kitchen table before retrieving a bottle of glue, wood pol-ish, a pair of wire cutters, pliers, and several rags.

"You've got to be kidding," Brooks said. "All the glue in China couldn't fix *that* guitar."

"Oh, but I *will* fix it," Rob said, splitting the larger pieces of the instrument into smaller and smaller pieces. "And I may not need to use a single drop of glue."

Outside, Paul sat in his underwear on the muddy driveway, saying goodbye to his *friend*. His thoughts, how-ever, quickly turned to a far more serious issue. He had just lost complete control, in front of his best friends, and worse, in front of Tara. He had very possibly destroyed their whole mission—all over six wires strung over a few pieces of pressed wood. To erase just a small portion of the damage would take the world's greatest apology. He immediately began preparing his apology.

The damage to the grape arbor was minimal. Tara walked to the front drive, where she and Paul sat in si-lence, staring back at the house's candlelit windows, Paul working on his apology and Tara contemplating some-thing that had been weighing heavy on her mind for quite some time.

"Paul, I need to talk to you about someone named Steven Garrett," Tara mentioned. "It won't be easy, and now obviously isn't the time, but someday—I'd like to talk to you—about Steve."

"Sure," Paul replied.

Tara leaned over and kissed his injured cheek before returning to the house. Paul shook his head. As often occurred in his life, a friend had reminded him the world did not exactly revolve around *him*. He set aside his work on his apology to contemplate Tara's relationship with someone named Steve.

Dave and Brooks exchanged a few words with Tara as they passed on the porch then joined Paul on the driveway.

"Aron's sound asleep," Dave mentioned to Paul.

"We think he's staying," Brooks added, "that if he was really leaving, he'd already be gone."

"That's good news," Paul replied. "I guess."

"Of course it's good news," Brooks said, "I've got a book to write, and I certainly didn't want it ending like *this*."

"Hey, Paul!" Rob yelled, stepping off the porch and walking toward his friends, "I'll need the rest of your guitar if you want me to fix it."

"Yeah, right," Paul said, eyes falling to his instrument's lifeless carcass. He wasn't sure what Rob had planned for the shattered guitar, but *he* certainly had no further plans for it, so he lifted it up toward his friend.

"I should have it fixed by tomorrow morning," Rob added, taking the pieces. "Oh, and Brooks and I've decided to watch Aron the rest of the night. I've got *this* little project to keep me busy."

Brooks tapped his pen on his pad. "And you and Aron have just given me quite a bit of material to work on tonight."

Suddenly, Paul felt quite naked. "Listen, guys," he said, standing, "I'm really sorry for what I did, and I'm working on a more formal apology for our next briefing."

"None necessary," Rob laughed. "This is the most excitement we've had since Detox. And I know Aron had a good time—he was in there laughing."

"Thanks, Rob," Paul replied, "but just the same, I think I'll continue working on my apology."

The men climbed the porch stairs then stepped around the flattened screen door.

"Doors surely don't last long around here," Rob commented.

"Guitars, either," Dave mentioned. "I think I'll keep mine locked in the trunk of my car until Aron's through withdrawal."

"Put mine in there, too, would you?" Rob asked.

"Smart, guys," Paul complimented, "I wish one of us had thought of it yesterday."

Paul changed into dry clothes, reattached the screen door, and checked on Aron before unrolling his sleeping bag on the front porch. The following morning he was awakened by the sound of laughter. He walked inside the house and found everyone but Aron sitting in the living room drinking coffee and admiring Rob's latest masterpiece circling above their heads. The splintered pieces of Paul's guitar, along with the instrument's disassembled keys and frets, had been polished to a fine gloss and hung like Christmas ornaments from six straightened and brightly-painted coat hangers. Cut pieces of the guitar's string connected the ornaments to the hangers. Paul's entrance stirred the air, causing the smaller segments of the mobile to rise, dip, and swirl within its wider orbit. At times it stretched 15 feet wide. Rays of sunlight shot from an open window, and the ornaments dipping through the light glistened.

"What do you think?" Rob asked Paul.

"I think it's amazing, but I don't see how I'll play Dylan on it."

"That *will* be a problem," Rob admitted.

"I love it, Rob," Tara said. "You should donate it to the Austin Museum of Art so more people will be able to enjoy it?"

"Donate!" Brooks echoed. "We worked all night on that masterpiece."

"What do you mean *we*?" Rob asked.

"I polished a piece or two," Brooks replied.

"Mr. Brooks, please tell me you see something in this work besides money," Dave said.

Brooks stood and walked in a slow circle beneath the mobile, studying it seriously. "Okay, I'll tell you what I see. Picture someone placing a stick of dynamite inside an acoustic guitar and lighting the fuse. Now film the explosion, stopping the film a second into the blast, just as the pieces are shooting away from the center. Now visualize the debris moving in a slow, three dimensional orbit around the center of the explosion. *That's* what I see."

"The big bang theory," Dave commented dryly. "An angry guitarist's interpretation of the big bang theory."

"That's it!" Brooks replied. "That's it *exactly*."

Dave made the sign of the cross in front of the mobile. "I hereby christen thee, *The Big Bang*."

"Rob, you're sitting on a perfect work of art with a name that interprets it perfectly. It'll be a cinch to market. Hire me as your agent, and I'll get you five figures, somewhere in the neighborhood of $50,000."

"You're hired, but we should probably give the angry guitarist a cut."

"He'll get a percentage," Brooks agreed.

"Don't forget I named it," Dave reminded.

"You'll get a much smaller percentage," Brooks replied.

"Don't forget it's *my* guitar," Paul lamented.

"You'll get a percentage," Brooks said.

"Hey, you're throwin' around percentages like it's Christmas time," Rob complained. "How much is my agent gettin'?"

"Thirty percent's about average," Brooks answered, "but my exemplary services will cost you thirty-five. Don't sweat the extra five. I'll squeeze it from *their* cuts."

Paul reached up and gently pushed one end of the mobile, watching it transform itself as it turned. "Not the sort of Christian burial I had in mind, but if it'll make me rich."

"What do you mean by *rich*?" Brooks asked.

"I mean that regardless of its present condition, Mr. Brooks, it's still my property. I'll take 90 percent."

"What!" Brooks replied.

"Ninety percent!" Rob echoed. "I spent all night sweatin' over that mobile, and you want to give me *10 percent*, to divide amongst these thieves?"

"I beg your pardon," Brooks objected.

"I appreciate your artistic talents," Paul replied, "but you said you were going to *fix* it."

"You only paid fifty bucks for that guitar," Dave reminded. "How about we give you a flat hundred? That's twice your initial investment."

"You're offering me a hundred bucks out of a $50,000 profit?" Paul asked.

"I'll handle this, Paul," Brooks said. "Dave, you have no interest in The Big Bang and no authority to negotiate in the artist's behalf. That's my job."

"I came up with the name, and I'll thank you not to use it until I've received my cut."

Paul smiled, listening to his friends' banter. But as his thoughts turned to the previous night's altercation, his face saddened. "I hate to interrupt this little party, but I have some rather unpleasant business to discuss."

The room grew quiet as Paul walked up to a window to collect his thoughts. "Growing up, I had a pretty hot temper. After one of my tantrums, my aunt told me I could be the greatest person in the world, or the worst, depending on my ability to control my temper. With my mother's help, I slowly learned the difference between reacting and overreacting. Last night I overreacted, big time. I lost my temper and physically and verbally attacked our patient—not exactly the better form of treatment Tara was searching for. I also physically attacked my best friends, and I don't exactly feel like the greatest person in the world. I'm ashamed of my behavior, sorry for the trouble I caused, and it'll never happen again."

As Paul took a seat, Tara stood and walked to the window. "Apology accepted, and I, too, would like to apologize." She faced Paul. "I'm not in the habit of reacting physically, of striking those I—care most about." She focused on the scar on Paul's face. "And of all the places I could have hit you. Never, have I felt so low. I'm sorry for my behavior, and it will never happen again."

"Tara, I'm glad you stopped me," Paul replied, "any way you could."

Tara's eyes dropped to the floor.

"But I understand what you mean about feeling low," Paul added, "and lousy aims, and wishing you'd reacted differently, and your apology is of course accepted."

Tara's face brightened.

Brooks propped his feet on the coffee table then crossed his hands behind his head. "Well, now that *that* messy business is over with . . ."

"Not so fast, Mr. Brooks," Aron said, walking into the living room. "I'm afraid I, too, have some crow to eat." He glanced up at the mobile, grinned, then stared at his guitar. "And I know just where to begin."

Aron picked up his Martin, put his head through its strap, and strummed its perfectly tuned strings. He closed his eyes, picturing an old juke box with two hundred 45's flipping left to right. He smiled broadly, opened his eyes, and slid his hand up the guitar's neck, fingers forming the first chord. He began tapping a moderately fast beat against the pick guard with his thumb. Satisfied with the tempo, he strummed the first two chords of the song as faces brightened. He played the chords again then began singing "Jailhouse Rock."

Paul immediately recalled an old black and white news reel of one of Aron's first concerts, performed in a high school gymnasium full of awkward, insecure, and self-conscious teenagers. Those same two chords caused the entire student body to stand as one, kick off their shoes, and rush down the tall bleachers. Paul recalled those teens running across the polished floor and sliding to a stop before the band stand, tossing their inhibitions out the gym's high windows as they hopped, spun, and danced with the leader of that brand-new phenomenon called rock 'n' roll.

At that moment, Paul had little trouble identifying with those teens. Throughout the living room, fingers snapped, feet tapped, and bodies danced, right where they sat. Even The Big Bang dipped and turned in perfect tempo with the King's gyrations.

As the last chord faded, Aron stared up at the spinning mobile and grinned. "Anyway," he continued, "my behavior last night was pretty . . ." He looked at Brooks for help.

"Despicable?" Brooks suggested.

Aron laughed. "Despicable," he agreed, "and pretty commonplace since my arrival here, and goin' through withdrawal's not all that good of an excuse. I'm really sorry."

Heads slowly nodded.

"Apology accepted," Tara replied.

"Paul, I know you loved that guitar," Aron continued, "and I know this one can't replace it, but just the same, I'd like ya to have it." He lifted it over his head and handed it to Paul.

Paul stared at his expensive Martin without budging. "Thanks, Aron, but I can't . . ."

"As you recall," Aron interrupted, "I left Memphis in sort of a hurry, so this is all I have to give." He glanced up at the mobile. "And you *do* need a guitar."

Paul hesitated then carefully grasped the warm guitar. His friends watched as he lowered the instrument to his lap and stared at it wide-eyed like a child on Christmas morning.

"Unbelievable," Dave said, shaking his head. "First, you escape the kidnapping charge, and now the felony theft."

"You should have stolen his Ferrari," Brooks joked. "He'd be giving you a fifty-thousand dollar sports car right now instead of a silly guitar."

"I'm happy with the guitar, thank you," Paul replied.

"Good," Aron said, reaching up and pushing the mobile. "By the way, Paul, I'm a little puzzled about your use of the word *business* last night. What did you mean when you said, 'if *this* is your only *business* here, I think you should leave?'"

Paul closed his eyes, replaying his angry words in his mind. "I didn't mean anything by it. It was just a phrase, like your motto, Taking Care of Business. Why?"

"No reason. It just jogged a memory of something that happened back in Memphis." He reached up and pushed the other end of the mobile. "Anyway, back to eatin' crow. After last night's fight, I was given a break from my aches and pains, and during that break, I realized that I *do* have business out here, other than bustin' guitars. I know it's not gonna be easy. My craving's have already started to return. I also know I've probably overstayed my welcome. But just the same, I'd like to stick around until my business here's done, if the invitation's still open."

"Of course it's still open," Tara said.

"Great. That's great. Can I have a couple Valium?"

"Yes, you may," Tara answered, leaving the room and soon returning with his sedative.

"Thanks," Aron said, swallowing the pills. "Now, if it's okay with my kidnappers, I think I'll inspect the storm damage to our hiking trail."

Again, heads slowly nodded.

"Oh, and if anyone's goin' to town later on, can I hitch a ride to the library. I'd like to do some readin' up on dream interpretation, along with a few other things."

"It just so happens, I have some books to return," Tara replied.

"Great, just yell, whenever."

As Aron left the house, faces beamed.

Dave shook his head. "Need I remind you folks that we've witnessed such miraculous recoveries before, only to find ourselves rolling around on a lockup floor the next day."

"Thanks for robbing us of our *one* moment of glory," Brooks replied.

"Just don't want anyone thinking we're out of the woods."

"Perhaps not," Tara replied, "but I think I see a clearing, and I have a strong feeling the worst is over."

"And not a minute too soon," Brooks said, glancing at the damaged wall and the doorless doorway. "I think we can kiss our security deposit goodbye."

Paul strummed a few chords on his new guitar, grinning broadly. "I agree with Tara. I think the worst is over. But just in case we're wrong, I'll be keepin' my new guitar locked in the trunk of my car."

"Good thinkin'," Rob agreed.

Tara glanced toward the kitchen. "Did I mention I make the best french toast in Texas?"

"Did I mention I'm starving?" Dave asked.

"I'm hittin' the sack," Rob said. "And this afternoon, I'll be startin' a new paintin', if anyone wants to buy tickets."

"I'm goin' for jog," Paul announced.

"I'll go with you," Brooks replied. "I haven't run in weeks."

Paul and Brooks changed into jogging shoes and shorts then used the porch railing to stretch their legs. On the way to the road, they cleared the puddled driveway of its larger twigs and branches. The tree trunks lining the drive had darkened from the hard rain, contrasting perfectly with the fresh splotches of light-green grass suddenly highlighting the earth below. Tiny, yellows, blues, and pinks were opening everywhere. At the road they paused a moment then turned left. Steam rose from the warm blacktop and swirled around their legs as they ran.

"Paul, you said some things to Aron last night that struck me as a little unusual," Brooks commented.

Paul's body tensed. "Yes, in the middle of my tantrum, I said a lot of pretty stupid things to him, about his life and career, and now that I've had more time to think about it, I think he was probably right—his life is really none of my business."

"None of your business? That sounds kind of strange coming from someone who just kidnapped him."

Brooks waited for some response, but none was given. They jogged in silence for a half mile before Brooks broke the silence. "You know, I was never a big Elvis fan. I liked a few of his first songs and movies, but we were only six years old when the Elvis phenomenon hit America. I was more into Superman and Zorro. But not you, Paul. You were an Elvis fan, big time."

Brooks gazed down the long blacktop and smiled. "I remember this one particular Saturday afternoon, sometime around 1962. We would have been eight or nine, and you were dragging me to see *Girls, Girls, Girls* for the

umpteenth time. The theater was packed with excited
fans, and I found the fans more interesting than the movie. I still remember their hypnotized faces, dilated pupils,
and druggedlike smiles, brightening in the screen's flickering light. And when the King sang "Return to Sender," a
tornado could have torn the roof off that movie theater
and no one would have noticed."

Paul's face beamed as he recalled those early highs
experienced while watching *Elvis*.

"It didn't matter that the film's plot was weak and
overused," Brooks continued, "or that the hero's antics
were quite silly. It didn't matter that the King wasn't the
greatest actor in the world or that most of the movie's
songs were, shall we say, less than hits. It didn't matter
that the movie had been the only one showing in our
one-theater town for three months. The only thing that
mattered was that they be allowed to enjoy their Elvis fix,
undisturbed, for just one—more—second."

They began feeling light on their feet as they entered
the second mile.

"It was a powerful drug, Paul," Brooks admitted. "I
was almost pulled in, myself, and I wasn't even a fan. But
you certainly were. Aron's music, his movies, and his career have had a profound affect on your life, so I'm having
a little trouble believing you now feel his life is none of
your business?"

"That was then," Paul replied. "This is now."

Brooks studied Paul curiously, deciding on a different
angle. "Can you believe the stark change in Aron's atti-
tude this morning? Suddenly, he has important business
out here and wants to stay until it's completed. All of a
sudden, he wants to go to the *library*, and *not* by way of

the pharmacy? Aron's changing, Paul. He might even become our friend one day, and as his friend, I'll have a ton of questions to ask him, and the first one will be, What in the world *happened* after that movie theater in 1962? What on earth could have possibly caused him to drop *so* low, *so* fast? Wouldn't you like to ask him that?"

"No!" Paul said, abruptly stopping to face Brooks. "No, I wouldn't! I'd feel *awfully* uncomfortable asking him that. I'd feel like it was none of my business."

Brooks gave Paul a puzzled look, took a few steps, then sat in the center of the hot pavement. Paul searched the road in both directions before sitting beside his friend.

"But Paul, I'm a *writer*," Brooks continued. "I want very much to know what happened. I want to know who, what, where, when, and most of all, why, and I can assure you, the rest of the world wants to know."

"That's great. Maybe it's their business. Maybe it's your business. But it's not mine."

"But . . ."

"Listen, Mr. Brooks, surely you realize I've asked those same sorts of questions countless times over the years. But not once was I ever happy with the answers I came up with, and I doubt I would've been satisfied with Aron's answers either, and now I'm beginning to understand why. I think I've been asking the wrong questions. I think I should've been asking, what's happened to *me* since that movie theater in 1962. At this moment, I think I should be asking if it's at all possible I kidnapped Aron, not for Aron's sake, but for my own—if it's at all possible I was drawn to this place, to this point in time, not to heal Aron, but to heal myself?"

Brooks stared at Paul in disbelief. "To heal yourself from *what*?"

Paul gazed out over the large track of farmland stretching between them and the horizon. "I'm not sure. I don't have all the answers. I don't even have all the questions. But I'm pretty sure that's the real reason I'm here."

Brooks gazed across the farmland then shook his head. "Well, whatever your illness, you certainly hide it well."

Paul smiled. "I've had lots of practice."

Brooks slowly nodded then looked at his friend. "I wish you luck, Paul, with your answers, and if I can be of any help . . ."

"Why thanks, Brooksie, but you've been helping me for quite some time. Like the time you invited me on that first Saturday morning treasure hunt. And the time you helped me balance my screwed-up checking account. And now, with *this* little adventure. You've been helping me since the third grade, and none of your good deeds have ever gone unnoticed—*or* unappreciated."

"Holy moly, Paul, are you trying to make me cry?" Brooks joked.

Paul laughed.

A big crow landed on a power line just above their heads. Brooks motioned toward the bird. "Looks like Mr. Crow's looking for some road kill."

The sound of spinning tires drew Paul's attention toward a distant tractor-trailer headed in their direction. "He'll have a field day if we don't get our butts off this blacktop."

The men stood and stepped to the side of the road, turning their faces away from the swirling dust and noxious fumes. As the truck faded into the distance, the disappointed crow flew off in search of food elsewhere. The joggers returned to pounding the pavement, stopping briefly to exchange a few words with two linemen, one of whom assured them their power would be restored by late afternoon. A mile later they noticed their nearest neighbors waving from the front porch. After a brief discussion, Paul and Brooks decided to stop and introduce themselves.

"Hello," Paul greeted, stepping through the open gate. "I'm Paul Roberts, and this is my friend David Brooks. We're your new neighbors."

"How do," Mr. Johnson replied. "I'm Sam Johnson, and this here's my wife, Lucille."

"Howdy, boys," Lucille greeted. "Welcome to the neighborhood."

As everyone shook hands, Sam and Lucille stared at Paul's injured face.

"What happened to . . ." Sam asked.

"Would you boys like some iced tea?" Lucille interrupted.

"Yes, ma'am, that'd be great," Paul answered.

"I'll be back in a jiffy."

"How do y'all like The El Dorado?" Sam asked.

"El Dorado?" Brooks replied.

"Y'alls house. The rancher that built it was a big Edgar Allen Poe fan. Named it after one of his poems."

"We call it *The Vineyard*," Brooks said, "and we like it just fine. It's really big, and it's a good thing because there's six of us living there. We're students at the University of Texas."

"Are you, now?" Sam replied, staring at Brooks suspiciously. "You're a *fur* piece from the university."

"It's a long commute, all right," Brooks agreed, "but Austin's becoming really crowded, so we thought we'd try life in the country."

"How much you payin'?" Sam asked.

"Pops, that's none of your business," Lucille said, stepping onto the porch with a large pitcher of tea surrounded by ice-filled glasses garnished with mint and sliced lemons. She poured the tea.

"Three hundred a month," Paul answered.

"Three hundred!" Sam replied.

"Is that too much?" Brooks asked.

"Too much!" Sam huffed.

"Last renters paid $400.00," Lucille explained, handing the men their tea. "Renters before that paid $500.00. They didn't stay very long. They never do." She stared in the direction of The Vineyard. "Some folks in these parts believe there's spirits in that old house."

A large lemon seed lodged in Paul's throat, causing him to cough until it was dislodged. "It's haunted?" he asked.

"Don't pay 'em no mind, hon'," Lucille replied. She gave her husband a cross look. "Some fools'll believe anything."

"Is your electricity out?" Brooks asked, changing the subject.

"Yep," Sam answered. "Quite a storm last night."

"Ours, too," Paul said. "Two linemen down the road said we'd have power back by this afternoon."

"We heard screams last night," Sam mentioned.

"Pops, will you cut it out?" Lucille scolded. "They're miles away."

"Noises carry out here," Sam replied.

"It must have been the television," Paul said.

As Paul gulped his tea, Sam and Lucille studied the strange bruises on his neck.

"I guess we'd better run," Brooks said, setting his empty glass on the tray. "Thanks for the tea."

"Yeah, thanks a lot," Paul said.

"You're surely welcome, boys," Lucille replied. "Y'all come back anytime."

"Thanks," the men replied.

At the road the men turned right and jogged toward home, Brooks staring at Paul disgustedly.

"What are *you* looking at?" Paul asked.

"Must have been the television?" Brooks mocked. "We don't even have a television, and you just told them our electricity was out."

Paul shrugged. "I never *was* much good at lyin'."

As they continued their run, Paul stared at Brooks disgustedly.

"What are *you* looking at?" Brooks asked.

"A hundred thousand ranch houses in Texas, and you had to pick a haunted one."

"Hey, you said you wanted something *big* and *secluded*. You never said anything about not wanting ghosts. Besides, maybe they're good ones. They've already reduced our rent from $500.00 to $300.00 a month."

"That's great, we can use the savings to buy burial plots."

Back at the ranch they informed the others of their visit with the Johnsons.

"I told them we were UT students," Brooks mentioned, "and that Austin was getting crowded so we thought we'd try life in the country. Sam Johnson said they heard screams last night. Paul told him it must have been the TV, right after he told them our power was out."

"Way to go, Paul," Dave said. "What else did you tell them?"

"I told them Elvis was cookin' meat loaf tonight and invited them over for dinner. What do you think I told them?"

Tara looked out the window. "I can't believe they heard us from so far away."

"Noises carry out here," Brooks said, "to quote Sam Johnson. And they're both dying to know what happened to Paul's face and neck."

"Perhaps you could pay them a visit and repair the damage," Paul suggested to Tara.

"You read my mind," Tara replied. "The sooner the better."

A half hour later Tara cheerfully introduced herself to the Johnsons. She told Sam and Lucille a little about herself, her friends, and their jobs at Detox, where Paul had recently had a nasty run-in with one of their more violent patients. She mentioned that one of their friends, Aron, was recovering from a drug addiction and that because Austin wasn't the best place for recovering addicts, they opted for a change in scenery. Tara said she thought there was something healing about country life and that The Vineyard was having a positive effect on all of them. Sam and Lucille were quite taken in by Tara's frankness and warmth and were soon giving her a complete tour of their farm.

"And what are you kids eatin' over there?" Lucille asked, noticing Tara's thin arms and legs.

"Today, peanut butter sandwiches, chips, and sodas, but we're trying to improve our diets."

Tara returned home with two burlap bags full of corn, potatoes, tomatoes, and squash. She announced her visit a success and was soon looking forward to her next visit with the Johnsons.

While the others spent the afternoon taking part in a hotly-contested football game, Tara and Aron drove to the library. Aron studied Tara curiously as she negotiated the winding roads toward Austin. "Tell me, Tara, would you have ever kidnapped me, if not for Paul?"

"Probably not. I would have continued my search for a better form of treatment and sent it to Graceland with my blessing."

"So, you let Paul pull you in to this crime?"

Tara laughed. "In my defense, he was pretty convincing—wouldn't take no for an answer. There was also something else transpiring at the time. Just between the two of us, I was falling in love."

"Hmm," Aron mused, "so you had *three* motives— saving me, searching for a better cure, and you were falling in love with Paul."

"What makes you think I only had *three*?" Tara asked.

Aron laughed. "That's exactly my point. You had a lot of strong motives, just like anyone attempting something that crazy would have. And durin' my first morning at The Vineyard, you told me your friends had their ulterior motives—plural. Paul insists he had only one, but I'm not buyin' it. The kidnapping was *his* idea, he pulled everyone else in, and he took the greatest risk by breakin' into

Graceland alone, and yet he insists his only motive was to save me. Doesn't that strike you as kind of strange?"

"Yes, it does. And you've discussed this with him?"

"I've tried, but he says there's nothing to discuss, so I guess I'll be searching for answers someplace else."

"Like the library?"

"Like the library, and thanks to last night's fight, I now have a lot of other questions, not only about Paul's motives, but about our relationship, his use of the word *business*, and a strange trip or dream I vaguely remember havin' before leavin' Memphis. I might have to enroll to get all my answers."

Tara laughed. "UT would be lucky to have you, especially the music department. And *you're* in luck, because I've become quite adept at finding my way around their libraries." She glanced at the baseball cap and sunglasses resting on the seat. "Don't forget your disguise."

"Just call me Curly, hon'," Aron joked, putting on his cap and glasses.

Later that night Aron lay in bed, staring at the ceiling and listening to the faint sound of laughter rising above his window fan's steady hum. He smiled as the day's events floated through his mind, chuckling at the fact that nobody at UT's undergraduate library even gave him a second look. His mind drifted to his early-morning performance of "Jailhouse Rock" and his apology to his kidnappers. He recalled his inspection of their hiking trail and discovery of a huge, uprooted oak tree, which he was eager to show Paul. For the first time in quite some time, Aron was looking forward to something besides drugs. To his surprise, he was looking forward to tomorrow.

Tara took part in a quick briefing then checked on Aron before leaving for work. Aron's other kidnappers entertained themselves by telling jokes and stories on the front porch. The porch light began drawing bugs, so Brooks turned it off and lit a candle, turning the porch into a perfect place for ghost stories.

"By the way," Brooks said, "The Vineyard's haunted."

"What?" Dave replied.

"All right!" Rob said. "And just when this place was startin' to get boring."

"What do you mean by haunted?" Dave asked.

"Some folks believe there's spirits in that old house," Brooks answered, "to quote Lucille Johnson."

"She said the house's previous renters didn't stay too long," Paul added, "and that our landlord's reduced the rent accordingly."

"Well, that's just great," Dave grumbled. "As if we haven't got enough problems."

"You're not afraid of a few ghosts, are you, Dave?" Rob asked.

"There's no such thing," Dave answered.

"Ten bucks says Dave sleeps with his baseball bat tonight," Brooks joked.

"Twenty says he sleeps in the trunk of his car with his guitar and teddy bear," Rob replied.

"What kind of spirits?" Dave asked, "and please tell me no one was murdered in *my* room."

"Just a poor UT medical student," Rob joked. "Had his throat slit with his own scalpel."

"You don't keep sharp instruments in your room, do you, Dave?" Brooks asked.

Dave rolled his eyes, nonchalantly scratching a sudden itch on the front of his throat.

"The Johnsons didn't elaborate as to what kind of spirits," Paul answered Dave.

"I'll tell you who's haunting this place," Brooks said. "Who's been wreaking havoc on it since Day One?"

"Aron?" Rob asked.

"Aron's not a ghost," Dave said.

"Oh, so now you're an authority on the subject," Brooks replied. "A second ago you were saying there's no such thing."

"So I drove to Memphis, broke into Graceland, kidnapped Aron's ghost, and drove him all the way to Austin?" Paul asked.

"Maybe you did," Brooks replied. "Maybe you got there a little late. Maybe Aron had already died of an overdose, which left only his ghost, a ghost more than willing to say adiós to Graceland."

"Maybe you're crazy," Dave said.

"Graceland did, in fact, look more like a mortuary than a rock star's mansion," Paul mentioned.

"I think Brooks is on to something," Rob agreed.

"What about the body?" Dave asked. "If Paul just nabbed Aron's ghost, that would have left 260 pounds of dead Elvis lying in Graceland. Don't you think his guards might have reported something by now?"

"Maybe they were afraid," Rob guessed. "Maybe the guard that stuffed the King's last envelope got scared and hid the body."

"Or maybe he didn't even die in Graceland," Brooks said. "We read he sleepwalks. His body could be lying in a cornfield somewhere, or floating face down in the Mississippi, halfway to New Orleans by now."

Paul's shoulders slumped. "So my miraculous kidnapping wasn't so miraculous after all. I showed up too late to save the King but just in time to become his stooge. I feel so—used."

"Hey, you got there as fast as you could," Rob consoled, patting his friend on the back.

Dave shook his head. "So Aron's ghost allowed us to lock him in Detox then attacked Paul to get out, when all along, he could have walked right through the door."

"Ghosts aren't known for their good behavior," Rob replied.

"He couldn't leave Detox without us," Brooks commented.

"And why's that?" Dave asked.

"Because he needed our help."

"Oh, yeah, nothing worse than a ghost addicted to prescription drugs."

"Don't be ridiculous, Dave," Brooks replied, "ghosts can't ingest drugs. He needed our help with something far more important."

"Which was?" Dave asked.

Brooks reflected a moment. "There's only two reasons why a ghost would stay behind, rather than move on to— wherever. Ghosts stay behind either to settle a score, or to get a message back to their loved ones. If Aron's ghost had wanted to settle a score, he'd have hung around Memphis, or gone to Las Vegas, or California. But he didn't do that, did he? He followed Paul to Austin, and the reason why is obvious. He wants to get a message back to his loved ones, fifty million loved ones to be precise, the King's fans." A sudden breeze stirred the candle flame. Everyone but Dave stared wide-eyed at the flame. Dave glanced at his friends then shook his head.

Brooks cleared a sudden lump that had formed in his throat. "Okay, where was I? Oh, yeah. So Aron accompanied Paul to Austin to get a message back to his fifty million fans—not an easy task if you're a ghost. He was thrown into Detox and introduced to Paul's fellow kidnappers, all of whom foolishly thought they had nabbed the King."

"I feel the fool," Rob said.

"You *are* the fool if you believe any of this," Dave said.

"But while in Detox, Aron's ghost learned that one of his kidnappers was a gifted writer, the perfect individual to help him with his important message."

"Well, well," Dave laughed, "Mr. Brooks has just become the hero of his own story. What a surprise."

"Every story needs a hero," Brooks replied, "and every ghost story needs a victim, and if you don't want to become that victim, I suggest you take this story a little more seriously."

"Yeah, right," Dave said. He casually glanced at the dark woods surrounding the porch, a cold chill climbing up his back.

Paul rubbed his chin. "So that's why our patients and staff inside Detox never discovered Aron, even when he was going ballistic, because ghosts only appear to those they want to appear to."

"Exactly," Brooks agreed. "He appeared to us because he needed us. But he didn't need us in the Detox unit of The Austin State Hospital, a terrible place for a ghost to work on an important message. An old haunted house in the country, however, would be the perfect place, so he went along with our little adventure, played the part of the addict struggling through withdrawal, then attacked Paul specifically to encourage us to quickly leave Detox and move to our *safe house* in country, and like pawns in his diabolical chess game, we played right into his hands."

Paul looked toward the front door. "So that emotional, kneeling-in-the-doorway performance during his first morning here was just an act."

"Just an act," Brooks agreed, "from someone who's had quite a bit of acting experience, I might add."

"And this morning?" Rob asked. "All that bull about overstaying his welcome, and having important business out here, and please can I stay till it's done?"

"All an act," Brooks answered. "That one probably won him a standing ovation from the other ghouls haunting this place."

"That explains all those strange, late-night noises we've been hearing," Paul commented.

"I thought that was flatulence," Dave replied.

Brooks studied Dave, eyes narrowing. "Some individuals find talk of ghosts disturbing. It brings out their worst fears. They use humor to mask their fears. Humor can sometimes provide, some degree of comfort."

"Thanks, Doc," Dave joked, reaching for his billfold. "I feel better already. How much do I owe you?"

Paul stared toward the dark living room. "All kidding aside, I've noticed a strange sort of *energy* around this place from the first moment I stepped foot here."

"Energy, my butt," Rob said, "this place is *haunted*, with *ghosts*, and we brought the biggest ghost with us." He looked at Dave. "And hidin' our heads beneath the covers *ain't* gonna make 'em go away. I say we confront them."

"Show me the ghosts, and I'll be happy to confront them," Dave said.

"That's what we've been trying to do," Brooks replied.

"So what's the important message?" Paul asked. "What's the King want to tell his fifty million fans?"

"I don't have a clue," Brooks replied, peering toward Aron's bedroom. "But I know this," he added, voice falling to a whisper. "If we want to live through another night here, I suggest we quit screwing around with trying to *save the addict* and start trying to figure out what exactly he wants to tell his fifty million fans, or next time it won't be someone's guitar splattering against the wall, it'll be someone's head."

"I bet he's holdin' his own little briefing right now," Rob said.

All eyes turned toward the living room.

"Spiking someone's soda with all the Valium he's been stashing," Paul guessed.

"Choosing their next victim," Brooks agreed.

The candle flame burned perfectly still as the men looked at each other. A lone cricket chirped.

"Don't look at *me*," Paul said, massaging his neck, "I was his first victim."

All eyes fell on Brooks. "Don't look at *me*. He needs *me* to craft his important message to his fans."

All eyes fell on Rob. "Bring 'em on, but I'm already a believer. All they have to do is ask, and I'm on board."

Heads turned toward Dave. A sudden breeze blew. The candle flame flickered. Everyone froze—even the cricket.

"Ahhhhh!" Aron screamed, kicking the screen door off its hinges before leaping onto the porch. "Ahhhhh!" he yelled again, wildly swinging a guitar inches above their heads.

Chairs crashed to the floor, as Aron's kidnappers sprang to their feet. Paul and Rob raised their tightened fists, focusing on the monster's head. Brooks clutched his pen as if it were a dagger, focusing on the King's throat. Dave swung a leg over the porch railing and was just about to jump when Aron's sudden burst of laughter filled the porch.

"Whacha doin', boys?" he asked, roaring with laughter, "tellin' ghost stories?"

All four men glared at Aron, pulses racing, lungs heaving, fists—slowly—relaxing.

"Holy cow, Aron!" Dave shouted, hand over his chest. "Are you tryin' to give me a heart attack!"

All heads turned slowly toward Dave. The sight of their friend straddling the porch railing, gasping for air with his hand over his heart, was too much for them to handle. Everyone burst out laughing, Dave included.

"Where ya goin', Dave?" Aron asked. "Story time over?"

"He mounted that railing like it was a horse," Brooks commented.

"He mounted it like he was gonna have sex with it," Rob said.

"One last screw before his death," Aron guessed.

"That's it exactly!" Brooks laughed. "He reacted purely on instinct. Having written off himself, he was quickly trying to reproduce so his species might survive."

"With the porch railing?" Rob asked.

"You need a horse, Dave," Paul joked. "How far did you think you'd get on that railing?"

"A horse!" Rob said. "He needs a woman!"

"Explain yourself, Dave," Brooks demanded. "Were you trying to reproduce, or ride that railing out of town?"

"I was cutting my losses," Dave replied, swinging his leg back to the porch side of the railing, "saving the brains of the outfit to fight another day."

"To *run* another day," Brooks joked.

"Well, look at *you*," Dave replied. "What were you planning to do with that silly pen?"

"I was going for the jugular," Brooks replied. "Don't forget, I'm the hero of this story. I was embarking on a noble fight to the death."

"Congratulations, Aron," Paul said, between laughs. "You got us good, and in the process, seemed to have crossed over from *patient*, to one of the boys."

"I liked him better as a patient," Dave said, "and *one of the boys* will be getting the pee scared out of him as soon as I figure out where and when."

"I'll help you," Brooks agreed.

"Sorry, *boys*," Aron apologized, "but I couldn't resist. I was having trouble sleepin' and thought I'd see what my kidnappers were up to. Imagine my shock at learning I was dead—that 260 pounds of *dead Elvis* was floatin' face down in the Mississippi, halfway to New Orleans by now.

You boys should be ashamed of yourselves, especially *you*, Mr. Brooks."

"I *am* ashamed of myself," Brooks admitted.

"What a terrible thing for a poor addict struggling through withdrawal to have to stumble onto," Aron continued, "and by the way, I'm a trim 240, if your bathroom scales are right."

"You could have sucked up 20 pounds of water on the way to New Orleans," Brooks replied.

"Yeah, and that gator attached to your butt could have added a pound or two," Rob said.

"I found the whole story offensive," Aron replied, "and regardless of my weight, y'all were wrong, *dead* wrong."

"I think I speak for everyone when I say we're very sorry for our behavior," Brooks apologized.

"I think I speak for everyone when I say this was all *your* fault, Mr. Brooks," Dave replied.

Aron leaned against the railing as the others picked up the door and tipped chairs. Rob inspected the door's torn hinges, giving Aron a disgusted look. "I think I speak for everyone when I say it's high time one of the boys started pulling his own weight around here, and he can start by reattaching this door."

"I'll be happy to, Rob," Aron replied, "my next briefin' with my *ghouls* isn't scheduled until midnight."

"Something tells me we'll never hear the end of this," Brooks grumbled.

"You'll find my tool box under the kitchen sink," Rob said, as Aron studied the broken door.

After repairing the door, the men took turns describing other big scares in their lives. The stories and laughter lasted until well after midnight, when Aron grew too sleepy to continue. "By the way," he said, slowly standing, "who's watching me tonight?"

"Rob and I have the first watch," Dave answered. "Why?"

"Just wanted to fix you boys a couple of sodas before turnin' in."

"That's *real* funny," Dave replied.

"Oh, and if any of my little pawns catch me sleep-walking tonight, would ya mind pointin' me away from the Mississippi?"

"No problem," Rob replied.

"Away from the Mississippi and toward the Colorado," Dave joked.

"Ya sleepin' in the trunk of your car tonight, Dave?" Aron asked.

"You sleeping in a lifejacket tonight?" Dave asked.

During the next four weeks, Aron continued struggling through recovery, but by mid-April he was able to sleep through the night without sedatives or painkillers. His diet improved, thanks in part to the Johnsons' freshly harvested vegetables, and his healthful diet combined with his daily hikes and frequent games of two-below helped him shed another twenty pounds. When not involved in group activities, he enjoyed lengthy phone conversations with his daughter, frequent trips to the UT library, and of course, singing and playing guitars.

Aron's improved health brought a number of wel-comed changes to The Vineyard. His kidnappers' round-the-clock watches were discontinued, and their daily briefings changed to weekly meetings, which included Aron. Those with houses or apartments in Austin wiggled out of their leases and made permanent moves to the country, freeing up even more time to spend on more personal interests.

Brooks began dating Beth, who enjoyed helping him with his wild *fiction* about a humanitarian kidnapping of the King of Rock 'n' Roll. Dave landed a second date with Susanne, which led to a third and a fourth, and on those occasions when Dave and Brooks entertained their dates at The Vineyard, Aron was taken on road trips to small, Central Texas towns offering good food and lively music.

UT's board of regents voted to allow the sale of alcohol at The Cactus Cafe, a popular on-campus hangout, and Rob became the cafe's first bartender. The Cactus attracted a gold mine of beautiful coeds, many of whom were happy to help Rob make up for those long, celibate nights at The Vineyard.

The drives to and from town began taking a heavy toll on everyone's cars, Paul's in particular. Although he was not the best mechanic, he was better than his friends and was soon spending much of his free time working on their clunkers, a job he grew to hate. He much preferred hiking, jogging, reading poetry, or contemplating the possible obstacles preventing his and Tara's relationship from evolving to the next level.

Tara continued monitoring Aron's progress through recovery while expanding her research into addiction. She quit her job at Detox, confident that communal life in the country would help her stretch her savings. She also began filling out applications to three in-state and six out-of-state graduate schools of medicine. When not reading or spending one-on-one time with Aron, she enjoyed caring for The Vineyard's grapevines, a few of which had begun to bear fruit. She also enjoyed her increased one-on-one time with Paul.

The thunderstorm that plummeted The Vineyard in March marked the end of the Texas drought. April and May brought ten inches of rain, and during one of these showers, Tara and Paul sat together on the back porch, watching the rain and listening to one of Aron's classics floating from an open window. Aron rarely sang traditional versions of his old hits, preferring to experiment with new creations or fresh renditions of earlier classics. But on that particular afternoon, the rain had spurred him to play "Pocketful of Rainbows." Paul's face brightened when he recognized the old tune, but Tara's face saddened.

"Bring back some sad memories?" Paul asked.

"Yes," Tara answered. "Of Steve. Steven Garrett. 'Pocketful of Rainbows' was our song."

As Tara's mind raced back to the beginning of her relationship with Steve, her face brightened. "Steve was a junior in high school and I was a freshman, when we fell in love. I worshiped the ground he walked on, and he worshiped me.

"His parents owned a thousand acre ranch south of San Angelo. On his seventeenth birthday, they bought him an expensive quarter horse named Sunny, and we spent the entire summer riding." Tara closed her eyes, smiling broadly. "I remember the bright sun glistening off Sunny's auburn coat, and Steve reaching down low and pulling me up high."

Tara opened her eyes to study the rain-drenched trees a moment before continuing. "As much as I loved the rides on Steve's horse, I loved the rides in his blue, '57 Chevy convertible more. Immediately after the last bell

rang, we would race to his car to fly over the back-coun-
try roads—radio turned high, wind blowing through our
hair, laughing at anything and everything as we fell deeper
in love. We loved each other so much, nothing else mattered, or so it seemed.

"Financially, my mother and I were just getting by.
Steve's parents were quite wealthy. You've heard the story.
Steve's mom and dad didn't approve of our relationship
and worked hard to break us up, but we held on tight. We
argued, fought, begged, and after all else had failed, vowed
to elope, but on the night of our planned elopement,
I backed out. I was underage and knew Steve's parents
would call the police. I also knew running away would
crush my mom, so I crushed Steve instead, and I don't
think he ever understood how, if I loved him so much, I
could have backed out.

"Several weeks after our planned elopement, IBM organized a job fair at San Angelo State University. My mom
attended, and after interviews in San Angelo and Austin,
she was offered an entry-level position with good pay, excellent medical benefits, and numerous opportunities for
advancement. IBM even insisted on funding our move to
Austin. For my mother, it was a golden opportunity. For
me and Steve, it seemed like the end of the world.

"One month later a loaded moving van sat in front of
our house beneath a long band of dark clouds. The final
bills had been paid, every room emptied and cleaned,
and all our farewells said—all but one. Steve and I had
put off saying goodbye until the last moment, and when
that moment came, we were sadly unprepared. My mom
greeted him with a warm hug then sat in our car to give
us some privacy.

"We embraced in the front yard, without saying a word, as the moving van slowly pulled away. A light sprinkle fell then quickly turned into a steady downpour. We held each other tightly, as if to shut out the rain, the numerous fights with Steve's parents, our looming good-bye, and the cold injustice of it all. We didn't care that we were getting soaked, or that Steve had left his convertible's top down and its radio on. We didn't care that a local disc jockey had picked that instant to play 'Pocketful of Rainbows.' The only thing we cared about was holding on to that moment so tightly, it would never be able to slip away.

"Eventually, I realized I would never be able to go through with it unless I acted fast, like pulling a tooth—except the string attached to the doorknob was wrapped tightly around my heart. I gently pushed myself back from Steve's grasp. I told him I'd never forget him, that I'd always love him, then kissed him on the cheek and ran to our car. I said goodbye the only way I knew how, and to this day, I'm haunted by the shock and pain in Steve's eyes—haunted by the hurried goodbye that he was forced to shout after me as I ran away.

"Our car radio was tuned to the same station as Steve's, and to my surprise, my mother was crying—hard. I think the pressure of the new job, move to Austin, and weeks of packing and cleaning had pushed her very near the edge. I think the combination of the hard rain, emotional love song, and sad scene taking place in her rear view had pushed her *over* the edge. She was quite beside herself. Between sobs, she said we didn't have to move, she could turn down the IBM job and get her old job back, we could have a state trooper turn the moving van around, and that we'd better hurry and tell Steve before he did something foolish. She was talking crazy and reaching for the door handle when I grasped her arm. It was one of those strange moments, in a mother-daughter relationship, when roles are temporarily reversed. I reminded her Austin was only four hours away, Steve and I could call, write, and visit often, and told her everything would work out, one day we'd get be back together. Although I managed to convince my mom, I did not at all convince myself. As we drove through the pouring rain, I had a sinking suspicion my relationship with Steve was suddenly, forever changed.

"During the next few months, Steve and I called and wrote religiously. Steve made several trips to Austin, and I made several trips to San Angelo. But his letters began to change. One day, he canceled a trip to Austin. One day, I canceled a trip to San Angelo. He never mentioned it, but I knew he'd found someone else. And I never blamed him, because my priorities were also changing. Mom's job entailed numerous business trips to Denver and Los Angeles, which left me alone with my newfound freedom and independence. I quickly made new friends, and we were soon enjoying after school activities, Austin's wild nightlife, and frequent trips to Corpus and South Padre. We began attending UT sponsored events and were all looking forward to attending UT after high school graduation.

"My first semester at UT, I heard Steve married a local girl from San Angelo, someone his parents loved. The marriage, however, was not a happy one and quickly ended in divorce. Steve moved to Austin to get away from his family and ex-wife, and because he still had strong feelings for me. We dated for a while, but things just didn't work out. When we first met, we were so young and growing up so fast, I guess, in different directions. Apparently, Austin wasn't far enough away from San Angelo for Steve because his next move was to Colorado. The last I heard, he had remarried and was working on a ranch somewhere in North Dakota.

"I'm no longer in love with Steve, but I still love him, if that makes any sense. I realize our passionate relationship was not meant to continue as it had once existed, and on one level, that chapter in my life is over. But on another level, it's not. On another level, I'm continually haunted by that sad goodbye in the rain. I wish with all my heart the Tara of my youth could reach out to the Steve of his youth and have one more shot at that goodbye. I wish with all my heart we could both have another shot at that goodbye."

With her story told, Tara bowed her head and burst into tears.

Paul held her close, staring intently at the water dripping off the porch's eaves. He waited until she was finished crying before speaking. "Tara, after your move from San Angelo, when you and Steve were writing and calling, did you discuss any of this with him?"

"No, at that point in our relationship, we were far more concerned about getting back together, than we were in how we had said goodbye."

"What about when Steve moved to Austin and the two of you were dating again? Did you discuss it with him then?"

"No, he had just been through another close relationship, a failed marriage. He was busy processing through all that. My problem didn't seem so important."

"So you've never talked to him about any of this?"

Tara burst into tears. "You don't understand. It didn't matter—until—it *did* matter. This whole thing has been like a deep splinter working its way upward, slowly growing and building in importance, as evidenced by the strong hold it has over me now."

Paul nodded reflectively. "That's a very good analogy, Tara. And I'd say that splinter has worked its way very close to the surface. I'd say now would be a very good time for you to contact Steve and tell him everything you just told me."

"But . . ."

"But what, Tara? Too much time has elapsed? You're different people now? He's married? It might be uncomfortable? Those excuses might have worked okay in the past, when the splinter was small, but in case you haven't noticed, they're not working all that well anymore. I think you should talk to him, in person, and not just for your sake, but for his. What if he's being haunted by the same memories? Like you said, shouldn't you both be given another chance at that goodbye?"

Tara responded by taking a deep breath then slowly nodding.

"I'll go with you, if you like," Paul offered. "He shouldn't be that hard to find," he added, with a shrug. "How big can North Dakota be?"

Tara smiled, wiping away a tear. "Thanks, I'd appreciate that." She glanced toward the living room where Aron had begun another song. "Perhaps when we're done slaying this dragon, we can journey north and slay another."

"All for one, and one for all," Paul joked, stretching his stiff arms and legs. He stared into the woods. "Let's go for a hike?"

"In the rain?"

"I've got some slickers. There's something I want to show you."

Paul and Tara soon stepped off the porch and into a light rain. The forest's thick canopy dispersed the drizzle into a fine mist, blanketing the hikers as they walked. As their pace quickened, their bodies warmed, spurring them to shed their slickers and tie them around their waists. The steamy woods and spongy earth was a stark difference from the cold, hard porch and heavy story about Steve, as evidenced by their broad smiles and lifting chins.

"There it is," Paul said, motioning toward a huge, uprooted oak tree, leaning at a 45 degree angle across the trail. The tree rested on its exposed roots to the left and crushed branches to the right. A large hole sat beneath its unearthed roots. Several tiny waterfalls poured over the roots, turning the hole into a small pond. The sound of trickling water grew as they neared. A much larger hole now appeared in the forest's canopy where the tree's branches once stretched. As the clouds thinned, long rays of sunlight shot through the hole, causing the tree to glisten.

"It looks like a fallen dinosaur," Tara commented, inspecting the tree's fat leaves. "But judging from these, its still very much alive."

Paul focused on the oak's lower branches, many of which were split and embedded into the soft earth—perfect stair steps to the tree's thick trunk. Tara focused on its upper branches defiantly reaching toward heaven. The dinosaur was screaming to be climbed, and like children at recess, Paul and Tara were happy to oblige. They cast off their slickers, scampered up the tree's lower branches, and leaped onto its fat trunk. Like suddenly liberated monkeys, they jumped, swung, and raced from branch to branch toward its highest limb. The rain had stopped, but each disturbed branch created a cold shower and loud screams. Snagged clothing, sudden slips, and unexpected falls drew bursts of laughter. Paul found the perfect branch for chin-ups. Tara found the perfect branch for hanging upside down.

While they played, Tara's wet clothing grew uncomfortably tight and restrictive. She remembered experiencing a similar feeling as a small child climbing on her neighborhood's Jungle Jim. She recalled resolving the problem by stripping off her clothes and tossing them to the ground, much to the amusement of the adults watching from below.

Tara glanced up at Paul, who was preoccupied with another climb to the top. While balanced on the tree's trunk, she grasped the bottom of her wet T-shirt and pulled it over her head. She next removed her wet bra and cutoffs, almost falling as her underwear snagged on the toe of her boot. While stretching her chest, shoulders, and arms skyward, every molecule in her body began to jump with excitement. She studied Paul's bulging muscles as he began another set of chin-ups. She bent over, grasped a wet branch and hung as her long legs stretched toward the earth. She dropped, boots quietly sinking into the wood's soft carpet.

A tickling sensation pulled at Paul's groin as he strained to complete just one—more—chin-up. He quickly wrapped his legs around the branch and hung upside down to rest his screaming arms and shoulders. His eyes searched for Tara, who was hidden by thousands of healthy green leaves. Tara stepped back from the tree and watched as Paul swung from limb to limb before dropping on the far side of the tree, twisting his ankle, and falling. He quickly sat up and began massaging his injured ankle.

"What a shame," Tara said, with a laugh. "And just when I was about to suggest a little game of If You Can Catch Me, You Can Have Me."

Paul's eyes began tracing every curve and line of Tara's nude body as she turned in a slow circle. He glanced at her discarded clothing, looking for further proof that his eyes were not deceiving him. Although he had imagined this moment a million times, his imagination had never quite done her body justice. He could not help staring. If his ears had not deceived him, every inch of her wet body was suddenly his for the taking. The only thing standing in his way was a few thousand pounds of fallen oak and a slightly sprained ankle.

Paul slowly stood. "You *do* realize, I'm a lot faster than you, even with a sprained ankle."

"Ha! In your dreams."

Paul shifted his weight to test his ankle before looking for the quickest route though the tree's broad limbs and wide branches. He took a step forward.

"Wait!" Tara said, taking a step backwards. "How about removing your clothes, too? Racing through the woods, naked, *does* have its disadvantages, and I know you want the game played on a level playing field."

Paul glanced at a nearby cactus standing groin high and laughed. "Nice try, but I'm a lot more concerned about protecting my privates, than I am about playing on a level playing field—speaking of which—weren't you just laughin' at my sprained ankle?" He took a quick step to his left.

"I *was* not," Tara answered, also taking a quick step to the left to keep the tree centered between them. "I was laughing at how ridiculous you looked falling on your face."

Paul braced to leap up to the tree's trunk.

"Wait!" Tara shouted, stepping back. "At least take your shirt off, Tarzan."

Paul glanced at his wet T-shirt then closed his eyes to pull it over his head. When he opened them, the only thing left of Tara was a distant flash of bare skin and the sound of racing footsteps. The whole forest suddenly became their playground as they leaped over cacti, brushed aside branches, and plunged through wet cobwebs. To Paul, there was something extremely exciting about having to suddenly work so hard for a prize that had until now had required waiting so long. To Tara, there was something extremely erotic about racing nude through a rain-cleansed forest as her energy waned and her love steadily closed the distance between them.

Their wild chase took them in a large circle back to the fallen tree, where Tara leaped onto its trunk. Paul lunged for her foot, slipped, and fell face first into the pond. Tara burst into laughter as she climbed to the highest branch. Her chest heaved as she stared down at the earth far below, teetering between jumping to a lower branch, or surrendering. Her foot slipped. She screamed and reached for nothing but air. A strong arm quickly encircled her waist and pulled her back to the safety of the tree. She spun as her slick body slid against his. They embraced, kissed, and soon lay on their slickers beneath the tree's outstretched arms, falling deeper and deeper in love.

*   *   *

Steven Garrett sat in a crowded truck stop just outside of Boise, Idaho. A hard morning rain had filled the diner with noisy travelers, but Steve was oblivious to the ringing cash register, dropped silverware, and noisy conversations—oblivious because he was thinking of Tara. Perhaps it was the strange dream he had had the previous night, or the Elvis song that had awakened him that morning, or the hard rain now tapping against the truck stop's window, but whatever the reason, his thoughts had again returned to Tara.

A plate crashed to the floor, forcing his attention back to the diner. The front door swung open as two more drenched travelers rushed inside. Steve turned his attention to his truck and horse trailer parked outside the big picture window. He studied the strong back of the purebred stallion that he was hauling from Boise to Fargo. He thought about the horse's bill of sale, medical records, and registration papers locked in the truck's glove compartment. He contemplated the long drive home and mound of paperwork waiting. He thought about Sandy, the most important person in his life, and smiled.

Suddenly, the first chords of "Pocketful of Rainbows" reached out from the diner's radio, wrapped themselves around Steve's heart and jerked him back to San Angelo, back to Tara's front yard, back to that exact moment she spun and ran away. The diner blurred as his coffee cup slowly lowered to the side of its saucer. The cup tipped, sending warm, black coffee across the white countertop.

At the song's end, the pay phone hanging near the front door rang loudly. A waitress raced by, arms filled with hot plates of warm pancakes. The cook glanced up before breaking two more eggs over his hot grill. Again, the phone rang. As if in a trance, Steve gradually stood then slowly walked across the busy diner, picking up the jelly-coated phone long after it had stopped ringing. He reached out to return the sticky receiver to its holder, but it seemed glued to his hand. He recalled the previous night's phone conversation with Sandy, and smiled. He put an index finger inside the zero and drew a slow circle. "I'd like to make a collect call, please."

"Morning, Sandy?" Steve said, a few moments later.

"Hi, honey," she replied excitedly. "I was hoping you'd call this morning. Did you get him?"

"I got him," Steve replied, glancing out the window. "He's the most beautiful stallion I've ever seen."

"I can't wait to see him. Did you get caught in the storm?"

"Yeah, I'm sittin' in a truck stop outside of Boise right now, waitin' for it to pass."

"Blue skies, here, but they're forecasting rain tonight. I guess you'll be bringing it with you."

"I guess so. Listen, hon', I know this is going to sound kind of strange, but I have to make a trip to Texas, I have to talk to Tara, and I'd like you to come with me."

Another wife might have had serious reservations about such a request, but years earlier Sandy had experienced a similar pull back in time to see her first love. She recalled stepping off the plane and her parents giving her a warm hug before asking her to sit down. She remembered the tragic news of an automobile accident the night before and recalled that sick, nauseating feeling in the center of her stomach, right before throwing up.

Sandy would never wish that feeling on anyone, least of all, her husband. "Just a second," she replied, flipping back the pages of her busy engagement calendar. She stopped at the first empty week and smiled at the beautiful picture of Texas bluebonnets opposite the blank page. "I've nothing scheduled for the first week of August."

Chapter Seven

Each spring WCT at Lakeway, a tennis and golf resort near The Vineyard, increased its staff of servers for
the summer season. Paul and Brooks applied, were hired,
and quit their jobs at Detox. The resort's bar and restaurant stood on a high hill overlooking thirty tennis courts,
sixty condominiums, and an 18-hole golf course. A tennis
racket-shaped swimming pool pointed toward Lake Travis
in the distance. Lakeway's servers enjoyed a guaranteed
20 percent gratuity, discounted meals, and free after-hour
use of its pristine courts. They also enjoyed numerous
opportunities to meet some of the world's greatest tennis
players.

Paul and Brooks quickly fell in love with the resort
and tried to persuade Dave and Rob to apply. Dave was
tempted by the good pay, but his interest in medicine was
leaning toward drug abuse and addiction, so he decided
to stay at Detox. Rob, too, decided to stay at his present
job, saying he was having way too much fun working at
The Cactus, much to his friends' chagrin. Because The
Vineyard was still without televisions, stereos, and telephones, Rob's paintings and the stories surrounding them
had become a valuable source of entertainment. His ap-

petite for beer, during and after work, was exceeded only by his appetite for young coeds, leaving little time for his art. His friends missed watching him paint, worried about his changing priorities, and worried more about his intoxicated, late-night drives home on the commute's dark and winding roads. After attempts to talk to Rob about their concerns failed, they decided to address the issue at a weekly meeting.

"This is startin' to sound like an intervention," Rob grumbled.

"That's because it is," Brooks joked.

"We're just a little concerned about your drinking and driving," Tara explained.

"I appreciate your concerns, but I'm a big boy, and I don't drink that much anyway."

"Lakeway's looking for bartenders," Paul mentioned. "They're just fifteen minutes away, so on those occasions when you've had a little too much to drink, you can hitch a ride with me or Brooks."

"Thanks, but I'm working at the only bar on a campus of forty-five thousand students, half of them beautiful coeds, eagerly waiting in line for a chance to meet *yours truly*. Why would I want to work in a stupid country club full of old retired couples?"

"Because those old retired couples are filthy rich," Brooks answered. "I made sixty bucks in tips last night, for three hours work. How much did you make at The Cactus?"

Rob stared out the window without answering the question. He couldn't deny that poor college students were terrible tippers. Some nights he hardly made enough to pay for his gas to and from town. But the phone numbers left by UT's drop-dead gorgeous coeds more than made up for the small tips.

Tara focused on one of Rob's brightly-colored paintings. "Working closer to home would certainly free up more time for your art."

"I thought you'd planned to paint an abstract a week," Dave reminded.

"And hit the art world the way I hit the music world," Aron added.

Rob glared at Aron. "Et tu, Brute?"

Aron chuckled.

"Did I miss the *What's Best for Rob* meetin'?" Rob asked.

"No, we're having it now," Brooks answered.

"You should consider yourself lucky," Aron chuckled. "I missed the *What's Best for Elvis* meetin' and ended up in a lockup for two days."

Rob shook his head, eyes falling to his stomach. He'd gained 20 pounds from all the beer, and The Cactus had, in fact, become a big distraction from his art, albeit a sweet distraction. He looked up at his friends. "Okay. I'll think about working at Lakeway—maybe in the fall."

"The fall," Brooks echoed. "Lakeway needs bartenders now. They normally reduce their staff in the fall."

Rob shrugged. His friends knew he would need a little more convincing but decided to let the topic die, for the time being. A few weeks later, Rob received a little more convincing when he ran his truck off the road and into a tree. He had only consumed a few beers prior to the accident, and his injuries were minor, but his humiliation was great, especially after his long walk home. The following morning he interviewed for a bartender position at Lakeway and by mid-May was enjoying the resort's numerous employee benefits, including one unexpected perk; the Food and Beverage Director let him show one of his paintings in the restaurant's lobby. Two wealthy members purchased the abstract, and the sell spurred Rob to jump back into his art with great vigor.

"I've decided to create a tribute to Lakeway's rich doctors, lawyers, stock brokers, and real estate tycoons," Rob announced, calling everyone into the living room, "a group of individuals that Dr. Dave Turner will soon be a part of."

"Sign me up," Dave replied.

Rob picked up a dry brush and stroked the top third of a large, white canvas. "Up here I want the good doctor swinging a seven-iron on the ninth hole of the resort's lime-green golf course, with all his cronies watchin'. I'll have 'em wearing silly yellows, reds, and oranges, with tiny flashes of white slicin' and shankin' in every direction."

"I thought you said this would be a tribute," Dave said.

"Yes, well, good art *does* make us take a hard look at ourselves, doesn't it?" Rob replied, "which brings us to this part of the painting." He brushed the bottom third of the canvas. "Down here, I want the colors fading toward darker hues. Visualize a small, stuffy waiting room packed with Dave's patients, the sick and downtrodden, all staring at Norman Rockwells and wondering if Doc Turner might be able to squeeze one of 'em in between the ninth and tenth holes."

"I can see them!" Brooks said. "They're reading dated magazines and looking up hopefully every time the door opens. Hey, Lakeway might commission you to paint this masterpiece."

"Ha!" Dave scoffed. "Just what every country club needs, a crude satire of its wealthy members."

"Talk about bitin' the hand that feeds ya," Aron agreed.

"I'll avoid a detailed explanation of the painting until I've received my commission," Rob replied.

"You'll cause a revolt," Tara commented.

"Wow, a revolt of the wealthy class," Brooks mused. "That's something you don't see every day. You'd be making history, Rob, and here I am to document it all."

"Hmm, that gives me an idea for a second tribute," Rob said. "Picture Dr. Dave Turner standing like George Washington at the bow of his boat, three wood held high."

"Which three wood?" Brooks asked.

"His golf club," Rob answered.

"I'm seeing it," Brooks said. "The great doctor Turner, sporting a woody and leading the charge—chasing the gifted, yet misunderstood, abstract expressionist across Lake Travis and off Lakeway Properties forever."

"With his cronies crouched in the bottom of the boat," Rob laughed, "trying not to spill their martinis."

"I'm finding all this extremely offensive," Dave replied, as the others laughed. He studied Rob a moment. "But I have to admit, it's good to see you painting again, Rob. The Cactus' loss is our gain."

Judging from the applause that followed, the others agreed.

May 27 marked the end of UT's spring semester, and a huge sense of relief fell over campus as thousands of students walked from building to building, picking up their grades. Some, however, were feeling a huge sense of anxiousness. The A that Paul had received in his Perceptual Psychology class had temporarily lifted his spirits, but he desperately needed a C in Dr. Singh's Psychology class to maintain a B average. He slowly climbed the tall steps of the Psychology building and stood behind the other anxious students crowded around the grades posted near Dr. Singh's door. Paul's heart leaped at the sight of his grade. "Yes!" he shouted, running down the hall. "Yes!" he repeated, leaping down the building's steep steps three at a time. His feet hardly touched the ground as he raced to his car, eager to share the good news with his friends.

At that moment, The Vineyard was also experiencing a big sense of relief. Aron's kidnappers had taken on a huge project by attempting to save the King during the busy spring semester. From the beginning, their short-term goal had been to just make it until summer. Suddenly, summer had arrived, bringing with it a number of other happy announcements: Dave and Brooks aced their courses, Rob sold a second painting, and Aron announced the completion of his first drug-free month.

The living room was filled with laughter when Paul ran through the front door. "I did it!" he shouted. "I aced my final. I made a C in Dr. Singh's Physiological Psychology course—the hardest psych course at UT."

Applause filled the room as Paul traded high fives with his friends. "Dave, I couldn't have done it without you," he added, giving his friend a big hug."

"Boy, my boy," Aron laughed, "if a C makes ya *this* happy, what's an A do for ya?"

"You don't want to see it," Brooks joked.

"He can really be hard to live with," Dave agreed.

"Congratulations, Paul," Tara said, "and *we* have some happy news to report, too."

After hearing the news, Paul congratulated his friends by exchanging more high fives. "That's great, Aron! One month! Without a thing!"

"Without so much as an aspirin," Aron boasted, "and I'm *very* sure I couldn't have done it without *you*."

"So why are we wastin' all these great highs sittin' on our butts?" Rob asked. "Let's play some football."

"I'm in," Paul replied.

"I'll play," Brooks said.

"I'm in," Dave added.

They looked at Aron.

"I'm still recovering from last time," Aron said, rubbing his shoulder.

All eyes turned to Tara. "Sorry. I, too, am still recovering from our last game."

"What a bunch of spoilsports," Dave said, shaking his head.

The Vineyard's football field was most unforgiving. Months earlier, they had eradicated a large nest of fire ants and removed most of the cacti, but a number of bumps, dips, and gopher holes still remained. The players wore hiking boots to protect their feet and ankles, but the rest of their bodies were exposed to the elements, as evidenced by a growing assortment of cuts, scrapes and bruises. At that moment, however, they were not feeling much pain.

"I feel like Bob Hayes!" Paul yelled, after making a great catch.

"I feel like Roger Staubach," Dave said, as he and Paul jumped up and down.

"I feel like throwing up," Rob taunted. "Hurry up and snap the ball."

Tara and Aron sipped iced tea while watching from the porch. Tara's rocking chair was surrounded by spiral notebooks and thick textbooks. Aron's rocker was encircled with guitars and legal pads. He set his tea on the porch, picked up a guitar, and began warming up his fingers. Tara's attention was divided between the textbook in her lap, and the football game in the distance, but when Aron began singing one of his new creations, her attention was suddenly undivided. She smiled broadly at the song's end. "That was beautiful, Aron. I know you've been told a million times, but you're truly a great performer, and now it would appear, on your way to becoming a great songwriter, as well."

"Why, thanks, hon'," Aron replied, glancing at Tara's books, "and you're great at what you do. My first drug-free month is proof of that."

"Thanks," Tara replied, glancing at a filled legal pad next to Aron's chair. "How's *your* research coming?"

"Fine. It's taken me to some pretty interesting places. I've had some long conversations with Paul's fellow Musketeers and even coaxed Brooks and Dave to make a few long distance phone calls—to DeSoto and New York."

"Goodness, you *have* been doing some research, haven't you?"

"Yes, hon'," Aron replied, exchanging his guitar for his legal pad, "and right now I'm puttin' it all together into what's turned out to be a pretty interesting story."

Tara looked at Aron curiously. "You're not becoming a writer, are you?"

Aron laughed. "No, I think I'll leave the writin' to Mr. Brooks." He watched as Brooks caught a pass. "But we all have our stories, don't we?"

Tara gave Aron a sly smile. "Yes, we do," she chuckled, trading her textbook for a notebook. "Are you experiencing any cravings today?"

"Yes, hon', I'd love a fried peanut butter and banana sandwich right now."

"Any other cravings?" Tara asked.

"Yesterday mornin' I was cravin' uppers but managed to direct my attention toward a new song."

"Any physical problems?"

"My lower back's a little sore, from helpin' in the garden yesterday, and there's this blister on my thumb." He laughed. "Not exactly the sort of ailments I ever expected to be havin', but better than the ones I was feelin' my first weeks here."

"Come on, guys!" Brooks shouted, running toward the porch.

"I told you, I'm still recovering from last time," Aron replied.

"Ditto," Tara agreed.

"We've cleared the field a little more since then," Brooks replied.

"I *see* you have," Tara said, staring at the bright-red blood running down Brooks' leg. She stepped inside and soon returned with bandages, antiseptic, and her hiking boots.

"Yahoo!" Brooks yelled, as the others joined him near the porch. "Okay, Aron, now you have to play or the sides will be uneven."

"I'm afraid that's tough," Aron replied.

"Leave Curly alone," Rob shouted. "I'll play quarterback for both sides."

"Son, I thought I asked ya to quit callin' me that," Aron replied.

"Oh, so you can call us *son* and *boy*, but we can't call you *Curly*," Rob grumbled.

"*Son* and *boy* imply young, which is a compliment. *Curly* implies fat, bald, and stupid, an uncompliment."

"*Uncompliment*'s not a word, Curly," Brooks corrected.

"*Uncomplimentary* is," Tara suggested.

"How 'bout *unpremeditated*?" Aron asked, leaning toward Brooks with clenched fists.

"Ah, leave the old man alone," Dave said, "he'll probably just get hurt, anyway."

"Forty-two's not that old," Aron commented.

"Older than you think, if you don't get your butt out of that rocking chair," Brooks warned.

Aron stood, strolled to his bedroom, and soon returned with his boots.

"All right!" Brooks yelled.

"First captain," Paul said.

"Second captain," Rob replied. "Start pickin', it's your funeral."

"Aron," Paul chose.

"Oh, going for experience," Rob joked. "You should've picked Dave. You're gonna need a doctor."

"Just pick, loser," Paul replied.

"Brooks," Rob chose. "Why break up a winning combination."

"Tara," Paul said.

"Dave," Rob replied.

"Last again," Dave grumbled, shaking his head.

"Okay," Rob announced, "it'll be me, Brooks, and Dave against the weak sisters, Paul, Tara and Aron."

"Who are you calling *weak sisters*?" Tara asked.

"Which team has the only woman on their side?"

"Which team will have the big jock cryin' after the game?" Tara asked.

"Hey," Aron laughed, "Big Jock Cryin' sounds like a good name for a rock band."

"Oh yeah," Rob replied, "well, Big Jock Laughin' will be playin' tonight, and you'd better get your tickets early."

"Standing room only," Brooks added, as their opponents jeered.

"Okay, everybody listen up!" Rob said. "In light of last week's arguments, I'll make the rules simple enough for even the stupidest of players. The goals are that tree—and that stump. Two tags anywhere below the waist, and you're down. No tacklin', or it's an automatic ten yards. No rushin' the quarterback till you've counted to five-Mississippi, out loud." Rob glanced at his watch. "We play for one hour—starting—now. Any questions?"

"Just one," Tara replied. "How many points do you want us to spot you?"

For sixty minutes, endorphins flooded their veins, sweat soaked their clothing, and laughter filled the air. After the game, the porch resembled a hospital emergency room as Tara made her rounds, applying medicine to Brooks' knee, and ice to Dave's shoulder and Aron's lip.

"There goes my singing career," Aron grumbled, glaring at Paul. He lowered the ice from his lip to check for blood.

"It's not like it was on the rebound," Brooks joked.

"Thanks for that observation, Mr. Brooks," Aron replied, "but since you were never a big fan of mine in the first place, I can't say that I value your opinion."

"Now, who told you that?" Brooks laughed.

"If you keep that ice on your lip, it might slow the swelling," Tara suggested to Aron.

"I told you," Paul defended, "count to six Mississippi, turn, and the ball will be sittin' right over your right shoulder. What's so hard about that? It was a beautiful pass."

"I'm sure it was," Aron replied. "I wish I'd seen more of it, but when I turned, at exactly six Mississippi, the ball was already halfway down my throat. How 'bout I play quarterback from now on?"

"Be my guest," Paul replied.

Dave rubbed his sore shoulder, grimacing in pain. "That was fun, but I could have done without the dislocated shoulder."

"It was a blast," Aron agreed. "It reminded me of the games we used to play in front of Humes High, back when a good run, catch, or interception could make ya an instant star. Of course, that stardom only lasted until your first screw up." He leaned back and smiled broadly. "But when you made a miraculous catch, and all your friends rushed over to pat you on the back, it was a *really* nice high."

Smiles graced everyone's faces.

"What's the highest you've ever been, Aron?" Brooks asked. "Without pharmaceuticals."

Aron's thoughts drifted back to those football games at Humes, to his first car, to his high school dates at the Suzore movie theater. He thought about his earliest performances at the talent shows, high school gyms, and county fairs around Memphis. He recalled his first appearance on KWKH's Louisiana Hayride. The faint sound of a distant train whistle caused his face to brighten. He stood, stepped to the porch railing, and stared in the direction of the whistle. "August, 1954, on a train ride to Houston. Before then, we'd just played small fairs and roadhouses close to home. That was our first ride ever on a train."

"We?" Brooks asked.

"Scotty, Bill, and me. Bill played bass and Scotty, rhythm. We were the Blue Moon Boys. After loadin' our bags and instruments in the baggage compartment, we searched every car for girls, but all we found were old folks and a few military. At nineteen, we were the youngest ones on the train. Through Mississippi, we scarfed down sodas and candy bars while throwin' a small football across the seats. After our sugar high wore off, we read comic books and magazines before goin' over our song list for that night's gig. The train dragged through Louisiana, stoppin' at every hick town along the way and quickly puttin' us fast asleep. Somewhere past the Louisiana-Texas border, a noisy group of teenagers woke me up, but I fell right back to sleep. When I woke up a second time, another loud bunch of kids was boardin' the train. Scotty and Bill were still sound asleep, and I was about to do the same, when I heard somebody mention *Elvis*.

"This was before televisions had found their way into every American home, before my face had become so recognizable. But transistor radios had just been invented, and every teenager on the train had one, and that's where they'd heard about us, and about that night's show. The girls in particular were workin' themselves into a frenzy—sayin' women were fainting at our gigs, that a fight had broken out at one, and that I'd soon dethrone Frank Sinatra. One girl said that night would be the greatest night of her life. Another called me the *King*.

"My head began growin' to the size of a watermelon. But deep down, I felt more like a *big* part of a *really big* hoax. It was true that larger and larger groups of excited kids had been showin' up to hear us play. But it was also true older folks had been walkin' out, several club owners had asked us to never come back, and every bigwig in the music business had turned us down before we finally got a chance to record that first 45. As I scrunched lower in my seat, I didn't feel much like a king. I felt like a poor boy from Tupelo who had to pee so bad he was about to bust.

"Fifty miles outside of Houston, an even larger group of teens boarded the train. I used the commotion to wake Bill and drag him to the restroom at the back of the car. While we peed, I filled him in on what was happenin'. He reminded me that my flirting with the girls at a recent show had almost caused a riot. We decided to grab Scotty and hide in the back car until Houston, but when we left the restroom, we discovered Scotty had other ideas.

He resembled Jesus surrounded by his disciples, and his *disciples* were hangin' on every word.

Scotty told them he was a New York reporter doin' a piece on the Blue Moon Boys and that he'd been following us throughout the South and had become good friends with all the band's members, including the lead singer. He said for a kiss, he might be able to smuggle some cute little thing backstage to meet *Elvis*. The cat was so close to jumpin' out of the bag, I could feel its claws crawlin' up my back.

While the girls smothered Scotty with kisses, Bill and I slowly backed out of the car, raced through the speeding train, and hid in the last row of the last car. We slid down low, prayin' for Houston. Scattered, cotton ball-like clouds slowly passed by the train's long windows. An occasional building flashed by. The buildings began passing more frequently while growing taller and taller until the conductor finally announced Houston. We stretched our necks to peek over the seats in front of us, jaws quickly droppin'. An excited mob of teenagers was trampling over Scotty, frantically searching through the second to the last car of the train. After strikin' out, their heads lifted and turned as one, like a hungry pack of lions havin' just spotted their prey, and I felt like a deer caught in headlights. Bill grabbed my arm. We jumped to our feet just as the hungry pack exploded through the last set of doors separating us from them. We ran out the back of the car, shocked by the noisy wind, rumbling tracks, and engine exhaust. We froze on the last step as the train slowed into the station. Excited screams followed as the door at our backs slammed open. We jumped and rolled across the hard cement.

"The train station was the size of a small football field, and packed with rushing passengers. There was no time to choose sides or examine the playing surface. No time to discuss the rules or ask if everybody wanted to play. Only time to run. We raced through the station, jumpin' over mounds of luggage and long rows of chairs before bustin' through two tall doors and slidin' to a stop in front of five lanes of stalled, bumper to bumper traffic. Tall buildings stretched toward heaven as horns blared and black clouds of smelly exhaust lifted from a line of diesel buses. Muffled screams echoed from behind the tall doors. We spotted a winding path through the stalled traffic and ran. Just as we reached the other side, the traffic light changed, the cars raced forward, and the excited mob was left trapped on the other side of the street, jumpin' up and down and tryin' desperately to see over the speeding traffic.

"We raced down the sidewalk and into a huge department store, famous for having the city's first elevators. Just as one emptied, we jumped inside and pushed the highest number. Our chests heaved as we waited nervously for the doors to slowly close. As we lifted, our backs slid down the elevator's walls until our knees were tucked beneath our chins. We looked at each other and busted out laughin'. After our laughter died, the elevator grew eerily quiet, and it was at that moment, I got this sudden flash of where I'd been, where I was at that instant, and where I was goin', and I'm tellin' ya, it was a *really* nice high. A single *ding* broke the silence, announcing our arrival at the top floor. Again, we looked at each other and busted out laughin'."

Loud applause erupted as Aron returned to his chair. "Thank ya," he replied, "thank ya very much."

"That was a pretty fair story," Brooks complimented. "Pretty fair, indeed," he repeated, slowly standing, "but if I were you, I'd stick to singing and leave the *real* storytelling to the master."

Laughter, barbs, and insults followed as Brooks walked up to the porch railing. He gazed out across their field then closed his eyes, visualizing another football field in his not too distant past.

"There was always something magical about John Carrell Field," Brooks began, "the home of the DeSoto High School Fighting Eagles. The field sat across the street from my childhood home, so I considered it an extension of my front yard, my own personal playground. As a small child, I sat atop its tall bleachers while the groundskeepers mowed, fertilized, and connected long water hoses. I sat alone for hours watching the sprinklers shoot giant sprays over its freshly-mowed grass. In early fall, my grade-school friends and I sat in awe as the high school band and drill team performed elaborate routines. Each Thursday after school, our football team's practice was moved to Carrell Field, and every kid within a five block radius ascended the bleachers to copy homework, drink sodas, and watch our team prepare for battle.

"Saturday mornings after big home games, my friends and I always awakened early and met beneath the bleachers to search for pocketknives, watches, bracelets, money, and as a last resort, three-cent pop bottles. The most exciting games produced the most lucrative hauls, so during home games, you could always find us in the stands jumping, cheering, and encouraging fan involvement in hopes of ballooning our next day's bounty.

"As we grew, we bequeathed these Saturday morning hunts to younger students and graduated to jumping off the top row of the bleachers, an important step for any boy wishing to become a man. Practice jumps were allowed off lower rows, but the actual jump had to be made from the top row and witnessed by two or more upper classmen. The ground behind the bleachers sloped, thankfully, so if you dropped and rolled just right, you could avoid serious injury. To the disturbed parents rushing their son to the hospital, the jump had only proven their child's stupidity. But to the boy sitting in the back seat with ice on his knee and a big smile on his face, the jump had proven his courage, strengthened his bond with his peers, and propelled himself one giant-step closer to manhood.

"As we entered high school, that rite of passage was also bequeathed, and we awakened one night to find ourselves members of the same Eagle Band and Football Team we had worshiped so as children. We awakened on Homecoming Day, minutes before halftime, standing at attention behind the bleachers. Paul held his trombone. Dave, his sax. And I, my trumpet. Rob was huddled midfield with the rest of our team's offense. The Eagles had won their first five games and were now playing their toughest opponent, the Lancaster Tigers. We were down by seven when the crowd erupted and the loudspeakers announced that the Eagles had just scored a possible game-tying touchdown.

Weeks, months, and it seemed, lifetimes had been spent preparing for that day. Fight songs were memorized—yells, rehearsed—speeches, written. Railroad ties were soaked in kerosene in preparation for the homecoming bonfire, where a black and gold replica of the

Lancaster Tigers' mascot would be burned in effigy. Night after night, students and teachers stuffed napkins and crepe paper into chicken wire, to the tunes of The Doors, Led Zeplin, Jethro Tull, and ZZ Top.

The day before the big game, the whole town turned out to watch our team, band, and cheerleaders lead eight floats, four convertibles used to carry our class queens, three police cars, two fire engines, and every horse in the county down DeSoto's two main streets and into Carrell Field for the homecoming pep rally. At the rally our superintendent, a former Southern Baptist preacher, informed us that because of a slew of poor officiating, dumb luck, trickery, and help from the devil, the Lancaster Tigers had amassed a win-loss record identical to our own. He said never in the history of football had a clearer choice existed between right and wrong, good and evil, victory and defeat. He ended his speech by saying that in just 24 hours we would have a clear choice between the Eagle that soared and the Tiger that crawled, and with God's help, the Eagle would surely prevail.

"The night before the game, I was so excited I couldn't sleep so I snuck over to Carrell Field, climbed atop its tall bleachers, and prayed. I prayed for a flu to spread though the Tiger's football team. I prayed for a date with the homecoming queen. I prayed for a flawless halftime performance from our band and drill team. I prayed for just one more Eagle win, and I prayed that if I had to die, my end would come sometime *after* Homecoming Day, and I wasn't alone. I could almost see the prayers rising like chimney smoke from our town's rooftops.

The big night finally arrived, and we suddenly found ourselves standing at attention behind the bleachers, minutes before our halftime performance, waiting impatiently for the Tiger Band to complete its performance and leave the field. Our green and gold uniforms were freshly dry-cleaned and pressed. Our white shoes, polished. Every horn sparkled. The day's 75° high had dropped to 50°, announcing the arrival of fall. A wisp of smoke from the concession-stand's grilled burgers and dogs floated beneath our nostrils.

Our hot-tempered band director, a former Marine Band Drum Major, had cursed and screamed through countless rehearsals until every note, step, movement, and lack of movement met with his approval. We even practiced freezing at attention behind the bleachers, eyes forward, mouths shut, waiting for the drum major's one long whistle and three shorts, our command to march in place as the first row led us single file to the field.

"Relatives, friends, neighbors, and reporters from miles around had arrived to show their support. Anyone remotely connected to the game had played their part, and now it was time for us to play ours. We were nervous, excited, and growing extremely tired of standing at attention. The Tiger Band was known for taking its sweet time leaving their opponents' fields, and they had saved their slowest exit for us. The stadium grew deathly quiet as the large crowd watched. A light breeze lifted the streamers on the green and white floats surrounding the field. Above our heads, sixty-four gold plumes gently stirred. On the outside, we were cool, calm, and collected, but on the inside, we were high-strung horses chomping at the bit, desperately wanting to snap the reins and break free.

"Our band director stood uncomfortably close to my right shoulder, wearing a freshly-pressed black suit and

Marine-approved, black-rimmed glasses. His charcoal hair was styled in a traditional, Marine-approved crew cut. A familiar scowl was permanently etched on his face, the same scowl he wore the day he made us stand attention in 100° heat until fainting bodies and expensive band instruments began bouncing off the hard ground—the same scowl he wore the day he made an example out of our first-chair trumpeter by kicking him out of the band, forever, just for talking—the same scowl he wore the day he angrily picked up one of our football team's largest defensive lineman by the face mask because he had inadvertently fallen through our ranks. With just a few choice words, our director quickly reduced the lineman to the cowardly lion shaking before the great and powerful Oz.

"At one time or another, most every member of the band had expressed a desire to shove their fists through our director's face. Stark fear, however, prevented such aggression. I closed my eyes, easily picturing small, black horns protruding from his charcoal crew cut. I slowly inhaled that familiar mixture of stale cigarette smoke and cheap cologne floating over the band, tightening its grip, daring us to move, speak, or even blink an eye. I could feel the mounting tension begging for release when Allison, our second-chair flutist, and the most angelic member of our band, accidentally blurted out, 'Please, God, kick the bastards off our field before I piss my pants.'

"Poor Allison quickly covered her mouth but way too late to stop herself from speaking out loud. Laughter was suddenly spreading through our ranks like a high-wind grass fire. I, too, wanted to burst out laughing but could feel the heat rising from the madman standing at my side. To him, contemptuous, uncontrolled laughter was spreading through his band, threatening to destroy everything he'd worked for, fought for, and stood for, and the responsibility to snuff it out was placed squarely on his shoulders, and he was more than equipped to handle the job. All he needed was one, small place to begin. He took a hard military step forward, turned, took a second step, turned, and stepped right into my face. All of a sudden, my whole world was this short-fused, hot-tempered, demon from hell—red nose inches from my forehead, noxious tobacco breath suffocating my face, black Cobra eyes peering straight into the depths of my soul.

"Every molecule in my body wanted desperately to laugh, but I knew the slightest smirk, and the volcano would explode. I'd be banished from the band on this most important day, at this most important moment, with the most important people in my life watching. My mind raced, frantically trying to think of anything but Allison's humorous remark. I recalled a game my dad used to play with me and my brothers when we were small. He'd have us close our eyes and pretend we were flying straight up then stop us at different heights and ask us to look down and describe what we saw.

"In my mind's eye, I rose 20 feet above the band and peered down at myself and my band director standing face to face and toe to toe. Suddenly, he took a quick step back and turned. His hot breath vanished, replaced by a cool breeze. He stepped, turned, and immediately stepped into the face of another unfortunate band member. I closed my eyes and rose to 40 feet, watching closely as he moved from student to student, snuffing out the grassfire. At 60 feet, the packed bleachers, football field, and homecoming floats came into view. The Tiger Band resembled a long centipede, slowly dragging its feet across the white-chalked lines of the 30, 20, and 10. As I rose to 200 feet, the whole town appeared beneath me—four churches, three gas stations, two main streets, and one high school. At 500 feet, I spotted I-35's orange-tented lights curving toward Dallas. At 1000 feet, Big D's majestic skyline shot high above the dark horizon. I rose higher still as the bright lights faded and the earth shrunk to the size of a basketball, a tennis ball, a golf ball, and a twinkling star before vanishing.

"The view from space was spectacular, but I soon felt awfully alone. I remembered the old adage, 'You can never go home again,' and soon felt awfully homesick. I recalled my earliest memories of John Carrell Field, sitting alone on the bleachers while the sprinklers sprayed giant circles over its lush green grass. I began to fall as one of the small stars below me suddenly brightened. I thought of those Saturday morning treasure hunts and fell faster as the bright star turned into a planet. I recalled my leap-of-faith jump off the top of those tall bleachers as the planet beneath me ballooned. I spotted my band and drill team standing at attention and landed hard, eyes shooting wide-open, just as the drum major's one long whistle and three shorts pierced the night. I instinctively raised my left foot and struck it against the hard earth in perfect time with the rest of my band, feeling as if I'd just proven the old adage wrong, feeling very much like I had returned home, on Homecoming Day, and never had it felt so good to be home."

Loud applause lifted to fill the eaves as Brooks returned to his seat. Tara waited for the applause to quieten before standing and walking up to the porch railing. "Those were both very good stories, gentlemen," she complimented, gazing out across the field, "and they won't be easy to beat, but beat them I will, because I've been higher than the two of you put together." She turned her back on the laughter that followed, stepped inside, and soon returned with a small decorative box, which she carefully balanced on the railing before facing her audience.

"At age ten, I became very sick with mono," Tara began. "My illness lasted three weeks but seemed like forever. During that time, my mother cared for me around the clock, assuring me that I would recover. She was even confident of the date, November 17. I'd heard a new Elvis movie was scheduled for release in mid-November and guessed that was the significance of the date."

Tara smiled at Aron. "My mother and I were big fans of yours. Although the Elvis phenomenon disrupted quite a few San Angelo homes, for our home, you were a common denominator, a strong bond that helped usher us through my turbulent teens unscarred. We took great pride in learning everything about you. Mom had even won several radio contests with her knowledge of Elvis trivia.

"On November 17, two days after our family doctor pronounced me well, I found myself dressed in my finest clothes, riding in our family car toward Austin. Mom had secretly packed our bags weeks before, so I had no idea where we were going or why. At the Austin airport she asked me to sit and count stewardesses while she checked our bags. We were soon sitting in the First Class section of a jet destined for Dallas. Mom informed me Coach had been overbooked, so the nice agent had upgraded us to First. I had never stepped foot on a plane, so sitting

anywhere was exciting for me. My first takeoff was thrill-
ing, but when the captain forecasted forty degrees, high
winds, and rain in Dallas, I became quite anxious. Mom
was also a little nervous but hid it well and assured me
everything would be fine.

"The landing at Love Field was quite scary, but seem-
ingly routine for the other passengers. Inside the terminal,
Mom had me sit in front of a huge, plate-glass window
while she checked on something. Outside the window,
tons of gray metal stretched over an ocean of wet cement.
Everything was so cold, hard, and man-made—and at
that moment, awfully chaotic. Like pirañas at feeding
time, tractors raced in every direction, pulling long strings
of carts through curtains of rain. Drenched workers con-
verged on every arrival, furiously stripping the planes of
their cargo. Pushback tractors lumbered like big turtles,
pushing and pulling large aircraft with huge, whalelike
tail fins. The biggest whale of all, a 707, suddenly burst
through the low ceiling, leaned slightly, and floated toward the runway. Four gill-like engines hung beneath its
long, finlike wings. It glided gracefully then struck hard
sending giant sprays of water shooting high.

"My mom returned and led me through the crowded
terminal. I occasionally glanced back at the 707 as it zigzagged through a maze of lighted taxiways and onto the
puddled tarmac, following us on our journey to the end
of the terminal. The gate area was filled with friends and
relatives eagerly awaiting the arrival of their loved ones.
Mom suggested we sit and watch the passengers deplane.
Two gentlemen stood and insisted we take their seats.

A long line of passengers descended a canopied staircase then scurried through the rain to a metal awning

leading to the terminal. I focused on the first two passengers to enter the gate area, a young couple wearing brown sandals, white shorts, colorfully-flowered shirts, and dark tans. The lady wore a lei of pink and white orchids. The gentleman, a floppy straw hat. The green spiny leaves of two pineapples jutted from a white box in one of the gentleman's hands. Excited greetings and warm embraces welcomed the couple home.

A hundred passengers followed, all carrying colorful bags filled with Kona coffee, macadamia nuts, and brightly-polished island treasures. Straw mats, tightly-rolled and lightly-salted, poked from their carry-on bags. I could almost smell the ocean on their bodies, see the sunsets in their eyes. All the passengers wore big smiles. I glanced out at the cold, colorless, tarmac, wondering what it might feel like to be lying on a warm, straw mat—on a white, sandy beach—in the middle of the Pacific Ocean.

"Mom pointed toward the last two passengers, a woman and a little girl, and said, 'That'll be *us* in nine days.' I gave her a puzzled look. She explained her comment by saying, 'You know, Tara, you and I are really very fortunate. I realize it doesn't always seem like it, like last month when our doctor called and told us you'd tested positive for mono. But before I could even hang up the phone, a disc jockey announced that his radio station would now be giving away a nine-day, all expenses paid, First Class trip for two to Honolulu, Hawaii to the first caller who could name Elvis Presley's childhood idol, the comic-book hero who could access his superpowers by invoking his father's name. With the phone still in hand, I quickly dialed the station and shouted out the correct answer, Captain Marvel, Jr.'

"My heart leaped as Mom began pulling out hotel brochures, maps, and the most breathtaking pictures of the Hawaiian Islands, all of which fell to the floor as we jumped up and down with excitement. Not until we boarded the plane, did I truly believe we were flying to Hawaii.

"A beautiful, blonde stewardess resembling the good witch Glenda in *The Wizard of Oz* glanced at our boarding passes before ushering us to our seats. The other First Class passengers politely smiled and nodded as we passed. A nice couple helped us store our carry-on bags in the overhead. Everyone was so well-dressed and well-mannered. I gathered we were sitting with America's most rich, most powerful, and most famous. Shortly before the doors closed, four last minute passengers rushed on board to fill the last vacant seats in the front row of First Class.

"During the flight, *Glenda* treated us like royalty, serving Mom champagne, and me, this strange tropical juice mixed with coconut milk. Our drinks were followed by a scrumptious array of island delicacies. Mom and I kept looking at each other and laughing. Glenda asked if that was our first trip to The Islands. Mom told her the closest we'd been to *The Islands* was at the movie theater watching Elvis Presley's *Blue Hawaii*—but that we had, in fact, seen the movie ten times. Glenda laughed and asked if we were Elvis fans. I told her we were Elvis' biggest fans. Mom joked, saying perhaps we'd run into him during our visit to the Islands. Again, Glenda laughed. She then gave us the most angelic smile and said the strangest thing. She said, 'Perhaps you'll run into him a little sooner than that.'

"Glenda excused herself, turned, and as if riding inside a large, crystal bubble, floated toward the front of the plane. She leaned over and said something to a tall, dark-haired gentleman sitting in the front row. We watched as the handsome gentleman unbuckled his seat belt and stood. We stared in shock as Elvis Aron Presley followed her to our seats."

Tara took a deep breath, staring into Aron's eyes. "Glenda introduced us as your biggest fans and mentioned we were on our first trip to Hawaii. You politely shook my hand, then my mother's, and said we were in for a real blast. My whole body shook with each pounding beat of my heart. I was speechless. My mom, was also speechless, but that didn't stop her from blurting out the first thing that came to her mind, 'Small world isn't it, Elvis?' The matter-of-fact way in which she said it caught everyone off guard, and we burst out laughing.

"Glenda asked you if you would mind giving us your autograph. As you looked around for something to write on, she reached into her apron and removed a clean, white-linen napkin and placed it across my armrest. You knelt on one knee, looked into my eyes, and grinned. You wrote . . ."

"I wrote," Aron interrupted, "To Tara and Sara, my two biggest fans. May your first trip to Hawaii be filled with laughter. Love, Elvis."

Tara turned toward the porch railing and opened the decorative box. She delicately removed and unfolded the napkin then placed it across his lap. "Small world, isn't it, Aron?"

Chapter Eight

June's sweltering, 100° heat was especially torturous for the Hill Country's shade-tree mechanics. Paul squeezed his sweaty body between the dirt driveway and his Malibu's hot transmission, trying for the umpteenth time to tighten an almost impossible to reach bolt. The wrench slipped, and his knuckles crashed across the hot exhaust manifold, proving to be the last straw. He cursed loudly and struck the manifold with the wrench before turning it on the transmission.

"What's the problem?" Aron asked from the front porch.

"This stupid car's the problem!" Paul replied, crawling out from beneath the vehicle. "And I'm gettin' rid of it! Now!"

"What'll you use for transportation?"

"I'll walk!" Paul answered, stomping up the porch steps.

The slamming bathroom door echoed through the house as Tara stepped onto the porch. "What was that all about?" she asked.

"Car problems," Aron replied.

"I should have guessed," Tara said. "Working on cars never puts him in the best mood."

"No, and lately he seems to be takin' over the door slammin' where I left off."

"Yes, he does," Tara agreed.

After a quick shower, Paul dressed then located his car's title. The smell of antiseptic followed him onto the porch. "Tara, do you have time to follow me into town? I'm gettin' rid of my car."

"I have plenty of time," Tara replied, "and it's a lovely day for a drive."

"Mind if I tag along?" Aron asked.

"Not at all," Paul answered, "you can drive. If I get behind the wheel, I'll be too tempted to run the stupid thing into the lake."

"Where are we taking it?" Tara asked.

"There's a half dozen used car lots on Lamar. I'll take the first offer."

"Give me a second to change," Tara said, stepping inside.

Aron drove Paul's car around Lake Travis and over the Mansfield Dam while Paul road shotgun and Tara followed in her car. Paul propped his foot on the dashboard, glaring at his car's hood.

"It handles well," Aron mentioned, steering it around a tight curve.

"Yeah, right," Paul replied.

"How long have you had it?"

"Seven years."

"That's a lot of history. I bet you've got some good memories stored up in here."

"The bad ones outweigh the good."

Aron smiled. "It got ya to Memphis and back."

"Yeah, and almost gave me a heart attack when it wouldn't start in front of Graceland."

During the silence that followed, Aron noticed Paul's injured knuckles. "Ya know, you and I have a lot of history, too, don't we?"

"Can we talk about something else?"

"Sure, what would ya like to talk about?"

A chilly silence filled the car.

Paul directed Aron to Lamar Boulevard, where they pulled into Mike's Used Cars. Two rows of cars with prices painted on their front windshields sat in front of a small office and a two-stall garage. Most of the cars were priced between $499.00 to $799.00. One with *AIR CONDI-TIONED* underlined twice read $899.00. Paul wondered how much to ask for his Malibu.

A red '57 Bel Air convertible parked next to the office caught Tara's eye. Aron climbed out and opened Tara's door.

"Thanks, Curly," Tara said.

Aron shook his head in mock disgust. "Who gave me that name, anyway?"

Tara shrugged.

Curly no longer looked much like Curly, which made the nickname funnier still. He had lost 60 pounds since Memphis, his face had thinned, and his body was as tanned as Paul and Tara's. His brown hair had grown an inch since his buzz cut and had grayed at the temples. He kept it combed straight back, beneath his ever-present UT baseball cap and dark glasses.

Mike, the owner, stepped out into the shimmering heat to greet his customers. Mike was twenty-nine, lanky, with straight, black hair parted to one side. He wore a Texas Rangers cap, white T-shirt, and faded blue jeans.

"Howdy. I'm Mike."

"Hi, I'm Paul, and these are my friends, Tara and Aron."

As everyone shook hands, a little boy wearing blue jean overalls, without a shirt, stepped out of the office, closed the door, and walked over to stand beside his dad. He had sandy-brown hair and a slingshot poking out of his back pocket—Opie on The Andy Griffith Show.

"This here's Bobby," Mike introduced.

"Hi, Bobby," Tara said, smiling broadly.

"Hi," the little boy replied, smiling back.

"Lookin' for a car?" Mike asked.

"No, lookin' to sell one," Paul answered, motioning toward his car. He noticed a thin trail of bloodlike transmission fluid stretching from behind his car and suppressed an urge to laugh. "The transmission needs a little work, but the engine's in pretty good shape. So's the body and interior."

Mike had two other cars waiting for parts, but for the right price, he would consider almost anything. "Mind if I take a look?"

"Please do," Paul answered, opening the driver's door and pulling on the hood latch. "It's got a new water pump, radiator, and battery, but I drew the line at the transmission."

"Mind startin' her up?" Mike asked.

Paul sat behind the wheel, instantly recalling that uncomfortable moment at Graceland when the car refused to start. He closed his eyes. Please, God, I know this'd be the perfect time for one of your jokes, but I really need to unload this car. He held his breath, turned the key, and smiled broadly as the engine started. The two men stood in front of the car, watching and listening.

Mike knelt and watched the slow drip of transmission fluid before closing the hood and sitting behind the wheel. He checked to make sure Bobby was well out of the way before driving in reverse a few feet. He then drove forward a few feet, put the car in park, and turned off the engine. He studied the interior before climbing out and giving the car a slow walk-around. "How much you askin'?"

Paul glanced at the other cars and grinned. "Well, it's probably only worth about $399.00, but I'm askin' $499.00 because it was once driven by Elvis Presley."

Everyone laughed but Bobby, who stared wide-eyed at the car.

"Anyone else famous drive it?" Mike joked.

"No, just Elvis," Paul replied.

Mike smiled, shook his head, and chuckled. "Well, $499.00 is kind of high, and I'll need to take a closer look at that transmission."

As Mike looked toward his two cars waiting for parts, Aron casually strolled over to Paul's car and sat on the hood. He removed his cap and sunglasses then combed back his hair with his fingers. He closed his eyes, searching for the right song, then grinned. He took a deep breath before beginning an impromptu performance of "Can't Help Falling in Love."

Mike stared, hypnotized. Bobby slowly reached up and grasped his father's hand. Instantly, everything within an earshot of Aron's rich voice began increasing in value. The office, the garage, and the '57 Chevy suddenly glowed.

The little boy and father holding hands were now radiant. Paul and Tara's faces beamed. Even the used cars began to glisten as the shimmering numbers on their windshields scrolled upward. As the last verse of the popular love song faded, the Kings' audience stood motionless, fearing the slightest movement might somehow burst the euphoric bubble enveloping the car lot. Aron put on his cap and sunglasses, stood, and rejoined his friends.

"I'll take it," Mike said.

Everyone laughed.

"Do—you—have the title?" Mike asked, unable to take his eyes off Aron.

"Sure do," Paul answered, pulling it from his shirt pocket and handing it to Mike.

"Four—ninety—nine?" Mike asked.

"Four ninety-nine," Paul agreed.

Mike slowly released Bobby's hand. "I'll be right back, Bobby," he said, patting his son on the head. Bobby watched as his dad walked toward the office.

"Hey, Bobby, you want to help me clean out my car?" Paul asked. "You can keep all the money you find."

"Sure!" Bobby shouted, running toward the car.

Tara studied her own car. "Hey, Aron, would you mind driving my car on the way back to the Vineyard?"

"Not at all," Aron laughed.

As Tara and Aron walked over to inspect the red '57 convertible, Paul opened his car's doors, trunk, and glove compartment. He found two paper bags and began filling one with old newspapers, receipts, and soda cans, and the other with maps, sunglasses, and other personal items.

"Yahoo!" Bobby yelled holding up a quarter.

Paul grinned then nonchalantly tucked a dollar bill halfway into the back seat. While removing trash from beneath the seats, his mind floated back seven years to that glorious moment he first laid eyes on the car. He smiled broadly, recalling all the lawns he had mowed for the $300.00 down payment. He remembered excitedly driving it home from the dealership and washing and waxing every inch of it before taking it on that first date. He recalled the thrilling moment his Malibu beat Jim Thompson's '66 Mustang in the quarter mile, with half the high school watching. And it was in that car's very back seat, he'd first gone *all the way*.

Paul chuckled. The joke was on him. There were, in fact, a lot of good memories stored up in that car, and like the other cars in the lot, his had also increased in value. He began having second thoughts about selling it until he again focused on the thin trail of transmission fluid stretching toward the road. No, he thought, eyes dropping to his injured knuckles, it's definitely time to let go of this one.

"What's this!" Bobby yelled, holding up a wrapped prophylactic. Tara and Aron stared at Bobby's hand then burst out laughing.

"You'll find out soon enough, Bobby," Paul answered, snatching the rubber and stuffing it into his back pocket. Bobby ran back to the car, spotted the dollar bill sticking out of the back seat, and screamed with glee. As Paul kneeled to remove the license plates, he closed his eyes and thanked his car for all the times, good and bad.

Mike stepped out of his office, check in hand. Bobby ran to show his dad his find. Paul signed over the title and handed Mike the keys before taking the check.

"Paul, ya ever ride in a convertible?" Aron asked.

Paul thought for a minute. "No. But I've ridden in the back of a pickup, if that counts."

"No," Aron replied, "that does *not* count."

"Can we test drive this '57?" Aron asked Mike.

"It's not for sale," Mike answered, a sudden grin brightening his face. "But you're welcome to drive it," he added, quickly pulling out his keys and handing them to Aron.

"Thanks," Aron said, opening the passenger door and politely stepping back for Tara and Paul to enter first.

Tara took a step forward then stopped. "Hey, Bobby, how would you and your dad like to go for a little ride?"

Bobby looked at his father, eyes big as quarters.

"Sure!" Mike said.

Bobby leaped into the front seat.

"Shotgun!" Tara shouted, jumping up front and nudging the little boy over as he giggled.

"I'll be right back," Mike said, running into his office to hang a "Gone Fishing" sign on the front door.

When Mike returned, Bobby was jumping up and down on the front seat, much to the adults' amusement. Mike jumped in the back seat and handed Tara two cassettes tapes labeled *ELVIS*. "Bobby," he said, looking hard at his son. Bobby stopped jumping and turned to face his dad. Mike placed his hands on the little boy's shoulders. "Bobby, I want you to listen to me real good now, you hear?" The boy nodded seriously. Mike motioned with his chin. "That gentleman right there is Elvis Presley. Do you understand? Elvis Aron Presley."

"Ain't nuttin' but a hound doggy!" Bobby shouted, as everyone laughed.

"Right," his father replied. "That's the one."

Aron turned in his seat to shake Bobby's hand. "Hi, Bobby, it's a pleasure to meet you."

"Hi, Elvis!" Bobby said, excitement pouring from his voice.

"And just where would you kids like to go?" Aron asked.

"To the bank before Mike changes his mind," Paul answered, pulling the check out of his shirt pocket.

"After the bank, let's drive to campus," Tara suggested. "Then up and down The Drag (Guadalupe Street) a few times. Then down town."

"How about Barton Springs and Town Lake?" Paul suggested.

"I bet the Hill Country's pretty today," Mike commented.

"Mt. Bonnell!" Bobby shouted.

Aron turned the key to *ACC* and watched as the fuel gauge swung to *Full*. He started the car, smiling broadly at the engine's low rumble, then put the gear shift into *Drive*. Tara pushed in the first cassette, and seconds later everyone was singing "His Latest Flame."

After the bank, they toured the UT campus, taking in Dobie Hall, the Tower, and Memorial Stadium, singing all the way. They next circled the State Capitol then crisscrossed downtown before following Town Lake on their way to 2222, one of the more curved routes out of Austin. During the drive, they stopped once to climb Mt. Bonnell, once for cheeseburgers and sodas, once for snow cones, and four times to use the restroom. After every stop, Bobby insisted on sitting someplace different, forcing the others to change positions, too.

Aron, however, usually sat behind the wheel. He drove his passengers high, he drove them low, and he drove them through countless sharp turns and gentle bends. And his passengers leaned way left, and they leaned way right, and they leaned into each others shoulders. And the wind blew their hair and the sun baked their skin and the music rarely stopped. At dusk Aron returned the red convertible, along with its exhausted passengers, to Mike's Used Cars—fuel gauge resting on empty.

"I'll take it," Aron joked, as the others laughed.

Bobby awakened from a short nap, lifted his head off Tara's lap, and looked around. He stared up at Aron, suddenly wide awake. "Thanks Elvis!" he said, smiling broadly.

"Yeah, thanks," the others echoed.

"The pleasure was all mine," Aron replied.

Everyone climbed out of the car and stood in a circle in the center of the lot, occasionally looking back at the convertible and smiling. As Aron handed Mike the keys, Bobby's ever-present smile turned upside down. Aron patted his near-empty pockets, looking for something to give Bobby. He pulled out a blue guitar pick, bent down, and handed it to the little boy.

"Thanks, Elvis!" Bobby said, giving Aron a big hug.

"You're welcome, Bobby," Aron laughed, returning the hug. "You're surely welcome."

Chapter Nine

"This is stupid," Tara said. "Really stupid."

"I have to agree," Aron said. "I'm a little old for this sort of thing."

"You two are surely making a big deal out of nothing," Brooks replied.

"Nothing!" Tara replied. "You want us to celebrate the 201 anniversary of our nation's birth by shooting each other with fireworks until someone gets maimed, blinded, or killed?"

"I think she's got the picture, boys," Dave said, rubbing his hands together.

"Tara, it's a Musketeer tradition," Paul replied.

"What's wrong with a picnic?" Tara asked.

"A picnic!" Rob echoed. "I want to shoot someone's butt off!"

"Well, it won't be mine," Tara said.

"Mine either," Aron agreed.

"Rob, I'll handle this," Paul said. "Guys, we've been celebrating the Fourth this way for nine years. It wouldn't be the Fourth without a bottle rocket fight, and it wouldn't be the same without everyone taking part, and, well . . ." He reached up and scratched the small scar on his cheek.

"Oh, please," Tara said, "haven't you got enough milage out of that little scratch."

Paul looked at Aron.

"Sorry, Paul," Aron laughed, "I'm afraid the milage just ran out."

"Way to go, Paul," Brooks scoffed, shaking his head. "Let me handle this." He studied Tara thoughtfully. "Tara, we may need a nurse."

"Ha! You may need a psychiatrist, too, but it won't be me."

"Nice job, Brooks," Dave said. "Let me handle this." He first stared at Tara, then Aron. "Look, guys, in nine years we've never had a serious injury." He reached down and scratched a sudden itch on his scarred knee.

Tara glanced at the scar then looked Dave in the eye.

"Well, almost never," Dave admitted.

"That's it," Tara said. "No way. Not even to pick up the pieces."

"Way to go, Dave," Brooks said. He left the living room then returned with three large sacks filled with fireworks, kneepads, elbowpads, sunglasses, squirt bottles, and lighters. As he emptied the sacks on top of the coffee table, the more excited rockets scurried to the floor. "We purchase the ammo a year in advance, just after the Fourth, when the prices have been slashed. We didn't just fall off the turnip truck here."

"No, you were probably pushed off," Tara said.

"You think ya got enough?" Aron asked, staring at the mound of fireworks.

"The best defense is a good offense," Rob said.

Brooks stood the squirt bottles in a neat row. "We use these to wet down our shirt sleeves. You don't want your clothes catching fire."

Paul picked up a pair of mirrored sunglasses. "We started using these a few years back to protect our eyes. They're rose-tinted—turn everything a cool pink—perfect for night vision. Try these out, Tara."

Tara hesitated then put on the glasses, half-smiling as the room turned pink.

"Where do these fights take place?" Aron asked.

"Different places," Brooks answered, "but always outside the city limits, outside the local cops' jurisdiction."

"How many arrests? Tara asked.

"No arrests or convictions at this time," Paul answered.

"Aron, try these kneepads on," Rob suggested. "You want them to be tight enough to stay in place when you're running, but not tight enough to restrict mobility. They should be comfortable."

"I see. You want my knees to be comfortable while I'm running from the Roman candle you're trying to shoot up my . . ."

"We get the picture," Tara interrupted.

"Sorry," Aron apologized.

"Quite all right," Tara replied.

"That's right," Rob answered, "you want 'em to be tight, but comfortable."

Dave scanned the coffee table. "Sunglasses, kneepads, squirt bottles—our fights have really evolved over the years."

"I wish your brains had evolved," Tara joked. "Perhaps if you put them together now, you can come up with a better way to celebrate the Fourth."

"What could be better than a bottle rocket fight?" Rob asked.

Tara shook her head, stood, and walked up to a window.

Aron stretched his sore back muscles. "I'm afraid someone else is gonna have to take over the weed pullin'."

"Okay," Rob said, "if that's y'alls final answer, we'll just have to throw the party without you."

"Four instead of six," Brooks lamented, shaking his head.

"Celebrating Independence Day without Tara and Aron," Dave said, with a sigh. "Why don't y'all move to Russia? Or China?"

"Why don't you grow up?" Tara asked. "You'll be a physician some day, probably treating fireworks' victims."

"We could call the whole thing off," Paul suggested, trying another angle. "That might make 'em happy."

"Now you're coming to your senses," Tara replied.

"I guess we *could* cancel it," Rob said. "I mean, it'd only be *fun*, and who'd want to be a part of *that*?"

Brooks stared at Paul and Rob. "You'd seriously cancel our *Tenth* Annual Bottle Rocket fight, just because these old geezers don't want to play?"

"Maybe they're right," Dave said. "Maybe it's time we grew up."

"Right," Brooks scoffed, "and even though they've given us some of the most memorable moments of our lives, maybe it's time to give them up."

Tara shook her head then looked at Aron. "I feel like we're talking to Peter Pan's Lost Boys." She scanned the others. "You know, growing up *might* be a good thing. It hasn't hurt me or Aron."

They studied Tara and Aron, unconvinced.

"Okay," Paul said, "in the interest of all for one, and one for all, I make a motion we cancel the Musketeers' Tenth Annual Bottle Rocket Fight, for something more—adultlike. Do I hear a second?" Heads dropped.

"I'll second the motion," Tara answered.

"All in favor?" Paul asked.

"Aye," Tara and Aron replied.

"All opposed?" Paul asked. Silence filled the room.

"The ayes have it," Paul announced. "I hereby proclaim The Tenth Annual Bottle Rocket Fight—canceled."

"There, that wasn't so bad, now was it?" Tara asked. "Shall we begin planning the picnic."

"I'm not hungry," Rob said.

"Me, either," Brooks agreed.

"You'll get your appetites back soon enough," Tara replied. "Who wants to make the potato salad?" she asked, picking up a pen and notepad.

No one answered.

"Unbelievable," Rob said, stepping up to the window. "Millions of courageous patriots will be reenacting our great country's fight for freedom by chasing each other with Roman candles and bottle rockets while we're sittin' on an old blanket eatin' cold potato salad with the ants and the flies."

"Does everyone like deviled eggs?" Tara asked, as she began her shopping list.

"What do we do with these?" Brooks asked, kneeling to return the fireworks to their sacks.

"Maybe there's a poor family out there somewhere," Dave suggested.

"How touching," Tara laughed. "A poor family in need of a couple thousand bottle rockets."

"Maybe they'll give some nice family the same joy they've given us over the years," Brooks commented.

"The same joy they would have given us *this* year if we hadn't canceled," Rob grumbled.

"May I suggest a meatless picnic?" Tara asked.

Aron picked up a Roman candle and balanced it at his hip like a six-shooter. "How far do these things shoot, anyway?"

"About fifty feet," Rob answered, "but every now and then, you'll get a dud or weak sister."

"Hey, Duds and Weak Sisters sounds like a good name for a rock band," Brooks mused, making a note.

"Boy, I'd surely hate to go into a fire fight with duds and weak sisters," Aron mentioned.

"That's why you keep two or more lit at the same time," Rob suggested. "I usually light four and hold 'em like double-barreled shotguns."

Aron picked up four candles, two in each hand, grinning broadly. He set them down and picked up a gross of bottle rockets. "What about these?"

"These are what separates the men from the boys," Rob answered. "Any rookie can hit the broad side of a barn with a Roman candle, but it takes a real marksman to hit a moving target with a bottle rocket."

"Do ya use bottles?" Aron asked.

"Glass isn't permitted," Brooks answered. "Too dangerous."

"You just pitch 'em," Dave said. "It's all in the timing. After a while, you sort of develop a sixth sense about when the rocket's about to take off. Right before it lifts, you toss it in the general direction of the enemy."

Paul picked up a rocket. "Toss it too early, and it falls to the ground, or worse, turns back on you. Hold it too long, and you'll burn your hand off."

Aron pulled a rocket from the gross and balanced it in his hand before turning it toward Paul.

"No shooting rockets within twenty feet of the enemy," Brooks added. "Thirty feet for Roman candles."

"The fights have really become quite civilized," Dave mentioned, glancing at Tara.

"Mind if I practice with a few of these?" Aron asked, pulling a dozen rockets from the gross.

"Practice for what!" Tara asked. "The fight's been canceled."

"Can't it be uncanceled?" Aron asked, rubbing his itchy thumb across the top of a lighter.

"No, it can't be uncanceled! *Uncanceled*'s not even a word!"

"*Reinstated*'s a word," Brooks commented.

"*Reinstated*'s a great word," Rob agreed.

"You—juvenile delinquents!" Tara said. She faced Aron. "And *you're* a Benedict Arnold."

Aron stretched his arms high over his head. "I think my back's startin' to loosen up a little."

The men stared at Tara hopefully. Paul nonchalantly scratched the scar on his cheek.

"Oh, all right," Tara said, throwing up her hands. "I'd hate to rob you boys of an opportunity to kill yourselves."

"Yahoo!" Brooks yelled.

"You won't be sorry," Dave said.

"I'm already sorry," Tara replied.

Paul gave Tara a big hug. "I make a motion we give Tara an extra dozen bottle rockets. All in favor?"

"Aye," everyone but Aron replied.

"What's *your* problem?" Tara asked, glaring at Aron.

"*I'm* not gettin' an extra dozen," Aron replied.

"I'll give you an extra dozen right now," Tara said, grabbing the lighter and rockets from Aron's hands.

Brooks snatched the lighter from Tara's hand. "Sorry, no practicing before the Fourth."

"Okay, let's get down to business," Paul suggested. "Mr. Brooks, have you located a suitable site?"

"Two possibilities, but I'm not happy with either one. I'll look again after we're done here."

"Rob, do we have enough ammo for six?" Paul asked.

"No way. We'll need twice this. And more kneepads and elbowpads. Try these mediums on, Tara. I might need to get you some smalls."

Tara reluctantly strapped on the kneepads while Paul and Rob helped her with the elbowpads.

"Don't forget, we ran out of punks and lighters last year," Dave reminded.

"I'll get the warm beer," Paul said. "One can each," he added for Tara and Aron's benefit. "Another Musketeer tradition. Okay, what's next?" No one answered.

"I'm going site hunting," Brooks said, standing.

"I'll go with you," Rob offered.

"No, you won't," Brooks replied.

Rob's eyes fell to the floor.

"You don't want Rob's company?" Aron asked.

"The night before rocket fight Six, an errant Musketeer snuck out to the site and stashed a rather large supply of extra ammunition for himself," Brooks explained.

"There were no private-stash rules at the time," Rob defended.

"Well, we have them now, and to remove any temptation, I'll be keeping the location a secret."

On the night of the Fourth, just as Austin's bright bursts, loud booms, and shrill whistles began to fade, Brooks drove his friends out Mopac, an under-construction freeway that cut through west Austin. After passing several *ALL LANES EXIT RIGHT* signs, he slowly squeezed his car between two *DANGER! END OF HIGHWAY!* signs before turning off his headlights.

"Where are you taking us?" Tara asked.

"You'll see," Brooks answered, "and rest assured, Ares himself could not have come up with a better site for battle."

As the pavement ended, the car dropped onto a long stretch of crushed white rock, which led to the battle site, a massive, under-construction cloverleaf intersection. As they neared the site, sixty tall, Stonehengelike columns slowly ascended from the flat earth, some stretching 200 feet high. These columns would one day support the intersection's curved ramps and overpasses, but at that moment, their only purpose was to provide cover. Big Caterpillar tractors, cement trucks, and dinosaurlike cranes lurked between the columns, eagerly awaiting their chance to join in the battle. A large, brush-covered hill rose from behind the columns. The white earth glowed from the cool, artificial moonlight emitting from four tall moon towers. Everyone smiled.

Brooks stopped his car a safe distance from the center of the site and turned off his engine. As their heavy boots crunched into the loose rock, their smiles broadened. As they hiked, they slowly turned, soaking it all in. Aron and Tara had already armored themselves with kneepads, elbowpads, caps, and sunglasses, and everyone carried heavy backpacks filled with explosives. They resembled a small band of futuristic warriors having just landed on some distant planet—easy to spot when moving across the white surface, but completely vanishing when freezing inside the columns' long shadows.

The warriors dropped their packs and branched off in six directions to scope the place out. Hands moistened, arms tingled, and pulses quickened as they searched for the best places to hide, launch attacks, and suck the enemy into an ambush. Faces glowed as they returned to the center of the intersection.

"Brooks, you're a master," Dave complimented.

"You really outdid yourself, Brooksie," Paul agreed, patting his friend on the back.

"There's a million places to hide," Tara added.

"Hollywood couldn't have come up with a better site for battle," Aron remarked.

"*This*, my friends, will be the mother of all battles," Rob announced.

The battle site was rough and dangerous. The night, hot and muggy. Ground fog crawling in from the surrounding fields had begun to make visibility less than ideal. But to a man and woman, everyone agreed the conditions for battle were perfect, perhaps a little too perfect because a skirmish soon broke out over the boundaries, rules, size of the teams, and everything else under the moon towers until Rob had heard enough. "Would everyone just please shut up a minute while I try and sort this mess out!" he shouted. He shook his head in disgust as the commotion reluctantly died. "Okay, first we discussed two teams of three each, but Dave insisted on something more original. Then we discussed three teams of two each and spent fifteen minutes arguing over who'd side with who. It seems our more timid fighters were squeamish about shootin' at poor little Tara, but took particular delight in the prospect of shootin' at my big butt."

"That's exactly why I didn't want you beside me," Dave chuckled. "Your big butt tends to draw enemy fire."

"Not to mention, flies," Brooks added.

Rob glared at Dave before turning his attention to Brooks. "Then, Mr. Brooks came up with the brilliant idea that we have two teams with one spy and one king on each team, the identity of which would be unknown to the opposing team. We'd then use our explosives and whatever other means necessary to capture the other team's members, one by one, and take them to a designated area where they'd have to declare whether or not they were their team's king or spy. Capture a king, you win. Capture a spy, you lose. And that's when we all agreed Brooks should keep his big mouth shut during all further discussions."

"It was a brilliant idea," Brooks defended, "just a little too complex for this group of morons."

"Then I suggested we spread out in six different directions," Rob continued, left hand sliding into his back pocket. "See who sides with who. A sort of natural selection. Darwin would've been proud. But *Darwin's*, y'all ain't." Rob lifted his backpack over his shoulder. "So this is what I say," he concluded, thumb rubbing the top of his lighter. "I say it's every man—or woman—for him or herself, and may the best man—or woman—win, as long as it ain't you, or you, or you, or . . ."

With each *you*, Rob took a step backwards. Suddenly, bright Roman candle bursts began exploding from his fists as his friends ran for cover.

"Foul!" Brooks yelled, as a blue burst just missed his head. "We haven't proclaimed the beginning of the fight!"

"I hereby proclaim The Tenth Annual Rocket Fight begun!" Rob laughed.

"Ahhh!," Dave screamed, as a red burst caught him in the derriere.

"Yahoo!" Rob roared. "Whose butt's drawing fire now, Dave?"

A bright yellow burst exploded at Brooks' feet, spurring him to jump and dance as he ran.

"Hey, nice two-steppin', Brooksie!" Rob laughed. "If all that writin' doesn't pan out, maybe you can get a job dancin' at the Rose?" Rob pitched his spent candles and began lobbing smoke bombs around his perimeter. "Hey, where'd everybody go!" he taunted. "The war's this way!"

Paul quickly pulled out four candles and a lighter then peeked around the corner of the tall column pressed against his chest. Rob resembled John Wayne ascending from a three-foot layer of blue and gray ground smoke.

Paul quickly lit the candles and aimed them at the Duke's chest.

"Was it somethin' I said?" Rob taunted, running from the sudden barrage of candle bursts.

Paul dropped his spent candles and raced for higher ground. Halfway up the hill, the familiar swoosh of the night's first bottle rocket gave him pause. He turned to watch as bright orange flares floated across the battlefield, each swoosh followed by a loud pop. The sound of laughter and smell of burnt gunpowder followed him up the hill. At the top, he lay on his stomach to catch his breath and to watch the battle below. The sound of two intruders slowly following his path up the hill interrupted his break. He quietly removed two candles and flicked his lighter as the trespassers approached. "Freeze."

Tara and Dave jumped. Dave lost his footing and fell to his stomach. "Truce," he said, sucking in air.

"Truce," Tara echoed, dropping her heavy pack and collapsing between the two men.

"Y'all don't seem to be in the best of shape," Paul joked, lowering his candles. "You should try a little more jogging."

Tara gasped for air. "You—should try—not scaring us to death."

All three crawled on their stomachs to peek over the top of the hill—Indians peering into a deep canyon.

After catching her breath, Tara burst out laughing. "Oh, man, did you see Brooks? He looked like a square dancer caught stepping a little too close to the camp fire."

"I saw," Paul said.

"And *you*, Dave," Tara continued. "I bet your posterior's wearing a big tattoo right about now. I've got some antiseptic in my backpack."

Dave gave Tara a cross look. "Thank you, but that won't be necessary."

A stray bottle rocket flew up the side of the hill, causing Tara to duck.

"Rookie," Dave scoffed, shaking his head. "We're a hundred feet out of range."

"Look!" Tara said, excitedly pointing. "Is that Rob with his back to us, crunched behind that cement truck? He's a sittin' duck. We could hit him from three sides. I'd like to see the *big jock* doing a two-step." She frantically searched for her lighter, in vain, then dumped the entire contents of her pack all over the ground.

"Would you calm down?" Dave asked, as both men burst out laughing. "We've created a monster."

"I suggest we keep her on our side," Paul replied.

"I suggest we keep her way out in front of us," Dave joked.

"How about a decoy?" Tara asked, snatching up her lighter. "One of us can direct his attention forward while the other two attack from behind."

"Fine by me," Dave answered, "but can we take a break first?"

"A little more plannin' wouldn't hurt, either," Paul suggested.

"And while we're up here planning, our enemy's down there burning up their ammunition," Dave added.

"On each other," Paul chuckled.

"I like the way you men think," Tara complimented, quickly arranging her ammo in a neat row before plopping down between the men. They watched in silence as colorful flares and insults flew back and forth across the battlefield. Dave reached into his pack, causing Tara to jump.

"Relax," Dave said, popping the top of a freshly shaken beer.

"Dave!" Paul and Tara shouted, as the warm malty foam dripped from their faces.

"Shhh! You want to give away our position?"

"You want to point that thing some other direction next time?" Tara asked, wiping her face with her shirtsleeve.

"Give me that," Paul said, snatching the beer from Dave and turning it up.

"Give me that," Tara said snatching it from Paul to finish it off.

Dave turned the can upside down and watched as the last drop of foam fell to the ground. "Thanks, a lot," he grumbled.

"Shhh," Tara whispered, as a faint trickling sound rose from the battlefield.

"Sounds like someone's relieving themselves," Dave commented.

"I think it's coming from behind that yellow tractor," Paul said.

"That's where Brooks was hiding," Tara said.

"He's marking his territory," Dave joked.

"Oh, man," Tara laughed, "what I'd give to be down there with a lit Roman candle right now."

"Someone's beating you to the punch," Dave said, as Aron and Rob joined forces to launch a frontal attack on Brooks' position.

Bright bursts exploded against the tractor as Brooks zipped up his pants, grabbed his backpack, and ran. A direct hit lit up his back as he cursed and screamed.

"Nice shootin', Aron!" Rob complimented.

"Thanks, not bad yourself," Aron replied.

"I demand a rule prohibiting shooting during pee breaks!" Brooks yelled, lighting a fist full of bottle rockets.

"You're rulin' us to death," Rob taunted. "Come out here in the open and we'll talk about it."

"Talk about *this*!" Brooks said, lobbing the lit rockets at their feet. Rob and Aron began stomping the earth as if caught in a nest of scorpions.

"Ohhh!" Aron screamed, as a rocket ricocheted up has pants leg. "Boy, my boy, that Brooksie can get plum dangerous when he's angry!"

"We must have caught him at a bad time," Rob joked.

"Ya mean with his pants down and all?" Aron asked.

"Yeah, we should probably apologize," Rob suggested.

"Hey, Brooksie, sorry for tryin' to shoot off your weenie!" Aron shouted.

"It's not like you were usin' it for anything but peein'!" Rob joked.

Suddenly, a meteor shower of bottle rockets lit up the sky above the three men. While scattering, they found themselves running in the direction of twelve lit Roman candles. The ensuing war between the two evenly-divided sides lasted several hours. Time-outs were attempted, and truces called, but tensions remained so high, the simple click of a lighter usually sent everyone scattering. At half past two, just as the last rocket fell, Brooks declared The Tenth Annual Bottle Rocket Fight over, just in time for the arrival of two of Austin's finest.

Officer Porter, one of the city's more portly policeman, climbed out of the passenger side of his patrol car while his partner ran a check on Brooks' license plates.

"Quick," Paul said, grabbing Aron's arm. "We've got to get you out of here!"

"Why?" Aron asked.

"Come on!" Paul insisted, frantically pulling on Aron's arm.

Aron hesitated but soon found himself racing to the back of the hill. As he stopped to catch his breath, Paul grabbed his arm and pulled as they climbed. Both men crawled the last few feet to the top, lungs heaving, hearts racing.

"Are—you tryin'—to kill me?" Aron asked, gasping for air.

Paul ignored the comment as he peered over the top of the hill.

Aron rolled onto his back, sucking in air. "I can't believe I'm doin' this—runnin' from the Texas Rangers—hidin' out in the hills."

"Shhh," Paul whispered, "they're not Rangers, they're local boys, and they can be real pricks when they want to be."

"I thought Brooks said we were outside Austin's city limits."

"He lied."

"What!" Aron replied, rolling over to look for Brooks below. "That Musketeer lied to me? And *you* knew?"

Paul shrugged. "You and Tara were so squeamish about the whole idea. We didn't want a little thing like jurisdiction dampening your spirits." He scanned the war zone. "And you have to admit, it was a perfect location."

"Yeah, it was," Aron agreed, as a second patrol car rolled to a stop beside the first. "But I bet it's lookin' a little less than perfect to our friends right now."

"Really," Paul laughed.

Three policemen walked toward the center of the intersection, flashlights in hand. One light beam held the four warriors motionless while the other beams scanned the area, occasionally resting on a beer can, spent Roman candle, and charred bottle rocket. The smell of burnt paper and gun powder hung in the air. Officer Porter inhaled that all too familiar mixture of beer and body odor, eyes narrowing.

"Good morning, officers," Dave greeted, sounding more like Eddie Haskel than Eddie Haskel.

"How 'bout you let *me* be the judge of that?" Porter replied. "Drivers licenses."

Dave, Rob, and Brooks pulled out their wallets while Tara rummaged through her backpack.

"What exactly do y'all think you're doin' out here?" Porter asked, shining his light over the first license, "Mr. Brooks."

"Celebrating the Fourth?" Brooks replied, more as a question, than an answer.

Porter shined his light in Brooks' face. "Is that a fact? What's wrong with a picnic?"

Tara bit her lower lip.

"Nothing that I can see right now," Brooks answered, squinting in the bright light.

While one policeman took their licenses back to his car, Porter and his partner lit into the four lawbreakers.

"Yes, sir," Dave replied, when asked if he understood Austin's ordinances prohibiting fireworks within its city limits.

"Yes, sir—I mean—no, sir," Rob answered, when asked if he realized how easy it would be to put a person's eye out with a Roman candle.

"No, sir—I mean—yes, sir," Tara replied, when asked if she realized how easily the dry grass surrounding the intersection could catch fire.

"Listen to them," Paul whispered to Aron. "They're so flustered they've lost the ability to answer simple questions."

"What a bunch of wimps," Aron agreed.

Suddenly, Paul and Aron looked at each other and immediately received a glimpse of the big picture—the two of them playing the parts of escaped convicts, hiding high above the fray, while making fun of their captured friends squirming below. The sudden glimpse caught both men off guard, causing them to burst out laughing. A light beam raced up the the hill. The escaped cons covered their mouths and ducked.

"Just the four of you?" one of the officers asked.

"Yes, sir," Tara answered, a little too quickly.

"Oh—man," Aron whispered between laughs. "Tara lied for you. That girl's in *love*."

"No way," Paul replied. "She just needs someone on the outside to post bail."

The harder the men tried not to laugh, the more difficult it became, and they were soon rolling on the ground, hands pressed tightly over their mouths, sides aching, lungs heaving, eyes watering.

"Ya got any Roman candles left?" Aron joked.

Paul patted his pockets. "Fresh out."

"I guess they're on their own."

"It'll do 'em good."

"How long's Dave been usin' that Eddie Haskel routine?" Aron asked.

"Most of his life. It played pretty well in DeSoto, but right now, I think he's learnin' he ain't in DeSoto anymore."

Again, they peeked over the top of the hill, brushing back tears.

"Are we going to jail?" Dave asked.

Porter's light beam scanned the motley crew, highlighting the cuts, scrapes, and tattoolike splotches covering their sweat-soaked bodies. Porter's eyes narrowed as he studied their scorched shirts, drooping kneepads, and exhausted faces. "Son, what could we possibly do to y'all in jail that'd be any worse than what you're doing to yourselves right here?"

Paul and Aron covered their mouths.

The third policemen returned with the licenses and conferred with the other officers.

"Okay," Porter said, "there doesn't seem to be any property damage, and none of you hooligans have a rap sheet—yet—so this is what we're going to do. Y'all have exactly ten minutes to pick up every beer can, spent firework, and scrap of paper in the radius of my flashlight and get the heck out of here, or you'll be spending the rest of the night in jail. And Mr. Turner," he added, handing

Dave his license, "you have three outstanding parking tickets. I suggest you get 'em taken care of—pronto."

"Yes, sir. Sorry about that, sir. I'll take care of them first thing tomorrow morning."

Three large circles of light began scanning the war zone in search of trash. Four *hooligans* obediently followed, stopping when the light beams stopped to peck the earth for trash.

"This is gettin' hard to watch," Paul joked.

"It really is," Aron agreed. "Our friends have been reduced to four clowns in a three-ring circus."

"I'm seein' four fat chickens," Paul replied, "frantically peckin' the earth in hopes of finding a free-get-out-of-jail card."

"Look at the big jock," Aron said, "scampering to follow the cop's orders. What a wuss. Why, I'd have told that fat pig to take a flyin' leap."

"Really," Paul chuckled. "I'd have told 'em to get his fat butt back to the donut shop before someone gets hurt."

"Look at poor Dave, the *conscience* of your Musketeers. Can't even pay his parking tickets."

"Look at poor Tara," Paul laughed. "She wanted to celebrate the Fourth with a picnic. Look at her now."

"Hey, she's cleanin' up America," Aron pointed out. "What better way to celebrate the Fourth. I'd like to see Mr. Brooks pickin' up trash all the way to the Austin city limits sign. Lie to *me*, will he?"

The captured warriors picked up the last scrap of burnt paper, gathered their backpacks, and climbed into Brooks' car, which guiltily crawled back toward the completed section of Mopac. A more powerful light beam from one of the patrol cars circled the intersection before rising up the hill. Paul and Aron ducked, rolled over onto their backs, and watched as the beam rose high above them toward Orion. The patrol cars inched across the crushed rock, soon leaving the men in silence.

"Now what?" Aron asked, "and please tell me we're not gonna have to walk home."

"No, my guess is those hooligans will make a beeline for the closest burger joint then circle back after the coast is clear."

"Boy, I'd love a big, fat cheeseburger right now," Aron said.

"With fries, onion rings, and a chocolate shake," Paul agreed.

Their stomachs growled at the same time, causing both men to laugh. As their laughter died, they stared at the star-filled sky in silence. The sounds of exploding fireworks, screams, and laughter had suddenly vanished, replaced by the more subtle sounds of crickets, frogs, and spinning tires on a distant freeway.

Aron rolled over onto his stomach and stared across the war zone. "I hereby proclaim The Tenth Annual Bottle Rocket Fight a complete success."

"And still no arrests or convictions," Paul joked, also rolling onto his stomach.

Aron thought about Paul's fellow Musketeers. "I envy y'all, your long friendships. You met and grew up on common ground. My friends and I always struggled beneath the shadow of *Elvis*."

Paul grinned as he thought about his friends. "Yes, I've been pretty lucky."

"Pretty lucky in some respects, and pretty unlucky in others."

"How do you mean?"

"I was thinkin' about the loss of your dad."

Paul's eyes fell to the war zone. "Yes, that was unlucky, but my friends helped take his place."

"Yes, they did. Your friends—and *Elvis*."

Paul stared at Aron curiously.

Aron rolled over onto his back to stare up at Orion, the hunter, wondering if now might be a good time for a little heart to heart. He took a deep breath. "Paul, as you know, durin' my first month here, I became a little curious about your motives for kidnapping me. You weren't exactly an open book on the subject, so I started lookin' for answers elsewhere. One thing led to another, and before I knew it, I was researching our whole history together."

For Paul, the earth began to feel awfully uncomfortable. "Researching," he echoed, sitting up to stretch his suddenly tightening muscles. "Aron, we've only really known each other for a few months. What's to research?"

"Well, an awful lot, really."

Paul leaned forward to tighten his kneepads. "Aron, what are you talkin' about?"

"I'm talkin' about *us*, Paul. I'm talkin' about a sad death long ago, and kings and knights and shields and secret vows and betrayal—all leadin' up to a kidnapping on the Ides of March."

Paul's pulse quickened as the palms of his hands quickly moistened.

"Of course, being *Elvis* made my research difficult, but your fellow Musketeers were more than happy to help, and I even persuaded them to make a few phone calls."

Paul abruptly stood and stepped to the top of the hill, trying to hide his sudden anger. "A few phone calls to *who*?"

"Just to your mom, and a teacher or two. Oh, and we made a few calls to your high school counselor, a Miss Jamison."

"You what!" Paul shouted, whirling to face Aron. "Are you crazy! You talked to my *high school counselor*! You talked to my *teachers*? You talked to my *mother*? About *me*! Have you lost your *mind*!"

"No," Aron answered, "I don't think so."

Paul whirled to face the intersection, mind racing. How could his friends have done this to him? How could they have let Aron talk them into this? My *counselor*? My *teachers*? My *mother*? He spun to face Aron. "You're *insane*! What do *they* know about me, anyway?"

"Well, separately, not much—you *do* hold your cards pretty close to your chest. I don't think any of 'em saw the whole picture, but they each saw a part, and I was able to pull it all together into quite an interesting story."

Paul turned and inched closer to the edge of the hill, face turning bright red.

"Paul, you know we have to talk about this *sometime*. What's wrong with now?"

For Paul, there was plenty wrong with now. Right now, all he wanted to do was escape. He closed his eyes and imagined himself leaping over the side of the hill, racing across the cloverleaf intersection, and running far, far away.

"Please, Paul, sit down. You might find this entertaining."

Paul stared out across the war zone, torn between running, and sitting. He shook his head, angrily plopped down, and picked up a stick.

"I began my research by lookin' into kidnappings. I discovered most kidnappers are driven by either money or political reasons. A smaller number are driven by anger and frustration. And an even smaller number are driven by a desire to save a friend or loved one from some real or imagined danger. Once I knew what I was lookin' for, your true motive hit me square in the face. You were driven by anger.

Paul glared at Aron, tightly squeezing the stick. "You're crazy! You think I planned all this, broke into Graceland, risked gettin' shot, risked gettin' my friends thrown in jail, all out of *anger*?"

"Yes, that's exactly what I think. Anger's a great motivator, Paul. It drives people to do all sorts of crazy things. It's also something we share in common. I'm afraid you and I've both spent a number of years playing the parts of angry young men."

Paul looked away from Aron, stared down at his stick, then used it to dig into the hard ground.

"I had to fill in some of the missin' pieces with my own guesswork," Aron continued. "Since you're the only one who can really separate the fact from fiction, feel free to chime in whenever ya like."

Paul closed his eyes, searching for any reasonable excuse to leave, but nothing came to mind. He opened his eyes and continued digging.

"My story begins with the passing of your father when you were two years old. On our first hike, you brushed it off by sayin' you can't really miss something you never had. But I discovered you *did* have a father. You had a good father who held you close, sang you songs, gave you baths, rocked you to sleep at night, and more. And during the short time you had together, you formed a tight bond. Then, two months after your second birthday, that bond was broken, you suffered a great loss, and that's when you first experienced real anger."

Paul's stick snapped, forcing him to toss it a side and search for another.

"As you grew, you found yourself in a world full of grandmothers, aunts, sisters, a brother, and a loving mother. You were lucky to have 'em, but they couldn't begin to fill the void, only a father could do that. So, at the age of five, you began the most important search of your young life, a quest for a dad.

"You were so young at the time, you weren't even sure what a dad was, but I think, like all little boys, you wanted somebody strong, kind, honest, and smart. You wanted someone you could look up to and who others looked up to. Somebody male, of course, and most of all, somebody who'd never bail out on you. I think you wanted a person who had all the qualities of, shall we say, a good king."

"Right," Paul scoffed, "I wanted all *that* at age five?"

"Yes, I think you did. Of course, you couldn't completely understand what it was you wanted at that age, and you surely couldn't verbalize it, but I think you wanted all those things and more."

Paul shook his head, looked down into the small hole in the earth, and continued digging.

"I entered your life when you were six years old—I've read, the most impressionable period in a kid's life—and I entered with a bang. Your mom described to Brooks how awestruck you were by my first television appearances, how you couldn't take your eyes off the set, how you cried because my performances ended so fast. She described your excitement the day she bought you those first 45's, and your excitement the first time she took you to see *Elvis* on the big screen.

"Brooks, too, described those Saturday matinees— you sittin' in the front row, Coke squeezed in one hand, M&M's squeezed in the other, watching *Elvis* beat the heck out of the bad guys, race fast sports cars, and sing the most amazing songs you'd ever heard. From your perspective, everybody on the big screen wanted *Elvis*, everybody in the movie theater wanted him, and you wanted him. I think, like a lot of fatherless boys growin' up in the late fifties, you saw what you wanted to see, you saw what you needed to see. You watched as the enthusiasm for me grew. You saw my rising popularity, fame, and wealth as proof of my greatness—fifty million Elvis fans can't be wrong—and all of a sudden, your search was over, and how proud, how lucky, how happy you must have felt because your father was also the King, your father was Elvis Aron Presley, the King of Rock 'n' Roll.

Paul's heart leaped and his digging stopped as he recalled that glorious moment in time.

"From age six to eight, you reveled in your illusion. You applauded my hits, movies, and awards, criticized my imitators, and blasted every new sensation that you feared might have an eye on my throne. Rob said shortly after teachin' you how to box, he found himself in the peculiar position of havin' to pull you off of every kid that dared to cut me down in your presence. You literally fought for me, Paul, like a good knight."

"Okay!" Paul said, standing. "Okay! I pretended you were my father, that you were my king. I pretended I was your son, that I was your knight! So what! I was just a stupid kid! Just a stupid kid!"

"Stupid," Aron echoed. "Paul, you're a *psychology* major for Pete's sake. I'm sure you've read all about coping mechanisms, surrogates, and illusions. *I've* surely read more than enough on the subject the past few months. You coped, Paul. You adapted. Your loss was great, so your substitute had to be just as great. You were only six years old, and yet you dreamed up this grand illusion that not only shielded you from the cold reality of your life, but helped you fill a growin' void. I'd call it creative, imaginative, a little melodramatic, and maybe even genius, but never stupid."

"Right," Paul scoffed. "If it was so *genius*, why didn't it work?"

"But it *did* work. It worked great, right up until around age eight or nine when a crack began to form in your shield."

Paul turned, stared down the hill, then reluctantly sat.

"Rob, Dave, and Brooks all had real fathers who existed in the real world, fathers who were constantly doin' fatherly things for their sons, and I wasn't exactly wakin' you up to go fishin', was I? I wasn't takin' you to football games, explaining the facts of life, or teachin' you the difference between right and wrong, was I?"

Paul's head lowered. "No," he whispered. "No, you weren't." He picked up his stick.

"As you entered high school you started seein' my movies as silly and childish, and my latest hits as dull and stagnate. You read a tabloid article describing me as lazy, extravagant, and overindulgent—not exactly good traits for a king. You read another article about my use of appetite suppressants, cheatin' on Priscilla, and violent temper. You started seein' me as human, a little *too* human, and the crack in your shield began to grow. You found yourself torn between wantin' to drop the illusion and move on with your life, and wantin' to hold on tightly to your father and king. And your frustration and anger grew. You became angry at a world that was once again taking your dad, angry at yourself for creating the stupid illusion in the first place, and most of all, angry at me. You felt—betrayed."

Paul's jaw tightened.

"Your high school English teacher told Dave about an essay you wrote comparing me to a popular eighteenth century poet. In your essay, you warned that if I wasn't careful, I'd end up just like that poet—a gifted talent, givin' into drugs, alcohol, and depression and dyin' way before his time. You wrote that I should check myself into a Tibetan monastery to relearn integrity, fidelity, honesty, and all the other honorable traits needed to be a good king. Short of that, you said I should return to Sun Studios, lock myself inside with nothin' but a piano and guitar, and stay there until I'd rediscovered my creative genius. In an impersonal critique, your teacher reminded you that *Elvis* was, after all, just a rock star, that you were taking his plight far too subjectively, far too personally.

But your high school counselor, who had talked to you after a few of those after-school fights, knew something else was goin' on, that the whole thing was very possibly way out of your hands, that you couldn't help but see my fall from grace *personally*."

Paul angrily dug the hole deeper.

"During your first year in college, you learned I was spending more and more time in Las Vegas—without Priscilla and Lisa Marie. In a letter to Rob, you angrily accused me of abandoning my wife and daughter for Sodom and Gomorrah. You said I was suddenly livin' in ivory palaces, majoring in glitter and glitz, wearin' silly capes, scarves, and gemstone-studded jumpsuits, and even carrying a fake scepter. To your horror, I was being introduced by a hundred-piece orchestra playin' the theme song from *2001: A Space Odyssey*. You told Rob I was suddenly light-years from the raw, solo talent you'd admired so much as a child and that my whole life had become some sort of bizarre odyssey."

Paul's eyes narrowed as he glared at Aron.

"For Las Vegas, I was a Godsend—thousands were arriving by the busload—but you never bought that bus ticket, did you? You never bought into *Las Vegas Elvis*, did you?"

"No," Paul answered, fists tightening. "No, I didn't."

"You saw trouble on the horizon, and your fears were realized during your second year in college, when you learned of my ballooning weight, wild mood swings, and escalating use of prescription drugs. Tabloid reporters began writin' about my wild parties and careless gun play. One reporter got a hold of a letter that I'd written to President Nixon offerin' my help as an undercover agent in the

DEA's war against drugs. You told Brooks the letter was so poorly thought out, so poorly written, that I must have been on drugs when I wrote it. Overnight, I was becomin' a national joke. Every comedian, talk show host, and disc jockey in the country was makin' fun of me, and you took it personal. You took it very personal."

"*Yes*, I took it personal!" Paul shouted, leaping to his feet. "*Of course* I took it personal! Why wouldn't I! What were you *doin'* to yourself! What were you doin' to *us*! I could've killed you! I could've killed you!" Paul took a quick step toward Aron then suddenly realized what he was doing and froze.

From his prone position on the ground, Aron stared up at Paul curiously. "In your defense, you were probably right to . . ."

"No!" Paul shouted. "No! I wasn't *right*! You think I was *right* to dream up this stupid illusion! To hold onto it for so long! To get so angry! To want to kill you! It wasn't my *right* to judge you! No one asked *you* to be my father! No one asked *you* to be my king! It's not like we signed a stupid *contract*!"

Aron gave Paul a surprised look. "Wow. What a strange choice of words, because that's exactly what it was like. Oh, we might not have signed anything, at least not on this level, but on some level, you can bet a contract was formed between this knight, and this king."

Paul turned and searched the battlefield for some rebuttal. He shook his head, plopped down, and stared into the hole.

"Last year I was hospitalized for fatigue, constipation, and an intestinal flu. Cards and letters began floodin' into Graceland, and you feared the end was near, and there was no way a good knight could stand by while his king slowly died. There was also no way you could let me get away without untangling this web that was your contract with your king. So you kidnapped me and drug me to Austin where you suddenly found yourself torn between wantin' to guard and defend me, and wantin' to knock my head off, and when the police came tonight, your first thought was to rush the king to safety. What'd you think they were gonna do, Paul, arrest me? Elvis Presley? For what? A third-class misdemeanor? For shootin' off bottle rockets like a thousand other folks all over Austin? What were you thinking, Paul? What were you thinking?"

Paul's head dropped. "I just—wanted—to save the king. I just wanted—to save the king."

Aron rolled over onto his stomach, crawled up to the edge of the hill, and gazed out over the intersection. "Well, you certainly did that, and although you only really saved me from havin' to pick up a little trash and havin' to maybe sing my way out of jail, I'm very grateful. I can't remember ever laughin' so hard, over so little. I can hardly wait to ask our hooligan friends what it felt like to chase those light beams and peck the earth like a bunch of fat chickens while we watched their comical performance from high above."

A trace of a smile tried to break through the strained expression on Paul's face.

"Don't get me wrong, Paul," Aron continued. "Whatever your reasons, I'm glad you kidnapped me. I'm glad to be drug-free, in good health, and wakin' up most every morning pain free and with a clear head. I'm also grateful for my new friends and all the fun we've been havin' together. But most of all, I'm thankful to have had such

a good knight watchin' over me all these years. You've
fulfilled your part of the bargain with great honor, and
that begs the question, What about me? What about my
part?"

Aron stood and stepped to the top of the hill. "After
our last fight, I became more motivated to experience
life without all the drugs, to become healthy and to stay
healthy. But as I started researching our history together,
something else started happening. I began experiencing
a strange desire to be strong, kind, honest, and someone
my chief kidnapper could look up to, and now the reason
seems pretty obvious. I've been tryin' hard to be a good
king, to fulfill my part of this contract, so the contract
can end."

"No," Paul replied, his whole body slumping from the
weight of the news. "No. I don't want it to end."

"I'm not surprised—eighteen years is a long time—
but you know it must. I'll be leavin' for Memphis soon,
and I don't want to leave any unfinished business. And
you're a young man, Paul, with a degree in sight, a whole
world to hike, and a beautiful princess to hike it with. I
don't think you really want any old contracts holdin' you
back."

Paul knew Aron was right, that clinging to old contracts was wrong, not to mention unhealthy, but he was
a stubborn knight. He took a deep breath, lifted his tired
body from the hard ground, and stood beside Aron on
the top of the hill. He slowly unlatched his kneepads and
elbowpads and let them drop to the ground. "Okay. Okay.
But I can't let all this end without adding a few things to
your story."

"I was hopin' you would," Aron replied.

Paul scanned the war zone while gathering his thoughts. "First, about Las Vegas Elvis. While planning the kidnapping, I read quite a bit about the hardworking musicians, backup vocalists, and hundreds of other talented individuals who took part in those extravaganzas, not just in Vegas, but throughout the country. Like yourself, they strived to give their audiences what they most wanted—a great show—and judging from the reviews, they were pretty successful. Y'all should be commended, not scorned. Also, the clear majority of your fans loved the glitter, glitz, and bigger-than-life presence that you commanded on stage, and judging from the millions who kept returning, they weren't disappointed. I read a quote from a Las Vegas cab driver who said his tips doubled and tripled on the nights you were performing. Thanks to such testimonials, I now have a more *objective* view of that part of your career."

"You should try wearing a girdle," Aron joked.

Paul smiled. As he focused on the war zone's long shadows, his smile faded. "Second, the little boy in your story seemed so sad. A little too sad. I was not an unhappy child. I thoroughly enjoyed being your knight, especially early on. Illusion or not, it taught me honor, respect, loyalty, and obedience—and most of all, love. I might have experienced an early loss, I might have felt the sadness, confusion, and void that accompanies such loss, but as I look back, I see a happy child who grew up in a wonderful environment, surrounded by a loving family, great friends, and yes, *Elvis*. Looking back, I realize I wouldn't trade one minute of my childhood for anyone else's."

Aron smiled.

"Third, the little boy in your story seemed so alone. Too alone. Often, over the years, I've felt this strange connection to this large band of fatherless boys—riding nobly, attacking dragons, saving damsels, and striking out against the insolence of the court jesters. Our *contract* may have had its unique qualities, but I never thought for a second that it was the only one. I often pray for all the other little boys and girls, who, for whatever reason, entered into such alliances."

Aron bowed his head and said a quick prayer.

Paul searched the battlefield for anything he might have left out. "Oh, yeah. One more thing. About your music. For *this* boy, your songs did more than excite, awaken, and touch deeply. Your songs opened a giant window, through which, I experienced my first situational highs. To this day, I can't listen to one of those early hits without entering that same euphoric space I entered as a child. I realize I've been living in an illusion. I realize we no longer live in an age of kings and dragons. But that giant window was no illusion. Through it, I saw a unique talent, a hardworking perfectionist, a great performer, and a noble soul. I saw a good king, worth defending, worth protecting, and well worth attaching myself to. I'm deeply honored to have been able to serve you in this way."

Aron bowed politely. "I'm very honored, too, Paul."

During the still silence that followed, they stared across the cloverleaf intersection, neither man knowing what exactly to say next. Aron recalled their bottle rocket fight, grinned, and took a deep breath. "I hereby commend this loyal knight for the stedfast and faithful fulfillment of his part of this sacred contract, and by the authority vested in me as his king, do hereby release him from it's hold."

Paul's tired arms suddenly felt unshackled and rose slightly from his sides. His chin and shoulders suddenly lifted. He stared up at Orion, searching for the right words. He took a deep breath. "I hereby commend this king for the worthy and honorable fulfillment of his part of this sacred contract, and by the authority vested in me as his knight, do hereby release him from it's hold."

The muscles in Aron's back and shoulders instantly relaxed as a big smile suddenly graced his face. "Wow. I feel like I could fly."

"Me, too," Paul replied, raising his arms and leaning out over the edge of the hill. "You'd think something really dramatic would happen right about now."

"Really," Aron laughed. "Where's Hollywood when ya need 'em?"

"Look!" Tara shouted, jumping out of Brooks' car and pointing high above the hill. Her friends quickly climbed out and looked upward. Paul and Aron spun, just in time to witness a bright shooting star. The star floated in a slow, horizontal path across the night sky, pulling with it a long, bottle rocketlike tail. Faces brightened as the meteor slowly faded then vanished. For the four warriors standing on the battlefield, the shooting star marked the end of the Musketeers' Tenth Annual Bottle Rocket Fight, but for the two standing on the hill, it marked the end of a contract between a knight and his king.

Chapter Ten

A few days after the bottle rocket fight, Aron called everyone into the living room for an important announcement. A stack of legal pads and six pens sat on the coffee table. "Folks, I've decided to throw a free concert, right out here, on August 1." He opened one of the pads to a one-page, handwritten outline.

"A concert!" Dave replied.

"Right out where?" Brooks asked.

"Really," Paul agreed, "we're living in a rental house with a back yard full of snakes and mesquite."

"What about your anonymity?" Brooks asked. "You want to trade *that* for a hundred thousand screaming Elvis fans?"

"A hundred thousand!" Aron laughed. "You obviously haven't read the reviews of my last couple of concerts. I was figurin' on around ten thousand, if that. And yes, I've enjoyed being anonymous, but my visit here is almost over, so my anonymity was comin' to an end anyway."

"What do *we* know about throwing a concert?" Dave asked.

"There's nothing to it," Aron replied. "I've helped throw thousands, in all sorts of venues, from carnivals to aircraft carriers."

"In *three* weeks?" Paul asked. "What about local ordinances, permits, and licenses? Don't those take months?"

"Yes, sometimes they do, but you'd be surprised what a little moolah placed in the right hands can do to speed things up."

"Did you say a *free* concert?" Brooks asked. "This'll cost a mint."

"What about all the work involved?" Dave asked. "We *do* have other jobs, you know."

"I suggest you ask for a few weeks off," Aron replied.

The room fell silent.

"Rob, you're awfully quiet," Aron commented.

Rob stood, stepped up to a large, freshly stretched canvas, and picked up a brush. "This is what I see," he replied. "Ten thousand Elvis fans makin' a long pilgrimage from Austin to The Vineyard to pay homage to the King. And five thousand of 'em are young, beautiful, sexually active women—all hot and bothered over *Elvis*—all suddenly intoxicated by his performance and lookin' for the after-concert party and a comfortable place to spend the night. And here I am livin' in this big, cozy house, with this big, comfy bed, and this big . . ."

"We get the picture," Tara interrupted.

"Welcome aboard, Rob," Aron laughed.

"You're sleeping with five thousand women?" Brooks asked.

"Some will have to wait," Rob admitted.

"They're welcome to wait in my bed," Dave offered.

"Mine, too," Brooks agreed.

"Welcome aboard, gentlemen," Aron said. "Tara, how 'bout you?"

"Thanks, but I prefer sleeping with Paul."

"And there's never any wait," Paul added.

"Very funny," Aron replied, studying his chief kidnappers. "Now tell me what you think of my idea? Ready to play a little game of a Grand Finale?"

Tara walked up to a window and closed her eyes, recalling the grand finales of Aron's old movies. Her stomach began to tingle with the same excitement she had experienced as a small child. She faced Aron and smiled. "I'm in."

Aron looked at Paul.

"You *know* I'm in," Paul replied excitedly. "I've never been to an Elvis concert."

"All right, then," Aron said, handing out pens and pads. "I've divided the event into three broad categories: Stage and Concert Site—Musicians and Workers—Parking and Security."

"You still haven't explained where we'll put ten thousand Elvis fans," Brooks said.

Aron stepped to the window facing the Johnsons' farm. "Right out there."

"The Johnsons' farm?" Tara asked.

"*This* I've got to see," Dave scoffed. "I guess you'll just waltz over there with your guitar, sing a couple of songs, and the Johnsons will give you their farm."

Brooks rolled his eyes. "He must think he's living in one of his old movies."

"Well, I don't mean to brag," Aron replied, "but I think I had 'em sold after the *first* song. Lucille was quite moved by my performance, and Sam said he suspected I was Elvis all along but nobody would listen to him. We've already picked out a great place for the stage. The bluffs are gonna make a perfect backdrop."

Dave stared at Aron in disbelief. "I feel like I've been invited onto a ship that's already set sail."

"You should be used to that feeling by now," Rob joked.

Tara shook her head. "We don't even have a telephone."

"I'm thinkin' six lines should be enough?" Aron replied, making a few notes.

"My sister runs a concert promotion company in Austin," Paul mentioned. "She might be able to help us cut through the red tape. And I'm sure my twin sister will want to help."

"I have an uncle who works for Texas Power & Light," Dave mentioned. "He might be able to help us run lines for the stage and lighting. Are we planning this gig for day or night?"

"Day," Aron replied, "from three till six." He grinned at Rob. "That'll give those ladies not sleepin' over plenty of daylight to find their cars and get back to town. But we'll need lights for the construction workers and dress rehearsal I'm planning for the night before the concert."

"What about musicians?" Rob asked.

"If possible, I'd like to take advantage of Austin's local talent. I'll need three or four guitarists, a keyboardist, drummer, and six or so backup vocalists." He smiled at Paul. "And a saxophonist for Paul's favorite song."

"Well, you're in luck," Rob said, "Austin's got almost as many musicians as politicians. I met a lot of 'em while workin' at The Cactus. And they're really talented, which means their weekends in August will be booked solid."

"August 1 is on a Monday," Aron replied. "I did my research and discovered that every weekend the rest of the summer was chocked full of music festivals, fairs, marathons, bike races, and concerts—some of 'em planned years in advance. I didn't want to step on any toes."

"Smart," Rob complimented.

"And considerate," Tara added.

"Where'd you say you were from?" Dave asked.

"Tupelo," Aron answered.

"Probably born after inbreeding lost its popularity," Brooks commented.

"Mr. Brooks!" Tara said.

"Back to the expense of this little project," Brooks said. "For those of you who missed our last business meeting, we have a grand total of $83.67 in our account. And *someone* hasn't paid their share of last month's rent."

"*Someone* masquerading as my *agent* hasn't sold a single painting," Rob argued.

Aron glanced at his watch. "In a few hours, money will be the least of our problems. Next?"

"What about our other neighbors?" Dave asked. "They may not appreciate seeing *Woodstock* out their back windows."

Tara stared out the window, reflectively. "If we bring them in during the planning stage, they'll be less likely to object. Lucille knows everyone within a five mile radius of this place. She and I can begin paying neighborly visits this afternoon."

"And if anyone needs a little extra persuading, just say the word, and I'll drop by with my guitar," Aron offered.

"What about advertising?" Brooks asked. "I know a few people at KLBJ, The Chronicle, and The Statesman."

"My brother works at the Dallas Morning News," Paul mentioned.

"I'd rather not," Aron replied. "Radio and newspapers can sometimes cause things to get way out of hand. I'd just like to thank a few thousand of my local fans. Oh, and I thought it might be fun to try out some of my new tunes on a younger audience."

"I can plaster the poles around campus with ads," Brooks suggested. "That's the locally-accepted form of advertising. The word *free*, alone, will bring out a couple thousand college students, but probably not much more than that. With Congress out of session and UT between semesters, Austin's a ghost town right now. I can also wait to post the ads until a few days before the concert. That should keep the numbers down."

"Perfect," Aron replied.

Worried looks crossed Paul and Tara's faces as they thought about the possibility of the exact opposite happening, the possibility of no one showing.

"I think your estimate of ten thousand is way too conservative," Dave said. "Even if there's only ten thousand Elvis fans in all of Central Texas, you can bet they'll be here August 1—*with* their friends."

"Well, we have the space for twice that number," Aron commented, "and planning for twenty thousand won't be that much harder than planning for ten."

The room grew quiet as they contemplated the size of twenty thousand fans.

"I'm gonna need a bigger bed," Rob commented.

"You're gonna need a bigger . . ."

"Mr. Brooks," Tara interrupted.

"What about parking?" Paul asked. "Even if they car pool, we're talking about five thousands cars."

"The Johnsons also own the sixty acres across the street," Aron answered, "and it's just been harvested. All we need is a little help constructing a few more entrances."

"We can shanghai our friends and relatives from DeSoto," Dave commented."

Brooks chuckled. "I guess it's time to tell Beth the wild fiction she's been helping me edit isn't quite as *fiction* as she thought."

"I owe my mom a *big* surprise," Tara grinned. "Perhaps I'll invite her out the morning of the concert."

"We can make her our honored guest," Aron suggested.

"And keep her in the dark till the last minute," Rob suggested.

"Boy, my boy," Aron laughed, "will *she* ever be in for a surprise."

"I'll stop by Mike's Used Cars and see if Mike and Bobby want to join in the fun," Paul mentioned.

"Lakeway's struggling to start a new catering business," Rob mentioned. "We could use 'em to feed the workers."

"We should document all this with photographs," Tara suggested. She looked at Aron. "To protect your privacy, we voted against cameras, but now that your privacy's being tossed out the window, I guess we can take as many pictures as we like."

"Be my guest," Aron replied.

Dave grinned. "I knew I took that photography class for some reason beside meeting girls and getting an easy A. And Susanne's an excellent photographer."

Tara walked up to the window and took a deep breath. "This changes everything. Cameras, telephones, construction workers, power lines, a stage, parking, thousands of Elvis fans invading our secluded little safe house." She looked at Aron curiously. "Why did you say we we're doing this, again?"

"Let's just call it a humanitarian gesture," Aron answered. "And this *temporarily* changes everything. The day after the concert, we'll pull the plug, pick up a little trash, and nobody will even know we were here."

"Ha, not if I have anything to do with it," Rob replied. "*This*, my friends, will be the *mother* of all concerts."

Everyone smiled.

Again, Tara studied Aron curiously. "And you're not harboring any ulterior motives for this concert?"

Aron shook his head in mock disgust. "Everyone's gotta be a shrink around here. Oh, all right, I do have one small ulterior motive—and one big surprise." He studied his friends. "For those of you who haven't noticed, two of my kidnappers have been moping around here like the end was nigh. I feared the situation would only get worse as the day of my departure neared, so I came up with a perfect solution—one that'd allow me to perform a kind gesture for a few fans and at the same time, keep my kidnappers so busy they wouldn't have time to dwell on the big goodbye."

Rob chuckled. "The tables have turned. Aron's become the doctor, and we've become his patients."

"I feel more like a kidnap victim than a patient," Dave grumbled. "Summers were made for being lazy, which I sometimes find very therapeutic. Now look at how we'll be spending the rest of it."

"Oh, quit your whining, Dave," Aron replied, "you might have a good time, or maybe you'd rather spend the summer talkin' to your lawyers about a very *real* kidnapping."

"Ouch," Brooks replied. "Shut up, Dave, you're making the monster angry." He looked at Aron. "So what's the big surprise?"

"Yisa," Aron answered, face brightening. "She'll be arriving in a few hours."

"*Lisa Marie*?" Tara asked.

"The *King's princess*?" Paul asked.

"In a few hours!" Brooks replied, scanning the messy living room.

"Yes, I'm afraid Yisa's missed almost all of my concerts. This was *one* I didn't want her to miss. I've got two close friends flyin' her out. They're also bringing my checkbooks, a few guitars, some clothes, and a mound of paper work for me to wade through." He looked at Tara. "I was hopin' ya might give me a lift to the airport, and perhaps keep Yisa entertained while I'm takin' care of business."

"I'd love to," Tara replied. "How much time do I have to get ready?"

Aron glanced at his watch. "Oh, about thirty minutes."

"Men!" Tara grumbled, leaping off the sofa and running toward the shower.

Rob stood. "I'm going into town to hunt for musicians."

"How about dropping me off at my sister's," Paul asked. "She's got a pickup we can borrow."

"I'll drive to Lakeway and inform our manager of the lucrative catering job we just scored for him," Brooks said. "Then I tell him we'll need the next three weeks off."

"I'll run to the pay phone and call my uncle," Dave said.

Aron quickly found himself alone in the living room listening to the sounds of starting cars and the bathroom shower. His thoughts passed from the thrill of seeing his daughter to the excitement of throwing a free concert. He thought of his friends hurrying off to tackle their new assignments and chuckled. He propped his feet on the coffee table then rested his head against the back of the sofa, wondering if he had time to sneak in a quick nap. Sometimes, it was nice being the King.

By the second day of Rob's search, he had interviewed five musicians, none of whom believed his wild story about *Elvis* throwing a free, outdoor concert. Three of the five were scheduled to play at Threadgill's that night, so Rob invited Aron out for a late dinner. After Lisa Marie was safely tucked into bed, the two men drove to the popular restaurant where a wailing saxophone welcomed them into the parking lot. Aron had recently dropped another twenty pounds, as evidenced by his baggy jeans and loose-fitting burnt-orange jersey. Before climbing out of Rob's truck, he put on his baseball cap and sunglasses. Rob wore paint-splattered overalls over a Colorado football jersey. His long, red hair just touched his broad shoulders, and his red beard was neatly trimmed. Both men wore dark tans.

The restaurant's foyer was packed with customers pressed between an autographed picture of Janis Joplin on their left, and a velvet Elvis on their right. Rob and Aron chuckled at the likeness of Elvis before squeezing their way to the bar and two just-vacated seats. After ordering chicken fried steaks and longnecks, they spun and rested their elbows atop the bar to watch the band.

A tall, redheaded waitress serving customers near the stage caught Rob's attention. He studied the curves of her body as she leaned over the table to grasp a plate. To Rob's surprise, she immediately straightened, turned, and looked at him from across the room. Their eyes locked. She handed the plate to a passing bus boy, removed her apron, then took the stage. "Howdy," she said, ducking her head and shoulder through the strap of her guitar. "My name's Tanya Price, and I'd like to entertain y'all with a Nancy Griffith tune called 'Lone Star State of Mind.'"

As Tanya turned to talk to the band, her curly red hair fell across her guitar's apple-green pick guard. Rob tucked the image away for a future painting. Tanya's choice of songs—a local favorite about a homesick boy sittin' in a Denver bar, drinkin' California wine, and dreaming of his Texas heartthrob—struck a chord deep in Rob's heart.

Aron chuckled at Rob's awestruck stare. "I guess we've found our first backup vocalist," he joked, at the song's end.

Rob responded by standing and whistling loud enough to hail a deaf cab driver. As the band struck up another tune, Tanya grasped her apron and walked toward the kitchen, passing the bar on the way.

"Excuse me, miss," Rob said, stopping Tanya in her tracks. "That was a *great* rendition of a *great* song. Nancy Griffith would be real proud."

"Why, thank you," Tanya replied, smiling at Rob.

"I'm Rob Carpenter, and this here's my friend, Aron."

"Tanya Price," Tanya said, shaking hands.

"Howdy, ma'am," Aron said, heavy on the Texas drawl.

"Say, Tanya, we were wonderin' if you'd like to sing some backup vocals at a concert we're planning for August 1," Rob mentioned. "We can promise you a great time, a lot of exposure, and a large percentage of the gate, which will be nothin'."

"First rehearsal's tomorrow night," Aron added.

Tanya laughed. "Well, gentlemen, I'm working tomorrow night, and I'm not that excited about the large percentage of nothin', but how much exposure are we talking about?"

"Around twenty thousand," Rob answered. "Oh, and you'll get to perform with Aron."

Aron removed his sunglasses and gave Tanya one of his famous grins. The band's song ended. Loud applause erupted then faded as Aron replaced his glasses. Tanya stared in disbelief, caught between some sort of practical joke, and a childhood dream suddenly coming true. The band cranked out another lively tune.

"I think Rob's being a little optimistic about the twenty thousand," Aron continued. "I expect the number to be closer to ten thousand."

Tanya stared, speechless.

"We could sing a duet or two, if ya like," Aron added, breaking the silence.

Tanya blinked twice, as if to jar herself from her trance. "Sorry," she apologized, color slowly returning to her cheeks. "You—sort of—startled me." She looked at Rob. "Thank you, Rob." She looked at Aron. "Thank you, Mr. Presley. I've been a fan of yours for—for as long as I can remember—and I'd be very happy to help you with your concert in any way I can."

"Please, Tanya, call me Aron. And thanks. Thanks a lot. I look forward to seeing you tomorrow night. Oh, and we're not announcing the concert until a few days before."

"Whatever you say, Aron."

"Now, if y'all will excuse me, I have some more arm twistin' to do."

Tanya and Rob watched as Aron made his way to the stage.

"Whatdaya have to do to get a beer around here?" one of Tanya's impatient customers asked.

"Settle down there, cowboy," Rob said, setting Aron's untouched beer in front of the gentleman.

"I'd better get back to my customers," Tanya said.

"I wouldn't worry about *them*," Rob chuckled, motioning toward the stage. "In a few seconds food will be the last thing on their minds." He glanced at Aron's just vacated bar stool. "Please, have a seat."

Tanya scanned her tables, focused on the stage, and grinned. To her customers chagrin, she slowly sat as the apron in her hand fell to the floor.

Aron introduced himself to the surprised musicians before asking if they knew any of his songs. After a short conversation, he grasped Tanya's guitar and began warming up his fingers.

"Howdy, ladies and gentlemen," Aron said into the mic. "My name's Elvis Presley, and I'd like to entertain y'all with a few familiar tunes before tryin' out a couple of new ones."

A waitress' pen froze against her receipt pad. Four green beans hung motionless between a plate and a half-open mouth. Chins lifted. A few heads turned toward the stage. Threadgill's was known for its famous walkups—but *Elvis Presley*—no way. As the band played the boogie-woogie rhythm of "Don't Be Cruel," Aron crooned the first verse, and every head in the restaurant turned. A bus boy raced to the kitchen. Hot skillets jumped off burners, noisy faucets hushed, and a sharp knife dropped, sticking like a dart into the hard wood floor as the kitchen doors burst wide-open. Those customers waiting in the foyer rushed to fill the empty space between the bar and tables. Fingers snapped, toes tapped, hearts leaped, and whether they knew the words or not, everyone in the restaurant helped Aron with the chorus. At the song's end, the crowd stood and burst into loud applause.

Aron followed the first song with "All Shook Up" then surprised his audience with a solo set filled with creative originals. On the way back to the bar, he shook hands and signed autographs as every phone in the restaurant and two in the parking lot speed-dialed friends and relatives. The restaurant's employees reluctantly returned to their duties as their customers hesitantly returned to their seats. The polite crowd let Aron and Rob eat their dinners uninterrupted, but just as the last piece of pecan pie slid south, a bus boy begged the King for another song. Aron happily obliged with another set. Afterwards, he continued signing autographs as Rob drew Tanya and the musicians maps to The Vineyard. While leaving the restaurant, Aron paused in the foyer to thank the restaurant's manager for the great time and to sign the velvet Elvis.

During the next three weeks, Aron and his musicians and vocalists took part in twenty rehearsals. As they rehearsed, phone lines were installed, power lines strung, a stage erected, and portable water tanks and lavatories delivered. A sizable contribution was made to Austin's Fraternal Order of Police, and an Officer Porter took charge of safety and security. Although preparing for twenty thousand guests was a lot of work, Aron insisted on daily games of two-below, and four teams quickly evolved: The Construction Workers, Austin's Finest, The Musicians, and The Kidnappers.

As the number of workers grew, so did the gangs of children racing around the concert site. Beth, Susanne, and a number of parents organized the kids into teams and kept them busy delivering food and drinks to the workers, helping stock the first aid tents, and crafting two hundred backstage passes. Those children helping with the work were rewarded with organized games of soccer, hikes to the ridge, and tours of the Johnsons' farm, where Lucille and her friends could usually be counted on for snacks and a movie.

Aron and Paul continued their evening hikes, but their excursions were often cut short. Three days before the concert, they found themselves sitting atop the ridge overlooking the Johnsons' once peaceful farm. The familiar sound of rustling leaves and singing birds was now being drowned out by the truck engines, power tools, and the excited screams of children playing a spirited game of soccer. Paul and Aron laughed.

"I'm gonna miss this place," Aron commented.

"You're welcome to stay," Paul replied.

"Thanks, I know, but my work here's about done, and in case ya haven't noticed, my priorities are changin'." Lisa made a goal, much to the glee of her teammates. Aron's face beamed. "Yisa's growing up fast, and I'd like to spend as much time with her as possible, which will mean a lot of flights between Memphis and Los Angeles."

"If I'm not mistaken, those flights pass right over Texas."

"Yes, they do, and we're lookin' forward to our Austin layovers."

Paul pulled two apples from his pack, which they enjoyed while watching the soccer game below.

"Yisa reminds me a lot of myself," Aron mentioned. "Sometimes I worry that she might one day have to wrestle with the same demons. If that day comes, I hope you'll invite her out for an extended stay."

"Of course I will, but where do you think *you'll* be?"

Aron chuckled. "Sorry, must be our age difference. The older I get, the more I think about my own mortality."

"Need I remind you that you're healthier now than you've been in quite some time?"

"Thanks, and don't think I don't appreciate it."

Paul glanced at his watch. "Rob and I have to leave for town soon to pick up those extra batteries and two-ways. If this concert flops, it won't be for lack of communication."

"That's for sure," Aron agreed.

"Oh, and we need these autographed before we have 'em laminated," Paul added, pulling several bundles of backstage passes from his pack.

"Boy, my boy," Aron grumbled, "you lugged work all the way up here?"

"The kids did a wonderful job, don't you think?" Paul replied, handing Aron a pen. "And they'll make great souvenirs."

"Yes, they will, I just didn't expect our break to be over so fast."

The night before the concert, everyone connected with the event attended a final rehearsal followed by a Lakeway catered cookout at the Johnsons'. The kidnappers' close friends and family members elected to spend the night near the concert site, and by midnight, sleeping bags stuffed with tired bodies carpeted every inch of The Vineyard's porch. For most, sleep came easy. Aron's kidnappers, however, tossed and turned like children on Christmas Eve, eagerly awaiting the next day's big surprises.

On the morning of August 1, they awakened to a brilliant sunrise beneath a clear blue sky. After breakfast, they attended one final meeting, then headed straight to the concert site. To their surprise, a few eager fans had begun trickling in, six hours before the beginning of the concert. Aron and Lisa Marie shocked the early birds by welcoming them personally, presenting them with backstage passes, and putting them to work. After greeting these early arrivals, the King and his princess spent the rest of the morning thanking workers and wishing them and their friends and family members a great time.

Tanya and the other vocalists and musicians spent the morning tuning instruments and double checking the huge assortment of amps, mics, speakers, and recording equipment. Susanne loaded her backpack with cameras, film, and batteries and continued documenting the big event with photographs. Rob and Dave helped the police rope off a large area around the stage where two hundred workers would provide a human barrier between the King and his more excited fans.

Brooks and Beth elected to accompany Paul and Tara to the airport to pick up Tara's mother. At exactly 10 a.m. a long, white limo bounced over The Vineyard's cattle guard, and a tuxedo-clad chauffeur was soon opening doors for the two couples. During the ride to town, they informed the driver of the big surprise awaiting Tara's mom and the importance of keeping Aron's concert a secret.

*   *   *

Steve and Sandy Garrett slept in during their first morning in Austin then treated themselves to a buffet brunch in the hotel's luxurious dining room, which over-looked Town Lake. After brunch they found one *Tara Benoist* listed in the hotel's phone directory and had little trouble locating her address. Steve, however, was not op-timistic. As they climbed the steps to the second story apartment, he began second guessing his decision not to call before making the long trip from North Dakota. He glanced at his watch, guessing that at 11 a.m. on a Monday morning, Tara would be at work, on campus, or perhaps living in another state by now. Just the same, his pulse quickened as he reached for the doorbell. He rang twice, waited, then rang again, shoulders sagging.

The couple tried two other apartments before questioning a nice lady hoeing in a garden across the street. The woman informed them that Tara had moved to the country three months ago, had stopped by once to visit, but had neglected to leave her new address. The woman also said she thought Tara still worked at the Austin State Hospital. Steve's spirits lifted briefly after their conversation but dropped after a call to the hospital.

"She's quit the hospital," Steve informed Sandy, "quit the hospital and moved to the country. That doesn't give us much to go on."

"Let's drive to campus," Sandy suggested. "Perhaps we'll get some ideas."

Steve's head hung as they walked to their truck. He had missed Tara by only a few months and suddenly felt awfully guilty for all the years he had failed to pick up the phone or write. He put his key in the ignition, started the truck's engine, and gazed at the radio, which was playing one of Elvis' old classics. Twenty minutes later they were strolling across UT's luscious green, perfectly-manicured lawns.

"This campus is dead," Steve remarked,

"This campus is alive," Sandy replied. "The groundskeepers must be majoring in St. Augustine and graduating with honors. And look at the architecture," she added, pointing toward a tall, limestone building roofed with orange, terracotta barrel tiles. "Mountain peaks of burnt-orange jutting toward the deep blue sky. And it's so peaceful."

"A little too peaceful," Steve replied. "Where is everybody?"

As they crossed UT's campus, a strangely familiar tune floated from a third-story dorm window. As they neared the dorm, Steve recognized Elvis' "Pocketful of Rainbows." He froze, staring up at the window, quickly sinking into a whirlpool of emotions. "Why is this happening?" he asked.

"Why is what happening?"

"All these Elvis songs."

"Steve, you and Tara aren't the only Elvis fans in this town," Sandy reminded.

"I know. I know. I'm sure it's just a coincidence, but a pretty strange coincidence, considering "Pocketful of Rainbows" was mine and Tara's song."

As they continued walking, Steve briefly closed his eyes. Please, please help me find her.

A light breeze blew. A soft drink cup fell off the white limestone wall overlooking The Drag. A large sheet of paper floated like a Manta Ray, high above their heads—rising, dipping, gliding in a wide spiral, searching the ocean floor for the perfect place to land. It brushed the lawn in front of the couple then gently wrapped itself around Steve's legs. He stopped, picked up the advertisement, and read it to himself. His serious expression changed into a big grin. "I know where she is, Sandy. I know where she is," he repeated, handing her the ad, "and they've even drawn us a map."

* * *

Tara gave her mom a warm hug before introducing her to Paul, Brooks and Beth. The men insisted on carrying Sara's luggage from the baggage carousel to the waiting limo, saying she should not exert herself.

"My goodness, kids," Sara said, as the chauffeur opened her door, "do you treat all your guests this way?"

"Just our honored ones," Paul answered.

"Aron insisted on the limo," Brooks added. "He's been calling a lot of the shots lately."

"Ah, yes, Aron, the singer," Sara said. "How's he dealing with his—problem?"

"We think he's cured," Paul answered, as an Elvis tune played on the limo's radio.

"Congratulations," Sara said.

"Thanks," Paul replied, "but Tara deserves most of the credit. Tara and The Vineyard. It's turned out to be a good place for healing."

"So I've heard. Tara's told me all about it. Big wraparound porch. Surrounded by mesquite trees. Remote and secluded."

"That, it is," Brooks agreed, "but I'm afraid it won't seem all that remote and secluded today."

Beth nonchalantly kicked Brooks in the shin as she crossed her legs.

"How do you feel about eating out tonight, Mom?" Tara asked. "And perhaps some live music afterwards?"

"That'd be grand," Sara answered. "I gather Austin's still the Live Music Capital of the World."

"It certainly is," Tara replied.

As the Elvis song ended, Paul turned off the radio to prevent the disc jockey from spoiling Sara's surprise. A passing truck's North Dakota plates caught Tara's eye, carrying her back to a rainy day in San Angelo. The silenced radio and lull in their conversation created an uncomfortable quiet, which Tara quickly noticed. "Mom, you're always telling me California's the most exciting place in the world, and you haven't said a single word about it."

While Sara embellished the pleasures of living in Southern California, Brooks noticed Austin's lunch-hour traffic seemed unusually light. The traffic leaving Austin, however, seemed unusually heavy, spurring him to make a few notes on his legal pad. Thirty minutes later, the limo topped the hill overlooking Lake Travis then slowed behind heavy traffic.

"Good grief," Sara said. "A traffic jam—out here?"

"Lakeway must be having a tennis tournament today," Brooks said.

"*Must* be," Sara echoed. "I thought Tara said you and Paul and Rob worked at Lakeway."

"Oh, yeah, we do," Brooks replied. "We're off today, and now that I think about it, Lakeway *is* having a big tournament today."

Paul rolled his eyes.

As the traffic crawled past the resort's entrance, Sara studied Brooks curiously. "It seems your tennis fans forgot to make the turnoff to Lakeway."

The traffic stopped. "Must be an accident," Beth said, sitting forward to look out the front window.

Several drivers had parked on the side of the road and were pulling blankets and ice chests from the trunks of their cars.

"These folks don't appear to be going to a traffic accident," Sara commented.

A patrol car coming from the opposite direction, lights flashing and siren blaring, screeched to a stop beside the limousine. After a short conversation with the chafferer, the policeman escorted the limo the final mile to The Vineyard.

"Would someone *please* explain to me what's going on?" Sara asked, as the limo bumped over the cattle guard.

"I'll be happy to, Mom," Tara replied, "but let's first get you to your room where you can freshen up and perhaps change into something a little more comfortable."

While Paul and Tara helped Sara with her luggage, Brooks and Beth raced up the porch steps and straight to the back porch where they stood frozen, listening to the low hum resonating from the Johnsons' farm. Brooks' legal pad slowly dropped to the porch with a thud.

Paul and Tara showed Sara to her room then rushed to join Brooks and Beth on the back porch.

"Oh—my—Lord," Tara said.

A truck exited the back of the crowd and raced toward The Vineyard. Rob, Tanya, Dave, and Susanne were soon jumping from the truck and running through a cloud of dust toward the porch.

"What's it like coming in?" Rob asked.

"Slow moving all the way from Lakeway," Paul answered. "Stalled a half mile from here. Please tell me the parking lot's not full."

"No way," Rob said, "they're just bottlenecked at the entrances. Everyone will get in, eventually."

"Where's your mom?" Tanya asked Tara.

"Inside changing," Tara answered.

"Does she suspect anything?" Dave asked.

"She suspects *something*, but doesn't have a clue what."

Dave gazed toward the Johnsons' farm. "I'd say a few folks played hooky today."

"I'd say about forty thousand," Brooks said, in disbelief. "How could we have been so far off? I didn't even post the ads until three days ago."

"Well, we *did* have a lot of people working on the event," Dave reminded, "and people *do* talk."

Paul slowly shook his head. "I probably shouldn't have made those calls to The Statesman, The Chronicle, and The Dallas Morning News."

All heads turned toward Paul.

"I probably shouldn't have called those radio stations in San Antonio, Houston, and Corpus," Tara added.

All heads turned toward Tara.

"Have you lost your minds?" Brooks asked.

"We were afraid no one would show," Paul said, with a shrug.

A worker testing a mic on the stage caused the crowd to stir.

"Well, I hope you're happy with yourselves," Dave replied.

"A lot happier than if no one had showed," Tara laughed.

"We've created a monster," Brooks said.

"No, we've created a dragon," Rob corrected. "Look. That's its head to the left of the bluffs, and that's its long tail stretching past the Johnsons' barn all the way to the parking lot."

"I see it!" Brooks said. "Shimmering nervously, slowly bulging as it shoves the stage right up the side of the bluffs."

"Is the stage okay?" Paul asked.

"It's fine," Rob answered. "Nobody will get within 50 feet of it without a pass."

"Mr. Dragon seems friendly enough," Tanya commented. "We fed him a couple of appetizers, my knees knocking together the whole time."

"She had them eatin' out of her hands," Rob said.

"Thanks, Rob," Tanya replied, "but I don't think they came all this way for appetizers."

"Where's Aron?" Paul asked.

"On the way," Rob answered, motioning toward Sam Johnson's truck stirring dust in the distance.

"Oh—my—Lord," Sara said, stepping onto the porch.

Everyone turned.

"That seems to be the general consensus," Dave commented.

"Who's performing?" Sara asked, focusing on the stage.

"That's the answer to today's big quiz," Tara replied, facing a rocking chair toward the back steps. "Please take a seat, Mom. The rest of your welcoming committee is on the way, then I'll introduce you to everyone."

"Thank you, dear, but am I the only one sitting?"

"You're the only one who'll need to be sitting, Miss Benoist," Dave joked.

Tara stepped inside to pour her mother a glass of iced tea, returning just as Aron and his entourage arrived. Sara's face brightened at the sight of the children. Lisa Marie wore blue jean cutoffs and a flowered shirt. Bobby wore jeans and a Dallas Cowboy T-shirt. Aron, Sam, and Mike wore white T-shirts, western boots, cowboy hats, and sunglasses—farmworkers having just come in from the field. Everyone stood in a wide arc between Sara and the growing crowd. Sara studied the handsome group, took a sip of tea, then set the glass by her chair.

"I think I'll begin from left to right," Tara said, "with Mr. Rob Carpenter, our resident artist. Rob, this is my mother, Sara Benoist."

"How do you do, Mr. Carpenter," Sara replied.

"It's a pleasure to meet you, ma'am?" Rob greeted, stepping forward to shake Sara's hand.

"If those are your paintings decorating every wall in the house, the pleasure's all mine," Sara replied. "You're a very a talented artist."

"Thanks, ma'am," Rob replied. "I hope the works are as much fun to look at, as they were to paint."

"If you'd like to make a purchase, I'm Rob's talented agent," Brooks commented.

"Brooks *was* my agent," Rob corrected. "If you'd like to make a purchase, you can speak directly to me."

"Thank you, I will," Sara replied, "and Mr. Brooks, I'm sorry to hear about the loss of your job."

"Thanks, but it wasn't exactly making me rich."

"And this is Tanya Price," Tara continued, "a good friend and talented singer. As a matter of fact, you'll be hearing her perform this afternoon."

"How do you do, Miss Benoist," Tanya said, shaking Sara's hand. "Welcome to the show."

"Thank you, dear, I look forward to hearing you sing."

"It's a great opportunity for me, too. I'll try not to disappoint you."

"And this is Mr. Sam Johnson," Tara introduced. "Sam and Lucille are the good neighbors I've been telling you about."

"How do you do, Mr. Johnson?" Sara greeted. "My daughter's very lucky to have such good neighbors. I'm looking forward to meeting your wife."

"Thanks, ma'am," Sam replied, "but *we're* the lucky ones. Lucille sends her best and says you're welcome to watch the show from our back porch—the best seat in the house."

"Why thanks, I'd love to."

"And this is Aron," Tara introduced.

"How do, ma'am," Aron said, tipping his hat before shaking Sara's hand.

"How do you do," Sara said, searching for the gentleman's eyes behind the dark glasses. "Tara tells me you're a talented singer, too."

"Well, I surely try, ma'am," Aron replied, easily disguising his voice.

"The mobile in the living room is Aron's handy work," Brooks joked.

"I'm impressed," Sara said to Aron. "It's the most unusual mobile I've ever seen. So you're an artist as well as a singer?"

"No, ma'am," Aron answered, "I'm afraid Mr. Brooks is makin' a sick joke at my expense, one that he'll pay dearly for later. The mobile was Rob's handy work."

"And for sale, too, I might add," Rob added.

"And this is Dave Turner," Tara continued. "Soon to be, Dr. Dave Turner."

"Good afternoon, Dave. I hear you and Tara might become business partners someday."

"I'd consider it an honor," Dave said, "and judging from our success so far, I think we're headed for a bright future."

"And you've met Paul, Brooks and Beth," Tara continued.

Sara nodded politely, recalling the drive from the airport.

Tara next introduced Susanne and Mike before moving to the children. "And this young man is Mike's son, Bobby."

"The Kidnappers' startin' quarterback!" Bobby shouted, stepping forward and excitedly shaking Sara's hand as everyone laughed.

"We put together a football team called The Kidnappers," Rob explained.

"Hi, Bobby," Sara said. "The Kidnappers are very fortunate to have such a handsome quarterback."

"Thanks!" Bobby said, running back to stand beside his dad.

"And that brings us to Bobby's friend, Lisa. Lisa and Bobby were a great help in putting this little show together."

"Hi, Lisa," Sara said.

"How do you do, ma'am," Lisa Marie replied, stepping forward to shake hands. "We're very happy to have you here."

"Why thank you, dear, I'm happy to be here." She glanced at the bulging crowd. "Although I must admit, I *am* a little confused."

Tara scanned her mother's welcoming committee, making sure no one had been left out, then grinned at Aron and gave him his cue, a slow nod.

"So tell me, Sara," Aron said, "how was Hawaii?"

Sara gave Aron a confused look. "Hawaii?" she asked.

During the past twelve years, Sara had made four trips to The Islands, but did not recall meeting Aron on any of them. She turned in her seat to look at Tara, who gazed toward the Johnsons' farm. Sara studied the concert crowd, wondering who could draw an audience that large? Stevie Ray Vaughn? ZZ Top? Willie Nelson? Probably not. And those stars were common fixtures around Austin and certainly wouldn't be considered a big surprise. Sara retraced her steps back to the airport. She recalled an Elvis song playing as she stepped inside the terminal, and another Elvis tune playing in the limousine. Had the King traded Las Vegas for the Texas Hill Country? Not likely? Who else could draw a crowd that size? Perhaps several bands. Multiple acts playing outdoor venues had become quite popular.

Sara stared at Aron. How—was—Hawaii? She recalled the friends she had made during her most recent trip to The Islands. Her mind raced through her other adventures, stopping on her first trip, with Tara. She recalled meeting Elvis on the flight over, and their luxurious hotel, and the white, sandy beaches. She scanned the faces of her welcoming committee, wondering if any might hold a clue. She paused on Lisa. Lisa who? Tara had not mentioned the little girl's last name. Sara scanned the others. Tara had mentioned everyone's last name except Lisa's—and Aron's. Sara studied Lisa's striking resemblance to . . . .

Sara's lower jaw suddenly dropped. Her mind instantly filled with the most vivid image of *Elvis* kneeling in the first class section of that 707 destined for Hawaii. Her head began to spin as her eyes darted back to Aron. "Elvis?" she replied.

Aron grinned then removed his hat and glasses. "Small world, isn't it, Sara?"

Lisa Marie immediately ran over and jumped into her father's outstretched arms.

"Surprise!" Bobby shouted, as loud applause mixed with laughter rose to fill the porch's eaves.

"Good guess, Mom," Tara laughed, giving her mother a hug. "What gave it away?"

Sara took several deep breaths, trying to recover somewhat from her shock before answering. "There were just—too many Elvis coincidences—to be coincidences," she replied. She smiled at Lisa Marie. "And then—there was this beautiful little girl's striking resemblance to her father."

"Thank you, Miss Benoist," Lisa Marie replied.

"Please, dear, call me, Sara." She focused on Aron. "And, Mr. Presley, to answer your question . . ."

"Please, Sara, my friends call me Aron."

"Aron," Sara replied, with a big grin, "to answer your question, Hawaii was grand, every minute of it, thanks in large part to your kind gesture during the flight over. You have no idea what that meant to us."

"The pleasure was all mine, Sara, and thanks to your daughter's description of the flight, I now have a pretty good idea what it meant to y'all, and believe me, she's more than returned the favor."

Sara faced her daughter. "So *this* is the *Aron* you've been telling me about? Elvis Aron? And you kept this from me for *five months*—just to give me heart failure?"

"In Tara's defense, we were all sworn to secrecy," Dave said.

"Plus, Aron wasn't in the best mood for receiving guests the first few months," Brooks added.

"I've got the scars to prove it," Paul said, reaching up to scratch his face.

"Paul!" Tara scolded.

"I've got it all documented," Brooks added, tapping his legal pad. "Confrontational. Ill-tempered. Hostile."

"I *was* not!" Aron protested. "I was a little grumpy, like any victim of a kidnappin' would be."

"Kidnapping!" Lisa Marie echoed.

"I'm afraid so, hon', and that's not the half of it. One night I caught Brooks trying to convince everyone I was a ghost."

"A *ghost*!" Bobby echoed, staring wide-eyed at Brooks.

"*My* dad's not a ghost!" Lisa Marie said, frowning at Brooks.

"Getting to the root of your father's problems required ruling out all other possibilities," Brooks replied, "regardless of how ridiculous."

"Speaking of problems, has anyone noticed the size of the concert crowd lately?" Paul asked.

All heads turned.

"They'll be easy enough to handle," Aron replied. "But first, I think our honored guest deserves a prize for guessin' the correct answer to today's quiz. Sara, how'd ya like a little preview of this afternoon's show?"

"Thank you, Aron, but I wouldn't think of imposing on you in that way."

"But if she *would* think of imposing, she'd probably like to hear something from *Blue Hawaii*," Tara suggested.

*   *   *

Steve and Sandy parked their truck on the side of the road and began walking. As the blacktop rose, they received their first glimpse of the huge crowd. As the futility of their task hit them square in the face, they burst out laughing.

"I hope she hasn't changed her hair color," Sandy joked.

Steve noticed a dirt driveway pointing in the general direction of the concert. "Let's try a shortcut," he suggested, leading Sandy over a chained cattle guard. Seconds later the sound of Elvis singing "The Hawaiian Wedding Song" floated down the mesquite-lined drive.

"At least, now we know why every radio station in Austin's been playing *Elvis* today," Steve commented.

"What a beautiful old house," Sandy said, as The Vineyard came into view.

Steve noticed a red '57 Chevy parked near the front porch and smiled.

Sandy motioned toward a long, white limo. "This must be where the King's staying."

The song grew louder as the couple rounded the side of the house. Elvis' deep, rich voice was flawlessly clear, and the tune was being sung with acoustic guitar only, unlike other versions of the hit. As they arrived in the back yard, they glanced at the small crowd standing on the back porch. Sandy focused on the gentleman crooning the last verse, guitar in hand. "Steve!" she said, grasping her husband's arm.

Tara heard the woman's voice and slowly turned toward the couple. She focused on the tall cowboy. Their eyes locked. "Steve?"

*   *   *

Everyone making the pilgrimage that day had their reasons for attending. Most Texans had always enjoyed a special affinity for the King—in 1955 Aron played eighty gigs throughout the Lone Star State, and in 1958, during a five month period between March and August, the King called Ft. Hood, Texas his home. Many came because they had never seen Elvis perform live, and many came because they had. A large band of fatherless boys rode in to pay homage to their king. One couple from North Dakota came in search of a high school love. A large number of Austin's younger concertgoers made the pilgrimage because they just did not like Mondays, and a free outdoor concert by *anyone* was a good enough excuse to play hooky and leave that Monday far behind. But whatever their reasons, they came, sixty thousand strong.

Aron stood in the wings with Lisa Marie, his kidnappers, and twenty or so of his close friends. At exactly 3 p.m. Tanya took center stage, confidently blowing a puff of air into the mic to make sure it was turned on. "Ladies and gentlemen," she said, pausing to tease the King's followers. "I'd like to welcome a gentleman, whom a few of you may already know." The dragon's stomach rumbled as a fire deep within its belly burned. "A poor boy from Tupelo who quickly became one of this country's most talented performers." Several loud whistles broke through the growing rumble. "An individual who took this country by storm, who captured fifty million hearts, and who holds many of them still." The dragon took a deep breath, lifted its head high, and opened its mouth wide. "It is with great honor—I present to you—the King of Rock 'n' Roll—Elvis Aron Presley."

The whole stage shook from the dragon's mighty roar. Tanya stepped back from the mic as if hit by a sudden tidal wave of emotions. Aron walked from the wings wearing boots, faded jeans and a dark-blue, long-sleeve shirt, rolled up at the sleeves. He gave Tanya a hug as she passed, then nonchalantly picked up his guitar and ducked his head and shoulder through the strap. His guitar's blue pic guard matched his shirt perfectly, making the whole instrument seem like an extension of his body.

"Welcome to the show," Aron said, leaning forward to adjust his mic.

Aron's audience applauded loudly then hushed respectfully as he introduced his musicians and backup vocalists. The King then whisked his fans on the ride of their lives, lifting them high with creative renditions of local favorites, surprising them with spirited, upbeat originals, and moving them to tears with recently-created love songs and duets. Throughout his performance, he gave his followers glimpses into the past with well-placed classics.

Paul and Tara watched most of the concert from the wings, but during the last set, they noticed Lisa Marie and Bobby getting a little antsy. After a brief discussion, they invited the children to step down into the belly of the beast. Four of Aron's biggest fans climbed down from the stage, held hands, and were soon zigzagging through the King's excited subjects, occasionally pausing to watch and listen. At each stop, Paul and Tara lifted Bobby and Lisa Marie onto their shoulders so the children could enjoy different perspectives of the show. As they neared the back of the crowd, Aron announced his last song, much to his fans' dismay. At the song's end, he politely thanked everyone for attending then vanished into the wings as sixty thousand exhausted fans screamed for just—one—more song.

"Is it over?" Lisa Marie asked.

Bobby's ever-present smile quickly turned upside down.

"Not quite," Paul answered. "There's one song your dad hasn't played."

As they distanced themselves from Aron's admirers, the earth rose slightly, giving them a panoramic view of the crowd, the stage, and Aron walking back to the mic without his guitar as his audience erupted. On cue, the band's saxophonist began wailing the introduction to an old classic that many in the crowd had been requesting for quite some time. "Sorry, folks," Aron joked, "I seem to have forgotten one." As his backup vocalists sang the tune's chorus, Aron began snapping his fingers and twisting back and forth, just as he had in the movie *Girls, Girls, Girls*. He then began crooning the first verse of "Return To Sender."

Lisa Marie and Bobby instinctively mimicked Aron by dancing The Twist as Paul and Tara laughed. Tara's eyes lifted from the children dancing at her feet, to the sea of fans stretched before them, to the King performing the show's last song. "Paul," she said, face beaming, "remember the grand finales of Aron's old movies? Remember the camera rolling back farther and farther, and higher and higher while taking in the whole festive scene?"

"Yes, I remember."

"Remember the entire cast gathered in the forefront—dancing, laughing, and soaring high as *Elvis* sang one of his latest chart-busters."

"Yes," Paul laughed, "I remember, "it was all I could do to keep from jumping out of my seat and into the picture?"

"Me, too!" Tara laughed. "Me, too! And *now* look at us. Look where we're standing—this instant. We've somehow done it, Paul. We've somehow jumped right in the middle of the big picture."

As Aron and his band repeated the song for those fans who had always felt the tune was a little too short, Paul took Tara's hand. "Care to dance?"

Chapter Eleven

After the concert, Aron and his friends hiked to the ridge to watch the dragon slowly shrink. It soon transformed itself into a long snake, decorated with a thousand red lights—brightening, dimming, and flickering as it curved its way through the hills back to Austin. Brooks wrote furiously in the fading light.

"Mr. Brooks, now might be a good time to talk about the royalties from our book," Aron commented.

"*Our* book?" Brooks replied. "Which chapters did *you* write?"

"None, but I'm guessin' I'm in enough of 'em to entitle me to half the royalties."

"Half!" Brooks echoed.

"How many chapters am *I* in?" Dave asked.

"More than I'd care to admit," Brooks answered.

"What about the rest of us?" Paul asked.

"Yeah!" Bobby shouted, "what about the rest of us!

"There's not that many halves," Brooks replied.

"We don't expect a cut for our small part," Sandy said.

"Thank you," Brooks replied, "you're setting a fine example for the others."

"But, I hope you'll devote a chapter to the greatest concert in the history of concerts," Steve added.

"Consider it done," Brooks replied.

Everyone applauded Aron's performance, again, then took turns describing their favorite moments during the event.

Tara occasionally glanced at the big red sun, which was nearing the horizon. "Negotiating the woods in the dark might be a little tricky."

Aron quickly grasped Lisa Marie's hand as she leaned over the steep drop-off to look down into the darkening woods.

"Good point," Paul agreed, "we should probably head back."

"No!" Bobby protested.

"Hey, Bobby, we're having a cookout tonight," Aron reminded. "Ya like cheeseburgers, don't ya?"

"Cheeseburgers!" Bobby shouted happily.

During the following three days, the stage was disassembled, tents removed, and tons of trash hauled to the dump. While they worked, Tara and Steve resolved a few issues concerning a sad goodbye in the rain while Paul entertained Sandy with a detailed description of a March trip to Memphis.

Cleaning up after sixty thousand fans was not how Aron's kidnappers had imagined spending their last days with the King, but the work did, in fact, keep their minds off the looming goodbye. Unfortunately, that goodbye arrived all too soon on the fourth morning after the concert. Aron, Lisa Marie, Sara, and Aron's kidnappers wished Steve and Sandy a safe drive back to North Dakota then watched as the Garretts' truck vanished through the trees.

Paul Pullen

Aron's kidnappers filled their back packs with a few going-away gifts then helped Aron, Lisa Marie, and Sara load their luggage. The King and his princess took one more slow walk around the porch while the others waited in the van, Brooks behind the wheel.

During the drive to the airport, Aron insisted that Sara visit Memphis soon and promised her a comfortable stay at Graceland. Sara accepted the invitation and invited Aron and Lisa Marie to stop in for a visit during their next trip to Los Angeles. Inside the airport terminal, warm hugs and cheerful goodbyes were exchanged before Sara boarded her flight to California.

While waiting for Aron's Convair to arrive, Tara presented the King and his princess with their first going-away gift. "We wanted you to have the masters of the concert," she said, pulling two large reel to reel tapes from her backpack.

"Why, thanks, hon'," Aron replied, grasping the tapes. "Of all my concerts, this was the most fun, and I surely wanted it documented. I hope y'all made copies for yourselves."

"Oh, yeah," Paul replied, "and I'm afraid there might be a few hundred bootlegs floatin' around Central Texas by late this afternoon."

"And California," Tara added.

"And North Dakota," Rob chuckled.

"Boy, my boy," Aron laughed, "and just when I thought I was gonna get out of this state without havin' to call the cops."

"What's *bootlegs*, Daddy," Lisa Marie asked.

"It's sort of like kidnappin', hon', except instead of stealin' the artist, you're stealin' his works." He shook his head. "I can't wait to tell the Colonel. He'll see this as one of the most expensive free concerts in the history of concerts."

"Tell him to think of it as the gift that keeps on giving," Dave joked.

Paul pulled a football from his pack and pitched it to Aron.

"No way," Aron said, catching the scuffed, grass-stained pigskin. "I can't take this."

"Sure you can," Paul said. "It's not like we don't have three others."

"Plus, you'll obviously be needing all the practice you can get," Brooks added.

"Ha," Aron replied, "the only time I lost was when *you* were on my side."

Lisa Marie snatched the ball from her dad and pitched it to Brooks, who pitched it back.

Rob pulled a large sketchpad from his pack. "This is your personal copy and sneak preview of my next painting, *Five Months in Texas*, destined to be my greatest work ever. The finished masterpiece will be around eight feet by twenty—a lot's happened durin' the last five months. It'll take at least that long to paint."

Aron sat to open the large sketchpad as the others crowded around to better see.

"Those in the know can read it from left to right," Rob explained, "from our first day at The Vineyard, to the concert. Colored pencils don't do it justice, so try and imagine it in bright oils."

Aron studied a small dark form kneeling before bright yellow. "That's me, isn't it?" he asked, face brightening. "Our first morning at The Vineyard?"

"You have a keen eye," Rob complimented.

Aron slowly turned the large pages until he had reached the end. A large, blue figure on the last page appeared to be slaying a big, green dragon. "Wow, I seem to have grown a little."

"I think we've all grown a little during the past five months," Tara replied, reaching up to brush away a tear.

"Now, Tara," Aron scolded, leaning over to give her a hug. "I thought we voted there'd be no tears."

As the others studied the last picture, Lisa Marie flipped back the pages to something she had noticed earlier. "What's this?" she asked, pointing toward a half-dozen streaks of orange flying across the page.

"It looks like the start of a bottle rocket fight," Aron answered.

"A bottle rocket fight!" Lisa Marie echoed.

"Yes, hon', it was a real blast. Four *big chickens* almost got arrested."

"I beg your pardon," Tara replied.

"What!" Lisa Marie asked.

Tara placed her hands on Lisa Marie's shoulders. "Lisa, listen to me very carefully. Four noble warriors stood to face the music while two *big chickens* ran away to hide in the hills."

"Ouch," Paul replied.

"It wasn't *my* idea to run," Aron protested.

"I was just tryin' to save the King," Paul argued.

"You can read all about it right here," Brooks said, handing Lisa Marie a copy of his nearly-completed manuscript.

"Thanks," Lisa Marie replied. "Is this the book about my dad's trip to Texas?"

"It certainly is," Brooks answered, "and you're in it, too."

"Really!" she asked, opening the thick manuscript to the first page.

"It wouldn't be much of a book without you," Dave replied.

"I'm still working on the last chapters," Brooks said to Aron, "but I wanted your input and thought you might like something to read on the flight back."

"Thanks, Mr. Brooks," Aron said, leaning over his daughter's lap to inspect the manuscript. "I can hardly wait to start makin' changes, especially in the first few chapters."

"Changes," Brooks echoed, with raised eyebrows.

"Would you mind takin' out the part where I gave you that black eye?" Paul asked.

"Not at all," Aron answered, checking his shirt pocket for a pen.

"You gave my dad a black eye!" Lisa Marie asked, looking wide-eyed at Paul.

"Yes, well, it wasn't like he wasn't askin' for it," Paul joked.

"How about that uncomfortable scene where I slapped Paul across the face?" Tara asked.

"Consider it gone," Aron replied.

"You slapped Paul!" Lisa Marie asked Tara, jaw dropping.

"Yes, well, it wasn't like he wasn't askin' for it," Tara replied.

"My little drinkin' and drivin' episode doesn't add a whole lot to the story, does it?" Rob asked.

"It never happened," Aron answered, checking his pants pockets for a pen.

"What about me running scared in the middle of Brooks' stupid ghost story?" Dave asked. "Could that maybe be Brooks hightailin' it to the hills instead of me?"

"All I need is a pen?" Aron answered.

Pens quickly appeared from four directions.

"Give me that!" Brooks said, reaching for the manuscript.

"No!" Lisa Marie shouted, leaning over to tighten her hold on the book.

"Oh, calm down, Brooksie," Aron said, "you'll still be the hero."

"Just a little more flawed than you first imagined," Rob chuckled.

Dave pulled a large photo album from his pack. "Susanne and Beth helped me put this together."

"Wow," Aron said, opening the thick album. "How many pictures did y'all take?"

"Over four hundred. We removed the duds and weak sisters, which left three hundred of the best for your album."

"Look, dad!" Lisa Marie said, pointing. "That's you and me playing soccer! And there's Bobby! And Bobby's dad!"

The photographs documented every day of the three-week event, triggering lots of smiles and laughter, and a few tears. Tara looked away to stare at a small dot in the sky, which quickly turned into the King's Convair.

"Please tell Susanne and Beth thanks," Aron said to Dave, as he closed the photo album.

"I will," Dave replied.

"I almost hate to ask if you made copies?"

"A limited number," Dave answered, "before locking up the negatives to protect ourselves from bootleggers. We're not stupid."

"Oh, so you're implying I *am*?"

"Now did I say that, Curly?"

"Didn't I ask you to stop calling me that?"

"My mistake," Dave replied, as Aron's plane slowed to a stop outside the big window.

"Thanks, folks," Aron said, scanning the gifts, "and not just for the presents, but for everything."

"Yeah, thanks!" Lisa Marie echoed, clutching the photo album.

"You're very welcome," Tara answered.

Big lumps formed in a few throats as everyone but Brooks stared at the floor.

"For Pete's sake, they're just going to Memphis," Brooks reminded, "and we *did* vote to keep a telephone or two."

"Thank you, Mr. Brooks," Tara replied, smiling. "That *does* take some of the sting out."

"And don't forget our layovers between Memphis and Los Angeles," Aron reminded.

"We're coming back next month, right?" Lisa Marie asked, searching her dad's eyes.

"We surely are, hon'," Aron answered.

Goodbyes and hugs were exchanged before Aron and Lisa Marie gathered up their gifts and exited the terminal. At the top of their Convair's stairs, they turned and waved. Tara managed not to cry, until the plane's wheels lifted off the runway. Her friends immediately enveloped her in a group hug.

Paul watched until the airplane vanished, then burst out laughing.

Dave frowned at his friend. "Did I miss something."

"Yes, as a matter of fact, you missed a *big* something," Paul replied. "I would've filled y'all in earlier, but I was sworn to secrecy until now."

Paul stared at a point in the sky where Aron's plane had vanished then casually sat on the carpeted floor. He leaned back on his hands, closed his eyes, and focused on the tickling sensation in the center of his stomach. His friends waited impatiently.

"Okay," Brooks grumbled, "you have our attention."

Paul slowly opened his eyes. "Mr. Brooks, your days of fretting over The Vineyard's account balance are hereby over. Aron has deposited six million in our account, one million for each of us, and an extra million for Tara's clinic."

Everyone studied Paul seriously, searching for any sign he was joking.

"Six—million—dollars?" Brooks asked.

"You're kidding, right?" Rob asked.

"No," Paul replied, "I'm not kidding."

One by one, they slowly sat, right where they had stood.

"I'm a—*millionaire*?" Brooks asked, staring at Paul in disbelief.

"*We're* millionaires," Paul corrected, smiling broadly.

"We're also not taking it," Tara said. "You *do* realize how wrong this is. We didn't do this for money."

"No, we didn't," Paul agreed, "and yes, it *is* wrong, and I said as much to Aron in a lengthy argument, which I lost. He said the amount might seem large to us, but that it wasn't that much to him and that he wanted to pay us back for the services he received during his visit, except for maybe the rough treatment in Detox."

Paul's friends smiled.

"Tara, he said to remind you of our first ride to the pay phone, and you saying he had a lot of positive traits, like generosity, positive traits that would help him arrive on the happy side of this country's 50 percent success rate. He said now that he was on the happy side, he was a little concerned about those still falling on the unhappy side and that the sooner you opened your clinic, the better."

Paul scanned his fellow Musketeers. "Dave, he said he wanted to help you with your student loans and parking tickets. Rob, he said anyone wanting to hit the art world should certainly consider opening his own art studio. And Mr. Brooks, he said he wanted to invest heavily in your book to increase his share of the royalties. As for me, he said the sky was the limit and he didn't want a little thing like no money slowing me down."

Silence hung over the group.

"Six—million—dollars," Brooks said, still trying to come to grips with the huge amount.

"It's a—king's ransom," Dave joked.

Everyone looked at Dave and smiled.

"Yes, it is," Tara agreed, her smile fading, "and like all ransom money, it's tainted. I took part in this venture to search for a better form of treatment, to return a favor, and to help Aron turn his life around—*not* to steal his money."

Dave nodded reflectively. "Well, I have to admit, I *am* feeling a little guilty. It seems like only yesterday I was calling you folks stupid and crazy and saying we'd all end up in jail and that I didn't want any part of it."

"If it'll make you feel any better, I'll take your million," Brooks offered.

"Really," Rob laughed. "If it'll make you feel any better, we could still go to jail for the bootlegged tapes."

"What bootlegged tapes?" Dave asked, holding up his bare hands.

"I make a motion we give the money back," Tara said.

"I make a motion we adjourn this meeting so I can start investing my million," Brooks replied. "You *do* realize every day we keep it in our checking account we're losing thousands in interest?"

"We appreciate your concern," Tara replied.

"Giving it back won't be as easy as you might think," Paul said. "He got a hold of our social security numbers, contacted the IRS, and sent them a fat check covering all the local, state, and federal taxes."

"What!" Brooks replied. "The money's *tax free!*"

"Tax free," Paul answered, "and he threatened to put twelve million in our account if we tried to give it back."

"No way!" Brooks said. "You mean if we give the six million back, he'll punish us with *twelve* million! I hereby second Tara's motion to give the money back. All in favor?"

"Mr. Brooks," Tara scolded, "we're discussing how to return the money, *not* how to abscond with more."

"Speak for yourself," Brooks laughed.

"I will," Tara said, standing. "I'm calling him the minute we get back. And I'll be informing him that in regards to my share, thanks, but no thanks." She reached down and grasped Paul and Dave's hands. "Come on, my little millionaires. I'm sure you have quite a bit of soul-searching to do during the drive home."

"Would you mind if I searched for mine at that Porsche dealership we passed on the way in?" Brooks asked.

"Porsche!" Tara laughed. "I kind of pictured you in something more—frugal."

"I'm seein' him in a used VW," Rob agreed.

Two hours later, Tara was speed-dialing Graceland. "I appreciate your generosity, Aron," she began, "but I can't accept your money."

"Sure you can," Aron replied. "Listen, Tara, y'all risked a lot by kidnapping me, and made a lot of sacrifices durin' the past five months, while refusing to accept a single cent in return. I'm just payin' ya back. And the bottom line is, it's a done deal. Any attempt to give the money back will surely fail. All you'll be doin' is makin' my lawyers rich while wastin' my valuable time—time better spent on more important things like havin' fun with Yisa and flyin' to Texas to visit my rich friends."

Tara lost every point in their lengthy debate before reluctantly agreeing to accept the money. She thanked Aron profusely for the large gift then passed the phone to her friends so they could do the same. Aron again thanked them for the going-away gifts before passing the phone to Lisa Marie, who had a ton of questions, including whether or not she would be allowed to take part in next year's bottle rocket fight. Before saying goodbye, Lisa asked Tara for Bobby's phone number.

Tara hung up the phone, scanned the living room's damaged walls and furnishings, and laughed. "I wonder if The Vineyard's for sale."

"Of course it's for sale," Brooks replied, "and now that we're wise to the fact that it's haunted, we should be entitled to a considerable discount."

"Cheap to the core," Dave said, shaking his head. "Don't forget to tell him about the holes in the walls. Maybe you can get him to knock a couple hundred off the selling price."

"Good idea," Brooks agreed, "I'll tell him the damages must have been caused by the ghosts that he conveniently forgot to tell us about."

During the next few days, numerous phone calls were made between Graceland and The Vineyard. Aron changed doctors, hired a personal trainer, and terminated his contract with Colonel Parker, convincing his manager that they had reached a point in their relationship where they would make better friends than business partners. He immediately canceled the rest of his concerts for the year so he could spend more time with Lisa Marie. The King and his princess became almost inseparable. They enjoyed taking Harley rides into the country, hiking a popular state park along the mighty Mississippi, and playing soccer, football, and baseball with friends and relatives. Lisa expressed an interest in playing the guitar and they began experimenting with writing upbeat songs for children. They discussed the possibility of throwing a free, outdoor concert near Memphis and began preparing speeches to persuade a few of their Texas friends to help stage the event.

Although Aron's gift was given with no strings attached, his kidnappers enjoyed keeping him informed of their larger purchases, investments, and financial goals.

Paul met with a UT counselor who helped him set up a schedule that would assure him a degree within nine months. He purchased an electric guitar, began taking guitar lessons, and discovered a strange knack for turning Edgar Allen Poe's old verses into lyrics for newly-created songs. He also awakened one morning experiencing a strange desire to help other young adults trapped inside of tight bonds—strange, because helping such individuals would undoubtedly require the continuation of his college education another three to four years. Paul mentioned the irony to Aron, and both men had a good laugh. Paul's most expensive purchase was a used, late-model Land Cruiser.

Rob transferred his transcript to UT and registered for two advanced art classes. He bought a ton of art supplies and began searching for commercial property in Austin, suitable for an art studio. He immediately purchased an expensive new truck.

Brooks hired a financial adviser and began investing heavily in stocks, bonds, and a local publishing company. He began the final edit of his book, with Aron's more serious suggestions in mind. Mr. Brooks opted not to waste time or money on new transportation.

Dave paid off his student loans, became Lakeway's newest member, and was soon taking golf lessons from one of the resort's pros. For his following semester's thesis, he began researching the physiological damages caused by the long-term ingestion of amphetamines. When not golfing or preparing for the fall semester, he enjoyed browsing Austin's Mercedes-Benz dealerships.

Tara had The Vineyard appraised and made their land-lord an offer he couldn't refuse. She compiled a list of the nation's best drug rehabilitation clinics and made travel arrangements to meet with the clinics' directors. A professor at UT's Graduate School of Psychology informed Tara that her application was making steady progress through the department's committee. Tara celebrated the news by purchasing a burnt-orange BMW convertible.

More money often means more responsibilities, and on a hot day in mid-August, Paul and Tara spent the entire morning meeting with accountants, bankers, and the IRS—and most of the afternoon getting inspection stickers and license plates for Tara's new car. By 3 p.m., however, their errands were completed, and they were rewarded with a scenic drive home in Tara's convertible. Paul effortlessly maneuvered her orange sports car through the purple and blue hills as the wind blew their hair and the sun warmed their skin. Tara rested her head on Paul's shoulder, gazing up at the passing rock formations, twist-ed mesquite trees, and a graceful turkey vulture circling high above. She turned on the car's radio and smiled as the King began singing "Heartbreak Hotel." They im-mediately joined in with the chorus. A second Elvis song followed, causing them to laugh at their good fortune.

"KLBJ's still paying homage to the big concert," Paul guessed.

"Or they just opened the bootlegged tapes I sent them," Tara laughed.

Paul slowed to negotiate a tight curve, popped the clutch, and slammed on the gas. They laughed as the rear tires squealed and the car shot out of the sharp turn. As the vulture circled lower, a third Elvis classic played, uninterrupted. The couple stared at the radio curiously. KLBJ, Austin's progressive rock station, rarely played old Elvis songs, and concert or not, they would never play three in a row, unless perhaps it was the King's birthday, which it was not. As the vulture's large shadow flashed across the car, Tara quickly changed the station. Another Elvis tune played. Tara's eyes darted to Paul then back to the radio. Paul lifted his foot off the accelerator. Tara changed the station again and again, eyes instantly filling with tears. At that moment, every radio station in Austin was playing *Elvis*, and there could only be one reason why. She burst into tears.

Paul pulled the car to the side of the road, turned off the engine, and quickly changed the station back to KLBJ. They listened in shock as the disc jockey confirmed their worst fears. The King was dead. Because an autopsy had not yet been performed, rumors were running rampant. Suicide. Murder. Drugs. Heart failure. Cover-up. One disc jockey even speculated the King had faked his own death to free himself from the hassles of being Elvis. Tara turned off the radio, buried her head in Paul's chest, and sobbed. "He—never should have left—The Vineyard," she cried, her whole body shaking. "He—never—should have left."

Paul caressed Tara in his arms, staring at the expensive new BMW, staring at the expensive new Rolex decorating his arm—suddenly realizing how worthless money can be. At that moment, he would have gladly traded every penny of his for the power to roll back the clock five months. He let Tara cry undisturbed for some time before suggesting they drive home. "If the others haven't heard, we should be the ones to tell them."

Tara lifted her head from Paul's chest then slowly nodded, dark mascara running down her cheeks. Paul waited for the traffic to clear then pulled onto the road, mind racing. They would need to contact Lisa Marie, perhaps fly to Memphis, probably plan for those returning to The Vineyard, which had suddenly become the site of the King's last concert. They should probably consider organizing their own memorial service—and on and on. For Paul, dealing with the loss, personally, would have to come later.

Aron's chief kidnappers returned home to find their driveway filled with cars and a short line of mourners standing in the doorway. Rob, Brooks, and Dave were leaning against the porch railing, anxiously awaiting Paul and Tara's return. A light breeze swirled the dust at the couple's feet as they walked toward the house. Tara made it halfway up the porch steps before bursting into tears. The men helped her to the nearest rocking chair, consoling her as best they could while trying to keep their own emotions in check. The sounds of ringing phones, radio news reports, and sad discussions of the latest rumors spilled out onto the porch.

"We need to talk," Paul said.

Another car pulled up the driveway, followed by a van full of flowers.

"Where?" Brooks asked.

Paul motioned toward the woods. "Ten minutes, and we'll have all the privacy in the world." Heads nodded. "Tara, if you don't feel up to it, we can fill you in when we get back."

"No. Thanks. I'll be okay. You're right, we need to talk."

Paul's eyes fell from Tara's sad face, to her brightly-colored dress and heels. "We can wait while you change into something more comfortable."

Tara nodded then slowly stood.

"Beth and Susanne are on their way," Lucille Johnson called from inside.

"Thanks," Brooks replied.

"Tanya's on the phone from New York," another voice echoed.

"Thanks," Rob replied, opening the screen door for Tara and the others.

As the wind picked up, the woods grew as noisy as the house. Tara stared at the agitated trees as they hiked, which caused her to trip and skin her knee. The men helped her to her feet, and Paul insisted on holding her hand as they continued walking.

"Where are we going?" Dave asked.

"There's a good place up ahead," Paul answered.

The sight of the fallen oak gave Tara pause. She re-called her first sighting of the defiant tree months ear-lier—its fat, green leaves glistening in the falling rain—thick, strong roots feeding from the pond below—sturdy branches reaching toward heaven. The tree's trunk now rested lower to the ground than she had first remembered. Its rounded shoulders drooped, and its arms hung low. Its boney fingers dangled noisily like bamboo chimes. The oak's last remaining leaves were pale, brittle, and holding on for dear life as the strong wind blew. A shallow grave below the tree beckoned. Tara looked away, a little late, and burst into tears. "I'm sorry," she apologized, between cries. "I'm sorry."

"For what?" Dave asked, giving his friend a hug. "You're allowed to grieve, Tara, any way you like."

Paul lifted Tara onto the tree's trunk then retrieved a bandage and antiseptic from his pack. As he doctored her knee, the others focused on the forest, which seemed to be growing angrier by the minute. A nearby mesquite took a swing at Rob's head. Rob reached up and snapped off the offending branch. The wind gusted, and the enraged tree lunged at Rob with all its might. The big jock shook his head. "I can't believe this is happening."

"I can't either," Brooks replied. "It doesn't make sense. We successfully kidnapped him. We saved him from drugs. We helped him turn his life around. And for what? So he could die with a clear head? It just doesn't make sense."

"We never should have let him go," Rob said.

"It wasn't our decision," Paul replied.

"Who talked to him last?" Brooks asked.

"Rob and I talked to him yesterday morning," Dave answered.

"I talked to him last night," Tara said.

"How'd he sound?" Brooks asked.

"Positive," Tara answered.

"Happy," Dave replied.

"He said he was keeping really busy," Rob answered, "and havin' lots of fun with Lisa Marie, and that they were lookin' forward to their next trip to Texas."

"Has anyone talked to Lisa Marie?" Paul asked.

"We've been trying since we heard but haven't been able to get through," Dave answered.

"I'll try again when we get back," Paul said.

"I'll bet you anything his Memphis Mob had something to do with this," Rob said, glaring at the forest.

"Someone who didn't like all the changes he was making around Graceland," Brooks agreed.

"They could have easily drugged him," Rob added.

Paul listened quietly as the men discussed the wild rumors pouring out of Memphis, but when someone mentioned the King was supposedly sitting on the toilet at the time of his death, Paul could take no more. "Stop it, guys. Please. What are we trying to do here, anyway? Solve a mystery? From a thousand miles away? He's Elvis Presley, for Pete's sake. It'll all come out, eventually, and what difference does it make now? Finding the cause won't bring him back. I think we should discuss—where we go from here?"

Heads slowly nodded.

"Should we go to Memphis?" Rob asked.

"Would we even be invited?" Dave wondered.

"They're probably blaming *us* for his death," Brooks guessed.

"Why would they blame *us*?" Rob asked.

"Lots of reasons," Brooks replied. "We helped him see his life in Memphis a little too clearly. We stole their golden goose. Our treatment was too rough and somehow caused his death. Who knows *what* they're thinking."

Paul stared sadly at the ground. "They're probably thinking sad thoughts. They just lost a son, a grandson, a father, a cousin, and a friend." He looked up at his friends. "They're suffering, just like us, and we should probably think kindly of them."

Again, heads nodded.

"Graceland will be bombarded with fans," Dave commented.

"So will The Vineyard," Rob added.

Tara looked toward their house. "I think we should have a memorial service here, for those returning to the site of his last concert. I'm sure Sam and Lucille will let us use their farm."

"Good idea," Brooks agreed, "but I'd like to go to Memphis, too. Even if the funeral's closed to the public, they'll have to have some sort of viewing for his fans, and it might be the only way to contact Lisa Marie. If all else fails, we can write her a letter and deliver it personally to Graceland."

Tara nodded. "I think I'll stay here, but I'm sure my mom will want to fly to Memphis."

"Then I'd better go, too," Rob said. "I have a feeling things are going to get really weird up there."

"I think I'll pay my respects here," Dave said. "This is where I knew him best—where we became friends."

"I feel the same way," Paul said, "but I'm sure there'll be others who'll want to attend both services. Maybe we can postpone ours until after Memphis has had theirs."

"How about next Monday?" Tara suggested. "We could schedule it for three in the afternoon, the same time as his concert."

"Perfect," Rob agreed.

As they planned the specifics of their service, Brooks took notes on the palm of his hand, having forgotten his legal pad. He quickly filled his hand then began writing on his arm. He paused, staring at his suddenly tattooed arm and hand, eyes moistening. "This is *not* how I wanted the story to end—not at all how I wanted it to end."

"It's not how any of us wanted it to end," Paul replied, giving his friend a hug. "But it'll turn out okay. You'll see. Everything will turn out okay."

Brooks and Dave both stared at Paul curiously. During the hike home, they pulled their friend aside.

"You're taking this awfully well," Dave mentioned to Paul.

"*Awfully* well," Brooks agreed.

Paul took a deep breath. "Yes, I am, and for good reason. We have a lot of work to do. I want to make sure everyone else gets through this okay. I'll grieve later."

Dave nodded reflectively. "Well, sir, I wish you luck with that. Just promise me you won't wait *too* much later."

"Thanks, Dave, I promise. I won't."

"And if *later* comes sooner than you think, we'll be here," Brooks added.

"Thanks, Brooksie, I appreciate that."

Aron's kidnappers returned home to find the line of mourners stretching down the windswept driveway and toward the road. Politely tipped hats were snatched and sent sailing. Long locks stung unsuspecting faces. Dresses were uncomfortably lifted. Tears, torn from red eyes. Someone had propped open the screen door to keep it from flying off its hinges. Inside the house the angry mobile swooped and swirled, occasionally striking the heads and shoulders of the taller mourners. Uncomfortable silences were shattered by overturned vases and ringing phones.

Tara changed into a black silk dress. Paul changed into black slacks, a white dress shirt, and a blue tie. The couple spent the rest of the day hugging well-wishers, thanking them for the cards and flowers, and informing them of the planned memorial service. Brooks and Beth scanned the growing number of cards and letters, selecting those appropriate for reading during the service. Dave and Susanne assembled a montage of concert photographs suitable for displaying at the service. The concert's musicians and vocalists arranged a list of songs to be sung live or played from the concert recordings. Rob helped ferry distraught fans from the airport.

As darkness fell over the house, the procession thinned, and by 11 p.m., vanished. Before leaving on his final trip to the airport, Rob stretched the chain across the cattle guard while Brooks attached a poster announcing the memorial service and asking fans to please leave any cards or letters in the mailbox. An hour later Rob first picked up Tanya, then Steve and Sandy Garrett.

"I hope y'all don't mind staying with the Johnsons," Rob said to their friends from North Dakota. "They already have a house full, but Lucille had her mind set."

"Of course not," Steve replied.

"It was very kind of them to offer," Sandy added.

"They're such a hospitable couple," Tanya commented, "and quite used to entertaining large numbers of guests."

Steve and Sandy were soon unpacking their bags and visiting with the other guests gathered in the Johnsons' living room. Before leaving, Rob and Tanya spoke briefly with Sam and Lucille at their kitchen table. Tanya focused on the the couple's tired faces. "You folks have had a long day, haven't you?"

"Yes, dear, we have," Lucille replied, pulling a crumpled handkerchief from her robe pocket. "And I'm afraid it's going to be a longer night. Sam and I insisted that those wantin' to sleep over stay at our house, to give you kids some privacy, but now we're not so sure that was a good idea."

"It's gotten really spooky over there," Sam explained. "All the lights are off, one candle lit, windows closed up against the wind. I'll be glad when mornin' gets here."

Lucille lifted her handkerchief to her eyes. "Tara's closed up like a clam, and the poor thing looks terrible. After the last vase broke, she had every flower in the house banished to the pantry." Lucille looked up at Tanya. "Perhaps you could talk to her."

"Of course I will," Tanya replied, resting a hand on Lucille's.

"We're worried about all you folks," Sam added, looking at Rob.

"We'll get through this okay," Rob replied. "A little scarred up, maybe, but we'll get through it just fine. And we *do* have the best neighbors in the world helpin' us."

Sam and Lucille smiled, but as a hanging basket struck the front of the the house, their smiles faded.

"Is that darn wind *ever* going to let up?" Lucille asked.

"It doesn't seem like it," Tanya replied.

At the cattle guard, Rob unhooked the chain while Tanya fought the wind to the mailbox. "Oh!" she said, pulling her hand back from the mail. After sucking away a small drop of blood, she carefully removed three red roses, several cards, and a half-empty bottle of cognac. "How strange," she said, holding the roses against her chest while walking back to the van.

As the van bumped along the narrow driveway, The Vineyard's angry trees scratched at its doors and windows. Tanya rubbed the goose bumps from her arms. At the sight of the dark house, Rob shook his head. They held hands while climbing the porch steps to the front door. A gust of wind followed them into the living room, twirling the mobile and shaking the lone candle flame.

Paul and Tara were sitting on the sofa staring blankly at the flickering light. Paul's curly hair cast a spidery shadow up the wall and ceiling. Tara's face was white, drawn, and void of any expression. Her bright green eyes had changed into dark orbs—open wide, but no one was home. Brooks and Beth were sitting on the other sofa and smiled at Rob and Tanya before closing their tired eyes. Dave was sitting in a big arm chair, head nodding sleepily, Susanne asleep in his lap. The entire group was positioned in a large semicircle around the candlelit coffee table as the mobile's ghoulish shadows floated above their heads.

"Who ordered the seance?" Rob joked.

Tanya smiled then set the flowers, cognac, and mail on the coffee table before whispering a few words of encouragement to Tara. The trace of a Mona Lisa smile flashed across Tara's face.

Rob closed the front door, walked across the stuffy room, and cracked a window. "Anybody want a drink?"

"I'll take some water," Tanya replied.

Rob stepped into the dark kitchen and opened the refrigerator. His tired boots cast long shadows across the floor and up the wall. He stared at the catsup, mustard, and mayonnaise bottles, which were still clinging tightly to Aron's fingerprints. He chugged a beer, filled a plastic glass with cold water, then grabbed another beer before returning to the living room. Rob handed Tanya her water then sat on the floor with his back against the wall.

Tanya took a few drinks before setting the half-empty glass in front of Tara and Paul. She then sat between Rob's legs, back against his chest, head cuddled beneath his chin, watching as the candle flame grew eerily still.

Again, Rob shook his head. He knew his friends would get through this okay, but he didn't particularly care for the way they were going about it. He could almost feel the house's ghouls entering the living room one by one. He opened his beer and took a long drink, resting his head against the wall. Outside, an empty rocking chair kept time against the porch railing. The rustling mesquite provided accompaniment and along with the chair, waited patiently for the lead vocals to join in.

Just past 2 a.m. three loud knocks broke the living room's silence.

"Paul!" Lucille called out. "Tara!"

Eyelids slowly opened.

"Sorry to bother y'all so late," Lucille said, "but we just found this letter with yesterday's mail. It's from Aron."

Eyelids opened wider.

Tanya stood and answered the door. "Thanks, Lucille," she greeted. "Thanks, Sam. Please, come in. That was very thoughtful of you."

A strong wind followed the Johnsons into the room, tipping the glass and sending water across the coffee table. Tara reached out then paused, fingertips suspended inches from the glass. As if suddenly realizing it didn't matter, she slowly returned her hand to her lap, staring blankly at the tipped glass.

Lucille's eyes quickly moistened. She reached into her dress pocket for her handkerchief, along with the envelope. "It was in another letter addressed to us. He asked that we give it to y'all if anything happened. He said the poem was for you, Paul."

"Thank you," Tanya said, closing the door and taking the envelope.

Everyone watched as the letter passed from Tanya's hand to Paul's. An uncomfortable silence followed.

"Well, then, I guess we'll be goin'," Lucille said.

"No," Paul replied, a little louder than he had intended. "No," he repeated, voice falling. "Please, stay. I'm sure this was meant for y'all, too."

As Sam studied the shadows slow-dancing across the room, a cold chill climbed up the back of his neck. Lucille searched the room for someplace to sit. Rob and Tanya retrieved two chairs from the kitchen, then returned to their seats on the floor. The Johnsons sat, completing the circle of bodies surrounding the candle. Paul opened the letter, read the poem to himself, and grinned. He next opened Aron's letter and began reading aloud.

"Dear kidnappers,

"Since our return to Memphis, Yisa's been talking nonstop about her trip to Texas. She was quite taken in by her new friends and their old ranch house and is lookin' forward to her next trip. I hope y'all will encourage her to visit soon and often.

"For some time, I've had this strange premonition, which is the reason for this letter. Since you're reading it now, I guess my hunch was right, and I can just picture the sad scene taking place at The Vineyard at this moment. I hope the little story that I'm about to tell y'all will help cheer you up.

"My story begins in Graceland on March 15, somewhere between four and five in the afternoon, where I found myself in the middle of some sort of drug trip, dream, hallucination, or near-death experience. I'll let y'all be the judge, but for the purposes of this story, I think I'll call it a dream—a really bad dream, at first.

"In the dream, I'd just died and wasn't at all happy about it. I was screamin', cryin', and shoutin' that I had this huge amount of unfinished business. I wasn't sure exactly what the business was, but knew it was extremely important and that I couldn't leave until it was finished. When my screams didn't get anybody's attention, I fell to my knees and begged for anybody listenin' to please let me stay.

"Suddenly, the dream changed. I never actually heard or saw anyone, but immediately understood that I'd be allowed to stay. My anger and frustration quickly changed to happiness—happiness to the point of euphoria. Unfortunately, my euphoria didn't last very long. The next thing I knew, my shoulders and neck were exploding with pain. Some fool was shakin' me so hard I thought my head was gonna fall off. I remember pushin' him away and wantin' badly to return to my euphoric dream. I recall tennis shoes being squeezed onto my feet, and hard slaps across my face, and somebody saying something about Lamborginis, Harleys, naked women, and cheeseburgers.

"I don't recall too much about the trip from Memphis to Austin. The next thing I remember was wakin' up in a small room, head throbbing, stomach churning, guts exploding up my throat. All of a sudden, my whole world was that small cell filled with the most agonizing pain and intense cravings. All memory of the strange dream had vanished, never to return again, or so I thought.

"The pain I experienced in Detox followed me to The Vineyard and continued to torment me right up until our last fight, when Paul's use of the word *business* jogged a vague memory of that Memphis dream. During the next few days, I started recalling small flashes of the dream and slowly began to realize that I did, in fact, have business there, business more important than bustin' guitars and attacking those tryin' to help.

"Some of my unfinished business was obvious, like gettin' through withdrawal and recovery, and findin' other ways to tackle my health problems. But a lot of it wasn't so obvious. A lot of it I stumbled over during group activities with my friends.

"During our fast-paced football games, I discovered a new appreciation for situational highs. While listening to stories on the back porch, I was reminded of the importance of kind gestures and learned how one of mine prompted a little girl to return the favor, sixteen years later. During a fun ride in a '57 convertible, I was reminded of the strong influence I still have on others. And a naggin' curiosity led to the discovery of a strange bond between a knight and a king, and on a hill overlooking The Musketeers' Tenth Annual Bottle Rocket Fight, I learned the importance of seeing that bond resolved. And, of course, reconnecting with Lisa Marie and throwin' a concert for a few of my most loyal fans was a big part of my unfinished business.

"As I again think about the sad scene now takin' place at The Vineyard, I can just imagine the house's spirits havin' a field day—sayin' if y'all had somehow forced me to stay, I'd still be alive—that you helped me turn my life around for nothing—that you failed miserably in your lofty goal to save the King. All lies, of course, but then ghosts aren't known for their good behavior, are they? They are, however, known for being pretty convincing at times, so just in case anyone's been believing their lies, I'd like to set the record straight.

"My kidnappers succeeded in doing everything they promised that first morning at The Vineyard. You created a healthy environment where I was able to free myself from addiction. You gave me a long break from my brutal concert schedule, destructive lifestyle, and all the other pressures of being *Elvis*. You allowed me anonymity and gave me common ground to become your friend, and while doing all this, you unknowingly provided me with a great opportunity to complete a whole lot of unfinished business. You did everything you promised, and more, and for this, I'm deeply thankful.

"In closing, I'd like to add one more thing. In the middle of one of our hotly-contested football games, right after one of my miraculous passes, I got this strong feelin' that we'd played that game before, not there, but in some distant time, and some distant place, and that we'd surely play it again. I realize that déjà vu feeling could've been nothin' more than a side effects of my situational high, but just in case it wasn't, just in case I was given a small glimpse at the big picture, I want y'all to know I'll be waiting for each of you on the other side.

Love, Aron."

Paul looked up to find everyone in the room smiling.

Aron's ghost, sitting on the floor a few feet away, was also smiling. He bowed his head and prayed for each of his friends before standing to leave. As he passed the coffee table he paused, grinned, and righted the tipped glass.

Everyone in the room witnessed the glass right itself, and everyone in the room jumped when a sudden gust of wind blew open the front door. Tara leaped off the sofa, ran to the doorway, and pushed open the screen door. She raced to the porch and clutched the railing with both hands. Her long hair and black silk dress whipped behind her like flags in the wind as she lifted her chin high and shouted, "We love you, Aron! We love you!"

Paul was next to race to the porch, with his friends close behind. "Thanks for all the highs, Aron!" he shouted. "And for all the laughs! And for *more* than filling the void!"

"Thanks for your music!" Tanya yelled. "And for all your concerts! And for the greatest of all concerts!"

"Thanks for the adventure, Aron!" Rob shouted. "Thanks for the mother of all adventures! And take care of that arm! We're going to need a quarterback!"

"Thanks for your life!" Susanne said. "And for letting us be apart of it!"

"We'll play the game again, Aron!" Dave yelled. "We'll certainly play it again!"

"Take care of yourself, Aron," Beth said. "Take care of yourself."

"Thanks for the book!" Brooks shouted. "I couldn't have done it without you. I couldn't have written one word without you!"

"We love you, dear," Lucille said, staring into the dark night. "We love you, dear."

"Hurry back, anytime, Aron," Sam whispered. "You hear me? You're welcome back, anytime."

"Goodbye, Aron!" Tara shouted.

"Goodbye!" Paul and the others shouted over and over.

"Goodbye!"

"Goodbye!"

Chapter Twelve

The Vineyard's memorial service was held beneath a clear blue sky. A light breeze blew to cool those gathering for the service then calmed just as the first speaker stepped to the mic. Even the mesquite stood unusually quiet as Aron's friends took turns addressing the crowd. Cards were read, stories told, songs sung. The service ended appropriately with the concert version of Aron singing "Return to Sender." Afterwards, the King's kidnappers and a few friends hiked to the ridge to watch the crowd disperse.

The memorial service, along with Aron's emotional letter, helped spur his friends toward recovery, but just as every loss is unique, so too, is every recovery from loss.

Brooks' progress was hampered by a large number of still unanswered questions. The doctor performing the autopsy on the King listed cardiac arrhythmia as the probable cause of death, but other doctors present at the procedure pointed to multiple drug ingestion and clogged arteries as contributing factors. Brooks could not believe it. A heart attack? At forty-two? Impossible. Clogged arteries? The Kidnappers' starting quarterback? No Way. And how could Aron have died of multiple drug ingestion? When he left Austin, he was drug free and enjoying every minute of it. Brooks was also having a difficult time with the ending of his book. Tara read the book for him, loved it, and said the only reason he was having trouble with the ending was because he was not quite there yet. Brooks continued writing, which for him, was always the best medicine.

Rob found drinking large quantities of beer helpful but knew he was only masking his sorrow. He decided to begin his grandiose abstract, *Five Months in Texas*, and soon discovered the activity lifting his spirits. He also found dining with Tanya at Threadgill's to be quite thera-peutic.

Dave remained pretty upbeat after Aron's death, but when occasional thoughts of the King's passing caused his mood to drop, he took Tara golfing. Tara had little interest in golf, but Dave convinced her it would be good for both of them, and it was. They often found themselves laugh-ing so hard, they had to step to the side of the fairway so Lakeway's more serious golfers could play through.

Tara believed Aron's Memphis dream was, in fact, a near-death experience, that he was given five months to wrap up his unfinished business then taken as originally intended on the Ides of March. This belief, however, did little to soften the blow. For Tara, helping others was the best medicine. She helped Brooks by reading his book and offering suggestions, she helped Rob by becoming a sounding board for his painting, and she helped Dave by learning to play golf. Helping Paul, however, became her greatest challenge.

Paul's road to recovery required fighting a number of demons still lurking around The Vineyard. As the team's leader, he should have insisted Aron undergo monthly physical exams. A strict, low-fat diet and more aerobic exercises might have gone a long way to preventing his death. And even if Aron's early passing had, in fact, been predestined, what about all the other mistakes Paul had made? Why had he not insisted Lisa Marie visit months earlier? He had literally robbed the little girl of four precious months that she could have spent with her dad. He had robbed all of Aron's friends and family members of the last five months of the King's life and felt extremely guilty for the theft.

The biggest demon of all, however, was the one keeping Paul and his fellow kidnappers from contacting Lisa Marie. Brooks, Rob, and Sara attended Graceland's public viewing, but all attempts to speak with Aron's daughter failed. They were forced to give a letter to a guard, who placed it with the thousands of other cards and letters flooding into Graceland. Paul left phone messages and mailed letters to Lisa's three known addresses, but his efforts were in vain. A Memphis radio station reported that Priscilla and her daughter had left the country immediately after the funeral.

Paul recalled Aron asking him on several occasions to keep in touch with Lisa Marie. It had been Aron's only request. Now, Paul felt that every day that passed without contacting her was another day he was letting both the King and his princess down. This situation lowered Paul's spirits even further. He lost his appetite for food, began having trouble sleeping, and preferred spending time alone. He took some solace in his frequent jogs to the ridge, but even that normally healthful activity grew unhealthful as he ignored his shin splints, cramps, and other signs he was pushing himself too hard. His friends indulged his behavior to a point, but when he began losing more and more weight, and hiking later and later into the night, they intervened with an emergency meeting.

When informed of the meeting, Paul was on his way to the ridge and did not appreciate the interruption. "I know what this is about," he grumbled. "You're having a *What's Best for Paul* meeting, even though I've told you a million times what's best for me. The only problem is—nobody's listening."

"We're listening now," Brooks commented.

"Leave me alone!" Paul replied.

Silence filled the room.

Rob shook his head. "Paul, we're your friends. We don't like watchin' you suffer."

"I'm *not* suffering. I'm *grieving*. Dave, didn't you tell Tara she had every right to grieve any way she wanted? Don't I have that same right? You're each dealin' with this *your* way? I have every right to deal with it *my* way!"

Paul had made a valid point, but it was completely overshadowed by his drawn face and Don Quixote frame. Tara stared into his sad eyes. "Paul, you're skipping meals, you're not sleeping, and you've lost interest in everything but hiking alone to the ridge. You've also lost thirty pounds. Your *way* doesn't seem to be working."

Paul shook his head, spun, and walked away. At the door he paused, took a deep breath, then faced his friends. "Listen, guys, I need space and time—and I'm not gettin' either one here. I appreciate what you're trying to do, but I'd appreciate it a lot more if you'd just leave me the heck alone."

"We've tried that," Tara replied. "Now we're trying something else."

Paul searched Tara's eyes, turned, and stormed out of the house. Tara followed.

"Wait," Dave said.

Tara spun. "For what? For his condition to improve? For him to resolve this on his own? It's not happening, Dave. He at least, needs to eat, if we have to force feed him."

"I agree," Dave replied, "I just think we should give him some time to digest everything that was just said—let him sleep on it. If he hasn't come around by tomorrow morning, I'm all for discussing other options."

"Perhaps some professional help would be in order," Brooks suggested. "I'm not saying we've reached that point, but suggesting it would certainly get his attention."

"Hey, there's always that female shrink that makes house calls," Rob suggested. "We can invite her out for dinner and won't even have to mention she's a shrink until she's passing him the mashed potatoes."

Dave chuckled. "And if he balks, we'll tell him she's not here for him, but for *us*, that we were having trouble understanding the way some individuals deal with loss."

Tara smiled. As she stared toward the woods, her face saddened. "Okay," she conceded. "I'll give him one more night, but that's it." She watched until every head nodded.

Paul's pace quickened as he reflected on his latest argument with his friends. Halfway to the ridge, he broke into a run, twisted his ankle, and fell hard. The sharp pain in his hands and chest was nothing compared to the pain in his ankle. He tried massaging the joint, but the slightest touch was painful, and putting just a little weight on it was excruciating. He hobbled up to a big mesquite, plopped down, and carefully removed his shoe and sock. As his ankle ballooned, he leaned back against the tree's trunk and looked up through its gnarled branches. He studied the sky's darkening pinks and blues, chuckling at the strange irony. He had just turned his back on his friends by *demanding* space and time, and there he sat, with an injured ankle, miles of rough country between himself and home, and nightfall quickly approaching. Suddenly, he had all the space and time he could have ever hoped for. Again, he chuckled, but as he focused on his ankle and the darkening sky, his face saddened. "What a world," he whispered, shaking his head. He watched an armadillo burrowing its nose beneath a rotting stump. "What a world," he repeated, resting his tired head against the tree, eyelids slowly closing.

Paul opened his eyes in dreamland, startled to find the big mesquite smiling down at him. He was even more startled when the tree bent down, carefully snaked its bony fingers beneath his thin body, and lifted him high. He felt a sudden tickling sensation in the center of his stomach, followed by the unexpected sight of a billion bright stars splattered across a Milky Way sky. Suddenly, his body dropped as the tree leaned way back like a pitcher preparing to throw a 100-mile-an-hour fastball. He opened his mouth to scream, but he was too late, he was already in flight, tumbling wildly as the night sky whirled by, as if in a Van Gogh painting. As he fell, he instinctively curled into a tight ball, hoping a good roll might soften the blow, but just as he neared the ground, a second tree snatched him up and threw a curve ball. Laughter bubbled up from the center of his stomach as he spun. Several tosses later, he realized he was being relayed in a zigzagged route all the way to the horizon. As the sky lightened, the bright stars faded and the first rays of morning light exploded from behind The Vineyard. The tree making the last grab held Paul high, as if to show the catch to the umpire.

From Paul's high perch, he spotted Tara picking big red grapes in The Vineyard's back yard. He heard giggling and spotted the most beautiful little boy and girl playing at her feet. They looked like a little Paul and a little Tara. They looked like twins. Paul's eyes moistened as his heart smiled.

Paul thought about Dave and saw his friend parking a Mercedes-Benz in a reserved space in front of a beautifully-designed building nestled somewhere in the Hill Country. As the driver's door opened, a golf ball jumped out, bounced down the sloped driveway, and vanished into the woods. "You couldn't wait until we got to the links?" he asked, with a chuckle. He picked up a stack of thick books before retrieving a Norman Rockwell from the back seat. Paul grinned as Dr. Dave Turner walked past another reserved space labeled *Dr. Tara Benoist*.

Paul looked for Rob and immediately saw the artist wearing paint-splattered overalls and standing inside a large art studio on Sixth Street. A crowd of art enthusiasts listened intently as Rob explained why he had used that particular shade of pink for the bull's gonads.

Paul thought about Brooks and spotted the writer sitting behind a desk inside UT's Co-op Book Store. He was wearing jeans and a short-sleeved, plaid shirt, feet crossed over the desk, arms tucked behind his head, waiting patiently for a store employee to open another box of books. A long line of students stretched through the front door and down the Drag's bustling sidewalk.

Paul thought about Aron and immediately saw a small, blond-haired boy dragging a toy guitar. The child was singing the strangest song Paul had ever heard—somewhere between Reggae, Latin Rock, and Southern Blues. As Paul hummed along with the song's lively chorus, the little boy quit singing, stopped, and turned. "I *thought* that was you, Paul," he said, with a grin. "How's that ankle doin'?"

Paul's jaw slowly dropped. "It's—fine—now. How are *you* doin', Aron. *Where* are you doin'? I mean—*what* are you doin'?"

Aron burst out laughing. "What do you *think* I'm doin', son?" he replied, reaching down and picking up a small football. "I'm waitin' for my kidnappers, so I can teach 'em how this game's *really* supposed to be played."

Paul burst out laughing. During the long conversation that followed, both men spent a lot of time laughing.

"Paul, wake up," Dave said, kneeling beside his friend.

Paul heard the words but felt glued fast to the hard earth.

Dave shook his friend's shoulder. "Paul, wake up."

Paul opened his eyes, squinting at the bright light shining in his face. As the light beam lowered, his eyes slowly adjusted. "Dave!" he shouted, sitting straight up. "You're never going to believe what just happened! Never in a million years!"

"Oh, I don't think I'll have too much trouble believing it," Dave replied.

As Paul's eyes adjusted further, he spotted Tara and his other friends standing behind Dave. "Tara! Brooks! Rob! I left my body! I time-traveled! It was just like in some fantastic dream! Except it wasn't a dream! It was real! This tree picked me up! And threw me to another tree, and another, and another, all the way to the horizon! And *you* were there, Tara. And *you*, Dave. And *you*, Rob. And *you*, Brooks, and . . ."

"If you're auditioning for *Dorothy* in *The Wizard of Oz*, you've got the part," Brooks said dryly.

"No!" Paul replied. "It wasn't a dream! I swear! It was real. I was thrown into the future, and you were all there, only a little older. *Dave*, you're practicing at Tara's clinic. *Tara*, you're a psychiatrist. *Rob*, you're a successful artist with a studio on Sixth Street. *Brooks*, your book's a best seller, and you're autographing copies at the UT Co-op. *Tara*, we have *twins*! A little boy and a little girl! And they're gorgeous! Just like you! Can you believe it! We're parents!"

"Aren't most parents married?" Tara asked.

"We *are* married, Tara! We *are* married!"

"No, we're not."

Paul reached up and grasped Tara's hand. "Tara, will you marry me?" he proposed, staring into her startled eyes. "Please, Tara. Please. Say you'll marry me."

With the ball squarely placed in Tara's court, all heads turned.

Tara smiled at Paul through the unexpected tears welling up in her eyes. "Why, of course I'll marry you, Paul. I've wanted to marry you from the first moment we met."

"Great!" Paul replied excitedly. "Great! That's great!"

"Well—I'll—be," Dave said.

"Congratulations, folks," Rob said, "when's the wedding?"

"We haven't exactly set a date, yet," Tara replied, blushing.

Paul's eyes darted toward the horizon. "And *Aron* was there, too! He was just a toddler dragging a toy guitar, but I recognized him, and he recognized me, and we talked for a long time, and he's okay. He's okay! Do you hear me! Aron's *okay*! Everything's going to be *okay*! Everything's going to be *okay*!"

"Yes, we hear you loud and clear," Dave replied, moving the light beam from Paul's swollen ankle to his squinting eyes. "You didn't by chance hit your head, did you?"

Tara inspected Paul's swollen ankle, frowning at her fiancé. "Paul, you had us worried sick! What if you'd hiked off the trail? What if you'd gotten *lost* or bitten by a *snake*? What if we hadn't found you? Would you just *look* at your ankle! Do you have any idea what time it is!"

"How's married life?" Rob chuckled.

"No complaints so far," Paul answered. He patted Tara's hand. "It's just a sprain, 'hon."

"A sprain!" Tara replied.

Brooks rolled his eyes. "One of his mesquite trees must have X-rayed it for him."

"Judging from the color and swelling, I'd say you have a broken bone or two," Tara said, "at the very least, torn tendons."

"I'm afraid, I concur," Dave said, searching for a branch to use as a splint.

"The good news is, you might have just escaped an extended stay at the Austin State Hospital," Brooks joked.

"And won a free trip to Aunt Bea's room at the Brackenridge," Rob added. "I wonder who's playin' tonight."

"I hope the cafeteria's open," Paul replied. "I'm starvin'! I'm so hungry I could eat a horse."

While his friends splinted his ankle, Paul continued describing every minute detail of his wild dream, much to his friends' chagrin.

Dave peered at Paul over the rim of his glasses. "Your euphoria's bordering on the obnoxious."

"Really," Brooks agreed, "I think I liked him better depressed."

"Mr. Brooks!" Tara scolded.

Tara and Dave led with their flashlights as Rob and Brooks half-carried, half-drug their injured friend through the dark woods.

"Ouch!" Paul shouted, as his foot bumped against a fallen branch. "Careful, boys, you're not just haulin' hay here."

They lifted him a little higher.

"Oh, by the way," Rob said, "while you were out breakin' your ankle, you missed an important business meeting."

"Sorry, what'd I miss?"

"Oh, nothing much," Tara replied, "except that Lisa Marie called."

"What!" Paul shouted. "Are you *kiddin'* me! That's *great*! Why didn't you tell me! Where is she! What'd she say! How's she doing! How's she takin' all this! How's *Memphis* takin' it! Where is she! Is she okay!"

"You can ask her yourself in a few hours," Brooks replied. "She and her mother are flying out for a little visit. It seems Aron mentioned to Priscilla that The Vineyard was a good place for healing."

"What!" Paul replied. "*Lisa Marie* and *Priscilla* are coming *here*! Tonight!"

"No," Rob replied, motioning toward the horizon, "they're coming here this morning."

Paul stared at the thin line of pink behind the thick woods. "Oh, no! You've *got* to be kidding. I spent the whole night out here? No wonder y'all were so worried. Listen, guys, I'm really sorry—and even *more* sorry for the past month. I'm afraid I've been a little, frustrated, lately, and takin' it out on my friends, and that was *really* wrong. How can I ever make it up to y'all?"

"Funny you should ask," Dave answered.

"In addition to Lisa Marie, you missed one other important item of business," Brooks mentioned.

"Perhaps we should wait until he's healed," Tara suggested.

"He's healed enough," Rob replied.

"Healed enough for what?" Paul asked, as a shoved branch whipped back and caught him across the face. "Ohhh!" he shouted, glaring at the tree.

"Sorry," Dave apologized.

"Brooks was at the grocery store the other day when he ran across the latest issue of *Rolling Stone*," Rob said. "Have you seen it?"

"No," Paul answered, "I'm afraid I've been a little, preoccupied, lately."

"The magazine contains some rather unflattering pictures of Bob Dylan," Tara commented.

"So," Paul replied, "Dylan never takes a good picture."

"Yeah, but these were different," Rob said. "Mr. Dylan's not lookin' too good lately."

"He looks—drugged," Tara said.

"Ohhh, no!" Paul replied.

"Wait till you read the reviews of his latest concerts," Dave said. "It's really sad."

"No way!" Paul replied.

"We're thinking' of payin' old Bob a little visit," Rob said.

"Oh yeah, well, you can count *me* out, " Paul replied. "How 'bout when you find *old Bob*, you just give him my regards."

"Robert Allen Zimmerman," Brooks corrected.

"We're thinking of calling him *Allen* for short," Dave mentioned.

"Hey, let's spell it with one L," Tara suggested.

"How serendipitous," Brooks replied. "Four letters like Paul, Tara, and Dave. Begins with the first letter of the alphabet. It says we're starting over. I like it."

"Please tell me you're jokin'," Paul pleaded.

"He's livin' in Upper State New York," Rob replied.

"I've already made some preliminary phone calls," Tara added.

"Oh, and he's a vegetarian," Dave commented. "You might want to use something else besides cheeseburgers."

"Perhaps we could lure him out with a big, fat carrot," Brooks suggested.

"Then hit him over the head with a sack of potatoes," Rob suggested.

"Rob," Tara scolded, "I hardly think that will be necessary."

*   *   *

Printed in the United States
114709LV00001B/4-12/P